HOTEL MAGNIFIQUE

EMILY J. TAYLOR

RAZORBILL

RAZORBILL

An imprint of Penguin Random House LLC, New York

First published in the United States of America by Razorbill,
an imprint of Penguin Random House LLC, 2022

Copyright © 2022 by Emily Taylor Creative LLC

Visit us online at penguinrandomhouse.com.

LIBRARY OF CONGRESS CATALOGING-IN-PUBLICATION DATA
Names: Taylor, Emily J., author.
Title: Hotel Magnifique / Emily J. Taylor.
Description: New York : Razorbill, 2022. | Audience: Ages 12 and up. |
Summary: Seventeen-year-old Jani and her little sister Zosa secure jobs at a glamorous magical hotel, but when Jani realizes that their staff contracts are unbreakable, she embarks on a mission to unravel the mystery of the magic at the heart of the hotel and free Zosa—and the other staff—from the cruelty of the ruthless maître d'hôtel.
Identifiers: LCCN 2021039042 | ISBN 9780593404539 (trade paperback) | ISBN 9780593404515 (hardcover) | ISBN 9780593404522 (ebook)
Subjects: CYAC: Hotels, motels, etc.—Fiction. | Sisters—Fiction. |
Magic—Fiction. | LCGFT: Novels.
Classification: LCC PZ7.1.T3849 Ho 2022 | DDC [Fic]—dc23
LC record available at https://lccn.loc.gov/2021039042

ISBN 9780593404515 (HARDCOVER)
1 3 5 7 9 10 8 6 4 2

ISBN 9780593524121 (INTERNATIONAL EDITION)
1 3 5 7 9 10 8 6 4 2

Printed in the United States of America

LSCH

Design by Tony Sahara
Text set in Lora

For Eric

PROLOGUE

The courier was given a single instruction: deliver the boy before the stroke of midnight. Simple—except, usually, she delivered packages during the day, not little boys in the dead of night.

The job paid handsomely, but that wasn't the reason the courier agreed. She took the job because she was curious.

She wondered why a well-to-do couple came to her of all people. Why the boy's father refused to write the address down and instead whispered it into her ear, why the boy's mother wept. Most of all she wondered who might receive this boy, considering the delivery location was not a home, nor an address to any physical structure, but the space in between two—an empty alley on the other side of town.

The boy seemed ordinary enough, with unblemished copper skin a shade deeper than her own. However, he hung his head as they walked, as if the thick night air pressed upon his shoulders.

The courier thrust her lantern at the gloom, beating back shadows with a growing sense of unease. Her grandfather's stories came to her: whispers of magic hiding in the corners of the world, and young children met with terrible fates.

She was too old to believe in stories, and yet she quickened her pace.

One block from their destination, the boy dragged his feet. Gripping his bony shoulder, she tugged him down the final street, and halted.

The alley was gone. A strange, slender building stood in its place, squeezed into the narrow space, fitting in seamlessly with the crumbling structures on either side.

A figure peeled away from a shadow near the entrance.

The courier drew the boy behind her. "Are you the person I'm supposed to meet?"

Whoever it was raised a slim object. A blood-red taper candle flared to life, illuminating a young man's blue eyes and pale face.

The courier searched for a match to explain the flame; no one could light a candle from nothing. Unless—

Shimmering golden smoke billowed from the tip. It spilled onto the street, snaking around the courier. Tiny globes buzzed and flickered like fireflies or dust motes catching moonlight. Or something else. Scents gusted by: peppermint oil, then burnt sugar, as if caramel were bubbling too long on a stove, followed by a whiff of citrus left to rot.

The man strode through the golden smoke and took the boy's hand, like a father would do. For a brief moment, the boy stumbled, unsure, but then he *willingly* walked with the man toward the narrow building.

The courier clutched her chest and felt her heart pound in an erratic rhythm—harder than it ever had before. This was all wrong. She lunged to stop the man, but golden smoke twined around her ankles, restraining her. She opened her mouth to scream, but no sound escaped her lips, not even a whimper.

Her hands wrapped around her throat as the man halted at the doorway of the building. She watched in horror as he smiled, sharp-toothed, then brought his striking face level with the boy's own. "Come along now," he said. "I have the perfect job for you."

The man opened the door and jerked the boy inside.

The moment the door shut, the smoke dissipated. The courier strained until she could move her feet. She hurled herself toward the building, skidding to a stop as the entire thing vanished before her eyes, leaving nothing but an alley covered with overgrown weeds and cast in shadows.

I often heard my sister before I saw her, and tonight was no exception. Zosa's supple voice spilled through the open window of Bézier Residence, sounding so like our mother's—at least until she began a raunchier ditty comparing a man's more delicate anatomy to a certain fruit.

I crept inside, unnoticed in the crowd of boarders. Two of the younger girls pretended to dance with invisible partners, but every other eye was fixed on my sister, the most talented girl in the room.

A special kind of girl rented rooms at Bézier Residence. Almost all worked jobs fitting of their foul mouths: second shifts as house grunts, factory workers, grease cooks, or any number of ill-paying positions in the vieux quais—the old docks of Durc. I worked at Tannerie Fréllac, where women huddled over crusted alum pots and wells of dye. But Zosa was different.

"Happy birthday," I shouted when her song ended.

"Jani!" She bounded over. Her huge brown eyes shone against a pale, olive-skinned face that was far too thin.

"Did you eat supper?" I'd left her something, but with all the other girls around, food had a tendency to disappear.

She groaned. "Yes. You don't have to ask me every night."

"Of course I do. I'm your big sister. It's my life's greatest duty." Zosa scrunched her nose and I flicked it. Fishing in my sack, I pulled out the newspaper that had cost me half a day's wage and pressed it into her palms. "Your present, *madame*." Here, birthdays weren't dusted with confectioners' sugar; they were hard-won and more dear than gold.

"A newspaper?"

"A jobs section." I flipped open the paper with a sly grin.

Inside were advertisements for jobs in fancy dress shops, patisseries, and perfumeries, positions that would never belong to a thirteen-year-old who didn't look a day over ten. Luckily, they weren't what I had in mind.

Skipping past them, I pointed to a listing that had appeared in papers across town an hour ago.

The ink was vibrant purple, like Aligney blood poppies or crushed amethyst velvet. It stood out, a strange beacon in a sea of black and white.

HOTEL MAGNIFIQUE

IS HIRING.

INTERESTED PARTIES INQUIRE TOMORROW AT NOON.
PACK A BAG FOR ELSEWHERE & PREPARE
TO DEPART BY MIDNIGHT.

The girls crowded around us, and everyone leaned in as the purple ink winked with an iridescence that rivaled polished moonstones.

No address was given. The legendary hotel needed none. It appeared every decade or so in the same old alley downtown. The whole city was probably there now, already waiting like fools for a chance at a stay.

Years ago, when the hotel last made an appearance, the majority of the invitations were delivered beforehand to only the wealthiest citizens. Then, the day the hotel arrived, a few more precious invitations were gifted to random folk in the crowd. Our matron, Minette Bézier, was one of those lucky few.

That midnight, the guests stepped into the hotel and disappeared, along with the building. Two weeks later, they famously stepped *back*, appearing in the same alley from nothing but thin air.

My fingers twitched and I pictured cracking the seal on my own invitation. But even if we were fortunate enough to win one, we'd still have to pay for a room—and they weren't exactly cheap.

Zosa's brows drew together. "You want me to interview?"

"Not quite. I'm going to interview. I'm taking *you* to audition as a singer."

It had been four years since I'd taken her to a singing audition—the first one hadn't worked out in our favor, and I couldn't stomach going through it again, so we didn't try for more. But today was her birthday and this was *the* Hotel Magnifique. Everything about it felt different. Perfect, somehow. "Hotels hire singers all the time. What do you say?"

She answered with a smile that I felt in the tips of my toes.

One of the older girls shoved a lock of greasy blonde hair behind her pink ear. "That advertisement is a tease. It would be a miracle if any of us got a job."

I straightened. "That's not true."

She shrugged as she turned away. "Do what you want. I wouldn't waste my time."

"Think she's right?" Zosa asked, her delicate mouth turning down.

"Absolutely not," I said, perhaps too quickly. When Zosa's frown deepened, I cursed silently and dragged my thumb along our mother's old necklace.

The worthless chain was Verdanniere gold, rigid as steel. Maman always joked my spine was made of the stuff. I often fumbled for it when I needed her guidance with Zosa. Not that she ever gave it; dead mothers weren't any good for guidance.

"The hotel wouldn't run an advertisement if no one had a chance. Tomorrow, we'll show them what we've got. When they discover how brilliant we both are, we can kiss this place goodbye for good."

The thought felt like a bright coal smoldering in my chest.

My fingers trembled as I straightened one of Zosa's dark curls like Maman would do. "Let's show the advertisement to Bézier. She'll know more about the hotel than anyone here."

Zosa nodded, eyes gleaming. I plucked the jobs section from her fingers and took off. Girls raced behind me up two flights of stairs to my favorite room, the third-floor sitting room that used to house sailors before Bézier bought the building. It was stuffed with shelves of antiquated ocean charts and atlases for far-off places I'd often page through.

Bézier sat before her fire, stockinged feet propped on a window ledge. Outside, rain battered the port of Durc, turning the city I hated into a wet blur.

Her mouth pinched when we all streamed in. "What is it now?"

I handed her the page of newsprint. Purple ink caught the firelight and Bézier's pale face slackened.

"Is something wrong?" asked a girl behind me.

Bézier glanced above the hearth to the decade-old sheet of parchment sheathed behind glass: her invitation. In the low light, the purple ink shone with the same iridescence as the advertisement. "Hotel Magnifique is returning, I see."

Another door opened and a few stragglers squeezed in, jostling for a look.

"I've heard the guests sip on liquid gold from champagne flutes for breakfast," said a girl in back. More girls chimed in with their own rumors.

"They say the pillows don't have feathers, they're all stuffed with spun clouds—"

"Heard each night, you cross the world thrice over—"

"And all their fancy doormen are princes from some far-off land—"

"Bet they give fancy kisses, too." A girl with beige skin and ruddy cheeks made a vulgar gesture with her tongue. Thankfully Zosa didn't notice. Instead, a grin split her face.

Shame there was no way to know if the rumors were true; guests signed away all memory of their stay upon checkout. Besides luggage, the only thing guests returned with was a feeling of devastat-

ing happiness. Bézier once admitted to icing her jaw from all the smiling.

Curious, I glanced at Bézier. Her eyes had grown misty, as if the hotel returning somehow sparked a memory. I opened my mouth to ask about it until Zosa slipped in front of me. "Did you ever see the maître?"

The maître d'hôtel was the proprietor and as famous as the hotel itself.

Bézier nodded, smug. "The hotel came once when I was a young, pretty thing. The maître had the brightest smile I'd ever seen. Positively gleamed greeting the crowds. He plucked a flower from the air and tossed it to me." She pretended to catch a tiny bloom. "The thing smelled like blueberry pie then dissolved to nothing in my fingers. Over a decade went by before the hotel came again, and when it did, the maître looked exactly the same."

"Wearing the same clothes?" someone asked.

"No, you ninny. He *looked* the same. Same face. Same charm. Hadn't aged, not a day. Makes sense, I guess. He is the greatest suminaire in all the world."

Girls gasped at the mention of a suminaire: the old Verdanniere word for *magician*.

Outside of the hotel, a suminaire was the most dangerous thing in the world. Magic was said to build in their blood during adolescence until it flared out in an uncontrollable power, with the potential to hurt—or kill—anyone who happened to be near them at the time.

Some said it poured from a child's nose into a dark cloud.

Others said it looked like pitch-black fingers clawing up a child's throat. And there was no way to tell a normal child from a suminaire before their magic flared.

There were rumors of what to look out for, of course. Outlandish things like craving blood or tongues turning black. There were even children said to come back to life after a fatal wound only to discover they had magic in their blood. But no one could prove it.

Whatever the case, magic was so dangerous that for centuries in Verdanne, children suspected to be suminaires were either drowned or burned to death.

But inside the hotel, magic was safe. It was well known the maître somehow enchanted the building himself, allowing the suminaires he employed to perform astonishing feats without harming a soul. Nobody knew how he'd done it, but everybody wanted a chance to see it firsthand.

Before anyone could ask another question, Bézier clapped her hands. "It's late. Everyone to your rooms."

"Wait," I said. "Do you remember anything now that the hotel is back? Is it as magical as the rumors?" As soon as the words left my mouth, I felt silly for asking.

Bézier, however, didn't laugh or think it odd. Instead, she glanced at her old invitation wistfully.

"I'm certain it's more," she said with a bitter note. I'd be bitter too if I couldn't remember the most exciting time of my life. She tossed the advertisement in the fire, then stumbled back. "My god."

The paper caught, burning pink, then green, then crimson, turning the hearth into a dazzling display of rainbow flames. The flames shot higher, raging into the chimney, creating a more arresting sight than the storefronts of boulevard Marigny.

"It's *magic*," Zosa whispered.

My neck prickled. There was a reason Hotel Magnifique caused gasps and goggling. Normally, magic was rare, dangerous, and to be avoided at all costs. But somehow, inside that hotel, it was the opposite, and tomorrow we might finally have a chance to experience it ourselves.

2

The next morning, a wet southern wind covered the vieux quais in slippery algae. I gripped Zosa's hand as we skidded along the docks, past fishermen unloading pallets and mothers kissing their sailor sons goodbye.

"Jani, look." Zosa pointed at a ferry pulling into port. "Think it's ours?"

"Hard to say."

Four years ago, after our mother had passed, I spent an absurd sum of dublonnes to purchase passage on a similar ferry from Aligney, our small inland village up the coast.

The trip took five days. Zosa spent the time dreaming about all the frivolous things she'd buy in Durc, like fingerless lace gloves and the striped tins of crème de rose Maman would smear on her face. I couldn't stop smiling, convinced that my life was about to begin.

Things felt different the moment we disembarked. The docks were crowded. Zosa was only nine so I made her stay close. It had hit me then: everyone I cared about was either dead or in Aligney. We were alone in a strange city, and it was all my doing.

It was a mistake to leave home. For the past few months, I'd been saving every coin to buy passage back to Aligney. But at the rate I was going, I didn't want to think about how long it would take. The hotel would probably get us there years faster.

My breath stilled at the thought, and crisp, golden memories of home rushed to me. I could practically feel the uneven cobblestones I ran over as a child, my belly full from gorging on strawberries plucked from swollen summer bushes.

"Move," barked a pale-skinned woman clutching an otter fur stole, snapping me from my thoughts. She walked around us, careful not to come too close.

Zosa fingered the holes in her good frock. "She must think we crawled out from under the docks. Everyone is so glamorous today."

I took off my ruffled lilac hat. The style was terribly dated, but it was the nicest thing I owned. Bending, I fastened it on Zosa as if it were a crown.

"No one is as glamorous as us, madame," I said, and my heart lifted at her grin. "Now let's hurry. The maître d'hôtel himself is expecting us for tea."

Together, we walked past the vieux quais and into town. Streams of purple bunting hung from eaves while pink and green carnations decorated every doorstep. The celebration was unlike anything I'd ever seen, and all for the hotel.

"There's so many people." Zosa giggled as we rounded a corner near the famed alley. "I can't see my feet."

I maneuvered her out of the way of a large group. "If you don't watch it, someone will stomp on those pretty feet and I'll never hear the end of it."

She twirled. "I don't care. It's wonderful."

"Only until we can't find each other." The thought of losing her in a crowd always put me on edge.

"Are you trying to have no fun?"

"I made it a rule to never have fun until *after* lunch," I teased.

"Truly?"

"Come on, you," I said, and steered her into a clearing occupied by street performers in satin brassieres, faces hidden behind mâché masks. Zosa jerked back when one performer popped forward, tears of painted blood dripping down her mask as she sang for coin.

"A *suminaire called up la magie.*

And turned his wife into a pyre.

He scorched her eyes and cracked her bones.

Her fate was rather dire!"

I'd heard the same words sung many times before. Here, suminaires were still the subjects of songs and stories, even when nobody had seen one in ages. In the last few decades, sightings became so rare that people stopped worrying about magic hurting anyone, instead growing curious about it, and Verdanniere laws grew lax. The hotel only added to the allure. People were so eager to experience magic that fears about it were forgotten the way one might forget the threat of a lightning bolt striking you dead in a field.

"Do you think we'll see a suminaire today?" Zosa asked.

"Hopefully only *inside*. Where the maître makes it safe for everyone."

"I bet the maître's handsome."

"He's too old for you," I growled, and pinched her nose. "Let's keep moving."

A moment later, we passed two men with brown skin and giddy smiles. They each clutched thick envelopes. Invitations.

"Six winners this time!" someone shouted.

"They already picked the winners?" My face fell. I supposed the contest was good—it gave everyone hope. Still, I felt a stab of jealousy that I couldn't shake. Before I could take another step, Zosa tugged my sleeve so hard she nearly took my arm off. "Hey!"

"Would you turn your big head?" She pointed.

Then I saw it.

The hotel looked like it had spent its whole life sewn into the narrow alley between Apothicaire Richelieu and Maison du Thé. Clad in slatted wood, a single column of windows went up five floors. There couldn't be more than ten cramped rooms, tops. Above the door hung a sign too ornate for the shabby building, where a pair of words swirled with inlaid pearl: HOTEL MAGNIFIQUE.

"How quaint," I said with a twinge of disappointment. The hotel was unremarkable.

A single round window, twice as large as the others, sat up top and shelved several succulents. Lucky plants. Except I didn't understand how they got from place to place. Or the building itself, for that matter.

The hotel was rumored to visit every corner of the world. I knew my geography—Verdanne was the largest country on the continent, bordered by the jagged mountains of Skaadi to the north and

windswept Preet to the east. Beyond were more enormous countries, then oceans filled with endless places to see. The world was vast and unimaginable, and yet this single building traversed it all.

We both straightened at a woman's cry. "It's the maître!"

A young man stood at the entrance.

"Saw him giving away invitations," the woman went on. "Pressed duchesse roses to the first winner's palm as she entered."

"I knew it. He's magnificent," Zosa gushed.

I had to squint. With the sun shining directly on him, the maître gleamed like a newly minted silver dublonne. He wore a black livery that contrasted with his light skin.

Bézier was right. The greatest suminaire in all the world wasn't much older than me. Nineteen. Twenty, at most. Outrageously young. Or he looked it, anyway.

This man somehow enchanted the whole building, made it safe for the suminaires he employed to practice magic, safe for guests to witness it.

"Welcome." The maître plucked a tulip from the air and handed it to an older woman with brown skin and wide smile as she hobbled into the hotel clutching an invitation. "Pleasure, pleasure," he said to a light-skinned young woman holding another invitation, then, "Outstanding hat, mademoiselle," to her little daughter as they filtered through the door, followed by the pair of giddy men.

The maître cleared his throat. "Thank you all for stopping by. Please come again next time Hotel Magnifique arrives."

He bent in a flourished bow. When he came up, a handful of lilies dripped between his long fingers. He tossed them up. The flowers folded into tiny birds that dissolved into shimmering purple smoke with each wing beat. When I looked down, the maître was gone.

Incredible. Except for in his place was a rope barring the front door with a sign that read, *only guests and staff beyond this point.*

"Do you think interviews are inside?" Zosa asked.

"I don't know, but I'm going to find out." I eyed the sign. Surely I could take a peek. "Wait for me here."

Elbowing past the crowd, I climbed the steps and slipped under the rope. Three words no wider than a thumb were carved into the front door's black lacquer: *le monde entier.*

The whole world.

The words tugged at something inside me, beckoning.

I pulled the door open, but it was impossible to see a thing. I took a step forward. But instead of walking inside, I crashed nose-first into a wall.

Stumbling back, I trailed my fingertips over what appeared to be a sheet of glass filling the doorframe. At least I assumed it was glass, until a hand reached through and grabbed my wrist. With a shriek, I discovered the hand was attached to a young doorman.

I blinked, trying to make sense of the open doorway that was also a wall and this boy who simply walked through it.

No, not a boy. Much too tall, with lean muscles evident under his livery. The maître was blindingly pale, but this young man was the opposite. His warm copper skin accentuated the vivid brown eyes that stared down at me.

"Can I help you?" he asked in Verdanniere with an accent I'd never heard before.

I glanced up at the building and pictured all the atlases lining Bézier's sitting room, the blobs of land I would trace with my fingertips. It didn't seem plausible that such an old structure could travel far.

"Where were you yesterday?" I asked.

"A minute's journey from here," he said curtly. When I tried to inspect the wall, he shut the door. "Only guests and staff are allowed inside."

Right. That damned sign. "Where are the interviews?"

"You want to interview with the hotel?"

He seemed surprised, which made me bristle. I skewered him with a glare. "Obviously."

We both jumped when the hotel's door burst open. A group wandered out. A lapis necklace glittered against a petite guest's deep brown skin. She was followed by another guest with skin so close to white that it would char in a minute under Durc's summer sun.

They laughed and a wafting sultry scent made my toes curl. "What's that smell?"

"Desert jasmine. It's rather ordinary."

Ordinary wasn't the word I would use. I could gobble that scent for dessert. "It's exquisite. Where is it from?"

"I'm sorry, but I'm in a hurry. I really don't have time right now for silly girls."

"Excuse me?"

"You took the words right out of my mouth," he said with a smirk, then tried to duck past me.

I couldn't enter the building by myself and although he was infuriating, he was the only employee I'd seen besides the maître. I grabbed his arm. "Where are the interviews?"

"Don't you understand I'm busy?"

"Then hurry it up and answer my question."

He gave me a long look then scanned down the street. I tried to pinpoint what it was he searched for, but all I could see was a mass of people. My breath halted when he brushed a curl from the side of my neck.

"If I were you, I would go straight home. Pretend the hotel never came," he said in a low voice. Then he dipped past me, disappearing into the crowd.

3

Over the next two hours, the doorman wouldn't leave my mind, the way his vivid eyes seemed to judge me. The way he'd brushed me off. He probably warned me away because he didn't think I belonged in a place like the Hotel Magnifique.

I picked at my green-stained fingers. The dye from the tannery stank of harbor fug, as most things did in Durc. Some said if you lived here long enough, barnacles would sprout from your rib bones. I didn't doubt it. After a rare bath, my skin would still stink of rotting fish. But I refused to give up now. Maman always said I was too stubborn for my own good, but I couldn't help myself. The doorman's actions made me want the job even more.

"Could this line go any slower?"

"God, I hope not." Zosa swiped at sweat dripping from under the lilac hat.

The line outside Maison du Thé—the old teahouse beside the hotel, where we'd learned interviews were being held—was obscenely long. Unfortunately for my aching calves, we were at the end.

When we reached the teahouse entrance, Zosa pointed at a

gilded sign listing the open positions: stage performer appeared between musician and scullery maid. A man with fair skin dressed in a suit too elaborate for the heat didn't spare us a smile. Instead, he opened the door and practically shoved us through.

Inside, marble countertops held weighted silver scales. Tall glass jars covered every shelf, filled to the brim with brightly colored tea leaves.

"Next!" shouted a woman from the back room. The interview.

"Will you go first?" Zosa's voice shook with nerves, just like during that first audition years ago.

I straightened a ruffle on the hat. "Of course I will."

In back, a statuesque, olive-skinned woman greeted me. Her cropped brown hair matched the gleam of her velvet pantsuit. She dressed like a man but had more panache than all the men I knew. I liked her, I realized, until she wrinkled her nose at me.

"Not much to look at, are you?" she said, then held up a large bronze compass with a gleaming green jade needle. "Now hold still."

The compass's needle spun in dizzying circles, but it didn't stop once. The woman tucked the compass in her pocket.

"What was that for?"

"I ask the questions." She snatched my chin. "Your name?"

I swallowed. "Janine Lafayette. But everyone calls me Jani."

"What a boring name." Her lips tugged up. "I'm Yrsa, by the way." She released my chin. "Have you lived in this city your whole life?"

"I'm from an inland village up the coast called Aligney," I said, a tremor in my voice.

"Did you like your little village?"

When we were babies, Maman pointed our cribs toward the center of Aligney so our feet would always know the way back, a Verdanniere superstition that stuck with me.

Even now, I could perfectly picture the tight rows of houses that turned lemon yellow in the winter sunsets. I knew exactly when the poppies would bloom, and where our next dinner would come from. I had friends there—friends who *worried* about me. It felt like I hadn't taken a deep breath for the past four years, but in Aligney I could breathe with every corner of my lungs.

My only constant these days was the ache in my chest to return.

"I loved my village. I only brought my sister here after our mother died. I planned to go back when—"

"So your mother is dead." She cut me off. "What about your father?"

Maman never told us specifics. "He was a farmer."

"And where do you live now?"

I started to tell her about Bézier Residence until she fluttered a hand, dismissing me with a wave. "I've heard enough. Send in the next person."

Zosa shot up when she saw me. "Are you all right?"

"I'm fine," I lied. "Don't keep the woman waiting."

My sister dashed in back while I scrubbed tears from my eyes. It was foolish to let myself hope. I traced the hard outline of a coin in my pocket, left over from the newspaper. At least I could buy Zosa a tin of pastilles when she was through, help sweeten the rejection.

Minutes passed. I heard her muffled singing through the door. Eventually Zosa burst into the front, a blank look on her face.

"Well?"

She held up a sheet of parchment and my mouth went dry. The page curled at the corners, archaic compared to modern foolscap. A black line at the bottom told me exactly what it was.

One contract. For a single job.

Yrsa sauntered up. "I offered your sister a position. She'll be paid ten Verdanniere dublonnes a week singing for our guests."

Ten dublonnes was triple what I made. I had to bite my tongue to keep from tearing up. Of course Yrsa would think Zosa was extraordinary, especially compared to her lackluster sister.

Zosa couldn't go alone. If Maman were here, she'd be poking me to do something. But Zosa was grinning like the sun itself had risen inside of her, and I couldn't think of a single thing to say that wouldn't break her heart.

Yrsa placed a bronze-nibbed pen and purple inkwell on a table. Pulling out a golden pin, she pricked my sister's finger. A perfect bead of ruby blood welled.

My hands shot up. "What are you doing?"

"It's part of the contract. Even our guests sign something similar." Yrsa tilted the drop into the inkwell. Purple ink hissed while Zosa's blood dissolved. Yrsa dipped the pen and pressed it between my sister's fingers.

My eyes darted to the contract. I expected the page to be drafted in Verdanniere—the language of Verdanne and a fairly common tongue across the continent. This contract had a smattering of Verdanniere, but most paragraphs were in languages I'd never seen. At the bottom was an X.

Zosa's cheeks were flushed. "I've never had anything this exciting happen to me. Jani, I did it."

Jealousy swept through me. My fingers curled with a swift desire to grab the contract and sign it myself. I turned to Yrsa. "My sister is barely thirteen. She can't go by herself. We could share a room and I could work doing whatever you needed." *Let us both go.*

"Afraid that's not possible," Yrsa said. "I offered her the job. Only guests and staff can pass the threshold."

The threshold: that wall made of nothing. There wasn't a way to get past it together.

"It's all right," Zosa said. "We'll speak to someone. It'll all work out."

She didn't understand that I couldn't go unless they hired me, too. I put my face in my hands. When I looked up, Zosa had lifted the pen nib to the parchment and scrawled her name across the bottom of the page.

I leaped forward and knocked over the inkwell. Purple splattered on the table as I grabbed the pen and gave it back to Yrsa. I glanced down and almost gasped aloud. The purple well wasn't spilled or knocked over. It was capped. But I'd seen the ink spill, I was sure of it.

It had to be magic.

"Your sister will report to the hotel by six o'clock." Yrsa tucked Zosa's signed contract down her jacket and left.

*

"There's no way you're going," I said, putting my foot down, right on top of an old nightshirt Zosa was reaching for. The seams ripped when she snatched it, while pretending I wasn't there. "Hello. Right in front of you." I poked her forehead and she glowered. "See. Not so invisible, am I?"

Continuing to ignore me, she stuffed Maman's old sheet music down a grain sack filled with more of Maman's mementos. A spider hopped from the burlap onto her finger. She shrieked, flinging it off then flipping around to face me. "You never let me do anything I want to do."

"That's not true. Besides, I made a promise to watch over you."

She rolled her eyes. "That was before Maman died. I'm thirteen now. You weren't much older when you took the job at the tannery."

"Do you think I had a choice? Now I'm seventeen and know better." I waved a hand around the cramped room. "I pay for all this. I have a say."

"The soot, you mean? The beetles and smell of rotting teeth? You don't spend your days pulling out your hair, wishing it was your skin, so you didn't have to feel the itchy dirt. With ten dublonnes a week, I could send some back. You could move out of the vieux quais by next winter."

"How would you send me money from the other side of the world?"

"There has to be a way."

"I've never heard of one."

"If Maman were still alive, she'd let me take the job." Zosa's bottom lip quivered. "Jani, I thought you wanted me to sing."

"I *want* you to sing," I said, and felt a pang in my heart, but I didn't know what else to do. "But not like this, without me. I'm sorry."

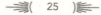

Zosa ripped off the lilac hat and chucked it into the hall. I took a step to grab it and stopped. A pearl peeked out of Zosa's sack.

Maman's pearl earrings.

When we were little, Zosa would clip them on and belt out a song, pretending to be a stage performer, while I crowed along like a tuneless donkey. I hadn't seen them since Zosa went on her first audition in Durc. Her only audition, until today.

The memory hit me. I'd thought the earrings would make her look older so I clipped them to her earlobes and put her in my old pink dress. She'd looked like a nervous little flower, but we'd needed money and Zosa wanted to audition more than anything.

Now I wished I could erase that day from both our minds.

I rolled a pearl between my fingers. Opalescent paint chipped away, exposing a cheap wooden bead beneath. After the audition didn't go as planned, I tried selling the earrings to a jeweler only to be laughed away. I never told Zosa how worthless they were.

"Listen to me. As soon as I save enough, I'm booking passage to Aligney." I took Zosa's hand. She tried ripping it away, but I held firm. "What if you're not back by the time I leave? Or something happens and I'm forced to go somewhere else? What if the hotel doesn't return for another decade?" I pictured returning from work to an empty room, and my throat thickened. "I don't want to be left alone," I admitted with a wince.

A tear slid down her cheek. After a few silent seconds, her small hand squeezed mine. She sat down. "My hair's a snarling mess from that hat. Would you help me brush it out?"

I let out a long exhale.

That evening, Zosa fell asleep early, while I lay awake, unable to close my eyes. When the Durc clock chimed eleven, my stomach rumbled; it had been hours since I'd eaten. I crept down the stairwell and stopped to pick up the lilac hat, now trampled with mud—the only casualty of the day, thank god.

Tiptoeing into Bézier's kitchen, I set the hat down and pillaged through leftover pantry scraps. Neck-deep in the bread shelf, I reached for a stale crust when the kitchen door creaked. I froze. It was late for girls to still be up. My fingers curled around a can of wooden spoons. Holding it like a weapon, I turned.

A man stood in the doorway.

"There you are. You're quite late, you know."

He inspected the banged-up lilac hat, then me. It was the young doorman from earlier. His cap was gone, no longer covering his shoulder-length black hair. When he tucked a dangling strand behind his ear, my breath caught. One of his fingers wasn't a finger at all but a finely carved and polished piece of wood.

It flexed.

Dangerous. The word flitted across my mind. I raised the can of spoons. He arched a brow. My arm drew back an inch. "What do you want?"

"Unless you were hiding this hat under your skirt earlier, I don't believe I'm here for you." He fingered a lilac ruffle. "I'm searching for the owner of this . . . thing. A young lady who signed a contract."

He meant Zosa. "She's not here."

Unconvinced, he stepped into the room. Too close. I launched the can at his head. It missed, hitting the wall, raining wooden spoons upon his shoulders.

"Excellent throw." He pulled a spoon from his collar. "As much as I appreciate a good game, there's no time. I've come to bring the hat's owner back to the hotel."

"Who are you?"

"My name's Bel. Now where is she?"

I didn't trust him as far as I could spit. "She's not going anywhere with you."

"So she is here after all."

I bit out a curse.

He turned to leave. I had to stop him. I reached under the butcher block and pulled out a thick, tarnished kitchen knife. Racing over, I flung myself between him and the door. Bracing one hand against the frame, I aimed the knife at his middle, and a thrill rushed through me. "Still think I'm another silly girl?"

"Of course."

"Oh . . . well . . . If you go any further, you'll regret it."

"I'm sure I will." He flicked his wooden finger. At the tiniest *snick*, a blade shot out. A switchblade.

He lunged at me. The kitchen knife clattered to the floor as he pinned me against the door, his face inches from mine. I felt his exhale against my bare skin. If someone walked in and saw us like this, they would get the wrong idea.

I flushed at the thought and struggled against him, but he held firm. With his switchblade at my throat, Bel bent and sniffed the air next to my neck. His nose wrinkled. "Isn't there soap in Durc?"

I reared back and spat on his face. He wiped his chin on his shoulder. The city clock chimed the half hour. Eleven thirty.

"Don't you have somewhere better to be?"

He swore, his blade clicking closed. "I'm not going to hurt you."

"Doubt it."

"Look. I'm taking your friend through the lobby door by midnight. She signed a contract. Deal with it."

I saw it then around the corners of his eyes, recognized it from my own face in the mirror; he was desperate. I knew from experience that desperate folk made foolish decisions.

"There are countless rooms here. You'll never find her in time. Give me a job as well and I'll take you straight to the owner of that hat."

He kicked the kitchen knife away and stepped toward me until my shoulders hit the wall. "You don't understand. It's nearly midnight."

Midnight was spoken with reverence: the hour the hotel left.

"I don't want to hurt you," he added.

I believed him. He didn't *want* to hurt me. But the look in his eyes told me he was willing to.

"Will you be punished if you don't bring her back?" I asked. There had to be a reason he was risking returning by midnight to find Zosa.

"I won't be punished. But don't you think it would be rude to deny the girl her job?"

Unbelievable. "After warning me away, how can you possibly care about whether my sister gets a chance to work?"

"Your sister?" he said. "And I don't care about her."

"If that's true, then give me a job, too."

"No."

"Then leave us alone."

A low growl escaped Bel's throat. "Enough. I have to find her, which means you have to move." He snaked an arm around my back, the other around my neck, his thumb catching Maman's necklace until it was on the verge of snapping.

I clawed at him. My fingers tugged something hard at his collarbone. It jolted me, and I clutched my wrist.

A thin chain holding a key had snuck out from under his jacket. I'd never touched magic, but there wasn't any other explanation for what I felt. I didn't understand, though—everyone knew magic ran through a suminaire's blood, not objects. He must be somehow enchanting the key.

"Are you a suminaire?" I asked.

Bel's mouth curved into a wicked smile, and my stomach dropped. He shoved the key under his shirt then glanced at my hand still wrapped around my wrist.

"Give me a job," I said again. Thankfully, the words came out sounding braver than I felt.

This time, an odd expression crossed his face, as if he were actually considering it. "Are you often this irritatingly persistent?"

"For you, always." Feeling emboldened, I flashed my teeth. "Will you take me?"

"It's not that simple. I don't carry ink and no one gets inside without first signing a contract or holding an invitation."

My eyes grew. "What if I could get myself inside?"

"How would you manage that?"

"With an invitation."

He released me. "Produce an invitation and I'll eat that ruffled atrocity of a hat."

"Then get a fork and give me five minutes."

"You have one minute."

I raced up the stairs to Bézier's third-floor sitting room. I ripped her framed invitation from above the mantel. Smashing the glass, I fished the paper out. I rushed down to the kitchen and waved it in Bel's face, breathless. "Will this work?"

He took it from me. "How old is this thing?"

"Will it work?"

"I've never seen anyone try to use an invitation this old before." He handed it back. "Now where is this sister of yours? We should have left ten minutes ago."

My blood pulsed. "You'll give me a job?"

"I don't exactly have a choice." Except he did. But for whatever reason, he was unwilling to leave without Zosa. His eyes settled on the invitation. "If we make it inside and that *thing* allows you entrance, I'll give you a trial run for a position."

"What does that mean?"

"You'll work for two weeks without pay, the same length as a guest's stay. Prove to me you're worthy to stay on and you will."

"At ten dublonnes a week?"

"Five."

Less than Zosa. But five was still more than I made now. "So you'll control my fate?"

"Let me guess. You have a problem with that."

"I don't," I forced out, even though the thought made my jaw clench. "So what if something happens?"

"You'll be out of a job." Meaning I'd be sent back here. Without pay and without Zosa. "It's a *very* generous offer."

"I'm sure it is." Three years ago I'd walked into Tannerie Fréllac desperate for work. Because of my age, I'd been given a trial run that turned into a long-term position. Just like Bel was offering me. I could do this. I glanced up. "How can I trust you?" He could easily be lying.

"I'm extremely trustworthy."

"I'm supposed to believe that?"

"Entirely up to you."

I wished Maman were here. She would know what to do. "Swear it on your mother," I said, thinking fast.

A pained look flashed across his face. "I don't remember my mother."

"Oh . . . Sorry," I said, awkward, while my heart gave a little twist. I barely had any memories of my own father. My gaze dropped to his key. "Then swear it on your magic."

"Fine. I swear on my magic I'll give you a job. Now we'll have to run if we want to make it on time."

Right. I pictured me and Zosa stepping out of the hotel and

into Aligney, returning home at last. Bel gave me an odd look when I giggled then slapped a hand over my mouth. I turned toward the stairwell and paused. If we ran, Zosa couldn't keep up with us.

"You'll have to carry her," I said, and flew up the stairs. Bel followed at my heels. Seconds later, he swung Zosa over his shoulder like a sack of winter turnips. She blinked awake, bucking, until I whispered the plan.

"Who is he?" she mouthed, then wagged her eyebrows at his backside.

God. "Stop that." I pinched her nose.

Bel looked between us.

"What is it?" I asked.

"You really wouldn't have let me take her without you." He sounded surprised.

"Like you said, irritatingly persistent."

His mouth twitched as if holding back a smile. "Don't drop the invitation until you're through the front door." He started down the hall.

Zosa's sack still sat on the floor filled with Maman's junk left over from her days as a music tutor. Those pearl earrings.

Then it hit me: Zosa would soon sing in front of a real audience, what she'd always wanted. All those years of scraping by were worth it after all.

In a few months we'd have enough saved to support us for years in Aligney. But we could travel with the hotel first, see some of the world. Everything felt too wonderful to be real.

"Would you hurry?" Bel shouted.

Footsteps creaked. Girls were waking up.

I hoisted Zosa's spider-infested burlap and raced after the doorman carrying my sister.

4

Maman once told me that a true gift tends to make itself known. The year I turned eleven, I finally understood what she had meant.

Aligney's Fête de la Moisson took place at the start of autumn. Grown-ups sipped vin de framboise under the stars and bartered their late summer crops, and Maman had her students perform to collect donations for the music school.

That year, Zosa had begged to sing at the fête. *Not yet, ma petite pêche*, Maman had scolded. *You're too young*. But I'd thought my sister was good enough to earn some dublonnes and we wanted to buy this tin of butter caramels we'd spotted in a shop window. They were exquisite—wrapped in golden foil with little adventure stories tucked beneath each label. Determined to have them, I tied ribbons into Zosa's hair and stole an apple crate from our cupboard. After sundown, we marched to the edge of town where the festival was held.

Everyone stood behind intricately painted stalls lit by flickering lanterns carved with fairytales. Embarrassed at our old crate,

I almost turned around. But Zosa refused, and I had splinters from hauling that awful crate. I hadn't wanted it to be for nothing.

Stealthily avoiding Maman, we crept to the end where the late arrivals were setting up. I recognized Madame Durand stacking aubergines from her garden. She turned up her ruddy nose when I kicked rocks to make a space. I put out the donation sign I'd painted along with an empty flour jar.

Old Durand had snickered, and I'd hated her for it. But Zosa ignored her. She hopped right up and began singing so beautifully that everyone stopped what they were doing to watch.

I'd been listening to Zosa sing for so long that her voice felt as ordinary as her snoring, but the people around us didn't have the same reaction. A crowd formed. *What a songbird! An angel! Remarkable little plum*, people murmured. Then Maman appeared, and she was covering her mouth.

That's it, I'd thought, *we're about to be hauled away by our earlobes*. But Maman's hand fell away and she smiled. Tears pricked her eyes, and I laughed in relief, and then at the sound of dublonnes clinking into our flour jar. All because of my sister.

I often wondered if Zosa remembered that day, if it had been as significant to her as it was to me. Now here we were, years later, standing before a prize larger than any flour jar filled with coins.

Moonlight cast Hotel Magnifique in shades of gleaming silver. Bel opened the black-lacquered door. With my hands gripping the invitation, the lights appeared crisp in a way they hadn't before. I pushed my fingers past the threshold. No invisible wall.

"*Greetings, traveler!*" A woman's obnoxiously effervescent voice chimed in my ears.

"Who was that?"

Bel glared. "Would you get on with it? You might be holding a sack of junk, but I'm holding a tiny person with rather sharp bones."

When I didn't make a move, he nudged me forward and I stumbled across the threshold. I opened my mouth to complain, but the words never came. The stink of fish was gone, replaced with floral scents and an undercurrent of oranges. And the sight . . .

This place wouldn't fit inside that old alley, nor a space fifty times that size.

The hotel was a palace.

A colossal staircase curved up the back. Candle-stuffed globes dripped from overhead like shining grapes. Above them, gold trim and filigreed fauna decorated every speck of ceiling, while the surrounding walls were papered in dark flowers. As I stared at the wallpaper, the petals *fluttered* as if blowing in a breeze.

The sights were almost too much to take in.

Mercury glass partitions hugged the perimeter, creating intimate seating areas filled with pink fringed cushions. One partitioned space contained a life-size chess set, its realistic queens dressed like goddesses in flowing robes.

Along a back wall, a series of alcoves housed plush banquettes. My eyes caught on a trio of huge, crescent moon–shaped lounge chairs near the door. They glowed as they bobbed, suspended in air.

Near the chairs, a row of luggage carts led to a grand concierge desk. No one worked the desk, and yet a multitiered cake covered in rose petals sat on the surface beside a tower of precariously stacked champagne flutes.

My breath halted as liquid bubbled from the top glass and spilled over the sides. Soon all the empty flutes were overflowing in a magical fountain of champagne, right atop the desk.

But behind everything was the greatest sight of all: a huge glass column shot to the ceiling, enclosing some sort of garden.

Moonlight filtered through white vines that climbed to where the column met the second-floor balcony. High above, a large bird swooped to a branch flush with more birds. It was an enormous aviary shooting through the center of the hotel.

There were storefronts along boulevard Marigny that kept exotic birds in cages. Zosa would giggle as they ruffled their brightly colored feathers. The aviary's thick glass blurred the view along the lobby level. Whatever was kept inside had to be unlike any bird in Durc.

The front door slammed. I turned and my sleeve snagged the branch of an orange tree that grew straight from the floor. Chunks of marble had crumbled away while thick roots twisted up from underneath. Branches hung with waxy leaves and gleaming oranges that appeared slick to the touch. Curious, I poked one. The orange swayed.

"Don't touch those," Bel said. He set Zosa down and looked from my neck to Bézier's invitation, a horrified expression on his face.

"What is it?"

"You're aging."

I lifted a hand and found myself unable to grasp what I was seeing. My skin was sallow. Each of my knuckles poked through loosening flesh. I ran fingers over my collarbone, shuddering at skin hanging where it should be taut. Age spots bloomed up my wrists. No, not age spots—they turned black and stunk, rotting and oozing. When a plump maggot wriggled out, I felt bile coming up my throat.

I wasn't aging. I was decomposing like a spoiled fish on the summer docks.

"Jani, what's happening?" Zosa scooted toward me.

"Don't," I croaked. Loose skin shuddered. At this rate, I'd be a corpse in minutes.

Before I could blink, Bel took off across the lobby. A sharp cramp stabbed my side. I stumbled, knocking the orange tree. An orange broke off, hitting the floor and smashing into shards. Even despite my current state, my brows furrowed. Fruit didn't shatter.

Another cramp struck me, and I sank to my knees. Bel returned a moment later with a sheet of parchment. A contract.

"Do something," I groaned.

Zosa whimpered.

He placed the contract in front of me, along with a large well of purple ink. With a flick of his switchblade, he stabbed my thumb and dripped my blood into the ink as the Durc clock in the square across from the hotel began its chime to midnight.

I managed to sign my full name by the eighth chime. Just before the tenth, Bel rifled through some big book leaning near the entrance. He pulled out his key and shoved it into the door's lock.

His forehead fell against black lacquer, the lean muscles on his back rising and falling at the eleventh chime.

I didn't look at my hands. I couldn't bear to see what was left. So I sat, dazed, waiting for that clock's twelfth chime to midnight. It never came.

Bel slid to a crouch, eyes locked on mine. I caught the edge of a smile before his forehead collapsed on his crossed arms. "Welcome back."

"He's right," Zosa said, amazed.

I touched my neck, my cheeks. My skin no longer sagged.

"Next time some fool tries to get in with an old invitation, remind me it's a terrible idea," Bel said, but I was too giddy with relief to let his words rile me.

"It's after midnight." Zosa hopped up and ran to the nearest window and tried to peek behind the shuttered drapes.

"We're not in that alley in Durc anymore, are we?" I asked Bel.

His brows drew together. "We're in *an* alley." Pushing up, he stepped toward me and stopped when his heel crunched against one of the broken orange shards. "You broke an orange? It seems you're not very good at following instructions."

I shot him a peeved look, but he was already kicking away the remaining shards, hiding all evidence of what I'd done. Then he studied me with an intensity I'd never experienced from anyone, let alone a man. My skin prickled. He leaned toward me, but didn't touch me. Instead, he grabbed my signed contract and swore.

"Is there something wrong with the contract?"

"Not exactly." He tucked it down his pocket.

"What's that supposed to mean?"

We both jumped at the click of heels on marble. "There isn't time to explain. I'll find you tomorrow before your orientation."

"When is that?"

He put a finger to his lips at the same moment Yrsa popped out from a back hall balancing a teacup on a saucer. "Ah, Bel! Glad you made it back, dearest. I was frightfully worried."

"We both know that's a lie," Bel said, his eyes never leaving her teacup.

"Because of you I had to send the gathering guests to bed early. Surprise, surprise. You're in a shitstorm of trouble."

"I retrieved your hire, didn't I?" Bel turned to Zosa, but it was me who caught Yrsa's eye.

"What's that one doing here?"

"I'm allowed to give out a contract every now and then under certain circumstances. Her sister refused to come without her," he said. Not exactly the truth, but I wasn't about to argue. "Don't worry. She'll be my responsibility. Besides, housekeeping needs the extra help."

"You're willing to take her on?" Yrsa sounded surprised and somewhat amused. "Very well. She can stay, but if she does something sublimely asinine, don't come running to me."

"She'll behave," Bel said, looking directly at me. A warning.

I thought of the two-week trial run and my stomach flipped. Luck got me here. Not merit.

Images poured through my mind—faces of workers plucked from the highest pedigrees. They'd all sense I was an impostor by tomorrow evening.

Stop it. You can do this, I told myself. No way I'd let anyone send me back now, especially Bel. He was probably already counting the ways I might mess up.

Zosa bounded over, skidding to a halt a foot away. She lifted an orange shard Bel had missed and yelped. The jagged piece bit into her palm. Blood dripped down her arm.

Yrsa set her teacup down and pulled a tiny vial of gold paste from her pocket. She uncapped it and scraped up the smallest bit. In one swift movement, she removed the shard and smeared gold into my sister's cut.

Zosa wiped her palm down her skirt, then lifted it to her face. "It's healed."

I inspected it. The cut was zipped up. Not even a scar.

Yrsa waved the orange shard at Bel. "Did you break a marvelous orange?" I'd never heard of a *marvelous* orange, but the look on Yrsa's face meant it was significant.

Bel shrugged. "Knocked it with my elbow when I carried the little one in." He cut me a look that said to keep my mouth shut. He was lying for me.

"Sorry if I made him break your orange, madame," Zosa added, clearly joining the charade to save my neck. I would have hugged her if Yrsa wasn't watching.

"Don't worry about it. It happens from time to time," Bel said, then turned to Yrsa. "Will you show these two downstairs? As you know, I have someone expecting me." He pointed to me. "And if that one tries to throw something at you, don't worry—she has appalling aim."

I could only glare at the back of his head as he stalked off.

"Good luck reporting to Bel. That boy doesn't care about anyone but himself." Yrsa picked up her teacup. "Now follow me."

She led us around the aviary. The glass went up forever, passing candlelit balconies. Around us, more orange trees grew from the marble. Haunting music filled my ears, but there were no musicians.

"It's all magic," Zosa whispered.

I nodded, breathless. With each step, the grimy film of my life in Durc seemed to drip away.

We barely blinked as Yrsa steered us down a staircase to an underground service hall lit by candles in slim sconces. The flames grew, turning mauve and casting the hall in dreamy pink. They stretched toward us as we passed. When one got close to my hair, Zosa batted it away.

"They're harmless and always curious of new staff. They'll stop soon enough," Yrsa said. "Here we are."

A door drifted open. The room behind it was tiny and perfect—it was like peering inside a dollhouse. Nothing was crooked or peeling or lived in. I was afraid to touch anything for fear I might corrupt it with my calluses.

Zosa rushed inside and flopped on a bed arranged with pillows. One bounced up and hovered an inch in the air, as if actually stuffed with spun clouds. The Bézier girls would squeal at the sight, but they weren't here. We were.

Yrsa turned to leave.

"Wait." She stopped. "Are we truly Elsewhere?" I asked. I knew her answer, but I needed to hear her say it out loud, that magic had taken me far from Durc, and one step closer to home.

Her hands curled around her teacup. It was filled to the brim with milk that miraculously swirled on its own.

"Welcome to Hotel Magnifique," she said with a smile, then sauntered off down the pink-tinged hall.

5

That night, I didn't dream of magic but simpler times in Aligney: afternoons scaling the village wall, fresh pain de campagne filling our bread box, Maman's fingers flipping through music workbooks on our sun-drenched kitchen table.

The dreams clung to the edges of my mind as I woke the next morning to Zosa's breath tickling my ear.

"You look worse than a rumpled troll," she said.

"Go away, goblin."

"Pixie-toed witch."

"I haven't a clue what that is." I cracked an eye and caught Zosa's grin. Slowly, I sat up. Zosa's old dress had been replaced with a white blouse tucked into a starched black skirt. "Where did you get those?"

"I found them in the wardrobe. They fit perfectly. Can you believe it?" She clasped her hands together and looked toward the ceiling. "Many thanks, oh divine goddess of the hotel."

"How do you think it works?" The wardrobe certainly looked normal. Zosa's sack sat on the floor. I was surprised she hadn't already decorated the room with Maman's things. Above the sack hung a maid's black frock. From the length, I could tell it was never meant for Zosa.

I would work as a maid.

I pictured my pretty sister singing to rounds of applause while I hovered in the shadows, a mop in my hand. *But you're here together*, I reminded myself as a wave of useless jealousy swept through me.

The dress was well made, at least. I ran my fingers over the white lace collar—silkier than anything I'd ever owned; I felt unworthy touching it.

"You look like you've been given a crown of diamonds." Zosa laughed and looked up once again. "Whoever is doing this, I gladly thank them." She then plucked a tarte aux pommes from a platter on the dressing table.

"Don't tell me a goddess dropped that off."

"They just appeared. Try a bite. They smell like destiny."

"Destiny doesn't have a smell."

"It does so, and a taste, too." She took a bite and moaned. "See for yourself."

I grabbed the pastry and took one bite, then another. Before I knew it, I was licking buttery crumbs from my fingers. Zosa smirked, but I ignored her and dusted off my old skirts. The fabric crunched like a stale wafer.

Zosa pointed to a slim door. "Washroom's there. Please change. I don't want *your* destiny anywhere near my pastries."

She was right. I nearly wept at the sight of a porcelain tub set with pastel soaps. After I scrubbed my skin raw, I changed into the black dress and spun, feeling fancier than I ever had. Tucking Maman's

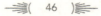

gold necklace beneath the constricting lace neck, I stepped out.

Zosa whistled. "Who knew you actually had a shape under all those lumpy frocks?"

"You shut up."

She snorted.

We both turned when a thick ivory card slid under our door. I inspected it. Gold letters printed across the front read:

Staff orientation begins at noon in the Blue Room.

Last night rushed back. Bel had promised to find me before orientation, explain why he'd acted strange at the sight of my contract. A clock hung above the bed. Already well after ten.

Bel could have forgotten his promise. But knowing him, he'd already written me off as a lost cause. The thought that there was something wrong with my contract made me uneasy, and I didn't want to wait for answers. I pushed my feet into the new boots beside the wardrobe and sighed at the perfect fit.

Zosa looked up. "Where are you going?"

"For a stroll." I pinched her nose. "I need to find Bel."

"Can I come?"

"It's your first day working. What if you're kept up late? You should rest." Plus, I doubted Bel would tell me anything with a pint-size gossip nipping at my heels. "I'll be back before you know it."

"But Jani—"

I cut her off with a single look. She groaned and flung herself on the bed. Pillows tumbled off and came to rest a hand's width above the floor. I fought the urge to peek inside one. *Later*, I promised myself and reached for the door handle.

"Don't look at the candles," Zosa blurted.

I walked over and swept a curl behind her ear. "There's nothing to worry about. This is the only place in the world where magic is safe, after all."

✳

After leaving the room, I took a service stairwell up, hoping it led to the lobby. But after I'd climbed it for five minutes, it strangely reversed direction and began taking me down.

Finally, I popped out in a candlelit second-floor hall strung with sleek umbrellas, each raining from the *inside*.

I plunged my fingers under one and wet wind dampened my cheeks. Walking quickly, I dipped my fingers under each umbrella I passed. Some rained tropical storms, others fierce gales. An aquamarine umbrella smelled like the summer showers from my childhood.

Beside it, a gloomy blue umbrella gusted with sea spray. I touched its waxed rib and immediately regretted it. It felt like I was rocking on open ocean. My stomach roiled. I was going to be sick.

A hand jerked me backward.

I spun to face a petite maid with light skin and rosy cheeks. She was near my age with blonde ringlets framing her pointed chin.

We wore the same uniform except a steel butterfly perched on her shoulder.

"You shouldn't touch the umbrellas," she scolded.

I wiped perspiration from my brow. "*Apparently.*"

Behind her were five more maids, each perfectly coiffed. I inhaled through my nose praying I wouldn't be sick all over their shining work boots. Thankfully, the wave of nausea subsided.

"Funny umbrellas, no? They only appeared yesterday."

"They did?"

"The halls change out constantly," the maid said, then perused my face. "I'm guessing you must be Jani. You're cleaner than I was expecting."

My eyes narrowed. "And who are you?"

"Béatrice," she said. "The head of housekeeping and your new boss."

But she hardly looked old enough to be anyone's boss. Bel's words came back, the trial run. If this truly were my boss, touching the umbrella would probably count against me.

Whatever expression I made must have been amusing because the other maids stifled giggles. *Wonderful.*

"Bel informed me that he brought you on to work under me." Béatrice looked me over. "I suppose no one told you that staff aren't allowed past the lobby unsupervised until after orientation."

Another rule I'd already broken.

My hands shot up. "I didn't know. I swear it."

The other maids whispered to each other, stealing glances at me. I fought an urge to run.

"Get to the laundry room, all of you." Béatrice shooed them off, then gripped my elbow. "Not you. I'll show you the way back to the service hall myself."

"Wait," I said. "Do you know where I might find Bel? Yesterday, he told me he wanted to speak with me before orientation."

"About what?"

"I'm . . . not sure exactly," I said quickly, not sure if I was supposed to mention my contract.

She gave me a lengthy look. "Well, Bel might be in the salon. I'll show you the way. Follow me." She led me down a staircase. Before I knew it, the stairs deposited us in the center of a lobby bursting with guests.

I'd never seen such a variety of people. Zosa and I had dark brown hair and olive skin like many southern Verdanniere folk, but the guests of Hotel Magnifique were every body shape and skin color imaginable. They were all draped in flamboyant fabrics and jewels, as if trying to win a costume competition before lunch.

I turned to follow Béatrice and ran straight into a guest with russet skin and large green eyes. "So sorry," I muttered.

With a harrumph, he unfolded a large pink fan made of dyed peacock feathers. He slung an arm over a fair-skinned man with tightly rolled curls that spilled past his shirt's tasseled shoulders. They both sipped champagne through silver straws.

"Watch where you're walking." Béatrice grabbed my arm. "If you upset a guest and the maître discovers it . . ." Her mouth tightened and I tensed.

"What a splendiferous morning," said a stunning older guest with skin a shade darker than Bel's copper complexion. She wore a hat piled with elaborate flowers and a tunic for the beach.

Everyone in Durc knew the invitations were good for a two-week stay, which meant fourteen different climates.

"If the hotel moves each night, how do they know what to wear?" I wouldn't know what to pack.

"Weather closets are scattered throughout the hotel, but the itineraries are the tool most guests prefer. They fill in when the maître decides on the next destination. Sometimes it's a day before we arrive, sometimes it's minutes." Béatrice's lips quirked up. "It's fun to watch guests scramble."

She pulled out a nearly blank slip of paper with *Itinéraire de l'Hôtel Magnifique* printed at the top, along with a kiss of rouge; someone had used it to blot their lips.

"I fish them from trash bins from time to time. Keep it. Now you can know what will appear out there." She pointed.

Twenty soaring windows stretched across the front, each one flanked by marvelous orange trees. Outside was a white-sand beach, but it was the windows themselves that stole my breath.

"Oh."

"They say the windows converse and decide on the single best angle to view Elsewhere, then repeat it across all the windows on this floor."

Each window didn't merely look out, but showcased the exact same frame-up of the beach. I stared when a woman in flowing crimson robes walked out the front door then turned, appearing through all twenty windows simultaneously.

Béatrice smiled. "It's something, no?"

Behind her, a sign was framed with gilded vines that twisted and coiled. For a brief moment, I thought I spotted a woman's face peeking out from beneath a golden leaf. The sign within the frame appeared ordinary in comparison. There were arrows pointing to the lavatories, the coat and raincoat check, the Ballroom of Astonishment, and an everlasting buffet. A liveried worker flipped the bottom arrow, changing the direction to the buffet to be to the left instead of the right.

Béatrice sighed. "The buffet moved again? I don't know how I keep anything straight anymore."

"You mean rooms move around at random?"

"Nothing is random. Rooms appear when they're needed. The game rooms, for instance, only appear during inclement weather and contain the most fantastical games. Certain ballrooms appear when a guest requests a fête. There are other rooms that sometimes pop up. Once there was a room filled floor to ceiling with porcelain plates." She frowned. "Never understood that one."

"Earlier, I took a strange staircase that shifted direction."

Béatrice nodded. "The hotel shifts to accommodate rooms, adding hallways, changing the layout. You'll get used to it."

As she continued speaking, I finally recognized her accent; ferries from the north would dock in Durc carrying wealthy folk who sounded just like her. "Are you from northern Verdanne?"

"You shouldn't say such things," she snapped. "Reminding a worker of their home when they're away from it for so long can be painful. It's rude to ask."

"I didn't realize . . ." My words trailed off as the lobby fell silent. Something rustled at my side.

"Seems the maître decided on tomorrow's destination," Béatrice said.

Everywhere guests reached into their jackets and purses, pulling out slim itineraries. Soon exclamations in a multitude of languages filled the air.

I plucked the rouged itinerary from my pocket and ran a finger over shimmering purple writing where it had just been blank. The woman's voice—the same effervescent voice I'd heard at the door—read the words as I touched them.

Itinéraire de l'Hôtel Magnifique
The city of Torvast, pinnacle of the Grimmuld Highlands.

Then the woman added, "*Secure your hats and knot your scarves. The wind is a notorious thief.*" A pause. "*Prepare to depart at midnight!*"

"Who is she?"

"You heard the woman's voice?" Béatrice's eyes grew. "No one knows. Odd you heard anything. She only speaks to guests."

I ran my thumb down the itinerary and pictured Aligney appearing in purple ink. When I looked up, Béatrice was a distance away. I raced after her, past the great aviary. Inside, white vines grew so thick it was impossible to see anything. "Where's the door?"

"There isn't one. The aviary is forbidden to everyone except the maître and Hellas, the Botaniste." Her expression darkened at the mention of Hellas. Apparently, she didn't care for him. "Let's move. The maître hates when maids dawdle."

As we walked the rest of the lobby, Béatrice pointed out alcoves named for such and such duchesse or dignitary. I forgot each name as soon as she said it, too taken by the sights to pay attention to words.

We finally stopped at a wall of glass café doors partitioning the lobby from a dimly lit room.

"Here we are," Béatrice said.

Inside, the ceiling reached two floors up, where crystal chandeliers dripped with those colored flames. A woman hung in the air above the stage, her feet balancing on what looked like glowing stars while she plucked a towering harp, lulling the guests. Above the doors hung the stained glass words *salon d'amusements*.

It reminded me of the first time I took Zosa to downtown Durc. We stood outside a restaurant sipping chocolat chaud and cackling as I made up stories about the fancy lives of the patrons behind the glass. But that restaurant was nothing compared to this.

"Bel was heading here earlier. If he's still inside, this is your best place to catch him," Béatrice said.

"Are maids allowed to go inside?" I didn't see a single maid's uniform among the guests.

"Only before lunch when it's slow. Good thing you work for housekeeping. Kitchen workers aren't allowed at all." She pointed to a stairwell. "That's the way down to the service halls. I'll go over your schedule at orientation." She then scurried off, muttering about soiled bedsheets.

I peeked inside the salon, but didn't see Bel. Yrsa made drinks behind the bar. She might know where I could find him. Before I could second-guess it, I walked in and sat on a barstool.

Blown glass bell jars glittered across the bar top, each one filled with a different color liquid. I spotted one filled with the same gold paste Yrsa had used on my sister's cut. Beside it, directly across from me, sat a peculiar vial swirling with silver smoke. I lifted its jeweled stopper and the tiniest plume snaked out.

Yrsa swooped over and corked the vial. "One minute here and you open *that?*"

"What is it?"

"Try a drop."

I jerked when a sunken face with hollowed-out eyes appeared through the glass.

"It's bottled nightmare," she said. "Any alchemist worth their salt has a vial."

"You're an alchemist?" I'd heard of alchemists selling cure-alls off street corners in the north of Verdanne, mixing elixirs that could easily be mistaken for magic. "But alchemy isn't—"

"Real magic?" Yrsa barked a laugh. "Most think that, considering nearly all alchemists' potions are fluff nowadays, crafted by suminaires and their magic so long ago they've been diluted a thousand times over. But not here." Her gaze roamed across the glimmering bell jars. "Most of these creations are new, and made by yours truly."

"You made the nightmare?"

"I made this bottle, but the recipe for it was created long ago

by a different suminaire. Some of the original stock still pops up at various destinations." She hid the vial, then slid over a drink the color of moonlit garnets. It glowed. "Don't worry, it's just juice."

"I'm supposed to believe you?"

"Believe what you want. I'm too busy to care." She left in a huff.

"Wait. I'm looking for Bel!" I called out, but she was already helping a guest.

Damn it.

Reluctant to leave, I lifted the glass of juice and took the smallest sip. My eyes fluttered. The drink tasted exactly like the tartine slathered with preserved apricots I'd gotten from a street vendor last summer—a handsome boy with deep tan skin and bright hazel eyes. He had smiled shyly at me and refused to take my money. I'd looked for him the next day, but his cart had gone.

I inhaled and thought I could smell his cologne mingling with sun-warmed skin. The drink grew sweeter, apricot exploding across my tongue. Before I knew it, the glass was drained and the salon was busier.

An amber-skinned server narrowed her pretty eyes at me. "It's late for maids to still be in here."

"Sorry." I pushed off the stool.

A firm hand touched down on the small of my back, holding me in place. "She's with me," said a sharp male voice.

The server startled. She curtsied and darted off.

I stiffened when Bel sidled down beside me and tapped the empty glass. "I take it you liked the juice?"

This morning he was freshly shaved, hair tucked behind his ears.

Striking, I admitted. The kind of man that would make most Bézier girls pout their lips.

At the thought, I lowered my gaze. Bel wore the same jacket as before, unbuttoned from throat to collarbone, that chain peeking out. When he caught me looking, I sat back on the stool, my neck heating underneath the constricting lace. The hint of a smile played on his lips.

"Don't smile at me," I said, flustered. When his smile grew, I scowled. Enough of this. "I saw your face when you grabbed my signed contract. You said you'd explain your reaction. If something is wrong with it—"

"Not here."

"So there *is* something wrong with it." My pulse jumped. "What is it?"

He brought his mouth to my ear. "I'm planning to show you later."

"Show me what?"

"What's your sister like?" He was clearly changing the subject.

"You met her earlier."

"I want to know more."

I felt compelled to say something. So I answered. In detail. I told him everything from Zosa's favorite song to the way she flicked me when I breathed with my mouth open. I pressed my lips together, but the words gathered behind them, pooling like saliva and aching to spill out. So I let them. Tears burned when I compared our life in Aligney to my days in Durc. Stealing from Bézier's pantry. How I was envious Zosa got to stay home while I scraped my fingers raw at the tannery.

Bel listened without interruption.

"No witty remark this time?"

"I'm sorry you went through all that."

He actually sounded sincere, which made me fidget. Wanting to switch subjects, I gestured to his switchblade hilt. "What happened to your finger?"

"It was removed," he answered curtly. "How old are you?"

"Seventeen." I looked him over. He couldn't be much older himself. "How many suminaires are in the hotel?"

He crossed his arms. "Too many. Where are both your parents from?"

"Verdanne. Where else?"

Blood rushed under my skin when he searched my face. "If your sister hadn't come, would you still want to be here?"

I tried to say no, that if Zosa hadn't come, I'd still be in Durc saving for the trip home. But I couldn't get the words past my tongue.

"Well?" he pressed.

"Yes," I said, then gasped, because it was *true*. It didn't matter whether Zosa was here or not. I was desperately curious about all the places outside the door. Yearning swelled in my chest, but I knew better than to listen to it. It was that same foolish curiosity that brought me to Durc, took us away from everything we knew.

Guilt clawed at me. I rubbed my eyes with the heels of my palms.

"What is it?" Bel asked.

"I was just thinking about my home."

He leaned in. "You miss it?"

That was an understatement. During the four years we spent in

Durc, I lived with a near-constant fear that I'd left behind the one place where I truly belonged. "As soon as this job is over, I'm taking me and my sister back to Aligney."

"I see," he said. "Does your sister want to go back?"

"I . . . of course she does."

He arched a brow. "Have you asked her?"

"Not exactly. I just . . . I . . ." I sputtered, and lost my train of thought as more questions bubbled up, filling my mind until it felt close to bursting. I opened my mouth and said the first thing that came out. "Why did you lie about that orange?"

Bel leaned so close I could feel his breath on my skin and my pulse fluttered. "Our maître tends to be overly concerned with the oranges. I think if he knew you broke one, he'd never let you leave. Now don't say anything more."

But the curious candles, the endless magic. The questions felt like knives cutting their way out of my throat. They needed out, now, else I might explode.

This wasn't me.

I wasn't secretive, but I was never this forthcoming with a man I barely knew, and certainly didn't trust. In fact, I never told anyone how hard my life was in Durc. I wasn't exactly proud of it.

Down the bar, I caught Yrsa's eye. A thought cropped up. An alchemist's trade was in potions to alter minds.

"What was in here?" I sniffed the dregs of the juice.

"If you're to be my hire, I had to know a few things."

That meant spilling the details of my life was planned. By him.

"You had her drug me?"

"I'm sorry, but there was no way around it. Yrsa usually handles the questioning, too, but I doubt you'd enjoy that option. So I talked her into allowing me the privilege," he said flatly.

He thought he did me a favor.

"Besides, it was merely a single drop of Truth mixed into the juice," Bel went on. "The drop allows Yrsa to uncover a potential hire's best ability in order to find perfect candidates for our open positions. It's usually dripped onto your tongue at the final stage of the interview."

Apparently I never got that far. But Zosa had. In the teahouse, she'd signed her contract so quickly. It must have been the drop of Truth affecting her—I could see how easy it would be to do something rash, with a feeling like this running through my veins. "How long will it last?"

"A few minutes, sadly." The hint of a smile flickered on his mouth. "In all honesty, this has been the highlight of my morning."

"You're despicable."

He cocked his chin. "You know, you're the first person with enough guts to call me that."

"You seem surprised."

"I guess I am," he said, almost to himself. "I'll find you about your contract later. If you want to work here past two weeks, you shouldn't be late for orientation."

Right. I rushed away clutching my throat, as if that would help keep any more unwanted words from spilling out.

6

The Blue Room was a sweltering space on the service floor, its only redeeming quality a sky blue ceiling painted with fluffy clouds.

I looked for Zosa. She wasn't in our room so I'd assumed she would be here, but I didn't see her. My worries only grew as I replayed everything Bel had told me. I pictured the maggot wriggling from my skin last midnight. If using an old invitation was strong enough to nearly kill me once, having something wrong with my contract could easily cause something worse to happen.

"Quiet, everyone!" A sharp voice sliced the din.

"Who said that?" whispered a worker behind me.

Someone pointed to a large, gilded mirror on a side wall. The maître's reflection appeared in it, but the spot in the room where he should be standing was empty.

"Welcome, everyone, to my hotel," the reflection said, and all the workers gasped. "My name is Alastair. And while I would love nothing more than to give you this orientation in person, I'm afraid I'm just too busy."

His mouth remained in an unwavering smile as he spoke. It reminded me of the too-perfect smiles painted on marionettes.

"What do you know of Hotel Magnifique?" the reflection asked the room.

"It's the only place in the world where magic is safe!" A fair-skinned boy in a doorman's getup shouted. "And it only stays one day in each place."

"Very good. Anything else?"

An older girl with smooth brown skin said, "We must be inside by midnight."

"What happens if we're caught out?" asked a pale-faced porter.

"At the entrance is the hotel's demarcation: the boundary between inside and Elsewhere. If a guest or staff member with a signed contract is caught outside when the hotel moves at midnight, they disappear. Unfortunately, they don't reappear anywhere else. It's a side effect of the powerful magic that keeps everyone safe inside the hotel."

The room went deathly silent.

Zosa had signed a contract.

In Bézier's kitchen, Bel was adamant about taking her. I'd assumed there was some selfish motive behind it. He'd saved her life, I realized, whereas I'd tried to stop him with that miserable knife. If I'd had my way, Zosa would be gone forever, and it would have been all my fault.

Standing on my tiptoes, I tried to look for her again, but there were too many workers. My pulse spiked. *Stop worrying. She's probably behind someone*, I told myself, but it was no use.

Zosa squeezed beside me, and I took a shuddering breath. "Where have you been?"

She didn't answer. Her eyes were glued to a beautiful woman with flawless light-colored skin near the mirror. She wore the same velvet uniform as Yrsa, but hers hugged each of her curves, giving way to a plunging neckline. Periwinkle curls bobbed from an enormous wig perched atop her head.

"Who do you think she is?" Zosa asked, awestruck.

"Someone who spends all her time in front of a vanity."

Zosa snorted.

"Hush," I said. We both giggled until Zosa tugged her shirt—the same blouse she wore earlier. Everyone wore uniforms except her. "Where's your uniform?"

"They said I would get it later."

"They?"

"Other performers. I still can't believe I'll be singing."

I was happy for her, I *was*, but for some reason, I had to force my lips into a smile. "Did they say when you'd start?"

She shook her head then elbowed my side as the maître's reflection cleared his throat. Candles flickered and everyone stilled.

"Now I'll have to warn you," the reflection said, that eerie smile as wide as ever. "Each of you is lucky to have your job, but the guests' experience is more important than any position here. If you break any rule, we won't hesitate to dismiss you. There are endless candidates vying for each of your places. Please remember that."

I squeezed Zosa's hand. The last thing I wanted was to be sent back to Durc.

"But," the reflection went on, "follow the rules and there will be nothing to worry about."

"What rules?" someone asked.

"You'll learn them from your supervisors in the coming days. They're merely precautions I take to keep magic safe. If you follow them, you will earn the privilege for trips outside where you'll experience for free what our guests pay dearly to see. However, if you can't wait, I'll void your contract and you can depart whenever you wish."

My heart thumped. That meant we could return to Aligney when the hotel got close. But we could work for a bit first, see some of the places from those itineraries. I bit my lip to keep from laughing.

"Now prepare yourselves for the most wondrous job you'll ever have." The maître's reflection swept a hand through the air. Glittery flecks shot from the mirror, landing across our noses. When they fizzled away, his reflection had disappeared.

Workers began gathering into groups by uniform. We couldn't find another performer, so Zosa stayed with me. Soon I spotted Béatrice standing in the center of a dozen new maids, young women with skin colors and body shapes as varied as the guests.

Béatrice pulled out a book titled *Monsieur Valette's Rules for Hotel Housekeeping, 4th Edition.* "Mornings are reserved for tidying guest suites," she read aloud.

That meant changing linens and scrubbing floors until they gleamed. Then I would spiff the candlesticks, dust the furniture, comb the carpets, and beat the rugs.

"After a quick lunch, you'll pick up where you left off. Of course, there are always odd tasks here and there. Cleaning ballrooms, sprucing lavatories . . ." Béatrice smiled sweetly. "Scrubbing toilets."

Zosa snickered and I poked her in the rib.

Béatrice described pre- and postdinner duties. She then gave a quick rundown of the guests, a dizzying plethora of nationalities. I learned the only similarity between them was their pocketbooks; the prized invitations were good for two weeks at a time, and those two weeks cost them dearly.

"Why does the maître need to charge the guests so much?" a taller, bronze-skinned girl asked.

"You'll learn that the guests' money has its uses."

I understood needing money to buy things, but the maître was the most powerful suminaire in all the world. "Why does he need maids, for that matter?" I added. "Can't he command the hotel to clean itself?"

"Not quite. There are enchantments that clean some spills along with other minor tasks. There used to be enchantments that made beds until a guest overslept and the bed made itself, trapping that *poor* wealthy guest under pressed sheets." She seemed to be holding in a laugh. "The guests are always changing, the rooms always adjusted for what we need. Enchantments aren't effective in an endless state of change. The maître would have to implement new ones constantly."

"Then why doesn't he?"

She shrugged. "He's told me enchantments take time. A team of

maids is more equipped to handle everything seamlessly without involving him. He prefers it that way."

As Béatrice spoke, sun rays began dancing across our faces. The painted clouds shifted to pinks and purples, as if the sun was setting inside this very room.

Béatrice looked toward the ceiling. "Here you will see magic unlike anything you've experienced. It's all to impress the guests, but that doesn't mean you can't appreciate it as well."

She stroked the steel butterfly on her shoulder. Its metal wings flapped on their own. She must be a suminaire.

Doors opened. The groups of new workers started filing out.

The maids began to move until Béatrice shouted, "One more thing! Every seventh evening we have a little soirée to bring on midnight. Tonight is the first of the summer and I can't risk new maids wandering through the lobby. You will take dinner in your rooms. Your work begins tomorrow at dawn in the second-floor laundry room." She then excused us so she could speak with a stout, pale woman in a chef's uniform.

Before I could take a step, the stunning, blue-wigged woman appeared at my sister's side. The same crème de rose paste Maman would use sparingly caked this woman's cheeks.

"You must be Zosa. Aren't you pretty? Follow me, sweet." The woman wrapped her fingers around my sister's wrist.

It was so sudden that, on instinct, I held Zosa back.

The woman smacked my hand away with a tasseled fan. "No fretting. This exquisite little morsel will be working for me nightly. She's my newest chanteuse." She looked me over while fingering something nestled in her cleavage, a silver bird's talon on a chain. "And who are you?"

"Her sister."

"Ah." Her lashes fluttered. She nodded at someone behind me. Béatrice appeared at my side. "If your new maid wishes to keep the position she has, she won't get in my way," she said to Béatrice.

Zosa's shoulders bunched. She turned to me, unsure, until her new boss took her arm and pulled her out of the room.

I stood there after the door shut, frozen. It felt exactly like the time Zosa had slipped under the eastern gate in Aligney's stone wall and disappeared. I'd run around, frantic, until an hour later when she turned up clutching fistfuls of wildflowers.

That same feeling screamed to run after her now. *Calm down. Zosa is perfectly safe inside*, I reminded myself. *You'll see her later.* Besides, the hotel wasn't open country.

"It appears your sister works for Madame des Rêves," Béatrice said.

Madame of Dreams. The title reminded me of the fanciful stage names decorating colorful posters around the vieux quais. It couldn't be the woman's real name. "Her uniform was similar to Yrsa's. Do they work together?"

"You could say that. The pair of them have worked very closely with the maître for as long as I've been here." Her mouth turned down as she spoke. "But they have different duties. Yrsa is in charge of the salon, whereas Madame des Rêves heads the performers and puts on the soirées."

"Does that mean Zosa will sing tonight?"

"Maybe." Béatrice led me to the door. "In the coming days, you can find her. Catch up. For now, I need you to go to your room. Dawn isn't negotiable."

I halted. "The coming days? But Zosa and I share a room."

"I heard about that little arrangement. Very last minute. There are endless rooms inside. Your sister will be given one near the other performers." With that, she shooed me away and shut the door in my face. I was too shocked to be offended.

I had my own room.

The closest I'd ever gotten to my own room was on my ninth birthday, when Maman surprised me with a bed she'd bought off the Beaumonts two houses down. The creaky thing was beautiful, with little vines carved into oiled walnut—a vast improvement on the cot Zosa and I shared, because it was all mine.

But that first night, the empty bed had felt strange. Zosa must have felt similarly because she weaseled her way under my covers. I pretended to be annoyed. She was my little sister. I wasn't supposed to want her in my bed, but I'd slept beside her for so long that it felt wrong to not have her there.

Now I had an entire room to myself.

Stunned, I walked the candlelit hall in a daze. Soon muted sounds came from nowhere and everywhere: the patter of rain, a kiss, the slither of silk stockings, and whispered curses. The sounds wrapped around me like a dream and left me disoriented. I wasn't sure what direction I was heading or if I'd walked this hallway earlier.

The halls could be rearranging, and I wasn't sure of the way back. Soon, I tiptoed down a hall with nothing but a single closet door carved with a sun and a snowflake, along with the words *Conditions Météorologiques Actuelles*. Current weather conditions.

Béatrice had mentioned weather closets. I opened the door expecting to see something spectacular, but it was only a supply closet filled with mops.

"Weather closets are only for guests."

I flipped around to face Bel clothed in evening livery, and my pulse picked up at the sight of him so close.

"I went to your room, but you weren't there."

"You did?" I looked around. "I thought I might be getting close."

"Your room is clear across the floor from where we're standing."

"Ah," I said, and turned toward the closet so he couldn't see the color creeping into my cheeks. "How does it work?"

"Promise to not go inside another one if I show you?"

I'd promise more than that. I nodded. He grabbed my hand. I tried to pull it away, but his grip was firm.

"I won't bite. Besides, I think you'll enjoy it."

A thrill snaked through me as Bel led me inside. He shut the door and I couldn't see a thing. This was a mistake.

"Now, don't move," he said.

7

I squeezed my eyes shut a moment before a cool breeze tickled my nose. "What's happening?"

"If you opened your eyes, it might be easier to see."

So I did and cried out. My hands scrambled up to grip Bel's shoulders.

"I could have sworn you didn't like me."

"Whatever gave you that idea?" I shoved him away and nearly lost my footing.

We stood on an ocean rock. Waves crashed and cool air gusted up my skirts. Below us, something large jumped from the water, its mouth filled with jagged teeth. I lurched forward and clung to Bel's jacket. His hands wrapped around me. This time, I didn't dare shove him away, even though his chest shook with laughter.

"This isn't funny."

"Oh, yes, it is. Don't worry. You'll be all right."

"Says the person I trust the least." I glanced out at the dark ocean. "Where are we?"

Bel pointed toward three buildings on the beach. Well, two

buildings, then a narrow structure squeezed in between.

"It's the hotel," I said.

Except the whitewashed slatted wood was replaced with a peach-colored clay exterior. The slim, single line of windows were in the same place, going up a quaint five floors, with a round window perched at the top. The hotel had the same bones but a different façade, like a snake that shed its skin at the stroke of midnight.

"Are we outside?"

"No. But this is what we'd see if we were at this very moment. The current weather." He knocked the open air and his knuckles *hit* something. "Technically we're still standing in a closet. So unless you want to be speared by an invisible mop, I suggest you stay still for the next few seconds."

It was an enchantment like the sunset ceiling in the Blue Room.

"Hold still." With his arms tight around me, Bel spun me to face the water.

My pulse leaped. I breathed in the night scents, the salt wind. I felt giddy.

"You all right?" he asked.

"No. Yes. It feels like I'm on the edge of everything," I said, and sneezed when a gust of ocean spray went up my nose.

Bel was quiet. I glanced back at him. A small smile played on his lips. He was enjoying himself, at least.

He shifted against me. "I take it you haven't seen many places like this?"

"Oh, one or two," I said, even though I'd been nowhere even remotely comparable. "I bet you've been to plenty."

"I have," he said. "But once you've seen one destination, you've seen them all."

"But that's not true."

"Oh?"

"No two places are exactly alike. In the sea south of Verdanne alone there are four chains of islands, each one with its own unique features."

He lifted a brow. "You like geography?"

I loved geography, but I was hesitant to admit it to him. He seemed more worldly than anyone I'd ever met. "There was a room in my boardinghouse stuffed with old atlases left over from sailors." My chest warmed at the memories of poring over each wrinkled page.

Sometimes those dusty maps would transport me to when I was younger. Back then, I dreamed of wandering on beaches with names I couldn't pronounce, lying naked on heated sand with only sunshine covering my skin. I'd wanted to experience the world with every inch of me. But that was before Durc, before I left home.

"What is it?" Bel asked.

"How often does the hotel visit southern Verdanne?"

"Are you thinking about your village again?" This time, his tone wasn't teasing.

"Why?" I looked up at him and froze.

He studied me with the same serious expression he wore when the orange shattered. He brought a hand up. The edge of his switchblade hilt grazed my chin. "I can already tell you're much too curious for this place." His hand dropped. "Here we are," he said

abruptly, then brushed past me, out of the weather closet.

I blinked. The beach was gone.

My hands scrambled to grip the walls for balance. "You could have warned me."

"What would be the fun of that?" he said with a wry smile, and darted up a nearby stairwell I could have sworn wasn't there before.

"Hey!" I sprinted to join him, coming to a stop on a landing carpeted with a pattern of sugared nougats and pastel bonbons. Chocolate scented the air.

"The nougats are sticky," Bel called out.

He was right. Prying my heels from the carpet, I caught up with him in front of an enormous caged lift.

"After you." He gestured to the open doors. I hesitated. "I thought you wanted answers about your contract."

I did. I stepped into the cage and onto a floor made of moving clouds. It felt solid enough. A filigreed dial on the wall pointed to *cirrus*. The other options were *cumulus* and *stratus*.

The lift's attendant didn't seem bothered by the clouds. He raised his tan hand. "Guests only on the lift tonight."

"Pleasure to see you too, Zelig. Six, please." Bel rapped his switchblade on the bars.

Zelig huffed but did as Bel said. The cage stuttered. When it came to a grinding halt on six, I fell against Zelig and then immediately righted myself.

"Seems you're destined to knock around kings tonight," Bel said once we were out. He glanced back at Zelig.

"Zelig's a king?"

"Was. Zelig ruled Isle Parnasse in the Seventh Sea. He's the reason the guests' stay only lasts two weeks. Alastair allows certain dignitaries he wishes to impress to pay absurd rates to stay longer, but never more than a month. Nothing like Zelig."

"How long did he stay?"

"Zelig emptied his coffers to stay for twelve years."

My eyes shot wide. Twelve years was staggering.

"Eventually, a distant cousin took over the throne and banished the hotel. Alastair wasn't pleased."

"But Alastair has the rest of the world. What does one island matter?"

"Trust me, it matters." He motioned down the hall. "This way."

The hall opened to a wide landing. The round sixth floor window hung in the center, huge and shining. I pointed to the view beyond it. "What's that?"

Bel watched me. "What do you see?"

A moon hung over water. But this moon was in a different spot than the one outside the lobby windows. It glowed murky yellow, illuminating hills to the west. Silvery sheets of rain pounded against the cobblestones. The docks gleamed like oil slicks in the distance.

From this angle, I could make out lights inside Tannerie Fréllac, then the dim gas lamps along boulevard Marigny. A small fire flickered on the third floor of Bézier Residence.

I pressed my palm against the window. Cold seared my skin. The glass rattled when a gust of wet wind flung up a sheet of water from

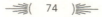

the port. I wrenched my hand away. My fingers were wet with condensation, and the cold still stung.

"Well? What's out there?"

"It's Durc," I said, because it was. It was also magic. Durc was likely on the other side of the world from us, but Bel didn't look surprised.

"The moon window is enchanted to show guests their home, where they'll return to upon checkout. One of the perks of paying for a stay." Durc wasn't my home, but the window didn't know that. Bel rapped a knuckle on the glass. "Judging from your face, it appears you're experiencing things like a guest would."

"But I'm no guest."

"No. You're not."

"Do I have magic?" I asked, and felt immediately silly. "I mean, I never thought . . ."

"Don't worry. You don't. Besides, I have magic and the moon window doesn't work for me."

"Then why—" I straightened. "My contract." It was the reason I was here, after all.

He nodded. "In the rush after you came inside, I grabbed the contract our guests sign. I didn't realize my mistake until it was too late."

"Right," I said, not quite understanding the implications. "So staff sign a different contract entirely?"

"Afraid so."

I thought of the woman's effervescent voice chiming in my ears.

The guests must experience much more magic than the normal staff. If I'd signed a guest contract, it meant I would see it all. Lightheaded, I glanced at Bel. My mood soured at the look on his face.

"What do you see?"

"The beach outside the front door, same as the rest of the staff," he said, and gazed out. With longing.

Béatrice warned me not to ask other workers about their homes, but I had to know. "Do you want to see your home?"

He didn't answer, but he didn't have to; it was painfully apparent. He must be from somewhere obscure where the hotel didn't frequent.

Alastair was cruel to not spare some magic so his staff could use the moon window, too. I felt sorry for Bel, but I didn't know what to say. Before I could fumble something out, Bel collapsed with a sigh on a velvet settee.

There wasn't another chair, only the spot beside him. My stomach fluttered, but I forced myself to sit. The velvet cushion hissed, moving under me like a stretching cat.

"God." I leaped up. "What in the hell is that?"

Bel's shoulders shook. He tried to hide his mouth, but the bastard was laughing at me again.

"I'm *thrilled* you find me so amusing."

"Believe me, so am I," he said, wiping his eyes. "Don't worry. It's just an enchantment. This place is dripping with them." He ran his fingertips along the tufts. "You can sit now."

"No, thanks." I crossed my arms. "Are we done?"

"Can't stand my company?"

"Not anymore," I said, then bit my lip. I did owe him for giving me a job, keeping me close to Zosa. I opened my mouth to excuse myself until he held up a hand.

"Look. I know you don't trust me, you don't have any reason to, but you have to keep your contract between us. If the wrong person were to find out—" His mouth pressed into a hard line.

I wasn't planning to tell anyone, but I hadn't thought it might be dangerous for somebody to find out. The notion sent a chill down my spine. I nodded.

"Very good." His eyes darted to a wall clock. "It's late. I should get downstairs."

As he spoke, music drifted up, along with sounds of clinking glasses and laughter. The soirée. I edged closer to the balcony, but I couldn't see a thing. "Will the soirée have a lot of magic?"

"More than you can comprehend. Then after everyone is dizzy with it, a handful of the most powerful suminaires put on a show to finish out the night."

My mouth fell open.

"What is it?"

"There were rumors in Durc that the most powerful suminaires are immortal."

"Immortal, huh? I guess that's one way of looking at it."

"Then it's true?"

"Somewhat." He touched a protruding vein on his wrist. "Our power is determined by the amount of magic in our blood. It allows us to heal faster than normal."

What he said made sense. "I've heard of suminaire children

healing after grievous wounds, coming back from death. It was said to be a way to tell a suminaire from a normal child . . . along with other rumors."

"What other rumors?"

"Craving blood," I blurted, and took a step back. "I mean, you don't—"

He laughed. "Don't worry. I don't have any appetite for your blood. The other rumor is closer to the truth."

"Coming back from the dead?"

"No one can come back from death, but there are suminaires who can heal from near death. Some think it's our body's defense mechanism for our own magic. Less powerful suminaires live a little longer and heal faster, but they still age and die. Very powerful suminaires, like the ones performing tonight, are different. Like you said, practically immortal."

"Like the maître?"

"Exactly." He straightened his jacket to go, then caught my shoulder, leaning in and pulling me so close that my heart crashed against my ribs. "If you have any more questions, please come to me first. For some strange reason, I don't trust that mouth of yours."

I wrenched my arm away with a scowl and nodded.

"Good." He gestured to a narrow stairwell. "The eastern stairs. They'll take you back down."

As he walked off, I lowered myself on the settee then cursed when the cushion began to *purr*.

Bel's laughter echoed down the hall.

8

As I descended the stairs, I couldn't get the pained look on Bel's face at the moon window out of my mind. Durc was the last place I wanted to see, but the idea that Zosa couldn't see it bothered me.

Our contracts were printed on thick parchment with paragraphs I didn't read. We'd signed them without a second thought. Clearly, there was more to them than I'd realized, and given what I'd learned so far, there were probably more clauses I wouldn't like. I should have asked Bel more, grilled him.

All thoughts of my contract evaporated when the eastern stairs didn't bring me to my room, but instead deposited me in the middle of the grand lobby. The soirée.

A wave of panic hit. Bel must not have realized Béatrice forbade me from setting foot here. The only way down I knew of was the service stairwell by the salon—clear across the lobby.

Quickly, I ducked past men surrounding card tables and women gambling jewels the size of eggs.

"So sorry," I said as I knocked into a woman with lustrous brown skin wearing a gown of silver fish scales. Beside her, a young light-skinned man with a shooting star headpiece yawned, oblivious of the fuchsia rouge smeared down his chin.

I jumped back as a stream of women ran past with feathered angel wings strapped to their shoulder blades. They were followed by a colossal sailboat made from champagne flutes steered by chic sailors on stilts. The entire thing rocked. Champagne sloshed and the revelers pressed in around me. I couldn't move, couldn't tell where I was or see the stairwell. My palms turned clammy.

"Here." A guest with fair skin and brunette hair handed me an empty champagne flute then blinked, revealing glossy lips painted on each of her eyelids. Another woman with warm brown skin kissed her naked shoulder.

I gasped with relief when the guests parted, until I realized it was only to make room for a bright red piano played by a woman with deep amber skin wearing a silver tux. She stood, playing the air while the keys continued to compress in time with her fingers. I wiped sweat from my temples and shoved past more suminaires.

A bronze-skinned man juggled fire on a saucer. A pale, freckled girl with the reddest hair I'd ever seen poured endless liquid from a thimble into guests' cups. A tawny-skinned, tattooed woman ran an emerald feather under her nose, inhaling color through her nostrils until the feather was leeched to a bone white. Then she *blew*. A stream of green rolled off her tongue like smoke from a cigarillo. Guests clapped when the smoke hit a pair of men, changing every item on them deep green, including their eyebrows. When I looked back, the feather gleamed citrine. Zosa's jaw would be on the floor.

At the thought of her, I glanced around. I couldn't see any singers, but I spotted the service stairwell, thank god.

I pushed toward it and nearly jumped out of my skin when a champagne flute smashed near my toe. The floor buckled, swallowing the glass with a mouth of white marble. A guest noticed it and giggled, while another guest lurched away.

In fact, the guests' reactions to the magic were as varied as their speech. It made sense; each nation would have different views on magic based on their own thorny histories with suminaires. The one thing it seemed we all had in common was fascination.

"Maids aren't usually allowed at the soirées," someone said. I turned. A short olive-skinned server glared at me.

"I—I was on my way downstairs." I pointed toward the service stairwell.

A pair of hulking men stood on either side of it. Identical twins. They mirrored each other's movements as if they shared one mind. Bald heads pivoted in synch to scan the crowd. In place of one eye, they each had a line of flesh sewn shut with black thread that stood out against their pasty white skin.

They blinked in unison. I jerked.

"Who are they?" I asked the server.

"Sido and Sazerat. They're suminaires who report to the maître. I'd find another stairwell if I were you," he said, and dashed off before I could ask where that stairwell might be. *Damn it.*

A guest's jacket lay forgotten on a chair. That would do nicely. I tossed it over my shoulders to mask my uniform. The crowd began shifting. Quickly, I ducked into an alcove to wait out the soirée.

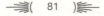

Once all the guests headed to their rooms, I should be able to sneak downstairs unnoticed.

As I pressed myself out of sight, I spotted a small wall plaque hidden in a shadow. Most of the letters were rubbed off, but three words were still visible: *artéfact guide you.*

The words were Verdanniere, except I'd never heard the word *artéfact* before. It could be a very old directional sign.

The lobby fell silent. I looked up to see Alastair stepping out— rather dramatically—from behind a star-spattered curtain near the door.

"Greetings, travelers," he shouted. "Welcome to Hotel Magnifique, where the whole world awaits!"

Everyone cheered.

"As you cross continents and seas, we will do our best to pique your curiosities, to fill your mind with wonder, and to deliver infinite happiness that will live on in your heart long after your stay is forgotten. Now, let the show commence. We depart for Elsewhere at the stroke of midnight!"

Lights dimmed and a circle of guests formed nearby. It was too dark to see if the twins still guarded the service stairs. Too dark for them to see *me*. Swallowing down nerves, I slinked toward the circle.

A woman with beautiful brown skin and glittering lips stood motionless in the center, sheathed in navy velvet. She held a purple flower bud to her nose. Her unyielding posture reminded me of the Durc street performers who powdered themselves bronze, pretending to be statues.

A man beside me squeezed a card.

"May I?" I asked.

He passed it over. Silver embossing ran across the front: *Le Spectacle de Minuit*. The Midnight Show. The back of the card read like a program.

> The *Illusioniste* will begin with a flutter of smoke,
> followed by the *Botaniste* with a feat of paper.
> For those needing a refreshment,
> Madame des Rêves and her *chanteuses*
> will perform on stage in *Salon d'Amusements*.
> But hurry back, *mesdames et messieurs*, hurry back.
> For at the stroke of midnight,
> the *Magnifique* will take us Elsewhere.

My fingertip hovered over the word *chanteuses*. Zosa was probably performing in the salon, but I'd be a fool to try to go there now.

I scanned the rest of the card. All the other titles must be of suminaires, which meant the woman with the flower bud was the Illusioniste. Except she wasn't doing much.

I looked up and gaped.

Eight versions of the woman now stood smelling the unopened flower. Then they moved in unison, touching index fingers to the petals. Guests cried out when the buds bloomed into *wings*.

Moths, butterflies, and bees began pouring from their open

palms, forming clouds that covered the ceiling. The women clapped their hands and the clouds changed color. Mauve. Peach. Blood-red. Silver. Indigo. Guests looked stunned at the spectacle. But the show had only just begun.

The lights flickered and the women vanished.

"Look!" someone shouted.

High above, the eight women descended from the clouds on an enormous chandelier in the shape of a ship. Their gowns were replaced with corsets and pantaloons dripping with silver netting. They began to speak in unison.

"I am the Illusioniste hired to astonish you. In my last trick, I'll become a tempest on the ocean blue. Revel in my underwater merriment. For after checkout, you will forget all of it."

They clapped their hands and the lobby filled with blue light. A salty breeze rolled through. A nearby guest squealed as bubbles fluttered out of her nostrils. Another guest's skirts billowed as if underwater.

My own skirts swirled up, exposing my calves. I tugged them down. When I looked up, the chandelier was gone, the lobby returned to normal.

The eight women now stood on the floor. I blinked and the women changed to one. She bent to take a bow, and a man wearing hotel livery came up.

The crowd erupted in applause until shouts drew everyone's attention.

A young man stood across the lobby. His silver hair reached down his back and leaves painted on his cheekbones glittered against the deep gold color of his skin. Around him, red flowers grew up from white squares on the marble.

"Do it again, Botaniste," said a guest in accented Verdanniere.

The Botaniste. The title Béatrice had mentioned. She'd said only Alastair and Hellas, the Botaniste, were allowed inside the Aviary. She didn't seem to like Hellas. *This* suminaire.

Hellas shuffled a deck of cards and held up a jack of spades. He tossed it forward. It landed on the ground and grew into a white vine covered by black spade-shaped flowers, matching the card's suit.

An older guest stepped on a flower and it shriveled back to a card. "It just crumbles to nothing. The suminaire's magic is weak!" he shouted.

The crowd gasped. Hellas smiled and snatched the guest's fedora.

"Give it back." The guest flailed, but I supposed it served him right for being so rude.

Instead of returning the hat, Hellas pushed a playing card inside and tossed it up. When the fedora hit the ground, the marble parted. Roots coiled around the guest's feet, growing into a white paper tree. The guest howled. Thankfully, bark grew over his mouth and bloomed with blossoms the exact hue of the fedora's sapphire feather.

"Never doubt a suminaire of Hotel Magnifique, else you'll find yourself losing things besides mere hats," Hellas said without any hint of humor. I decided right then that I would never cross him.

The crowd clapped then began backing up, making room around the lacquered door.

"The Magnifique should be here any minute," said a guest. "I

heard he's the most powerful suminaire here, besides the maître."

A stage had been wheeled in front of the door. Oil lamps were lowered on pulleys, brightening the entrance. Alastair stepped out alongside Madame des Rêves.

She had changed into an outrageous gown decorated with peacock feathers. Her wig was no longer periwinkle but pure white and twice as tall. She still wore the silver bird's talon at her bust, but her fingers were wrapped around a delicate oval hand mirror.

She fanned herself with it until Alastair plucked it away and carefully pushed it down his jacket pocket, as if it were precious to him.

Madame des Rêves cleared her throat and the entire lobby darkened. "Esteemed travelers! Please welcome the suminaire whose glorious magic moves us each night." Des Rêves raised her arms. "The Magnifique!"

Lights flickered. The Magnifique stepped onstage wearing white gloves and a cape. I'd pictured a gentleman with a waxed mustache, but this was only a brown-eyed young man with a key dangling from a chain, a key I'd *touched*.

The Magnifique was Bel.

Last night, he locked the door. I didn't realize *he* was the suminaire responsible for moving the hotel. Bel had said powerful suminaires were practically immortal.

He'd meant himself.

No wonder he seemed surprised when I'd called him despicable in the salon. No one would dare speak so candidly with a powerful suminaire. I buried my face in my hands. I'd fought with him, spit on him. I'd even threatened him with an old kitchen knife.

Reaching behind the orange tree, Bel pulled out the same book he'd paged through last night. The spine cracked as he flipped through it.

"Two minutes to midnight," whispered a guest. She held an itinerary where one filled-in destination glimmered purple.

Guests knew where the hotel would appear, but this was more thrilling than any speck of ink. To think, we were all about to blink through the world in a century-old building, and I could barely see.

I elbowed my way forward until I could tell that the book was a strange atlas filled with cobbled-together maps, some on smaller pages, some scribbled on newsprint.

Bel stopped at a large map and dragged his hand down it with a reverence similar to how I'd treat Bézier's atlases. Then he pushed his key inside the door's lock, turning it clockwise. A second passed, then another.

"Here we are," Des Rêves said. She elbowed Bel out of the way and opened the door. Outside wasn't a beach but an expansive city, glittering and vast. Tiny snowflakes fell through the air. My lips parted.

Alastair and Des Rêves bowed to deafening applause.

Bel stood behind them and gazed outside with the same enthusiasm I witnessed on the guests' faces. *Once you've seen one destination, you've seen them all*, he had said. Clearly that wasn't the truth.

After a minute, he shut the door and rubbed the back of his neck,

tired. Understandable considering he moved this place every night. At least he only had to make a ridiculous show of it for the soirée crowd every seventh night.

When Alastair and Des Rêves took another bow, Bel quietly slipped away.

9

The following morning, I woke alone in a bed for the first time in my life.

It felt like some of the magic of this place had fluttered away with my dreams. Zosa wasn't beside me, and I didn't like it. *She's probably still tucked in bed, snoring away*, I tried to remind myself, to put her out of my mind. But after the information I'd learned last night, it was impossible.

My fingers fumbled with my buttons as I dressed, my mind too preoccupied with everything Bel had told me. But there was one crucial detail he'd left out: he never actually answered me when I asked about visiting southern Verdanne. The maître's guarantee that we could depart whenever we wished meant nothing if we didn't travel closer to Aligney than Durc. I couldn't bear it if we were dropped off even farther away from our home, and yet I didn't ask about it.

I should have questioned Bel more about the places we stopped, but I was too distracted by all the magic. Part of me wanted to corner a worker and demand answers, but I'd promised Bel I wouldn't speak to anyone else. As tempting as it was to ignore him, I knew

I couldn't. Not only was he a powerful suminaire, but he'd saved Zosa; I at least owed him enough to keep my promise. My only option was to watch for him as I started my shift.

This morning, Béatrice gathered all the new maids then led us through a maze of dim halls dotted with guest rooms titled like poetry. We passed the *To Tangle in a Labyrinth Suite* and *A Taste of Sin and Chocolate Suite*.

"Are the rooms themed?" asked a maid behind me.

Béatrice nodded. "The maître tailors each suite for our more prestigious guests. He shifts the colors, the décor, even the scents and sounds behind each door."

A fragrant smell wafted from an open door labeled *A Breath of Blooms Suite*. The scent calmed my nerves. I peeked inside.

Dahlias formed clouds across the ceiling. A bed frame made of delphinium stalks somehow supported a mattress. Along a dressing table were glass-domed cloches with enchanted floral scenes. In the closest cloche, moss swans bobbed on a forget-me-not pond.

I spotted a golden button the size of my pinkie nail on the wall. Beside it, an equally dainty Verdanniere sign read *Press for Champagne*.

Curious, I lifted my hand.

Béatrice popped over. "Unless you want to clear away a bucket of champagne the size of a bathtub, I wouldn't touch that."

I didn't believe it. "An entire bathtub?"

"At the press of a button." She stepped back to address all the maids. "Each guest room is filled with surprises. Especially the one you're all about to clean."

We lined up as she barreled her laundry cart through the most massive suite door of all.

"Voilà, the *Ode to a Fabled Forest Suite.*"

The suite was aptly named; the room could have been sculpted from my childhood storybooks. I swept my hand across a dressing table carved with horned beasts. Lichen bloomed where my fingers touched.

A purple velvet box sat on top. I flipped the lid revealing guest paraphernalia: a pair of filled-in itineraries and a series of luggage tags. I unrolled a scroll of paper with A *Packing List for Elsewhere* printed along the top. The list called for items like cravats and dinner jackets and things I'd never heard of: a fog umbrella, hosiery for bathing in salt water, a trundletvist.

"What's a trundletvist?" I asked.

The other maids looked equally confused.

"Some posh doodad from wherever that guest calls home," Béatrice explained. "The Packing List for Elsewhere is unique to wherever you arrive from."

I smiled at a smaller packing list for pets, should you choose to bring yours along.

"Where's the room key?" It wasn't in the box.

"We don't use room keys," Béatrice said. "The suite doors are enchanted to open for guests during their stay, then for staff once the guests check out. Each door is also equipped with an interior lock, but don't you dare turn it. They tend to trigger more enchantments."

Béatrice then pulled out a crate filled with everything from washing soda to chloride of lime. "Time to work," she said, and left us to show a couple girls to another suite.

I soon found myself piling armfuls of linens on the floor.

"Soiled linens go in the laundry cart," said a maid.

"Sorry." I looked the maid over. She was tall with beige skin that looked sallow, like she hadn't slept well. "I'm Jani. What's your name?"

She blinked at the question, so I repeated myself. Finally she said, "Sophie. It's Sophie."

"Are you sure about that?"

"Of course," she bit back.

Her strong reaction struck me as strange. "Sorry I asked."

With a petulant huff, she picked up the pile of soiled linens, leaving behind a throw pillow hovering in the air near my ankle.

I lifted it. A thread stuck out and I tugged it. Probably not the smartest thing to do, but I couldn't help myself. The seam began to unravel, opening a tiny hole in the pillowcase.

The other maids gathered around, awestruck. Evidently, the pillows weren't stuffed with spun clouds.

I held my hand above the opening. Feathers poured through my fingers, traveling up, up, combining in a single white stream that billowed across the ceiling.

Girls giggled, dancing their fingers through the weightless feathers. The laughter turned to an abrupt silence when Béatrice returned.

Sophie pointed at me. "That girl did it."

Béatrice was silent. I could practically feel her turn through punishments, judging whether she should get the maître, send me away.

Stop it, I told myself. It was just a silly pillow. But I still froze until a younger, amber-skinned maid plucked a single feather from the air.

"How does it work?" she asked, and Béatrice seemed to relax.

"Most of the magic you'll see inside are enchantments penned by the maître himself. He is the most powerful suminaire here," she said. I wanted to know how one man penned all of this into existence, but I didn't dare ask because Béatrice fixed her steely gaze on me and clapped her hands. "Now back to work."

Over the next few hours, I discovered a host of little enchantments that made my job easier: the tissues replenished themselves, the pillows remained perfectly fluffed, even my boots never left a scuff. I tried to be happy with how marvelous it all was, but my mood was slowly spoiled by a series of odd behaviors from the other maids.

I asked a second girl her name and she reacted similarly to Sophie. Then every time I attempted a conversation, the maid would trail off mid-sentence, or wander away, or busy herself in a task, following each rule like her life depended on it.

It went on throughout the day. The maids' behavior left me so unsettled that after Béatrice excused us to our rooms late into the evening, I had a hard time falling asleep. Zosa's absence only added to my growing unease.

The next morning, after a series of disturbing dreams, I bolted awake, a terrible feeling still squeezing my chest. Though my first day in the hotel had been filled with wonder, that was beginning to fade the more time I spent here. Everything I'd learned from Bel, the behavior of the other maids, all of it was beginning to gnaw at my thoughts. Something wasn't right about this place. But aside from conversations, there was nothing tangible I could point to that would prove what I was feeling.

After dressing for my shift, I decided to take a different route to the laundry room and stumbled upon a small gilded chest labeled *Wishing Box*. Engraved words instructed guests to bring their lips to the keyhole and whisper a wish for something they wanted the maître to create. I turned down another hall and passed a suminaire handing out presents. Guests peeled back striped paper to uncover fistfuls of rose petals that ignited into miniature firework displays in their palms.

The magic seemed harmless enough, and all to heighten the guests' experience. Still, the enchanted sights didn't stop the feeling that something was terribly wrong.

"We need to make a quick stop on the fifth floor," Béatrice announced after I arrived in the laundry room. Of course none of the other maids asked where we were going, so I kept quiet as well.

We soon arrived outside double doors padded with ostrich leather and tufted with pearls. A sign above read SALON DE BEAUTÉ.

"Lovely, no?" Béatrice caressed the tufts then swiped at the corner of her eye, batting away a tear at the sight of the door. Her reaction seemed a bit much. "Madame des Rêves modeled this room after Atelier Merveille."

"Where's that?" someone asked. I'd never heard of the place.

"It's only the most famous ladies' store in Champilliers. Where Des Rêves purchased all her wigs. Madame re-created the famed dressing rooms here." Béatrice stroked a tufted pearl. "I'd love to see the real ones."

"You haven't been?" I asked. Champilliers was the largest city in Verdanne, renowned for its canals on the river Noir. Surely the hotel visited.

Béatrice shook her head. "There's a list of places we don't travel. Champilliers is on it. Maître's orders, unfortunately. If we ever visit, I know exactly where I'll spend the day . . ."

She smoothed her hands along the doors then pulled them open to a plush pink space filled with dress forms and curios stuffed with silks. In the center, workers fussed around a guest.

"L'Entourage de Beauté." Béatrice gestured to workers. "Suminaires skilled at amplifying a guest's *beauté*."

The tawny-skinned suminaire with the citrine feather was a member of the entourage. She inhaled color from her feather, then blew puffs of yellow along the guest's bodice, while another suminaire smoothed a bobbin of thread around the guest's waist. The thread wove itself into a pattern of embroidery, while a third suminaire pulled a porcelain brush through the guest's hair, creating perfect curls from nothing.

Everything was magical, and shades of pink. Even the members of L'Entourage de Beauté wore pink livery.

When I was younger, Maman assumed pink was my favorite color for no reason at all. I didn't hate the color. It just wasn't me. I preferred jewel tones, emeralds and sapphires as deep as oceans, colors captains wore when they helmed ships and heroines when they sneaked away to meet their secret lover in the dead of night. Blazing peony pink was Zosa's favorite color. She'd probably burst into a giggling fit at the sight of all this.

I tensed at the thought of her. Béatrice had said she'd be warned of everything that might get her in trouble. And after the strange behavior from the other workers, that was all I could grasp onto to keep from panicking. I'd look for her room this evening. Knowing Zosa, she'd hunt me down first.

"The top latch broke again." A worker waved her pale, chapped hands at a towering glass cabinet, its top door hanging crooked.

Béatrice twitched her wrist. A tiny tin canister dislodged from her sleeve. She popped the lid. We all took a step back as a glinting cloud of gears shot from her tin toward the cabinet.

"You're a suminaire," I said.

I'd suspected it, but aside from the steel butterfly she wore that occasionally flapped its wings, I hadn't seen a speck of her magic until now.

"I am, and skilled at repairs. Since the maître doesn't like to be bothered with matters like these, I'm always called. It's why I'm head of housekeeping." She waggled the canister. "All suminaires are put in higher positions based on their specific abilities."

"So your ability is fixing things?"

"Usually. But these cabinets are tricky." She twitched her wrist again and again. The gears shifted, clattering against the cabinet's handle, but nothing else seemed to happen. "The cabinet door is quite stuck." She sighed and the gears streamed back into her tin.

I stared at the tin—another magical object, just like Bel's silver key. The pink-liveried suminaires with the spool of thread, the brush, the feather—more objects.

"How does your tin work?" I asked. She had to be enchanting it somehow.

Béatrice opened her mouth then closed it, her expression turning guarded. "You know, it's not wise to concern yourself with suminaires and their magic."

End of discussion. The workings of magic must be an off-limits topic.

The worker waved at the broken cabinet again. "What's taking so long?"

Béatrice gave us a sidelong look. "Why don't you all head down to the laundry room. This will take longer than I'd hoped."

With quick curtsies, we dipped out. The other maids turned back the way we came, but I halted. Down the hall, a maid stood pinching her temple. It was Sophie, the maid from the guest suite.

I rushed over. "What's wrong?"

"Headache. Poor thing." A brown-skinned guest walked over trailing a turquoise fur coat. She waved around a glass of champagne. "I get terrible bouts of them myself."

"Have you had headaches before?" I asked Sophie.

"I—I don't know," she said.

"You don't?"

"I can't remember." Her lips trembled. "I think I'll go lie down for a bit." She wandered off clutching her head.

"I told her to go outside," the guest said. "Fresh air always does the trick, but she refused. Said she doesn't like to go out."

"What?" There were Bézier girls who worried the sun would ruin their complexions, but the hotel didn't always travel to sunny places. In fact, everyone in the teahouse line in Durc spoke nonstop about where they wanted to visit if they were hired. That was part of why we all wanted to work at the hotel: to see far-off places. The biggest perk of the job, aside from the magic. But that maid didn't like to go outside—didn't want to experience Elsewhere.

It seemed inconceivable enough on its own, but coupled with all the strange things I'd noticed, it set my stomach in knots.

The floral wallpaper lining the halls seemed to darken with my mood. Petals dropped from withering flowers. Too many things were just a little bit off, and I couldn't shake the feeling that there was something deeply wrong. I wanted answers about this place. I doubted I'd be able to sleep tonight without them.

I turned back to speak with Béatrice and halted, cursing under my breath as I remembered my promise to Bel.

The guest lifted her glass and grinned. Half her teeth were replaced with gold. "Want some champagne, darling? I pressed this little button, and poof! Now I'm drowning in the stuff."

"I can't. I—I need to find someone," I muttered.

"Good grief, you maids are no fun," she called out as I darted off.

I only had a handful of minutes before I was due in the laundry room, so I looped through the lobby looking for Bel. When I didn't spot him, I darted up a stairwell that deposited me in a familiar area on the second floor.

Béatrice had said halls come and go. Evidently the umbrellas had gone, replaced with a shadowy hall hung with white plaster intaglios of the same woman's profile, each showcasing different emotions like boredom, pleasure, and grief.

As I gazed at each profile, the woman's emotions muddled my own thoughts. My feet slowed to a stop and I swept a finger across the scrunched brow of one intaglio. I heard weeping and a swift sadness clotted my throat. My attention shifted to an intaglio on the bottom row. The woman held a single finger to her lips as if shushing someone. I leaned toward it. The hall darkened and candles guttered.

"Careful who you trust," a soft voice whispered from somewhere in the distance. A chill crept over me. Slowly, I lifted a hand to the intaglio.

"Those are only for guests to touch."

I spun.

The maître stood against a dark corner.

I stumbled, knocking an intaglio off the wall. I waited for plaster to shatter. For Alastair to demand my name, fire me.

Nothing happened. The intaglio hung as if it never fell.

He stepped toward me clutching a slim inkwell filled with shimmering purple ink. Unlike the large wells Zosa and I had used to sign our contracts, this one looked ancient and was capped with a silver stopper in the mold of a wolf's head, its jaws biting down as if the wolf feasted upon the well itself.

I glanced at his fingers. One stuck out crooked, the skin around it mottled and rippled.

"Leave," he snarled.

I did the only thing I could think to do. I ran.

10

The image of Alastair's hand squeezing the wolf-capped inkwell burned in my mind. His expression. It was the first time I'd seen him without a smile on his face.

There was no denying he was angry, but as far as I knew there was no rule preventing me from being in a hall. I shuddered. If I'd upset him, it didn't matter what the rules were. No one would look twice if he sent me back to Durc tonight.

I forced myself to walk, but all I could hear in my mind were those whispered words: *Careful who you trust.* I didn't know who I could trust here yet. I wanted to trust Bel—he was probably the closest I had inside to a confidant—but then he never told me he was the Magnifique. There had to be other secrets he was keeping—things he didn't want me to know.

The candlelit halls seemed to narrow, and I was all alone. A throb built at my temple and I had an urge to run, to find somewhere safe to catch my breath. I turned the corner toward the laundry room and stumbled into a cluster of maids carrying mops. Relief swamped me at the company. I braced myself against the wall, my chest heaving.

One fair-skinned maid's eyes grew at my empty hands. "No mop? Béatrice will chew your head off. All the maids were ordered to help clean up."

"Clean up what?" I asked.

"The sky started dumping sleet. Some guests refused to go outside so the maître ordered the performers to head up impromptu games."

My pulse ratcheted. "Which performers?"

"I'm not sure. All sorts."

If Zosa were part of the games, I had to find her. There were extra mops along the wall. I took one and followed the crowd.

The game room was as large as a grand ballroom and lit to look like a night sky sprinkled with stars. Dozens of box-shaped glass rooms filled the dark space, each containing a group of people.

My face fell. I didn't see Zosa in any of them.

"*Greetings, traveler!*" the woman's effervescent voice chimed in my head. "*Welcome to the Glass Puzzle, Hotel Magnifique's inclement weather game of danger and escape. The rules are simple: follow the clues to find the way out. But be forewarned, once you're inside a game, there is no stopping it until the exit is discovered. Bonne chance!*"

Each room held a handful of guests alongside a suminaire.

In one glass room, I spotted Hellas's silver hair and deep gold skin. The Botaniste fanned himself with his deck of playing cards while guests picked through a small forest of his white paper trees. In a different room, a young girl with brown skin and delicate features blinked bubbles from a monocle and braced herself as guests pushed against the walls, rocking the entire room back and forth. Another room held a miniature storm. Ladies floated a foot off the ground as a pale, liveried boy blew through a pocket-size weather vane. More magical objects.

In a nearby room, the red-haired suminaire from the soirée poured a stream of never-ending liquid from a thimble. A group of soaked guests—all with the same blonde hair and tan skin— searched the wet ground with their fingertips. My heart skipped a beat when the red-haired suminaire looked right at me. Then her gaze shifted back. I turned, but behind me was a wall.

"They can't see us," the maid shouted above the din.

"What do you mean?"

"Just what I said. Once you're in a game, you can't see out."

"But the walls are glass." I stepped forward to examine the room. The maid jerked me back. "Don't get too close."

"A group is coming out!" a voice roared.

We both jumped and the maid knocked into me. My hand shot out to brace myself against the room, but instead of stopping, it passed through the glass. I tumbled headlong, landing in a puddle of warm liquid. My right foot still poked outside. When I pulled it the rest of the way through, the ballroom disappeared. The glass walls turned opaque white. I knocked. Solid.

"How fun. A maid has joined us," said a guest in thickly accented Verdanniere. She twirled a costume mustache like a spy from some theatrical play. Her ruffled dress was soaked through.

The liquid felt like bathwater, but from the scent, I knew it was tea. The walls shined like ceramic. The opening of a spout curved across the ceiling. We were trapped inside a teapot. I counted. With eight people, the room was snug.

"Maids aren't allowed inside the games," said a high-pitched voice.

I turned. The red-haired suminaire stood in the corner. "I didn't mean to—"

"Des Rêves's in charge. If she catches you, you'll be fired."

She spoke so casually, but it managed to shake me to my core. "Can you let me out?"

Her fingers squeezed her tea-pouring thimble. "I'm afraid you'll have to wait. Once you're inside a game, there is no stopping it until the exit is discovered."

The same words as the woman's effervescent voice. Except the walls were solid with no exit.

A guest waved. "There's no clue that leads to the exit. We're doomed to drown."

"You're allowed one hint," said the red-haired suminaire. "Do you want it now?"

Everyone chanted, "Hint. Hint. Hint." followed by cackles of laughter.

"Very well. But the hint has a price." At her words, a series of letters pushed out from the wall.

"What's the price?" I asked.

The suminaire lifted her thimble. It poured faster, the tea climbing quicker. Right.

I didn't recognize the language of the hint, but I trudged over, trying to understand the puzzle so I could find the exit and leave.

"Look, the maid has come to save us all!" one guest howled, waving an empty wine glass.

"What could you possibly try that we haven't?" said another guest.

I agreed with him. I had no idea what to do.

I sloshed back to the suminaire. "What's your name?"

"Red," she said.

Made sense. Her hair gleamed like a ruby.

"Well, Red, I'm certain the guests have had too much to drink. You have to let me out." When Red didn't move a muscle, I wrapped my fingers around her thimble. It sizzled with magic.

"Don't touch my artéfact." Red ripped the thimble away.

Artéfact. It was the same word inscribed on that plaque in the lobby. I stared at the thimble.

"There was a plaque with the word *artéfact*—"

"Hush," she whispered, suddenly fearful. "That word doesn't leave this building. It was foolish of me to say it out loud."

Red was as cagey as Béatrice. Before I could question her further, she swiped back a clump of wet hair, revealing a circlet of small dots tattooed across her forehead. I'd seen that same pattern across the brows of sailors in Durc.

"You're from the Lenore Islands, aren't you?" The small chain of islands was a two-day trip southeast of Verdanne. Bézier once told me the tattooed dots mimicked the star formation directly above the main isle.

Her jaw tensed. "I don't recall."

"You don't recall where your home is?"

She turned away from me. "I need to get back to my job."

A tremor of unease moved through me. Béatrice and Bel had

both danced around answering any questions about their home. Now Red didn't seem to remember it. My worry was only growing the more I heard.

I grabbed the nearest guest, the mustached woman. "Where did you enter the hotel?" I asked. "Do you remember your home?"

"Stanisburg? Of course I remember it." She sniffed. "The maître promised me I wouldn't forget a thing until after I check out, and certainly not my home."

Of course. She would soon return home because she was a guest.

I shivered. At the moon window, Bel said workers couldn't see their homes. He never mentioned anything about forgetting where they were from. But then again, he never mentioned being the Magnifique, either. It seemed he'd left out a lot.

I remembered Durc perfectly, though. It must have something to do with the guest contract I'd signed. In that contract there were the paragraphs of languages—anything could have been hidden inside it. The maids would have all signed staff contracts. If those contracts altered their memories, it might explain their strange behavior.

I rubbed my face. Thinking about any of it now wouldn't do much good. If Des Rêves wasn't outside the room, she was on her way. If they sent me back to Durc before I could get to Zosa—

"Please let me out," I begged Red.

Her mouth tightened to a slash. "I'm not allowed. The only way out is to find the exit and end the game."

"How? I can't read the language the clues are written in, and the guests aren't in any hurry."

"I'm sorry, but you'll just have to wait."

"And be caught by Des Rêves? Fired?" I glanced around. "Can you at least tell me where a door might appear?"

She sighed. "I'm not allowed to tell you where the exit is, but I will say it's not a door." Her gaze flicked up to the inside of the teapot's spout above us.

"That's the way out, isn't it?"

Her lips pressed together.

It must be. "But there's no way to get up there."

"There will be once everyone solves the clues."

"What if we can't?"

She lifted her thimble and tea gushed out. "Either Des Rêves will let us out or we'll swim."

I wanted to scream. I looked around. There had to be another way up, but the walls were slick and the room was narrow. Then a thought struck.

"I figured it out," I said. I'd seen guests rocking a room. I shoved my shoulder against one wall, then rushed over and pushed on the opposite wall. "If we all push in unison, we could tip the room over and crawl out the spout."

"It's my job to make sure guests follow the clues to the exit," Red hissed. "I'll be in trouble if they don't."

Whatever trouble she might find herself in couldn't be worse than me getting sent back to Durc.

Ignoring her, I shouted, "Everyone push!" But the guests weren't listening. I couldn't tip the room on my own.

An older guest turned to me. "You're not very convincing."

His words gave me an idea. I cleared my throat. "The sooner we

tip over the room, the quicker you can all collect your prizes."

"Prizes?" a woman asked.

Red glared at me.

"Fantastical prizes," I said. "Better than a firework display in your palm. And"—I paused for dramatic effect—"you get to take them home with you *after* checkout."

Eight pairs of eyes widened.

I couldn't help but smile. "Don't just stand there. Help me rock the room."

Red didn't join in, but the rest of us moved in unison, heaving palms against one wall, then the other. The weight of tea sloshing back and forth added to our efforts. Soon, the entire room tipped sharply to one side. "Lean on the wall."

This time they listened. We pushed. Everything tilted, then tumbled over. Tea shot up my nose. I landed on the floor, sputtering.

Tipping over the room caused the walls to vanish. The entire game had disappeared.

Red sat in a wet heap a distance away. People gathered. I scanned their faces. Des Rêves wasn't here yet, thank god.

Next to me, the guests sat in a blubbering pile. I hobbled up and lifted the hem of my sodden skirts. I curtsied. "Congratulations. You may all collect your prizes in the lobby."

A hand grabbed my arm.

"This way. *Now*." Béatrice dragged me toward a potted palm, face twisted in rage. "Before she sees you."

Then I heard it.

Heels clicked. An orange wig bobbed above the rooms. Red sat across the puddle. I hesitated.

"Leave her," Béatrice said. "There's no time."

She was right. We ducked behind the palm just as Des Rêves rounded a nearby room, Hellas at her heel. They didn't see Béatrice or me; their eyes were too glued to the mess.

"This game wasn't supposed to end like this. What did you do?" Des Rêves bellowed.

Tears rolled down Red's cheeks. She hugged her knees, terrified. But Red didn't tip the room herself. Surely she wouldn't be punished.

Béatrice dug her fingernails into my palm to keep me still.

"I don't have an ounce of time for this." Des Rêves's eyes narrowed at Red. "Hellas, take that girl to the maître."

11

"I forbid you to speak." Béatrice dragged me along the service floor, then up a flight of stairs.

"It was an accident. I didn't know I wasn't supposed to enter a g-game." I hugged my arms across my dripping frock as a shudder ripped through me. "Will the maître really punish that suminaire?"

"What do you think?"

My shoulders sagged.

On the second floor, Béatrice knocked on a slim door. When no one answered, she ordered me to wait while she left, returning moments later with Bel in tow. My stomach clenched at the sight of him. He shook ice from his hair, nearly as sodden as I was, as if he'd been outside all morning.

"You asked me to watch over this girl, but it's impossible when she does reckless things," Béatrice said.

Bel looked me over. "What—" he started to ask.

"She entered a game." Béatrice cut him off. "A suminaire was taken to the maître."

"Yet Jani wasn't caught."

"Thanks to me." Her eyes were bright with anger. "Take the rest of the night off. Tomorrow you're scrubbing toilets," she hissed in my direction, and stormed away.

Silently, Bel led me inside the small room. My teeth began to chatter. Bel rifled through a closet by the door. "Here." He handed me an old maid's frock that looked two sizes too big then turned to face the opposite wall.

"You have got to be kidding."

"Freeze to death if you want." He shrugged. "One less thing for me to worry about the next two weeks."

I faced the door. "Don't you dare turn around," I said, and struggled to undo the wet buttons at my back. My hands shook from cold. "Damn it."

"Hold still." I gasped when strong fingers pinched the material at my nape. I squirmed, but Bel held me in place. "This isn't anything I haven't seen before."

"So you often help remove the dresses of frightened, helpless women?"

He snorted. "Daily."

Quickly, he undid all the buttons down my back. I spun around. "Face the wall," I ordered, and kept an eye on him as I peeled the wet dress off until it was a sopping puddle on the floor.

He started to turn.

"Not done!" I shouted, fumbling with the new frock. He huffed and turned anyway, hopefully only catching a glimpse of my bare legs before the black material fell into place. My hands still shook, but the rest of me was blessedly warm.

"Took you long enough," he said.

I rolled my eyes and looked around the room. There was no bed. "Is this your room?"

"No. Did you want to see my room?"

"I . . . No," I stammered. He managed a laugh. "I hate you."

"Right now, likewise." He gestured around the tiny space. "This is the map room."

Against one wall, a shelf was stuffed with dusty objects. A painting of a woman hung above a cold hearth. Delicate strokes created the woman's piercing eyes, light skin, and sharp nose. Her low neckline showcased a bronze pendant.

I knew her face. It was the same woman I'd seen repeated in tiny plaster intaglios in that magic hall where I'd run into Alastair. As I stared at the portrait, the floral wallpaper the woman stood against *bloomed*. Black petals bulged from the canvas. One tumbled to the ground.

The gilded frame looked expensive and the portrait was masterfully done. She must be someone very important. Or very rich. "Who is she?"

"I don't know."

Nodding, I fixed my eyes on a round table, painted with flowers from around the world. I traced my thumb around the purple petals of an Aligney blood poppy. There were papers scattered across the surface. One had a quick drawing of a signet ring. The giant atlas Bel used when he moved the hotel sat in the center, opened to a hand-drawn map labeled with delicate penmanship.

"Every map in that whole atlas was drawn by a single suminaire," he said, noticing where my gaze had landed.

"The woman in the portrait?"

"Perhaps."

He removed his jacket. His damp shirt stuck to his chest, outlining the panes of his muscles, and my skin tightened.

I swallowed and took a step back. "You look lovely," I said dryly.

"So do you." He gestured to one of my soggy locks. "You can't wander into escape games."

"I didn't wander in," I said. "I—" Thinking back to what had happened, the conversation I'd had with Red, everything I'd experienced in the past two days came crashing forward. "I've had strange conversations with a few maids. Then in the game, the suminaire didn't remember her home, but the guests do, and so do I. The only difference I can think of is that guest contract I signed. You didn't tell me everything the contracts do, did you?"

"I was planning to."

I crossed my arms. "Well, you can start now."

Instead of answering, Bel pulled a ball of linen from his pocket and carefully unwrapped it to reveal an old pair of dice etched with moons.

I shot him an incredulous look. When he ignored me, I was tempted to grab the dice and throw them at his head. Before I could do it, he plopped them in my palm. Magic hummed softly against my skin, different than Bel's key. Cool and silkier.

Somehow, mercifully, the magic calmed me. I exhaled and rolled the dice. They felt similar to Red's thimble. "Are they . . . an artéfact?" I asked, testing the word on my tongue.

"How do you know that?"

I told him how Red had accidentally said the word, then about that plaque in the lobby. "I've seen other suminaires using magical objects like these." I stroked the dice. "How do they work?"

"Artéfacts aren't magical themselves. They're reservoirs for magic. Every suminaire is given one the moment they come inside. They pull magic from our blood and transmute it into a single spell before it can hurt anyone."

"But I thought the hotel is enchanted to keep magic safe." It was the reason everyone felt comfortable coming here.

"The hotel has nothing to do with it." He touched the chain that held his key. "I don't need an artéfact with me at all times, but it would be dangerous to go more than a few days without one, or without using my magic in more basic ways."

Everything I knew about suminaires must be false. "What basic ways?"

"Healing is one. Outside of the hotel, some suminaires keep their magic from flaring up by healing themselves over and over." He shrugged. "But I've never tried it because I've always had an artéfact close by."

I couldn't believe it. All that hatred and fear of magic. This whole time, artéfacts could have put everyone in the world at ease and no one knew they existed. "Wouldn't it be better if Alastair spread the word about them? If people realized—"

"Not an option, unfortunately." He plucked the dice from my hand. Then, in one swift movement, he took my wrist and flipped me around. I struggled. "For god's sake. I'm not going to murder you."

"You're so reassuring."

He laughed. "Just try to hold still." My breath halted when he bent me forward. His hand slid down my arm to press my palm tight against the open atlas. "Feel that?" he asked against my neck.

My skin heated. I could feel his fingers encircling my wrist and the warmth radiating from him, but I doubted that was what he meant. I breathed in and focused my attention. Then I felt something else. Two distinct pinpricks of magic on the map's surface tickled my palm. "What are they?"

"Magical signatures. Sometimes they represent a suminaire, but more likely, they're artéfacts." He dragged my hand along the page. I felt two more.

Four artéfacts.

"Alastair told me the method to craft them was lost over time. It involved powerful suminaires, blood, and other things he can't figure out. So he doesn't make his own, thank god. Luckily for him, they were scattered around the world when suminaires were either killed off or forced to flee from persecution, and there aren't that many left."

He released my wrist and paged through the atlas. I recognized a couple of maps of cities on the continent. The rest of the maps were foreign.

"The magical signatures on these maps show me roughly where each artéfact is hidden, but they're still difficult to track down."

"You track down artéfacts?"

"Tracked down these just this morning." He shook the dice then shoved them in his pocket. "Besides using my key each midnight, it's my job." He flicked one of my damp curls. "Unlike *you*, I'm rather good at it."

I glowered at him.

"Please just listen." His eyes shifted to the atlas. "Somehow Alastair got his hands on a record of known artéfacts. He's searching for a number of them. The magical signatures dictate where we move the hotel each night."

I straightened at his words. Our destinations were all based on tracking down artéfacts.

"Is he looking for that ring?" I pointed to the scrap of paper on the table with the signet ring scribbled on it.

Bel grabbed the paper and stuffed it down his pocket. "Alastair is looking for many artéfacts."

He didn't seem pleased by that fact.

"If artéfacts are the easiest way to keep a suminaire's magic from hurting others, wouldn't finding them be a good thing? Alastair could take on more suminaires, keep everyone safe."

"The staff certainly believe that." There was something hidden beneath his words.

"But you don't believe it."

"Not entirely. Alastair is fanatical about safety, but beneath it all, I think he's greedy. But it's just a theory I have. Alastair doesn't want suminaires outside the hotel collecting artéfacts themselves. He's said there aren't enough left in the world to go around."

"How many are left?"

He didn't answer. Instead, he stared at me, his lip caught between his teeth. The silence made me suddenly aware of how close he stood, how small the room was. "You know . . . I'm not exactly supposed to be telling you any of this."

The way his eyes searched mine seemed significant somehow. My stomach danced with nerves. "Then why are you?"

"I'm not sure . . ." He looked down. "I guess I don't want you to do anything you might regret."

The way he said it—"Are you worried about me?"

"No," he said too quickly, and my eyes widened. "Don't flatter yourself."

Incredible. He *was* worried about me. Which meant he cared enough to worry in the first place. I tucked that thought away to turn over later, because right now there were answers I still needed. "So are you going to tell me about the contracts, or do I have to throttle the information out of you?"

Bel's expression flattened and he gave me a look I couldn't read. Instantly, I was on edge. "The staff and guests' contracts are opposites in most respects. The memory of this place disappears from the minds of guests once they check out."

"Yeah? So what? That's common knowledge."

"True. But what's not common knowledge is it's the reverse for the staff. Once a new worker signs a staff contract and steps inside, their memory of home disappears."

My eyes widened.

"It's why the moon window doesn't work for me." He gave me a pitiful smile. "Congratulations. Because of my mistake, you were spared."

I took a step back, the truth eddying through me. Bel's painful expression at the moon window wasn't because he couldn't see his home, but because he didn't even remember it.

Then there was Béatrice's reaction in the lobby when I asked about her home. Of course it was rude to ask. It probably triggered the same pain I saw in Bel, the same blank look on all the maids. It all felt too horrible to be real.

I squeezed my eyes shut, grasping for memories of Aligney. Its stone walls. The sunshine turning the fields of farmland gold. I could walk Aligney's grid of cobbled streets blindfolded. The thought of those streets ripped from my mind made my lungs burn.

Maman always joked that the soil under our village was part of my blood. I didn't know who I'd be without my memories of it. The village made me who I was, made Zosa who *she* was.

Zosa. She'd signed a staff contract, which meant she'd be like Bel for as long as she worked here.

There had to be hundreds of workers inside, their homes taken from them. Erased. The cruelty of it was staggering. But it didn't quite add up. Bel had just said Alastair was greedy, fixated on finding artéfacts, but that didn't account for why he took away memories of home from his staff. He had to do it for some purpose. No one was that heartless for no reason.

I pictured his smile in the Blue Room's mirror, and my stomach sickened. He'd promised us the most wondrous job we'd ever have. Certainly not this.

Then I remembered something else.

My ears rang as I walked to a small window in the corner. Outside, the sky was darkening. The view showcased a snow-covered topiary garden. Hedges were carved into animals that shouldn't exist: winged bears, fork-tailed cats, and four-legged swans. There were a few flamboyant guests wandering about but not a single person in hotel livery.

That word doesn't leave this building, Red had said. About arté-facts.

"Alastair promised everyone at orientation that if we do a good job, we'll be rewarded with trips outside. When will I be allowed out?" My voice sounded shrill.

"Only a small handful are allowed out at any given time."

"How small a handful?"

"It's not important."

My teeth clenched. "How small?"

He sighed. "Yrsa goes out to conduct interviews. Béatrice, but with an escort and only to purchase supplies. A couple others for security. Me."

He didn't say another name. My god, workers weren't even allowed outside.

"I'm sorry, but it's just how it is," Bel said gently.

A suffocating sensation crawled over me. It seemed like everything I'd been told since setting foot in this hotel was a lie. I had to warn Zosa, but I didn't know where she was. I'd left her by herself for two days. *Whatever happens, promise to watch over your sister*, Maman had begged me before she died. I could still picture the tears streaking down her wasted cheeks.

"I need to find my sister right now."

"You seem to find enough trouble as it is. Searching for her this late will only get you in more."

I couldn't believe it. "But she's my sister. I have to find her. You must understand—surely there's someone you care about inside this place."

He flinched, as if my words upset him. "The only thing I care about right now is for you to not do something else as reckless as the escape game. Have you seen the twins?"

"I saw a pair of bald twins each missing an eye. I—I almost ran into them."

"Why does that not surprise me?" He rubbed his forehead. "It's a good thing they didn't see you. Sido and Sazerat are Alastair's watchdogs. They each carry artéfacts that amplify their strength, two identical little stones they keep sewn into their uniforms. They're dangerous. And if they see anything suspicious, they'll alert Alastair."

"But Zosa—"

"You might work under Béatrice, but I gave you the job." He slid his hands around mine. When I jerked away, his knuckles knocked the table. "I'm responsible for you. Do you even know what that means?"

He didn't get it at all. "You might not think I understand responsibility. But I do."

"Sure you do." He began paging through the atlas.

My skin grew hot. "You don't believe me?"

"I don't believe many people. I wouldn't take it personally."

I never told anyone what had happened to bring us to Durc, but if he were my link to Zosa, it might help him to understand.

I steeled myself. "Four years ago, our mother died and left us with nothing but a smattering of junk."

Bel's fingers stopped moving. At least he was paying attention.

I cleared my throat. "After the funeral, I went through the house collecting things to sell and stumbled upon a crumpled flyer for a performance in Durc. The front was printed with a beautiful woman singing. I decided right then to take us there."

"Because of a flyer?"

"Yes," I admitted. "The woman looked so *happy*. I foolishly thought that if we went to Durc, Zosa would book singing jobs. Then we could have money to travel, find a more exciting place to live. I was only thirteen." I looked down at my hands. "Now it all seems too silly to say out loud."

"Hoping for something more isn't silly," he said quietly. "What happened next?"

"I bought ferry tickets. After we arrived, I used the last of our money for the room at Bézier's. The following afternoon, I dressed Zosa up and took her to audition at the venue on that crumpled flyer. She was only nine."

Bel watched me, an inscrutable look on his face. "Let me guess. She didn't land the job."

"She didn't sing. The venue manager took one look at her all dolled up and laughed. I wanted nothing more than to return to Aligney afterward, but I'd spent all we had to get us to Durc. We were stuck."

His expression softened. "I'm sorry you went through that."

I bristled. I didn't want his pity. I dropped my gaze to the open atlas, filled with far-off places. I thought I might see some of them before returning home, until a moment ago, when I learned I wasn't allowed outside.

"If something happens to my sister before we leave this place . . ." Guilt planted a foothold inside me. "Where is she?"

"Probably in her room. If she was hired as a performer, it's doubtful she'll work again until the next soirée."

That wasn't right. "But Des Rêves told me herself Zosa would work for her nightly."

"Nightly?"

"She's one of Des Rêve's chanteuses."

Bel stiffened. Something about his posture made me wary.

"What is it?"

"Nothing," he said quickly. I didn't believe him. Something was wrong, I was sure of it. Bel's eyes flicked to a wall clock. "It's after seven. Madame Des Rêves will be onstage in the salon. I'll speak with her later and ask after Zosa. You and I can talk in the morning. Now please get to your room." His eyes bore into mine. Those eyes weren't about to take no for an answer.

"Fine," I lied.

If there was something wrong, it would be my fault for not checking on Zosa. I'd speak with Des Rêves right now.

Bel let me pass. When the door shut, I took off. I raced downstairs and across the lobby, only slowing at the sound of singing. The salon was packed. No sign of Yrsa or the twins, so I crept inside. A man plucked a towering harp. Guests lounged, sipping glowing aperitifs, eyes glued to the stage where a trio of girls performed.

The first girl had brown skin, luminous against a pink chiffon gown tipped with marabou. The second girl was curvy with beige skin and blonde hair that curtained against a dusty blue gown sewn with iridescent feathers. Zosa was girl number three.

She wore a low-cut silk concoction disappearing into a skirt of feathers the exact shade of molten gold.

I shoved forward until she opened her mouth and sang. My feet stopped. With each word, her voice strengthened. I thought of the apple crate and the flour jar, then the venue manager who had laughed at her.

He wouldn't be laughing now.

Zosa hit a high note and all the guests in Salon d'Amusements gasped. Tears pricked my eyes. My sister was better than Maman. Better, I imagined, than that woman from the crumpled flyer. The guests probably assumed she was a suminaire, because her voice felt like magic.

The velvet curtains behind the chanteuses parted. Madame des Rêves stepped out in a sheath of ruffles matching her sapphire wig. The only part of her that wasn't blue was her pale skin, and that silver talon resting in her cleavage. I'd forgotten about the talon. An artéfact, I assumed.

"This is the best part," cooed a guest.

On the last note, Des Rêves touched the talon to Zosa's collarbone. The crowd went wild. In the span of a blink, Zosa folded, her dress scrunching up as she transformed into a tiny golden bird.

"Zosa!" I jostled forward, but there were too many guests. My mind screamed to get to her, but I was trapped in the center of the crowd.

A gilded cage appeared from nowhere, and I clutched my throat. It felt like I couldn't breathe. Des Rêves transformed the other two girls and placed them each inside the cage.

"Zosa!"

The curtains fell.

My arms slackened into dead weights. Everything had been so sudden that I wondered if Zosa knew what was happening. No, she couldn't know, because she'd never agree to this. But she didn't have to, I realized, with a sinking horror. The other workers performed their jobs with utter complacency, and Zosa was probably just like them now.

This was my doing; I'd brought her the newspaper, took us to interview. This place was supposed to be my shortcut out of Durc, and I was supposed to be the older sister who did something right for once, who took us home, kept us together. I squeezed my fist and could practically feel my sister's small, sweaty hand slipping from mine.

Black shadows crawled along the walls, swallowing the light. Everything Bel had told me—all the warnings, the staff contracts, Alastair's behavior—tore through my mind. I'd thought we were safe inside, so I let Zosa out of my sight. That had been my biggest mistake. I had to get to her.

Shoving past exiting guests, I climbed the stage and parted the velvet. No cage. Not a single feather. Nothing there.

12

"The stage is off-limits."

Madame des Rêves stood at a side door, perspiration smearing her crème de rose.

"My sister, the singer in the gold dress, where is she?"

Des Rêves's lips pursed. "I'm afraid, sweet, I don't know. Perhaps you should bring it up with the maître. His office is through there." She pointed to a door behind the bar.

Just then, the ground shifted. I fell hard on the salon floor as the stage walked itself behind the tasseled curtain.

Des Rêves laughed. Grunting, I stood up. No one stopped me as I dipped through the door behind the bar to a dark hall lined with more closed doors. Halfway down, I spotted one door cracked open. Lamplight flickered from within. Silently, I walked over and peeked inside.

Red, the suminaire from the escape game, lay across a table, her small, freckled arms splayed, crimson hair spilling over the sides. Yrsa appeared and placed her teacup beside Red's ear. The milk swirled on its own.

Unrolling a leather surgeon's kit, Yrsa pulled out a long knife. She held the blade tip over a blue candle flame, humming to herself. Then, with a detached nonchalance, she raised the heated knife, pulled back the pale skin below Red's eye, and sunk the blade tip into Red's eye socket.

Red's body jerked once before my own eyes squeezed shut. Instruments clanked. Sounds came: a low groan, a clatter, a wet pop. When I thought it might be over, I looked up, then bit down on the inside of my cheek so I wouldn't scream. Yrsa held Red's detached eye above her teacup. A tendril of white liquid that most certainly wasn't milk swirled *up*.

Yrsa flicked it down. She plunged the eye inside then pulled it out.

Red's eye—what was once an eye—now looked like a cast-off piece from a potter's studio that might snap in two if Yrsa dropped it. It had to be solid porcelain. If this was Red's punishment for the escape game—

I caused it to happen.

"My god," I think I said aloud. My fist flew to my mouth.

Yrsa muttered to someone. Footsteps shuffled toward the door. Stumbling back, I raced down the hall not caring where it would lead, just that it led away. The next door was unlocked. I ran in and slammed it behind me, shaking uncontrollably.

In this new room, a fireplace illuminated an enormous glass curio arranged with a collection of objects. I braced myself against it and felt faint vibrations sizzling through the glass. Artéfacts. On a high shelf sat the tarnished oval hand mirror Des Rêves had fanned herself with during the soirée.

A book snapped shut.

I spun around. Across the room, Alastair sat behind a desk littered with glass vials, some filled with shimmering purple ink, some empty. In the center sat his slim wolf-capped inkwell. "My office is off-limits. Who let you in?"

My tongue refused to make words.

"You're the maid Bel brought on," he said. "The girl with the sister."

The mention of Zosa focused my mind. "Her name is Zosa and she's a bird in a cage somewhere," I blurted. "I—I need to find her."

Before Alastair could speak, Sido and Sazerat burst in. Their combined pair of eyes trained on me. My throat tightened. Yrsa must have cut out their other eyes, too.

Alastair's features sharpened. "What is it now?"

"That maid saw Yrsa use her artéfact." One twin spoke while the other watched me with his dead stare.

"Wait outside," Alastair said. They left in unison. When the door shut, he pointed to a chair across the room. "Have a seat."

Sitting was the last thing I wished to do. "So you can scoop out my eye?"

"I don't know what you saw, but I promise that will never happen to you. Have a seat. Afterward, I'll take you to your sister."

This was all wrong. "Take me now."

Something hit the back of my legs. I sat down hard on a leather chair that had just been across the room. Its wooden arms felt like fingers gripping my wrists. I couldn't move. Chair legs scraped the floor, pushing me forward until I was opposite Alastair.

He lifted his wolf-capped inkwell, uncapped it, and filled an empty glass well, identical to the ones Zosa and I had used to sign our contracts. Purple ink poured from his inkwell in a never-ending stream just like the tea from Red's thimble.

That wolf-capped inkwell must be an artéfact. *His* artéfact.

When he finished, he pulled a book from a desk drawer, its leather binding covered in purple scribbles. Handwriting. *Société des Suminaires* was printed in tiny gold words amid the purple ink. I'd never heard of the society.

"What's the book for?"

His eyes flicked up. "My infinite ledger? It's enchanted to be a file cabinet of sorts."

He began flipping through pages like Hellas shuffling his deck of cards. But cards were only so thick. The ledger's pages were endless, as if Alastair flipped through a hundred books stacked atop one another. Purple writing flashed across each page. After flipping for more than a minute, he stopped at some arbitrary spot in the center. Opening the ledger wide, he plunged his entire forearm inside and fished around. Then he pulled out a sheet of parchment with a single purple signature scribbled across the bottom.

My contract.

"These were my invention," he said mournfully. "We all must do our part to keep magic safe—"

His words cut off and the skin along his jaw pulled tight. I swallowed hard when he took out a second, blank contract and laid it beside mine. They looked identical until Alastair ran a finger down the blank contract, stopping at a small line of Verdanniere near the bottom.

My eyes darted from the guest contract I'd signed to this blank one. Sure enough, the line he pointed to was missing from my contract.

Once a new staff member steps inside the hotel, they will forget everything they leave behind.

If this were a staff contract, Bel was right; it was the opposite of the contract guests signed, the contract I'd signed. Except *forget everything they leave behind* seemed all-encompassing.

That clause meant Zosa would have signed away more than just her memory of home. I ran through everything we'd discussed the morning of the last soirée. Not once had she mentioned Bézier's or Maman. She hadn't touched that sack filled with Maman's junk. Yet she remembered me—

Because she didn't *leave me behind.* We walked together through the front door.

In Durc, I'd asked Bel to swear on his mother he'd give me a job, but he couldn't. He said he didn't remember her. I thought it was because she had died, not because his memory of her had been *taken.*

Alastair filed the blank staff contract back in the ledger. He then grabbed a pen and dipped it into a well of purple ink.

My heart leaped. "What are you—"

"It seems you signed a guest contract instead of one meant for staff. But it doesn't matter anymore."

I didn't understand it until Alastair began writing on my guest contract. Amending it. Six purple sentences that made me feel ill.

I had to get out. Leaping up, I ran to the door and collided with a pair of muscled chests. The twins. They'd been waiting.

"Hold her," Alastair ordered. Their magical grip felt like steel claws clamping my shoulders. I couldn't move. Alastair lifted my chin, forcing me to meet his pale eyes. "Poking around where you aren't supposed to is a violation of the rules I've set in place to ensure magic remains safe." A look came over his features that I couldn't decipher. "I'll have to demote you. I have no choice."

I didn't think I breathed.

He released my chin. Both his hands were normal. Ten long, perfect fingers. No mottled skin like I'd seen in that hall. I must have imagined it. He then raised my amended contract. The fresh ink glimmered. "I promise this won't hurt. Afterward, you won't remember a thing."

No.

I struggled when his other hand touched the wolf-capped inkwell to my collarbone, just as Des Rêves had touched her talon to Zosa. Magic hummed in my skull and tightened around my neck, choking me, as those six purple sentences glowed hot then dissolved into the parchment.

> With this demotion, you will forget everything.
> Forget your home.
> Forget your position.
> Forget your friends.
> Forget your sister.
> Forget your name.

13

"**M**ol!"

Chef jabbed her finger, pointing past my shoulder. "You've worked in the kitchens for five weeks. Can't you tell when a pot's boiling over?"

Nine waist-high copper vats bubbled before me, the sixth one currently overflowing. *Damn it.* Drips of cream hissed against hot coals. Everything was hot. Sweat slicked the handle of my brittle wooden spoon. *Don't you dare snap, spoon.* I plunged it into the steaming liquid. My forearms strained as I turned the spoon in a slow arc. A circle. Soup sloshed up, adding to the mess of stains gathering across my kitchen frock.

Chef walked over and sniffed the sixth pot. "Burned. Entire thing is garbage. Too busy daydreaming, Mol?" When I didn't answer, her lip curled. "Mol?"

I swore under my breath. I'd been called that name countless times since that night in Alastair's office, but it still felt like someone getting my attention by slapping someone else.

After a demotion, a worker was always given a new name.

Although it didn't seem to matter. Aside from basic knowledge about the hotel, like the locations of the lavatories, demoted workers weren't supposed to remember a thing about working in their previous positions.

But I did.

Alastair had used his ink to amend the contract I'd signed and demote me. The ink should have worked, but for some reason that I couldn't figure out, it didn't take. I remembered everything. I just couldn't let anybody else know.

I wrinkled my nose at the burned soup. "I'm sorry."

Chef glared. "You've been here for weeks. You should know better."

"Give the girl a chance. She's still learning, aren't you, Mol?" Béatrice came around the corner.

Chef shifted her attention to Béatrice. "What are you doing down here?"

Béatrice held up a basket of empty satchels. "A duke in the *Of Mischief and Masquerade Suite* requested lavender for his wardrobe. I was hoping Mol might give me a hand." She grinned at me conspiratorially. "Surely you could spare her for a few minutes."

Chef wasn't a suminaire as far as I could tell, and it was an unspoken rule that suminaires had seniority over normal workers regardless of station. But that didn't stop Chef from giving the head of housekeeping one of her signature stern looks. "As long as Mol is back before another pot burns."

As Chef walked off, Béatrice threw a cross gesture at her back. I pressed my lips together to stifle a laugh.

Over the past few weeks, Béatrice often visited to check on a few kitchen workers, including myself. Maybe it was wishful thinking, but I sensed that she came down here because she felt guilt over my demotion; she seemed to be looking out for me, especially around Chef.

Whatever the case, I was grateful. She'd become a good friend, even in spite of her big opinions, and little respect for personal space.

She pinched my cheek. "You're looking too pale and thin, Mol. You should visit the forêt à manger."

She meant the dining hall on the service floor where workers took meals. It was an enchanted forest of honeyed meats and sugary cakes. The entire room was created for a guest fête, then repurposed for staff.

I'd gone once weeks ago. Never again. Working in the kitchens was difficult enough. The last thing I needed was to dine with someone who would call me Mol then run to Alastair when I mistakenly corrected them.

"I eat in my room."

"Suit yourself, ma chérie. But don't think you're off the hook that easily. You know . . ." Béatrice smirked. "I could always order L'Entourage de Beauté to put a little glow on your cheeks."

"You wouldn't *dare*," I said in mock shock.

"They could freshen your hair, tidy that rag of a dress."

"I'd never speak to you again."

"Then you'd be awfully lonely down here, weeping into soup, no friend to put up with your pouting."

"I'd make friends with Chef."

She barked a laugh. "What would you do? Braid each other's hair?"

I pictured that and snorted.

"Come on. Before Chef hears us." She took my elbow. Together, we walked past a group of liveried front-of-house staff stacking a filigreed service cart with glass boxes of pastel sweets.

I halted. Red, the suminaire from the escape game, stood with them.

I'd seen her from time to time. She never made eye contact, but I couldn't help staring. Her right eye—the eye I'd watched Yrsa gouge out—caught the kitchen light and gleamed a shade brighter than the other, nearly inconspicuous. If I didn't know what to look for, I'd never guess it was glass.

Thankfully she disappeared around a corner, the reminder of what I'd caused gone for now.

Ahead of me was aisle after aisle of sweltering cooks doused in flour and egg yolks and frosting, oblivious of their missing memories.

There were hundreds of questions I wanted the answers to, like if they craved the same food they used to before coming to the hotel, or laughed at the same jokes, or wore their hair in the same style.

After witnessing the maids' behavior, I assumed Alastair's ink changed a person on a deeper level, so it would make sense if it altered them more with each demotion. But only Alastair would know the truth.

Sometimes I would ask the other workers leading questions to test boundaries. There were a few subjects they avoided altogether: any talk of pay, changing positions, or going outside. Removing memories made workers more docile, more apt to not question anyone or anything. And yet I was spared, twice now.

The first time, because of Bel.

A swift image of him fluttered up: that last day in Durc when I met him at the door of the hotel, his mouth against my neck as he whispered in my ear that I should go home. He'd tried to protect me and Zosa from the beginning, but I was too stubborn to take him seriously.

That first day here played in my mind. Zosa's smile. How preoccupied I was. How envious. I'd thought we were safe inside, so I let my guard down—something I never allowed myself to do in Durc. I should have known better than to do it here.

"Hurry, Mol," Béatrice said near an enormous steel freezer door. Weeks ago, I learned one thing quick: never to go near it. Yrsa and Chef were the only two allowed inside.

In Durc, ice was harvested from ice fields during winter months and buried in underground cellars below many of the fancier establishments. The ice never lasted past June. No way to keep it cold when the world turned warm. But the deep freeze of Hotel Magnifique produced perfect blocks of ice year-round. I had thought it was an enchantment until one morning Chef shouted at something behind that door. I didn't know what was inside, and I wasn't eager to find out. Thankfully, we headed to the dry storage rooms.

Béatrice went in and brought out fistfuls of lavender. We began stuffing it in satchels. Our hands stilled at a clatter of metal.

Yrsa wheeled her drink cart toward the deep freeze. Her artéfact, the teacup full of milk that wasn't milk, sat on top. She eyed Béatrice. "What are you doing in the kitchens?"

"Satchels." Béatrice raised her basket, backing away when the not-milk swirled.

Reaching out, the alchemist ran her pinkie in a slow circle around Béatrice's right eye. "Maître's been too lenient on you, *Mechanique*. I could tell him not to be."

Béatrice's gears rattled. The head of housekeeping was nervous, as she should be. If she ever stepped out of line, I was sure Yrsa wouldn't hesitate to cut out Béatrice's eye and dip it in her teacup, like she'd done to Red's. I'd come to realize that all suminaires were fearful of the threat.

"Get back to work," Yrsa barked, then disappeared inside the deep freeze. The steel door slammed shut. We both jerked when something thumped from within.

"Let's find another shelf to stuff these." Béatrice hugged the basket of satchels, her fingers trembling.

After hours of hovering over soup, I changed my apron and prepared to run my nightly round of room service—the part of my shift I didn't mind. I scanned the delivery ledger. Tonight, most deliveries were for floor three, with a few stops on two, and one delivery for the library.

"At least this shouldn't take us all night," I said to a new kitchen worker with pretty dimples and skin the rich color of terra-cotta. He'd signed a contract this morning and Chef tasked me with showing him the ropes. I opened my mouth to ask him where he'd arrived from, then stopped myself. "Follow me."

At the lift, King Zelig—the name I'd taken to calling him— regarded us regally. "Floor?"

"Two."

As the lift ascended, the new worker toed the clouds curling around our feet. I pulled out the first delivery. It was for the *To Traverse a Forgotten Ocean Suite*.

When we arrived, a tan-skinned woman with sun-bleached hair, who I imagined to be a sea captain, answered the door in a nautical dressing gown. The worker presented her a whole fish on a platter.

Our next delivery was for the *On a Carousel of Wishes Suite*. A guest with light brown skin and hazel eyes answered. He didn't speak Verdanniere and waved us goodbye with his pinkie finger in a gesture I'd never seen.

The occupant of the *A Verdant Enchantment Suite* placed the same order the past three days: a jar of dried berries and seeds. The door swung open on the fourth knock. A girl with deep golden skin and a nest of hair nearly the same color stuck her head through. She snatched the jar and slammed the door.

"That was interesting," the worker said.

"You'll find most things here are."

On the third floor, I told him to finish the deliveries then wait for me in the kitchens, while I took the last delivery myself.

The library was a plush space near the salon. I pulled out the delivery of chopped fruit before I entered so the rustling parchment wouldn't disturb the library guests. Or the creature. Written on the parchment in Chef's hasty scrawl was a twice-underlined note: *Don't wake the bird.*

Great advice, for this particular bird was as large as my torso and fast asleep, its obsidian feathers tucked against its body.

The bird wasn't just pretty to look at, but proved useful; its coo soothed library-goers, and it squawked if a guest became too loud. Good thing its cage was kept out of reach; there was gossip about a kitchen worker who once startled the bird. Unfortunate for her, considering it bit off her ear.

I scaled the library's small ladder, opened the cage, and plopped the fruit inside. Thankfully the bird didn't wake. I climbed down and looked around.

Above me, stacks of books appeared to go up forever, connected by a web of ivory ladders and ornate catwalks. Robed guests populated the perimeter. Each clutched a pair of lorgnettes with filigreed handles, pressing the elaborate glasses to their eyes as they read.

It reminded me of Bézier's sitting room, how I would lose myself for hours hunched over books and atlases. Longing moved through me as I took in all the books. I supposed it wouldn't be difficult to borrow one now, then slip it back later. Guests did it all the time.

I ran a finger over a book embossed with a language I'd never seen, then a book in a different language made up of vowels mashed together. A pair of lorgnettes lay forgotten on a low shelf. I grabbed them. When I raised them to my eyes, the title of each book appeared in crisp Verdanniere. I scanned the shelf. No geographies, so I shoved a scandalous-looking romance in my pocket, along with the lorgnettes.

"What are you doing?"

I spotted his silver hair first. Hellas, the Botaniste, appeared at my side. He brought a playing card to my chin and tilted my face up with the sharp edge. Magic tingled where the card touched my jaw.

"I'm running deliveries, sir," I squeaked.

He glanced down. The lorgnette's handle stuck out of my pocket, and my heart dropped. He pulled the glasses out, along with the book. I expected him to grab my shoulder and drag me away, but he didn't. "Next time the maître will hear about it, understand?"

He was letting me go. I nodded.

"Now run along." He released me, then added, "Mol."

My eyes widened. The kitchens had at least two hundred workers. There was no way he remembered the name of one girl without a reason for it. He must suspect something.

But I'd taken every precaution since that night in Alastair's office; there wasn't anything I'd done to garner his notice. Besides, the closest I'd ever come to him before this moment was at that first soirée—when he'd practically turned a guest into a tree with the barest flick of his wrist at the midnight show.

Hellas ran his thumb down the edge of a glossy playing card.

I had to move. I could feel his eyes on me as I forced myself through the library entrance and into the lobby. Once I was out of sight, my shoulders collapsed against the wall. I clutched Maman's necklace, attempting to calm myself.

When my hands no longer shook, I skirted the lobby shadows until I found the small alcove a few feet from the entrance to the salon. It had served as the perfect hiding spot over the past few weeks, with a clear view of the lobby.

Hidden in shadows, I fished an itinerary from my pocket; like

Beatrice, I had picked up a habit of checking waste bins, so I never went long without knowing where we were.

As I traced a finger over each purple destination, the woman's effervescent voice chimed in my ears.

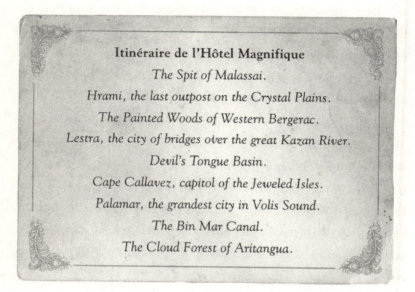

Itinéraire de l'Hôtel Magnifique
The Spit of Malassai.
Hrami, the last outpost on the Crystal Plains.
The Painted Woods of Western Bergerac.
Lestra, the city of bridges over the great Kazan River.
Devil's Tongue Basin.
Cape Callavez, capitol of the Jeweled Isles.
Palamar, the grandest city in Volis Sound.
The Bin Mar Canal.
The Cloud Forest of Aritangua.

Thank god Aligney wasn't on the itinerary yet. My heart couldn't take it if we traveled there when I could only experience it from behind the lobby windows.

Soon Zosa's voice spilled through the open salon doors.

As a kitchen worker, I wasn't allowed inside, and the layout made it impossible to see the stage from the lobby. My tiny sister had become nothing more than a far-off ripple of gold behind glass. She performed for Des Rêves nearly every night alongside the two other chanteuses, only to be turned into a bird and vanish as soon as the curtains closed.

When one song ended, Madame des Rêves's high-pitched voice rang out. "Aren't my little chanteuses wonderful? What song shall we make them sing next?" I could almost see the smirk on Des Rêves's lips.

My sides grew hot with a rush of anger, but I knew better than to ever show anyone how I felt. Along with Yrsa, Des Rêves was the maître's second-in-command. If I did anything to catch her attention, I'd probably be demoted again.

Over the past few weeks, I'd questioned Béatrice about Des Rêves without giving myself away. The woman turned the girls into birds for the spectacle of it and didn't bother to turn them back until it was time for her next show. Since Alastair approved of anything that wowed the guests, he let her do what she wished. With my sister.

Anxious, I walked the distance to the aviary and dragged my fingers against a section of glass I hadn't yet touched, searching for a door, a keyhole—some way to know if Zosa was kept inside between performances—but there was none. Alastair and Hellas were the only two who could get inside.

I rapped an angry fist against the glass and the woman's effervescent voice chimed in my head, "*Closed indefinitely!*"

"There you are."

The kitchen worker I'd left upstairs wheeled the delivery cart toward the aviary.

"You were supposed to meet me downstairs. That cart can't be in the lobby." I braced my hands on the handle, but he didn't move, too distracted by something behind me.

The windows.

Outside, the setting sun filtered through palm leaves the size of horses. A golden monkey sat on a guest's hat, claws peeling a bright blue fruit. The view was astounding, made even more so by the other nineteen identical views.

"They say the windows converse and show the guests the best view," I said softly.

His lips parted. "Skies above! The windows talk to each other?"

"Part of the magic." I turned to leave, but something caught my eye. An envelope sat under the delivery ledger. Snatching it, I tucked it in my pocket before he could see. "Was anyone at the cart?"

He gave me a strange look. "Not that I noticed."

"Are you positive?"

"Do you think I'm a liar?"

"No," I said.

I didn't think him anything. To me, this pretty boy with his light-up dimples was as blank as an empty itinerary, and he would remain as blank as an empty itinerary for as long as he worked here.

"Can you take the cart to the kitchens?" I feigned a yawn. "My feet won't make it."

He nodded. As soon as he was gone, I tore open the envelope and pulled out a card scrawled with handwriting I'd come to know as well as my own. A shiver went up my spine at the four little words that might mean everything, or nothing at all.

Meet me on six.

14

Five weeks ago, after the episode in Alastair's office, the twins had dragged me back to my room. I'd kept my mouth closed and my head down, praying they couldn't tell anything was amiss.

I couldn't sleep that night. I'd lain awake trembling, half convinced it was all a terrible dream that I'd wake from at any moment; it was hard to believe any of it was real.

In the hour before dawn, someone had knocked at my door.

"Just a moment."

I'd felt stiff, my limbs too heavy to move. *Get up*, I told myself. I dragged my body from the bed and staggered to the vanity mirror. A tear-stained girl with big, hollow eyes stared back. I took a moment to compose myself, to calm my frantic heartbeat. It didn't make a difference; as soon as I turned the door handle, terror gripped me at what might be waiting for me on the other side.

Bel stood across the hall.

I collapsed against the doorframe, relieved it was him and not Sido and Sazerat or Alastair. I waited for him to demand answers. Instead, he held himself at a distance, barely making eye contact.

Then it hit me: there was no way he knew Alastair's ink didn't work.

He gave me a cordial nod. "Good morning," he said. "I'm Bel. I've come to—"

"You could have warned me," I choked out.

"Warned you?"

A raw rush of anger rose up, forcing me to breathe through my nose. I gulped back a sob. "You could have warned me *before* I walked into Alastair's office."

His features sharpened. He gripped my forearms and pulled me forward, searching my face. "You remember me?"

"How could I forget the person whose neck I want to wring?" I managed, then sucked in air through my teeth as another sob wracked my chest. The green flames on the hall candles sputtered.

"Hush," Bel whispered against my ear. He pushed us into my room and shut the door behind him.

"What are you—"

"Chef is coming for you in a manner of minutes."

"Chef?"

"You work in the kitchens now," he said. I hadn't even seen the kitchens before. I opened my mouth to question him, but he held up a hand. "I want to help you, but first I need you to tell me about last night. Quickly."

Bel's face pinched as I went over the events leading up to Alastair's office, the purple ink. "My guest contract has to be faulty."

"It's not," he said. "Alastair's ink does exactly what he writes without fail. There must be some explanation for why it didn't work on you."

I tried to think of one, but I was too overwhelmed. My mind kept snagging on the image of Zosa onstage. Her pale skin and golden dress. Her voice. Then how easily Des Rêves had turned her into a bird, locked her away. And yet I *remembered* her. If Alastair's ink had worked . . . If it *had* worked, I would've lost my sister entirely.

I glanced at the bed. The pillows Zosa had knocked off were still scattered, floating above the floor. She had slept here the night before last, beside me like she had done every other night for as long as I could remember.

An image came to me of our last morning in Durc, waking to Zosa's slim fingers tangled in a lock of my dark hair. She would often reach for it in her sleep, like she was trying to hold on to me while she dreamed. Sometimes, instead of untangling her fingers, I would wait to see if she would let go on her own. Tears sprang up.

"Here." Bel offered me the edge of his jacket.

I gaped at him.

"I'm not your enemy," he said.

I believed him. Still, it would be much easier for him to cut his losses and leave me, and yet he stood there as I took his offering and wiped my eyes. I didn't know what to think about him, but I knew without a doubt that I was grateful for him.

"It gets easier," he said. I didn't see how, but I didn't have time to argue because a second later, he leaned close. "Now listen carefully. I'm going to give you a lesson in pretending to be someone you're not, and you must do exactly as I say."

Over the following five weeks, Bel sent for me every few days, always with a note slipped beneath my door. Tonight's note was the first one he'd left in my delivery cart.

Velvet darkness cloaked the sixth floor, giving way to a round slice of night sky. The moon window. As I waited, my fingers drummed against his note, those four little words. Minutes later, my nerves prickled at the sound of an exhale. I turned. Bel leaned against a settee, quiet as a wraith. He'd been watching me.

"Still find me endlessly fascinating?"

"Keep telling yourself that," he said. But his lips curved in a half smile and my pulse jumped, my body hyperaware of how close he stood. I bit the inside of my cheek until the feeling washed away.

"What do you see?" he asked. He wanted to know if Alastair's ink had suddenly taken hold.

I looked out the moon window. "An erupting volcano. Amazing we're all still people and not puddles of skin-colored goop."

"This isn't a joke, Mol."

"Don't you mean 'Jani'?" I winced when my real name echoed, *Jani Jani Jani.*

Before I could draw a breath, Bel was at my side. "Do you want me to stop meeting you?" he asked.

"Like you would dare."

He shrugged and started walking away.

"Wait. I'll behave. I promise."

"I don't believe that for a second," he said, but he didn't leave. *Thank god.*

As a kitchen worker, I was banned from setting foot inside the salon, but he wasn't. "How is my sister?"

"You first."

After that night in Alastair's office, our meetings became transactional; Bel brought me news of Zosa in exchange for a single answer.

I glanced out the moon window again and wished with everything inside of me that I could see Aligney. It would at least give me some comfort. Instead, rain pounded Durc's port. "The view is the same. My contract still doesn't affect me. Now how is my sister?"

Before Bel could say a word, the lift rattled. King Zelig's voice mingled with guests' drunken laughter. There were never guests up here this late.

I looked around for a place to hide, and started toward a settee.

Bel grabbed my hand. "Don't be ridiculous. There's nowhere to hide up here."

"Someone will see us," I hissed. "We'll be found out."

"We won't. Whoever it is will think we're here for another reason."

"What reason?"

I squirmed when his fingers pushed into my waist, facing us to look out. He pulled me against him. One by one, each button of his uniform pressed against my spine, and I understood exactly what the guests were supposed to *think*.

I could have murdered him.

"If they believe we're a couple, they'll give us privacy," he whispered in my ear. "No one will question us. It's the reason I chose this spot."

"You could have mentioned that earlier," I said through my teeth.

Bel sighed into my hair, and a searing sensation traveled up my spine.

"Remember it's an act," he whispered as the guests wandered up. I sensed a woman's eyes on me, on Bel's hands that smoothed their way up my hips.

It's only an act. It doesn't mean anything, I told myself as his lips pressed down on the back of my neck, and my stomach tightened.

"I think you're enjoying yourself, Mol," he whispered against my cheek.

I stomped on his foot. "Am not."

"Whatever you say." His nose trailed up the ridge of my ear, then he leaned into me, almost as if he were enjoying it, too. But he couldn't possibly be. This was only a means for him to get information.

"It's the Magnifique," a guest remarked under her breath.

We both stilled.

"A shame he's taken," someone else muttered. "I've heard the reason they call him the Magnifique doesn't have anything to do with moving the hotel, if you know what I mean."

A terrible choking noise escaped my throat. Bel must have felt similarly because he buried his face in my shoulder to stifle his reaction.

"Is that a new perfume you're wearing?" he asked at the sounds of the lift finally rattling down.

"Do you mean the boiled onions or the tarragon beef tips?"

"The boiled onions. Definitely the boiled onions. They accentuate your sparkling personality."

"You're an ass." I shoved him back, flustered. His useless banter didn't fool me. He was as calculated as they came, and yet I had to trust him. "How is Zosa?"

"She looked a little pale, but otherwise unharmed."

The words did little to lift my spirits. "Why can't I see her for myself?"

He shook his head and launched into his oft repeated warning. "Kitchen workers never go inside the salon. If you do, you'll be noticed, and you don't want to have the twins on your back. If Alastair ever caught us having this conversation . . ." Bel's jaw went rigid. "Here, no one is safe in their job. All the workers are replaceable, even the suminaires. You can't risk it."

"But what about before Zosa's performance? Or after? If you found an aviary key, I could see if she's kept inside. Check on her myself."

"We've been over this. Only Alastair and Hellas go inside."

"So what?"

He gave me a scalding look. "Even if your sister is kept there, I can't change her back without Des Rêves's artéfact, let alone release her from her contract."

He was right. If Zosa and I managed to get past the threshold, we would disappear into nothing the moment the hotel moved at midnight. We had to void our contracts first.

And that was impossible. But I had to find a way.

I suspected Zosa's contract was filed in that infinite ledger along with mine and all the others. But I didn't know how Alastair voided them. Whenever I brought it up, Bel told me that it wasn't as simple as ripping the parchment in two, that Alastair used powerful, complicated magic. He didn't know how it worked, or if we could repeat it ourselves.

I wanted to search for something that could help—do something other than feel utterly useless—but Bel told me that Alastair would notice if I even glanced in his direction for too long. I was to keep my head down, while he continued looking for answers and checking on Zosa.

But it wasn't enough. I was going out of my mind working in the kitchens. I needed to see my sister with my own eyes. "How hard would it be for you to get an aviary key? Let me peek inside?"

"I always thought you were pigheaded, never a complete fool."

"Zosa is my family. Can't you understand that?"

Bel flinched and my hand flew to my mouth. It was the wrong thing to say. Bel didn't remember his family or his home. Though he'd never told me outright, it was obvious he wanted what I still had.

"I'm sorry. I didn't mean—"

"It's fine. Drop it."

"Bel . . ." My heart stuttered. Despite how calculated he was, I'd finally felt like there was something growing between us. Tenuous as it was, it felt different than what I had with Béatrice. Bel knew my secrets. He understood me like no one else inside save for Zosa. Now I had to go and screw it up.

I reached for his hand, but stopped myself. Bel looked at my fingers dangling in the space between us. His brow arched.

What was I doing? My neck grew hot. *He's only a means to escape this place. Don't lose focus. All that matters is Zosa,* I told myself. I let my hand drop to my side.

"Anything else?" he asked after a little while.

"I saw the suminaire, Red, in the kitchens."

"And?"

"I only glanced at her."

"You have to pretend she's a stranger."

I pictured that teacup full of not-milk. "But the escape game was my fault. Her eye—"

"You didn't know it at the time. It's just what happens when a suminaire is demoted."

Bel had told me weeks ago Alastair used to demote suminaires the same way he did normal workers, until he erased one particular suminaire's mind too many times and it snapped. In an instant, the magic coming from that poor suminaire's artéfact magnified tenfold. A handful of normal staff were killed. Since then, Alastair became fearful about accidentally destroying his suminaires, so he stopped removing more of their memories during demotions.

Now, when a suminaire misbehaved, they were allowed to keep their position. Instead of demotion, Yrsa scooped out one of their eyes and dipped it inside her teacup full of not-milk, turning the eye to solid porcelain. A first warning. But what came next was worse.

Bel had witnessed Yrsa crack a porcelain eye once. The suminaire dropped dead a moment later.

"Did Red notice you watching her?" Bel asked.

"You mean when we danced a jig for everyone to see?"

"Just keep your head down," he said, unamused. "Here." He pulled out a bundle from his pocket.

"What's this?" I unwrapped it. It was a pair of lorgnettes along with a small book stamped with a silver compass rose. An atlas. It startled me. Bel brought me something that he didn't need to . . . because he knew I wanted it. The thought made me smile.

His mouth twitched.

"Thank you. But why—"

"There was gossip about a kitchen maid perusing library books."

"Oh god."

"Next time you're bored, please let me know." He straightened his jacket to go. "It's time I get back to work. It's nearly midnight."

"Already?"

"First you can't stand my company, and now you can't get enough?"

He was teasing me, but I didn't take his bait because a dead feeling had settled in my chest. "I'm not going to learn anything else tonight, am I?"

"I'm sorry."

"So I'm supposed to go back to my room alone and wonder if I'll ever speak with my sister again?"

"You could try to be patient for a change."

"You say that every time."

"Maybe I should stop saying it and tattoo it on your hand."

"Wouldn't make a difference. Irritatingly persistent, remember?"

I jolted when Bel took my shoulder. One of his knees crooked, brushing the pleating of my skirt. The skin on my leg tingled. "Can't

you just smile and curtsy when I tell you to do something like any other worker here would?"

"So you'd rather me be a mindless puppet you can pluck to your every whim?"

"Sounds like fun."

I scowled.

His attention shifted to my mouth. "You know . . . I think I'm growing fond of your scowls," he said. "Goodnight, Mol."

15

After my meeting with Bel, one week went by without any news. I did as he said and kept my head down. But as I stirred soup, my mind would wander to Alastair's ledger. I liked to imagine myself gleefully shredding everything inside to bits. His power was in those contracts. Because of it, my obsession with them grew into an itch that I wasn't allowed to scratch.

Soon the days felt like years, and the nights felt like eternities. I'd lie awake, churning through memories of my childhood, because I didn't know how much longer they would belong to me. The only downside was I would miss Zosa all over again. And the missing hurt, like mourning. I guess I *was* mourning in a way. She was my sister, but in Durc she was also my best friend. It was painful to not have either one.

Early one morning I passed the staff dining hall, the *forêt à manger*. The kitchen worker I'd helped with deliveries stood at a tree branch hung with glass dishes. He piled clouds of fluffy brioche on his plate, laughing as the pastry magically replenished.

I pictured Zosa beside him waving me over like she used to at

Bézier's when I was hesitant to join the other girls.

A maid I didn't recognize tapped my shoulder. "You going in?"

I shook my head and moved out of her way.

In the kitchens, Chef was already in a mood, barking orders beside a row of delivery carts stacked with everything from raspberry mille-feuilles to oysters on ice.

"What's going on?" I asked a pink-faced, sweating cook.

"Didn't hear? We're in Barrogne."

My blood chilled. Barrogne was a lakeside village in northwesternmost Verdanne, hugging the Skaadan border. Skaadi had staunch laws on magic and still executed suminaires.

Chef stormed by. "Two minutes and all delivery carts head to the lobby." She pointed at me. "Back of the line for you. I need all delivery workers manning carts. Maître's orders. Doesn't want to upset that fancy ambassador."

"Wait. The Skaadan ambassador is here?" Many in Durc assumed the young ambassador could convince the stodgy ruling party to reverse the Skaadan laws and allow the hotel entrance. It hadn't happened yet.

"The maître is sending out a welcome party, along with the ambassador's fee to let us into their backward country." Chef grunted. "Everyone was supposed to be outside twenty minutes ago. Get to your cart."

My eyes widened as her words sank in. "I'm going outside?"

Chef snapped a towel at my skirt and stormed off.

Minutes later, I stood at the rear of sixteen carts waiting to pass through the lacquered doorway. At the sight of sunshine, my heart sailed up, plummeting a moment later when Alastair appeared.

I'd snatched glimpses of him since his office but never this close. As he walked along the line of workers, his boots clicked an uneven rhythm—a limp I hadn't noticed before. Bel's warnings sounded in my ears. When Alastair got to me, I looked down, meek as a kitchen mouse, while he passed me by.

"Everybody move!" Yrsa boomed.

Behind me, suminaires surrounded a large object hovering beneath a silk sheet. A suminaire I'd seen at the escape games concentrated as he blew through his miniature weather vane, levitating the object, while the other suminaires coaxed it through the air. I tried to peek under the sheet, until Alastair and Yrsa joined them, starting the procession.

I forced my feet to walk. With a little muscle, I heaved my delivery cart across the demarcation and onto a stone walk that surrounded a mountain lake. The sunshine was blinding, but I gulped it in.

I was outside. Elsewhere.

"Move," Alastair said as he came through the door.

I pushed forward, past buildings surrounded by pine trees and framed by Skaadi's Bjor Mountains. But nothing compared to the dwellings on the water.

At least fifty bateaux manoir—mansion boats—filled the crystal cove like colorful floating palaces. There were two in all of Durc. Zosa would often count their decks on her fingers. If she tried to count these decks, she'd need more fingers.

Hundreds of locals stood on boat decks, watching us. But soon every eye turned toward the largest bateau of all—a gray monstrosity marked with a black fox, the sigil of Skaadi—where a single woman stood.

The ambassador's golden hair was the only thing soft about her. She was sharp from every angle, from jutting cheekbones to razor-thin brows. Her skin was stark white. Guards hung at her back, gleaming rapiers crossed against their hearts. More guards lined every level of the manoir's decks, crossbows aimed at the floating object under the silk sheet.

"Ambassador." Alastair gave the sheet a tug and the object glided forward on nothing but air. "This is for you."

The ambassador didn't look impressed. "If you expect my queens to grant your hotel access to our country, it costs coin, not whatever magic that is." She tossed a hand in disgust. "Where is the chest I was promised?"

"Right here." Alastair yanked the sheet away. Gasps rang out as sunlight glinted off tight stacks of pale pink coins: Skaadan urd, made from the metal urdiel mined in the Bjor mountains. The urd formed the shape of a great chest suspended in air.

Pushed into the toes of stockings, urd were said to lead you toward your fate. I wouldn't mind a pocketful myself. In Durc, pink jewelry hewn from melted-down urd was flaunted on only the wealthiest streets; a single urd was the equivalent of a thousand Verdanniere dublonnes. That chest was shaped from hundreds.

The entrance fee to Skaadi.

Weeks ago, Béatrice had said Alastair needed guests' money. It must be to bribe nations to loosen their rules on magic. Dignitaries around the world probably lined their pockets while Alastair stole their workers.

The suminaire with the weather vane blew down and the chest broke apart in a splash of pink. Two guards scurried over. "They're real!" shouted one. Rapiers and crossbows lowered.

"My end of the bargain," Alastair said. "I'll sign whatever papers you require over dinner. We'll plan for a stop next week."

"Not that soon," the ambassador said coolly. "You'll have access beginning in the new year."

It was still summer. The new year was months away.

For a moment, anger flashed on Alastair's face. Then he gave the same brilliant smile I'd seen in his reflection during the staff orientation. It didn't reach his eyes. "Surely you can let us visit sooner than the new year."

The ambassador crossed her arms. "Would you rather I forget about your hotel altogether?"

"Very well," Alastair said. "So we have an agreement?"

The ambassador didn't respond; instead she walked down the row of carts, stopping before she reached Alastair. Right beside me. "What do you do for the hotel?" she asked.

Hundreds of faces turned toward me. "I—I work in the kitchens," I stammered.

"Have you seen the magic harm anyone?"

"Ignore the girl," Alastair said. "She's just a kitchen maid. I assure you the magic is safe."

The ambassador lifted a cool brow. "In Skaadi, the *kitchen maids* prepare food that nourishes our people. Their opinions are held in higher esteem than any hotelier." Her pale blue eyes burned. "Answer my question, girl. Is the magic dangerous?"

My thoughts stumbled. I pictured Zosa. I could scream for help. The ambassador had guards. She could save us.

I caught Yrsa's glare. If Alastair suspected anything, I'd never forgive myself. "There is no danger," I forced out.

"There you have it," Alastair said cheerily. "Mark your calendars, everyone. Hotel Magnifique will arrive in the capital of Skaadi in the new year."

I straightened at the mention of the capital.

Alastair waved a fan of envelopes. "Now we hand out invitations!"

People ran off their decks. The quickest crowd I'd ever seen formed beside Alastair.

"All workers back inside!" Yrsa shouted.

I nodded and pushed my cart inside, lost in thought.

The capital of Skaadi.

I could still picture an old map I'd dug up at Bézier's of that city, the way it sprawled out like a six-pointed star stretching between mountains.

I'd seen that shape recently, and I think I remembered where.

Chef wasn't in the kitchens. Workers were still running around in the commotion. It would be a little while before anyone was looking for me. Before I could talk myself out of it, I slipped away.

16

Not ten minutes later, I pushed into the small map room Béatrice had led me to all those weeks ago. Luckily it was empty. Like before, the atlas lay open on the table.

I flipped past a few pages and stopped at the map I'd seen the first time I'd been in this room with Bel—a city in the shape of a star.

Slowly, I brought a hand to the page and recoiled. It was slathered with dozens of magical signatures. Tiny handwriting ran across the top.

Alpenheim.

The capital of Skaadi, and according to this map, a city brimming with undiscovered artéfacts.

Alastair was furious we weren't heading there soon. He already had a whole curio of artéfacts in his office—more than enough for every suminaire he took on. It shouldn't matter if we visited Alpenheim tomorrow or a year from now, but for some reason it did.

Beside the atlas were more scraps of paper. I lifted a scribbled drawing of a signet ring, just like the last time I was here.

Bel had said Alastair kept a record of known artéfacts, that he was searching for a few. Alastair could be looking for the signet ring, I supposed. It could be a reason why he'd seemed so desperate to visit Alpenheim.

Whatever the case, it wouldn't help me get to Zosa.

I slammed the atlas shut and paced. The woman in the portrait above the hearth seemed to watch me.

"Why does Alastair go through such lengths to trap everyone? Surely it's not just to keep magic safe," I said, half expecting her to answer me. "I bet you think it's hilarious when workers attempt to speak with paintings."

Rubbing my temples, I leaned against the shelf beside the fireplace. An old candlestick tumbled to the ground. I put it back and my eyes snagged on a small, dusty book jammed between the shelf and the wall.

The book was ancient, its spine embossed with *Société des Suminaires*, the same words printed on Alastair's infinite ledger.

I pulled the book out and flipped it open. It was written in Verdanniere. I ran my fingers over a bold, curving script on the inside page that read *May your artéfact guide you toward your soul's desire.*

Artéfact guide you were the same words from that lobby plaque. I remembered that plaque perfectly—the rubbed-off words. It could have easily once said the same thing as this book.

The rest of the page was a table of contents with sections labeled *Building Map, Code of Conduct, General Regulations, Artéfact*

Regulations, *Policy on Secrecy*, *Directory of Staff*, and *Information for Boarders*.

It read like a handbook. The embossed printing date on the bottom was over a century ago, during Renaissance de l'Acier, the Steel Renaissance, a period when all the great northern Verdanniere cities ballooned to their current size.

Back then the world was a cruel place for suminaires. If this society had let them stay on as boarders and kept them a secret, it would have meant the difference between life and death.

I flipped to the building map. The floors were made of rooms you'd expect to see in a society headquarters: various common rooms, two smaller kitchens, a series of offices. The top three floors were labeled *Boarding* and consisted of smaller rooms interspersed with lavatories, and rooms designated for artéfact practice.

The entryway on the first floor wasn't grand by any means—tiny compared to the other rooms—and labeled *Lobby*. I didn't think much of it until I noticed a landing on the sixth floor labeled *Moon Window*.

My lips parted. There was no mention of the hotel anywhere, but it had to be this same building. It was too coincidental. That meant this building used to house a society of suminaires—a secret society that no one outside the hotel knew existed.

There never seemed to be an end to the secrets in this hotel, no matter how much I learned. I knew every cranny of Bézier Residence. I'd walked nearly every street in Durc. That knowledge kept me grounded, whereas here I had the impression I was standing inside a shifting labyrinth; there were whole swaths of this building I hadn't explored, new halls and rooms popping up without notice and vanishing just as quickly. A mystery within a mystery.

I imagined that if I peeled back the floral wallpaper, I might uncover locked doors leading to secret drawing rooms and dimly lit libraries filled with tomes on magic. Members of this society once walked these halls—*lived* in these very rooms—practicing the very thing that would have gotten them killed. But the society wasn't here anymore.

If the hotel opened during the tail end of Renaissance de l'Acier, something clearly happened to it. It could have dismantled, I supposed, or perhaps it existed in secret somewhere else.

I paged through the rest of the handbook, past a section on lorgnettes. They were enchanted so suminaires could study books on magic in languages that weren't their own, under the belief that the workings of artéfacts shouldn't be exclusive to geography or culture. After that were various printed portraits of the old society heads wearing hairstyles from a different era.

I stopped at the last portrait of a woman, what was left of it. The top half of the page was ripped out from the nose up, leaving only the mouth, neck, and torso. Her fingers were wrapped around the wolf-capped inkwell. I recognized her mouth.

I held the book up. It was difficult to tell with the eyes gone, but the mouth was identical to the woman in the painting.

If this woman used the inkwell before Alastair, she might know something about voiding our contracts. But she could have died a hundred years ago, for all I knew.

I put the book away and rubbed my face. I thought I'd find answers here that might help me, not more questions. Frustrated, I flipped through the atlas again, letting my palm skim against the magic on each page. I was beginning to calm down until I jerked at a map in the center, and nearly bit off my tongue.

It was Durc.

Of course there would be a map to Durc; Bel had taken the hotel there. I'd hated the place, but right now I'd give anything to be back there with Zosa, pilfering stale kitchen scraps. Bézier was probably sipping afternoon tea in the third-floor sitting room now.

Bézier. If Bel took me there, I could tell her everything. She never liked me much, but she always had a soft spot for my sister. She might help me round up the authorities—

The wall clock chimed. Chef would notice me missing soon. I left the room and started down a dark hall.

"The crown molding on this floor is edged with gold leaf and over four hundred years old," Madame des Rêves's voice rang out. "It was excavated from a dilapidated palace in the Topaz Isles."

"Fascinating," someone exclaimed.

A large group of guests came around the corner, a cobalt wig bobbing in the center. Des Rêves was leading a tour toward where I stood. There was no reason for a kitchen maid to be on this floor without a delivery cart.

I started to turn until Bel stepped away from the group. A pretty guest with light brown skin and berry-stained lips ran a hand up the front of his jacket.

I shuffled back, into a sideboard. A vase crashed to the ground. *Damn it.*

Without pausing, I opened the nearest guest room door and ducked inside. Before I could get the door shut, Bel pushed himself into the room. He didn't look pleased.

"What were you thinking coming up here this early? Des Rêves could have seen you," he said through his teeth. "Now we'll have to wait until the tour is gone."

His tone made my jaw clench. "I was only looking for something that might help us." Kiss marks snaked up the side of his neck. I thrust my chin at them. "Considering *you've* been preoccupied."

He rubbed the marks, smearing red across his collar.

"Bel?" said a high-pitched voice from the hall. "Where did you wander off to?"

I shut the door and flipped the lock, too late remembering Béatrice's warning about locking guest suites.

The room darkened. The floor was covered in plush burgundy carpet. The walls were papered with curling vines and plump roses, but the grand space itself was curiously empty save for an oversize bed fitted with nothing but crimson sheets. I hadn't caught the title on my scramble to get in. "What's this room called?"

Bel's mouth straightened to a hard line. "It's not important."

"Look." I pointed. Glimmering sapphire smoke poured from under the bed and blanketed the carpet. My boots began to sink. I'd heard of rooms changing shapes and sizes, but I'd never heard of smoke.

We both jumped on the bed. A moment later, the floor fell away, replaced with darkness that seemed to go down forever.

"What's happening?" I asked.

"I don't know. This room is new."

I ran a hand across the sheets. They rippled under my palm. "Do you see this?"

He studied the surface of the bed. "It's shrinking."

He was right. The edges of the mattress were slowly dissolving, the sheets growing smaller by the second.

Bel took off his jacket and tossed it over the side. We both watched in horror as it fluttered down a good two stories before disappearing into the blackness below.

"Do rooms usually harm guests?" I asked.

"Not that I've heard of, but Alastair isn't exactly forthcoming."

"Make it stop."

"Trust me, if I knew how, I would."

The edges of the bed continued to disappear until it was the size of my mattress at Bézier's. My legs fell over the side. I planted my palms on the edge to shove myself back and cried out when the bed disappeared beneath them. I was going to fall.

"No, you don't." Bel grabbed my shoulders, jerking me back.

I landed on top of him, facing him, our arms tangled, and my nose pressed into the crook of his neck. My skirts had pushed above my knees, which were now on either side of his waist.

His stomach muscles flexed between my legs, and my neck heated against my will. He gripped my wrist. I struggled against him.

"Stop wiggling," he said. "*Look.*"

Chest heaving, I touched the edge of the mattress. Miraculously, the bed had stopped shrinking. "How?"

"I have an idea," Bel said, and let go of me.

The moment his fingers left my wrist, the mattress dissolved under one of my hands. I shrieked, and Bel wrapped his arms around me, his fingers threading through mine.

"It wants us to touch," he said. "Skin to skin."

The mattress was now the width of a banquette, but it wasn't getting any smaller. Instead, glowing star ornaments floated down from somewhere above us, transforming the nightmarish room into something out of a dream. It was achingly romantic.

Bel shifted against me, and I tried not to think about how closely I was pressed against him, so I looked away. At our entwined hands. *God.*

My pulse hammered, and I desperately hoped he couldn't feel it. When I didn't think things could get more awkward, soft music began playing and rose petals rained down from above, filling the room with a heady fragrance that made my mind swim.

I swallowed. "This is . . ."

"I know."

I tried to slide over so I wasn't directly on top of him, but there wasn't enough bed left. The skin on my neck burned, overly sensitive to every puff of air Bel exhaled against it. "How long are we stuck here?"

"Your guess is as good as mine." He shifted, tucking one hand under his head. His other hand wrapped around my waist, and I froze.

"What do you think you're doing?"

"We'll have to wait until the tour leaves regardless, so I'm getting comfortable."

I cut him a glare. "Let me guess, you've been waiting *weeks* for this."

The edge of his mouth lifted. "I dream of it every night. Your elbow jabbing my side, a murderous bed . . ."

It might have been nice lying here if I wasn't painfully aware of how every corner of my body pressed into his. I didn't dare move for fear of brushing something.

Bel tipped his face to the stars. The kiss marks along his neck were still visible, along with a shadow of stubble. My own mouth was inches away, and I couldn't help but wonder what it would feel like to kiss him there. Probably rough.

He drummed his fingers against my arm. "What are you thinking about?"

"Absolutely nothing."

A laugh shook him. "As long as we're trapped here, I suppose you could explain what exactly you were doing on this floor."

"I—I can do that," I said, utterly relieved to switch topics. I told Bel about Alastair's reaction outside, then about Alpenheim in the atlas and the woman in the painting matching the ripped page in the book, the wolf-capped inkwell in her hand. Bel wasn't surprised at any of it. Although he'd probably searched the room himself dozens of times. "There was also a sketch of a signet ring beside the atlas, just like the last time I was there with you."

His muscles tensed.

"It's an artéfact, right?"

"It's one of the artéfacts Alastair has me looking for. I don't know what it does, and I'm not supposed to speak of it. So please don't ask again," he said, bitterness tinting every word. Evidently the ring was a sore subject. "Is that it?"

"I also saw a map to Durc."

"We do travel there from time to time," he said dryly.

"That's exactly my point. You could take us back. I could find Bézier, tell her everything. She could call the authorities before the hotel moves at midnight."

"I can't. Alastair would be skeptical if I changed our destination so suddenly unless it had to do with finding an artéfact."

I groaned. "Then find another one in Durc."

"It's too soon. I'd be punished for not finding everything the last time we were there. Besides, going back would be a waste of time for many other reasons."

"What other reasons?"

"Too many to go over right now." His words were as sharp as a knife.

The way he said it felt final, as if I wasn't allowed to question him.

Everything that had been building inside me over the past two weeks bubbled to the surface. "You don't know how hard it is to pretend to be Mol, knowing the only person I care about is trapped somewhere in this place and I might never see her again," I said. "I don't know what to do with myself, or how much longer I can handle feeling this . . . *lonely*."

Shame barreled into me, and I immediately wished I hadn't said

the last part. Fortunately, Bel didn't seem to hear the end of my outburst.

"Shh," he said, his ear angled toward the door. "I think the tour left."

Gently, he scooted out from beneath me and slipped down the edge of the bed.

"Don't!" I lurched toward him. But instead of falling, his foot hit a black staircase. It carried him to the floor.

The moment both his feet were on the carpet, the bed returned to its previous size. Except I now sat in the center of a crimson bed with my skirts pushed up my thighs.

Bel dragged his eyes over them. His throat bobbed. "I have to get back downstairs. Can you find your way to the kitchens without any more trouble?"

I nodded.

"Good." He opened the door then hesitated. In a softer voice he added, "You might feel lonely, but I promise you're not alone."

With that, he left.

I sat there for a moment, allowing his last sentence to sink in. Then I composed myself and walked out. The room's title was em-bossed on a plaque beside the door. *La Suite Lune de Miel et Étoiles.*

The Honeymoon and Stars Suite.

17

There was a sharp knock at my door the next morning. I twisted my hair into a neat bun and turned the handle to find Béatrice standing in the hall, tapping her toe impatiently.

"I've already spoken with Chef. This morning, you're coming with me. There's a market at today's destination and I'm in need of supplies." She tossed me a ladies' pink cocktail jacket. "Put this on."

"You're taking me outside?"

"I'm allowed an escort. And the last I checked you were in *imminent* need of some sunshine and fresh air." Her lips curved up. "Don't get used to it."

Two whole days of going outside after being cooped up for weeks felt too good to be true, but I wasn't about to complain. I put on the jacket and followed her to the lobby.

Today, the marble expanse was flush with guests coming and going. I started toward the front door, but Béatrice held me back.

"Wait just a moment," she said, scanning along the perimeter.

I didn't see Alastair anywhere. "Is everything all right?"

"I think so. But I've also never taken a kitchen worker with me outside before, so I'd rather not run into anyone who might find that unusual."

It struck me as odd that Béatrice would risk her neck to bring me with her. She must feel guiltier about my demotion than I'd thought.

Together we walked toward the front. A worker held the door wide. We were nearly through when Béatrice came to an abrupt stop.

I turned. The twins flanked her, their sewn-shut eyes standing out against their pasty skin. Bel had told me Yrsa cut out their eyes long before she began replacing suminaires' eyes with glass.

"Alastair didn't give you permission to leave," said one twin, who I assumed was Sido considering Sazerat never spoke.

"I left him a detailed note." Béatrice's hands shook as she pulled out a mangled faucet. "The *Ode to a Fabled Forest Suite* is getting a guest and the silly faucet decided to protest. I tried repairing it with my gears, but these mechanics are quite persnickety." She flicked a bolt. "I don't have the parts inside to fix it."

When the twins remained silent, I added, "Doesn't the maître expect his guests to have running water?"

Béatrice kicked my ankle, but not before both twins' eyes narrowed in unison. "That one isn't allowed out."

"The maître permits me one escort." Béatrice rattled the faucet. "We'll be quick. Before a guest finds the hotel lacking."

The twins faced each other in a seemingly silent conversation. Finally, Sido released Béatrice's shoulder. "Two hours."

"That won't do," Béatrice argued. "Three hours. What if I can't find the proper part?"

"Two. Or we'll come looking for you." With that, they left us.

After being inside for weeks, two hours sounded like an eternity, but Béatrice didn't share my enthusiasm.

She jerked me across the threshold. "I suppose two hours will have to be enough. Because we're here."

I looked around. *Here* stole my breath. A large square stretched before us lined with cobblestones and flanked by fountains adorned with nude statues. Beyond was a city landscape carved from pale blue stone.

This color reminded me of the agate stones Zosa would dig up around Durc. Except those were rough-hewn and mucky with barnacles, while this—*god*—this wasn't any of those things.

"Pick up your jaw and move. The maître will be out soon with invitations, and we don't have much time."

Béatrice was right. Just like in Durc, a crowd of folk who looked no different than the residents of the vieux quais gathered around the hotel.

After witnessing the chest shaped from pink urd yesterday, it was clear that Alastair must demand a staggering price from guests in order to buy his hotel access. That must be why I hadn't seen a single guest inside who wasn't ridiculously wealthy.

The thought stopped me in my tracks. Lack of wealth was a barrier to entry, I realized.

Everyone had a chance at winning an invitation. It was part of the draw, why the hotel attracted the crowds it did, and why all these people stood here now, their eyes filled with hope. Most of these people looked no wealthier than me.

In Durc, wealthy people like Bézier had won invitations over the years, but so had many poorer folk, and I'd never heard of a single person being turned away. There weren't any poor guests inside the hotel that I'd seen. I didn't understand how this could work. More people began to crowd around us.

"This way." Béatrice dragged me to a shop at the edge of the square that sold fancy dresses and not faucet parts.

"Aren't we supposed to be in a hurry?"

"There's always time for a dress store," she said, her attention landing on a lavish silver skirt. The shop girl noticed and pulled it down, holding it up to Béatrice's waist until Béatrice shooed the girl away.

I knew wealthy guests left her tips. She had some means. "You could purchase a pretty dress and quit your ogling."

"I don't need one now."

"But I thought you wanted to impress a *certain* suminaire?"

Last week, Béatrice had strolled into the kitchens with swollen lips and a secretive smile, the lace collar of her maid's frock curiously changed from white to a bright shade of coral. Before I could question her about her collar, she eagerly confided that she'd become very close with the tattooed suminaire with the citrine feather.

I was thrilled for her. Béatrice deserved all the joy she could squeeze from inside that place. We all did.

She ignored my prodding and ran her fingers over another dress. When I gave her a pointed look, she sighed. "Something new is tempting, ma chérie. But not from here. I'm saving to shop somewhere else."

"Where?" I asked, but she had already wandered down another aisle. "I thought you had to find faucet parts," I called out.

"She doesn't. The faucet was my idea."

I jolted. Bel stood at the shop's entrance leaking blood from a split lip. His knuckles were grazed, his dark hair sticking out in all directions. His vivid brown eyes fixed on me. I wasn't prepared for the sight of him so soon after yesterday in that suite.

I cleared my throat. "What happened to you?"

He held up a floral brooch studded with sapphires and diamonds that looked like it cost a fortune. "Artéfacts aren't always the easiest to come by."

"Took you long enough." Béatrice swept up and proceeded to tell Bel about our ordeal with the twins.

"This was your idea?" I gaped at him.

He shrugged. "I'm not allowed to bring anyone outside with me."

But Béatrice was allowed an escort. "Why now?"

"I thought you might enjoy an afternoon away from the hotel," he said, but there had to be more to it. He was too calculated to arrange all of this for my benefit alone. He turned to Béatrice. "We'll meet you back at the hotel's entrance before the twins come looking."

"If either of you are late, I'll never let you forget it," she said, then darted down an aisle of dresses.

"Why am I really outside?" I asked once she was gone.

"For an afternoon away from the hotel," he repeated. "I thought about what you had said in that godforsaken suite yesterday. And, well, getting outside in the fresh air is the only thing that keeps me sane inside that place."

My eyes grew. "You mean, you planned all of this because I was upset?"

"Don't look at me like that. It's just for a couple of hours."

I nodded, too stunned to do anything but walk silently beside him.

He led me down a blue cobbled street lined with stationery merchants selling floral paper and wax seals. The heat was relentless. I stopped at a fountain to splash some water against my neck and peel off the pink jacket.

Bel eyed the jacket. "Is that yours?"

"No. Béatrice dug it up. Bright pink isn't exactly my favorite color." I ran a hand across the sleeve.

"What is it?" he asked.

"My sister loved pink, the brighter the better. She always wanted to stand out. But I never liked the attention much." Bel watched me, a small smile softening his eyes. For the first time in weeks, I let myself smile back. "Once, my mother forced me to wear some dresses a shade brighter than this. Never again."

Bel propped himself against the fountain and faced the sky. Sunlight lit up his features. I tried not to stare, but he was breathtaking. "Tell me about the dresses."

Oh god. They were embarrassing enough to think about, let alone speak of. "They're . . . not very interesting."

"They are to me." He squinted up at me. "I like to hear about your memories."

"You do?"

He nodded, and my heart ached for him.

I looked down so I didn't have to meet his eyes. "One year our mother misordered fabric for Zosa's winter dress and a huge bolt of peony pink muslin arrived at our door. It took all three of us to get it inside. There was no way Maman needed more than a fraction of it for Zosa. Unfortunately, I'd gone through a growth spurt and all the dresses in my closet barely covered my calves, so Maman decided to use the material to make me four more." I cringed at the memory. "They were so bright they practically glowed. With enormous ruffles."

"I can picture it perfectly."

"Stop it. I wanted to burn them all."

"But you wore them."

I groaned. "Yes. Maman hid my other dresses so I was forced to wear them or run around naked. People gawked at me wherever we went. I couldn't stand the attention. I tried to stuff myself at every meal in hopes that I would outgrow the dreadful things as quickly as possible."

"Did you?"

I hid my face in my hands. "Three years later."

Bel burst out laughing. I scooped water from the fountain and splashed his face.

"Sometimes you astound me with your maturity," he said, and then flung a handful toward me. I shrieked as it splashed against my neck, soaking my collar. His gaze dropped to my wet neck, then lower. He jerked his eyes up. "We should keep walking."

Right.

I buttoned the pink jacket over my wet dress. Four blocks later Bel stopped in front of an eatery with a plethora of flower baskets and cured meats hanging in the windows. A Verdanniere sign on the door read WELCOME TO CAFÉ MARGOT.

"Are we close to Verdanne?" I asked.

"We're on a small island a few days' boat ride north of the continent. But still close enough to get the occasional expat." Bel opened the door. "After you."

"You want to dine?"

"Béatrice only agreed to help me on the condition that I feed you properly."

"Of course she would say that."

I glanced down the busy street. It would be easy for the twins to walk by. At least the café front was somewhat obscured.

We walked inside to a narrow restaurant covered with knick-knacks. A beaded dress was pinned to one wall along with theatrical ephemera: multicolored show tickets, sequined headbands, play-bills, even an ornate Verdanniere lavatory sign. An olive-skinned boy stacked a teetering display of quiches behind a counter, while a light-skinned old woman played an upright piano.

"Nice little restaurant," Bel called out to the woman.

"You speak my language," she said in perfect Verdanniere. "Sit, sit. Let me bring out some food." She shooed us to a table then disappeared through double doors in back.

Bel didn't sit. Instead, he stepped to a hanging portrait. It depicted a woman dressed in an aproned uniform from a different era

standing in front of a gilded storefront. She must be a shop worker. A line of Verdanniere at the bottom said it was painted in Champilliers fifty years ago. But that wasn't what caught my eye.

"It's Béatrice," I said.

"It's not."

"What?" I leaned in. It looked like Béatrice, but Bel was right; there were small differences. The eyes were closer together, the forehead too high. "A relative?"

"I believe it's her sister. I discovered this painting when we stopped in this city years ago and I struck up a conversation with Margot, the woman playing the piano. Although she was younger then and I didn't need the painting to tell me what was right in front of me. She looked a little older than Béatrice, but nearly identical."

Slowly, I turned the words over. Margot was Béatrice's sister. "Margot's the reason you brought me here?"

"No. I brought you here to show you this." He touched Margot's right arm. She held it at an odd angle over an empty space.

"Why does her arm look like that?"

"I've seen a couple other paintings here and there with people posed similarly, as if they were holding someone's hand, or their arm was slung over someone's shoulder. Once I saw a portrait of a bride on her wedding day floating in the air above a chair, as if she were painted sitting on someone's lap." He tapped that empty space. "Originally I think there was someone painted right here."

"Béatrice?"

He nodded. "Until she signed her contract and stepped inside the hotel." Without missing a beat, he flicked out his switchblade and made a large slash across the bottom of the canvas.

"What are you doing?" I looked around, hoping no one noticed.

"The same thing I do every time I visit. Upward of twenty times now. Minutes after we leave, the painting will be back to normal, along with any evidence we were here. Margot will forget us by this evening."

I glanced at the painting, the missing space. "We disappear," I said. The words sounded hollow.

"From paintings. From minds."

"Does Béatrice know? You could have brought her here, shown her."

"I have. Many times. It doesn't matter. She doesn't recognize Margot, and Margot doesn't know her. They looked almost identical once, and yet they still refused to acknowledge the resemblance, like they couldn't see it."

"That means Bézier, all the boarders I lived with . . . No one I knew in Durc remembers me?"

Bel nodded. "I bet your old room is now bare and every spot you've worn on your furniture probably looks like new, as if you never sat on it. You may be immune to Alastair's enchantments, but I'm willing to bet none of your old friends are."

"Yesterday, when I asked about going back to Durc—"

"If I took you there, and you asked anyone to call the authorities, they would have laughed in your face. Trust me, I've tried it myself. I've tried nearly everything."

I sat down because I didn't think my legs could hold me up

another minute. If what Bel said was true and Zosa left without me, I would have forgotten her entirely.

"No one is looking for you. No one is looking for me," Bel went on. "No one keeps portraits of us hanging in dining rooms or hopes that we might drop in for afternoon tea or tears up when they think about us. No one *ever* thinks about us. Outside of the hotel, we're not even a memory. We don't exist." The last word came out choked. He threw a few coins on the table. "Eat whatever Margot brings. I need some air. I'll meet you outside in a few minutes." He stalked out of the restaurant.

I turned to the painting and stumbled back. The slash Bel made in the canvas had already smoothed over, the evidence we were here disappearing before my eyes.

I couldn't believe it. We were no better than ghosts floating through the world. No, that wasn't true; people remembered ghosts. Outside of the hotel, our lives had no permanence, no meaning, no power.

"Here you are." Margot walked up holding two plates of quiche. "Where did your friend go?"

"He left," I said, and faced the painting before she could ask more questions. "Is that you?"

Her wrinkled mouth pulled into a wide grin. "It is. Painted back when I wasn't as good-looking as I am now." She winked. "I was all moxie then. Told my family off after they tried to strap me to a wealthy neighbor."

"So you went to Champilliers?" I pointed to the text at the bottom.

"I did. To play piano."

"But you're painted in a uniform."

She shrugged. "I booked jobs around town, but it didn't pay the rent. Luckily, I knew a thing or two about baking. I took a daytime job as an assistant to a pâtissier in the café of a very famous ladies' store." She tapped the gilded storefront in the background of the painting. "I created the most outlandish towers of macarons that were only eaten by rich women in dressing rooms. It was tedious."

I thought of Béatrice's face when she showed me Salon de Beauté so many weeks ago, told me how it was modeled after the dressing rooms of the most famous ladies' store in Champilliers. Then today, how she was saving to shop somewhere else. I gripped the edge of a chair. "What ladies' store did you work for?"

"The famed Atelier Merveille, of course." She chuckled to herself.

"Ah," I said, and took a shaky breath.

If Béatrice was originally painted alongside Margot, she could have worked at the atelier, too, and felt some pull to it.

"I still don't understand why I took that absurd job. Or why I stayed on for so many years." Margot frowned. "Eventually I packed a bag and got as far away from the continent as I could."

In the painting, Margot's uniform grazed the ground. It was easy to imagine Béatrice dressed in an identical uniform. They would have looked so similar standing there together. But not in real life anymore.

Béatrice had a sister who was probably as dear to her at one time as Zosa was to me. A sister she didn't know existed. It struck me then how easily I could have wound up in the same position as Margot.

The door opened. Bel raced toward me. "We have to go. Now."

"Are the twins here?"

"Not them." He grabbed my arm, dragging me out of the shop.

"Who is it?" I asked at the same moment three brutish men with sharp features and olive skin surrounded us. Bel was tall, but these men made up for it in sheer bulk, with biceps like ham hocks. One of them had a thick knife in a holster at his waist.

"Jani, get back," Bel said.

He didn't need to. The largest of the three brutes shoved me so hard, I was knocked off my feet. The air left my lungs as I slammed against a vendor cart. I scrambled under it while two of the men held Bel down a few feet away, shouting.

The brute with the knife ransacked Bel's pockets. He pulled his hand out. A diamond and sapphire brooch glittered on his palm.

It was the artéfact Bel had hunted down. Although it was probably only a valuable bauble to them.

People yelled at the men to leave. Two of them took off running. The brute holding the brooch pocketed it, then bent over Bel a second time. He grabbed the chain that held the hotel's key and jerked it up, attempting to break it off Bel's neck.

Bel's face contorted in rage. He flicked out his switchblade.

That was all it took.

The brute unsheathed his thick knife and buried it deep under Bel's rib. It came out glistening. Blood dripped from the tip onto the blue stone.

One of the vendors behind me cried out. A scream built in my

throat until two pairs of hands grabbed the brute and wrenched him off Bel.

Sido and Sazerat were here.

Before they could see me, I pushed myself farther under the vendor cart. My palms slipped on grease from meat drippings. One arm lost purchase. I skidded sideways, slicing my wrist, but I swallowed the pain. I didn't dare make a sound.

The brute struggled as the twins held him by the shoulders, their thick fingers digging into flesh. My own shoulders bunched at the memory of their amplified strength.

The twins' eyes flicked to Bel's glistening wound. The knife had sunk deep. I didn't know how long suminaires took to heal, but that wound was worse than any I'd ever seen.

He'll heal, I told myself. He was a powerful suminaire. Practically immortal, or so he said. There was no reason for me to worry, but he looked pained and I couldn't stop myself.

"That man took an artéfact from my pocket," Bel said through gritted teeth.

"Can you get back on your own?" Sido asked.

Bel's eyes shot to where I hid under the vendor cart. His lips were blue-tinged and his hands trembled; he was obviously badly hurt. But instead of saying so, he pushed himself to standing. He staggered, but he remained upright.

It was a show so he wouldn't have to leave me here by myself.

"See. Perfectly fine," he managed to say. If I was any closer, I would have clobbered him.

The twins nodded in unison.

"Then we'll deal with this man," Sido said. Together, they dragged the brute away kicking.

Once the twins had turned down a side street and out of view, I crawled out from under the cart. A large crowd had gathered. People were shouting things I couldn't understand, pointing at Bel. Leering. Bel clutched under his rib. I tried to peek at the wound, but he groaned.

"We need to leave," he said. More people pushed in around us. "Will you . . . help me?"

He asked it like I might say no.

"Of course, you fool." I gripped his hand and gasped; his fingers were ice-cold. Carefully, I tucked him to my side. His head lolled, landing on my shoulder.

"That bad, huh?"

He answered with a grunt, his painful breaths puffing against the crook of my neck with every step.

18

I stopped to check the wound once as we backtracked toward the hotel. The gash bubbled and turned my stomach.

"You should learn to move the hotel while outside of it, save us some time," I joked. Bel didn't respond. His eyes fluttered. "Stay with me."

It was a nasty wound. Bel would have died on the cobblestones if he weren't a suminaire, and I wasn't ready to think about what that meant. Luckily holding him upright took all my concentration. Eventually we found our way back.

Béatrice slid out from a shadow near the entrance. I almost dropped Bel, I was so relieved by the sight of her. Then I thought of her sister, Margot, and I didn't know what to say.

"You're late. What happened?" Her face scrunched at the blood. "No, no, I don't want to know. There's no time. After you're across the threshold, take him to his room. His magic should help with the rest."

"So we just walk him in leaking blood?"

"Leave the details to me."

But the wound was bad. I opened my mouth to protest, but Bel squeezed my hand. "Don't be stubborn. Do what she says."

"I'm not the stubborn one who got themself stabbed."

He opened his mouth, probably with some sharp retort, until his face crumpled with pain.

"See? Now shut your mouth before you hurt yourself more." I hauled Bel higher up my side.

Béatrice's eyes widened. "No one talks to him like that."

"Time someone did," I said, and started up the stairs.

Before the doorman could spot us, Béatrice sent out a stream of gears and dismantled a mirror fifteen feet away. Glass smashed. The commotion pulled eyes away from the door long enough for the three of us to slip through it unnoticed.

Béatrice gestured to the lift. "His room is up. If the maître is here, I'll keep him busy. But hurry." She shifted Bel to lean against me, then headed for the salon.

Bel slumped then straightened when I poked his wound. "You're losing a lot of blood."

"How observant of you," he ground out, feet dragging.

Inside the lift, King Zelig tipped his hat. "Floor?"

"Six," Bel grunted.

"You live on six?" It was the same floor as the moon window. Bel didn't answer. Instead he swore when the cage jerked.

"Down the hall on the right. The very end," he said when we reached his floor. Luckily the door was enchanted to open for him. Bel staggered in and crumpled down on his bed.

Knee to the mattress, I eased him over and unbuttoned his shirt.

My fingers painted streaks through the mess of red, feeling along his lower ribs for the wound. Finally, Bel moaned when I hit a puncture the width of a knuckle.

I balled the bed sheet and pressed it to the gush, like fishermen did at the docks whenever a hook sunk through a finger. But this wasn't from a hook and it wasn't his finger.

"All right, suminaire. Now's a good time for that magic body of yours to do its thing."

Except nothing happened, save for Bel appearing a little blue.

"Heal, damn it," I said, and sucked in a breath, caught off guard by the sudden thought that I might lose him, that he might bleed out until he was gray and dead, his body tossed wherever we were.

For all his secrets and wry taunts, he was my only confidant. I couldn't bear to lose him.

I shook his shoulders and his eyes snapped open. They were glazed over. His lips fluttered. When I brought my face down to hear, I realized he was laughing to himself. "Durc," he muttered. "That horrible little kitchen."

"What about that kitchen?" I asked to try and keep him talking.

"I thought you were ridiculous. That rusty knife." He laughed again then winced with pain.

"You're delirious. Now hush," I said, and brought a finger to his lips.

He grabbed it. "You're stronger than I thought."

I gave him a long look then jerked when he brought his hand up and brushed his thumb against my mouth. It lingered there, and my pulse skittered.

"I wish . . ." His voice trailed off.

"What do you wish?"

His gaze pinned me for a moment. Then his eyes shut and he fell against the bed.

I hung over him, startled. "Bel? Can you hear me?"

He didn't move.

I touched his cheek and he groaned. Where his skin wasn't bloody, it was clammy. But he was supposed to heal himself. I couldn't do that for him. I knew how to scrounge for meals, but Maman was the one who bandaged our scraped knees. I needed her now. *Help me*, I begged. I ran a finger over her necklace.

My hand flopped down, palm bloody. At the sight, I suddenly remembered how Zosa's cut from the orange shard had miraculously healed. That vial of gold paste. That first morning here, I'd seen a jar of the same paste sitting on the bar top in the salon, hidden among the bell jars. If it were still there, I could grab it and run before anyone saw me. It would be risky; kitchen workers were forbidden to step foot inside the salon.

When Bel moaned again, I shot up. I had to at least try. "Don't go anywhere," I said. "And don't yell at me afterward. You're not allowed."

He didn't even open his eyes to look at me.

✳

Salon d'Amusements was packed with diners sipping on rose-tinted alchemical concoctions. I barely paid them any attention. The sticky blood between my fingers kept me focused. The bar. Yrsa wasn't behind it. Instead, Hellas was the barkeep on duty tonight.

His long silver hair was pulled into a knot. His uniform sleeves were rolled up while he mixed a drink. The golden paste sat behind him. I tugged on a vacant expression and walked to the bar.

He glanced up. "Are you lost, pet?"

"I—I'm looking for Yrsa."

"Oh?" His lion eyes narrowed. "Why is a kitchen maid wearing a pink jacket over her frock?"

Not good. I'd forgotten to take it off. Spots of blood dotted my sleeves. Thinking fast, I held them up for him to see.

"You're bleeding," he said.

"It's not my blood. There was an accident. Chef—" As if on cue, I whimpered. A guest turned.

Hellas shrugged. "Not my problem."

He wouldn't help a worker who was bleeding? I wanted to dig my fingernails in his silver hair and make him listen. I managed to keep my face blank until a voice rang out.

I couldn't believe it. I'd forgotten.

Zosa stood onstage between the two other chanteuses. I'd caught hazy glimpses of her through glass, but I hadn't seen her. Not like this. The two girls hummed while Zosa sang a song Maman would sing to wake us up so long ago.

All I wished to do was shut my eyes and disappear. When my sister finished her song, the trio began another.

"Shouldn't you be meeting the Magnifique soon?" Hellas said.

I blinked. "Excuse me?"

"It's confounding Bel would sink so low as to disappear with a kitchen maid."

He knew I met Bel. My blood pulsed. He must have seen us together. "I don't know what you mean."

"Of course you don't."

Something I recognized hid in his words. But when Zosa hit a high note, I lost my patience. "Let me take the gold paste to Chef."

Hellas arched a silver brow. "And how does a kitchen maid know what this does?"

Damn it.

"If Chef wants it so badly, she can get it herself."

"Please."

"No."

It was clear he wouldn't give in, and arguing was only going to waste my time. Time Bel didn't have. I gave Hellas a tight nod and left the salon in a daze, looking around. There had to be a way to get to the gold paste, something I could do to cause a commotion, a distraction, to get Hellas out of the way. Because he would never give the paste to me. It was clear he didn't like me, though I couldn't tell why. Even that day in the library—

The library. That giant bird. I rushed to the entrance. The room was near empty, the massive bird asleep.

I climbed the ladder. I tossed my jacket over its cage and heaved it off the high stand. The contraption weighed the same as a small child. Inside, the bird's obsidian feathers ruffled. I stilled. *Please don't wake up, bird.*

Carefully, I carried it along the edge of the lobby. When I reached the salon, I flung the cage door open and poked the bird awake.

Liquid black eyes darted around while its claws clicked, scrabbling its way out. It was nearly the size of a dog.

It stretched its long neck and took off into the dining room, straight for a guest's jeweled headpiece. It didn't take long for the effect I wanted. Chairs toppled as guests screamed and ran out.

Hellas swung an upended chair. But the beast of a bird continued to peck at the woman's head, while the clearly intoxicated man next to her giggled like a child, toasting his wine glass to the spectacle. Blue flames tipped toward the bird, away from the now-empty bar.

No one paid me any attention when I dipped behind it and grabbed the gold paste, slipping it down my pocket. When I glanced up, Zosa looked right at me.

I froze.

Seconds passed. She took a step in my direction. Her pink lips moved, like she was speaking my name, but she was too far away to hear clearly. My throat closed up at the thought that she still knew me somehow, that there was a chance I wasn't forgotten like I'd assumed.

Zosa was too thin. Her dark eyes shone like drops of oil. A tear dripped down my cheek, and I couldn't look away. It took everything inside me not to run to her.

Madame des Rêves appeared out of nowhere, an enormous lavender wig limp around her shoulders. She held that tarnished hand mirror—the same one from the maître's office. Fanning herself with it, she yanked on a tasseled rope to release the curtain, but two guests had wrapped themselves up in the velvet, hiding from the bird. The curtain wouldn't close.

Des Rêves grumbled then pulled a small cage from offstage. I blinked away fresh tears when she touched her talon to each chanteuse's shoulder.

Alastair burst into the room. "Who let the library bird loose?"

I dropped to my knees and scrambled under a café table.

"I don't know," Des Rêves said. "One moment, it was just there."

The salon door was close, but they'd see me if I left. I'd have to wait here until I could make my way out unnoticed—calling attention to myself now would be fatal.

The bird snapped at a guest. An angry vein bulged in Alastair's forehead. He plucked the silver mirror from Des Rêves's hand, just as he'd done at the first soirée. He ran a finger over it as if checking for cracks.

It seemed an odd thing to do, given the circumstances. Clearly the artéfact was precious to him, even though the inkwell was Alastair's main artéfact, the talon Des Rêves's. They must both be using the mirror for something. I wondered what. Another question I didn't have the answer to.

The bird shrieked.

"Enough!" Alastair mumbled something softly and stomped the ground with a resounding *crack*. A wave of marble moved out from where Alastair's heel hit, toppling café chairs, sending crystal crashing. The bird stilled.

Alastair leveled his glare at Des Rêves, at the three birds hopping around next to the gilded cage. "Where is Frigga?"

"Probably in her room. She isn't due for another hour," Des Rêves said.

"*Probably?* She's responsible for the birds," Alastair said, incensed. "Get her down here now. Have her put those songbirds away then remove that *thing.*" He pointed to the black bird as it chomped on a slice of mangled cake.

Responsible for the birds.

My mind reeled. "Frigga," I muttered to myself, memorizing the name. If she were responsible for the birds, she might know where Zosa was kept, how to get inside the aviary. Alastair and Hellas had keys, but there could easily be more.

Alastair's boots crunched over broken glass. Before he turned around, I darted toward the salon door, looking back once to see Madame des Rêves shooing Zosa toward the cage.

✳

"Are you alive?"

I opened my eyes. I'd fallen asleep hunched next to Bel's bed. He stood over me. His fresh shirt hung open, exposing his clean, muscled chest. He caught me looking and I forced my eyes down to his wound. This morning, it was nothing but a bright red scar.

Relief shot through me. I had an urge to spring up and wrap my arms around his neck, but I stifled it at the memory of his ramblings last night. I touched my mouth, remembering the feel of his thumb running across my lips.

"Do you . . . remember when I brought you up here?"

"I remember my door opening. The rest is a bit fuzzy." Bel skewered me with a wry look. "Why? Did I say something I should apologize for?"

"No, nothing," I said. My voice sounded too high. Bel tilted his chin, skeptical. "At least you're healed," I added quickly.

"You do realize I'm a powerful suminaire, don't you? On top of it, you used an entire jar of Morvayan Sacred Salve. The paste costs more than renting the *Ode to a Fabled Forest Suite* for a year." He wiped a thick streak from under my ear.

It made little difference. The gold paste was matted in my hair and smeared over his bed. I couldn't help it, I laughed.

"I'm glad you find this funny," he said, but he grinned, too. After his smile died, his eyes remained on me, his expression unreadable.

Warmth spread up my neck.

"I like your room," I said, reaching for something to fill the silence. Except I hadn't actually looked at his room.

Slowly, I took it in. It was lined with books. The titles I could read were all geographies, the floor littered with stacks of maps and atlases. A collection of little globes sat across one shelf, along with a few old compasses, a small brass telescope, and other worldly knickknacks.

My fingers twitched, wanting to inspect every shelf. It wasn't fair that he got to surround himself with all this treasure. I could easily spend days here.

I always thought Bel's room would be modern and spare. Not *this*. His room reminded me of Bézier's third-floor sitting room that I'd loved so much. Bel had professed to not care about a single destination, and yet this room was an altar to them.

The rest of the space was nice. Folded blankets, a worn leather chair. It even smelled like him: brass polish and orange oil. I inhaled a lungful.

Bel untied something at his neck—the cape he wore when he used his key.

"You got up and moved the hotel?"

"A midnight passed." He shrugged. "It's my job."

I nodded as everything came crashing back: Café Margot, the salon, Zosa. My sister had looked right at me, mouthed my name. Another name came to mind. "Who's Frigga?"

Bel stilled as if he knew something. "I think she helps Des Rêves, but I could be wrong."

My fingers balled into fists. "Is there something you're not telling me?"

"Of course not." He took my wrist, smoothing out my hand with his palm. "Would you relax?"

Relax? This was the closest I'd come to finding out how to get my sister back. I forced myself to take a deep breath. Bel was probably right. Zosa was still under contract. Besides, even if I found this Frigga, there was no way I could ask her about the aviary without revealing myself.

I picked at a snagged nail and thought of the aviary's thick glass, the woman's voice as I touched it. *Closed indefinitely.*

"I don't understand why the aviary is always locked." There had to be an explanation why Alastair closed it to guests, something driving him. "That day in the map room, you told me Alastair was greedy. What did you mean exactly?"

Bel shrugged. "I see his face every time I bring him an artéfact. Alastair's fanatical about hoarding them. More so, I think, than he is about safety. Once I caught him lining up artéfacts across his office floor, counting them over and over, like a dragon counting its hoard of gold."

"What about that signet ring you're looking for?"

"You're not going let it go, are you?"

"Did you honestly expect me to?"

He huffed a laugh. "Actually, I thought I'd have to explain it sooner. The truth is, I've searched for that miserable ring for years."

Alastair must want it badly. "What does it do?"

"I don't know," Bel said. "I've been looking for it for so long that I can barely stand to think about it. And yet Alastair still expects me to find it."

It must do something spectacular—but none of this explained the strictness around the aviary.

Bel swirled his thumb in a puddle of gold paste. "Now would you care to tell me how you came by the Sacred Salve?"

Here we go.

Bel listened, grim-faced, as I recounted the tale of the library bird. There was one more thing I wanted to ask, but I didn't know how. The thought alone made me sweat.

"Are you all right?"

I must have looked anxious because he took my hand and began idly scraping paste from my palm with the hilt of his switchblade. I prayed he didn't notice my full-body blush. But he definitely did. I wished to god my face wasn't so damned readable, especially by him.

"Hellas knows we meet," I said.

Bel's switchblade stilled.

I wasn't bothered by what Hellas said, but how he had said it. "Is he . . . jealous we meet?" As soon as the words came out, I wanted to take them back, melt into the floor. "Not that we're anything . . ." I added. *Oh god. Boil me.* "Forget it, forget it. Forget I even asked." I sat down on his sheet and cringed when gold paste squished under me.

Bel was quiet.

The silence was unbearable. My insides twisted. I forced my eyes down between my boots, as if the floor held all the world's secrets.

After a long while, Bel exhaled. "Hellas and I . . . We were together once. Long ago."

"I had no idea."

"Not many do. There was a time when I was closer to him than anyone, back when we were both trying to prove ourselves to Alastair." He frowned. "But then, slowly, we started to notice what was happening around us. I wanted to investigate, but Hellas was nervous to do anything that might get him in trouble. I would get so mad." A terrible expression crept over Bel's face. "But Hellas had a good reason for being nervous—a reason that I refused to acknowledge at the time."

I titled my chin, curious. "What reason?"

"It's . . . not important anymore," he said. "I don't like who Hellas has become, but I could never hate him for it. Looking back, the fact that our relationship ended as badly as it did probably nudged him to be the person he is now. And how it ended was all my fault. The things I said . . ."

He shut his eyes. I could tell it was hard for him to talk about, and my heart cracked open a bit. This made me see the Botaniste in a whole new light, and I couldn't help but feel sorry for him, and for Bel.

"Hellas is allowed to still be angry with me. Regardless, he reports to both Yrsa and Alastair, so promise me you'll be careful around him."

When I nodded, he exhaled and sat down beside me. His thigh brushed my skirts and my skin tightened at the contact. The silence in the room felt tense. I turned toward him, searching for something to say, but my attention shifted to his clean shirt that hung unbuttoned. A swath of his smooth, muscled chest peeked through.

Last night, I'd dragged my fingers over that same chest hoping his bleeding would stop, but this felt different. My cheeks warmed. He caught my eyes. His were dilated. My lips parted to tell him I should go, but nothing came out because his eyes moved to my throat. When my breath hitched, they moved to my mouth as if he might . . . as if he might kiss me.

I shot up and started toward the door.

"Wait." He took my arm. "Your cut."

The cut from the vendor's cart was now a puckered slash crusted with blue dust. I'd forgotten it.

Bel swiped some paste from my hair and smeared gold over the cut, erasing it before I could pull away. His fingers lingered against my skin. "Thanks," he said. "For the paste."

"Right. The paste," I repeated.

He then added, "Even though it was a horrendous idea to re-trieve it in the first place."

I scowled while he fished a towel from a shelf and held it out.

"I didn't ask for a towel."

"Washroom's in back." When I balked, he wiped a streak of paste from my lip. "You look like an overly lavish truffle. Walk around like that and the guests will try to eat you." He threw the towel at my head and left.

19

Bel had taken us to Morvay, one of the smaller nations east of Preet. I knew it not from the guests' flowing robes or understated wealth, but from the cats. Sleek Morvayan leopards, straight from Maman's bedtime tales, padded though the lobby leashed by ropes of twisted silk.

I hid in the shadows while the leopards drew everyone's attention, including Alastair's. He clapped his hands, ordering citrus-infused water to be put out. Staff scurried around setting down trays of raw meat. Leopards growled, fighting for the larger morsels. One fixed its ocher eyes on me. My heart beat furiously. Thankfully, I didn't pass another leopard before my shift.

"Decided to show after all," Chef said as I arrived in the kitchens. She placed a silver tray with an enchanted meringue decorated with blooming fondant flowers on the top of a delivery cart.

"I'm sorry, I didn't—"

She fluttered her hands. "Béatrice explained. Don't know how you're standing after tumbling down a flight of stairs."

Béatrice had covered for me. I started toward the soup station when Chef pulled me back.

"No soup. You'll be doing deliveries all night. Dignitaries from Morvay take dinners in their rooms. Each of them ordered extra food for their pets." Her mouth turned down in disgust. "I wouldn't bring a dog to dinner. Now they make us serve steak to their cats? Pomp, if you ask me."

Plenty of folk revered their pets. There had to be a reason the leopards were treated so well. But Chef didn't want to hear it. She handed me a delivery ledger and walked away.

"Wait," I called out. "Does Madame des Rêves have a girl reporting to her called Frigga?"

"Frigga? Reporting to Des Rêves?" Chef barked a laugh. "Hellas would cut off his hair before he'd allow that."

"Hellas?"

She pointed to my cart, to the jar of dried fruits and seeds destined for the A *Verdant Enchantment Suite.* "Funny you've never heard the name. You've delivered to Frigga for the past two weeks," she said. "Maître lets Hellas's sister live on the second floor, apart from the other staff."

I knew that suite. It was occupied by the girl with deep gold skin and hair, but I'd only seen her through a cracked door.

A sinking feeling settled in my chest. If she were Hellas's sister, Bel had to know who Frigga was, and yet he played her off like she was nothing. But she was responsible for the birds. She had to know a way to Zosa.

If I'd known about Frigga earlier, I would have searched for her. I hadn't seen my sister in weeks. And Bel knew about her—

Understanding washed through me. Bel wasn't a fool. He knew

that if I'd learned about Frigga earlier, I would have done something drastic to get to her, and possibly landed myself in Alastair's office. Again. And in the end, even if I hadn't, it wouldn't have made a difference, because we were all still trapped. Bel was only trying to protect me.

But my fingers drummed against my skirts. If Bel kept this from me, there could be other things he might be keeping from me still— other secrets hidden within these walls, secrets that might help me and Zosa get home—and I wanted to know every single one.

✸

A few hours later, it was dinnertime in the salon. Guests gathered around tables that had been set upright again, and the marble floor appeared whole, or as much of it as I could see through the glass.

Hidden in my alcove, I waited for Zosa to sing, but only piano music drifted out. There was never piano music in the salon. The piano was always saved for soirées.

I peeked inside. The suminaire from that first soirée stood atop her bright red piano. Workers darted between tables. I'd memorized some of the waitstaff's faces over the past weeks. But these were all strangers.

When a porter walked by, I grabbed his shoulder.

"Let me go." He brought a carved stone near my chin. Magic sizzled. I ripped it away and tossed it across the floor.

"I was supposed to deliver a package to one of the waitstaff. Minette." I said the first name I thought of. "She's not in the salon."

"I don't suppose they'd tell a kitchen maid."

"Tell me what?"

"A bird got loose last night. Caused a scene. The maître demoted all the salon staff." The boy smiled, smug. "He even reprimanded the Botaniste."

When he tried to pull away, my nails dug into his shoulder. "What about the birds?"

He was silent.

"*Tell me.*"

"I—I heard a bird flew out the door and never came back."

His words made my heart pound. "What did the bird look like?" I never saw Zosa go into the cage. If she flew outside before midnight . . .

He cringed and I realized my fingers were digging at bone. "You're hurting me, ma'am."

I let him go and ducked through shadows to the aviary glass, searching for a lock, a door. Anything. "*Closed indefinitely!*" rang the woman's effervescent voice.

"Shut up," I said, panicked. Guests backed away.

The delivery cart was where I left it. Shoving the jar of fruit and seeds in my pocket, I flew up the stairs to the A *Verdant Enchantment Suite.* The door cracked opened on the sixth knock and the woman peeked out. Frigga.

"Delivery." I held out the jar. She tried to snatch it, but I pulled it back. Her door notched open. Birds flitted behind her. "I need your help," I said.

Her forehead scrunched. She didn't know me, nor trust me, but if she had a way inside the aviary, I needed to know.

I rustled the jar. "Can we talk in your room?"

Frigga shook her head and a bee shot out from her pile of hair. She swatted at it. The hall candles flared bright blue and she shrunk back, nervous. Eyeing the jar, she pushed the door open. "You can't stay long."

Inside, open birdcages lined a far wall. White paper trees grew up from thick carpet. Birds flitted from the paper branches to a cast-iron slipper tub filled to the brim and covered with lily pads. The A *Verdant Enchantment Suite* wasn't so much a guest room as a forest made from Hellas's precious cards.

I handed over the jar. She poured its contents on the carpet. Birds flocked, jostling for a nibble, but Frigga's brown eyes never left me. "Why are you here?"

"I heard you're responsible for Des Rêves's songbirds. What does that entail?"

Frigga lifted her arm. A manacle encircled her wrist. She stepped to the wall of cages and touched the manacle to one. Metal bars melted together until there was no door. Her manacle was an artéfact.

"You work metal."

"I'm also good with birds." She whistled and a white bird flitted to her shoulder. "So the maître put me in charge of transporting them."

"Have you seen a bird with molten gold feathers?"

"I help with lots of birds."

I groaned. "A porter said a bird flew out last night. Do you know which one?"

"I . . . I heard the black bird from the library took off and didn't

come back." Her mouth pulled into a terrible frown. It was hard to imagine anyone could like that awful bird.

"What about the golden bird? Des Rêves's chanteuse?"

"I'm not sure. I didn't get down in time to see. I haven't checked—"

"Not sure?" My pulse picked up. "Is the golden bird kept in the aviary? Do you have a key?"

She backed off, skittish. "Hellas also has a key. You could go ask him."

Also.

She had to get me inside that aviary, but if she were going to help me, I had to put her at ease. I searched around. A letter sat on a dressing table, a name scrawled on top. "Who's Issig?"

"No one," she said, her attention focused on my soup stains. "You work in the kitchens. What's it like?" She lifted the letter. Her slim fingers danced over the paper. "Hellas forbids me from stepping a toe inside."

"It's hot. Look, I'll give you a tour if you'll show me the aviary."

"Hot?" Frigga stuffed the letter in an envelope. She stacked it on a pile of more envelopes, each one addressed to the same man.

"Issig is no one, huh?"

"He works in the kitchens."

I'd never met a cook by that name, but the kitchens were vast, and she was forbidden to enter. That gave me a bargaining chip. "If I delivered those," I said, "would you take me inside the aviary?"

Her eyes grew. They reminded me of Zosa's. "You would do that?"

"Of course." Right now, I'd do almost anything.

Fighting a smile, she bundled the stack with twine and handed

it over. "Deliver these, then meet me in the lobby near the aviary at eleven. Bring a piece of ice as proof."

My head snapped up. "From the deep freeze?" She motioned to the letters, the name Issig. It took one breath to realize what she was asking. "You have got to be joking."

"That's where he's kept."

The deep freeze. I'd been warned away from it, and from what I could tell, it had been for good reason. Béatrice had never been inside, nor Bel. But both Chef and Yrsa went in, and they were fine. And eleven was an hour away. "I'll do it," I said, shoving the letters in my pocket.

"All right, then. Tell me what he says." She whistled; her birds flew away from the door long enough for me to sneak through it. She then slammed it shut.

It didn't matter. Soon I would see my sister.

I exhaled and turned to face Hellas.

"Fancy seeing you again."

He pressed a playing card between my eyebrows. Thick paper vines grew over my nose and mouth. I clawed, trying to scrape them away, but it was like attempting to remove my own skin.

"I just visited Chef. She didn't know anything about an accident, or a *stolen* jar of Sacred Salve."

The paper vines kept growing, fusing my head to the door. I couldn't breathe. Hellas swiped away the bark at my mouth. I sucked in air, struggling, but I was still stuck.

"I don't have time for liars. Who was the gold paste for?"

"It was for me."

Bel leaned against the wall, liquid as a Morvayan leopard. A piece of hair escaped his ear. When he brushed it away, his switchblade flicked out with the softest snick. "Time you and I had a talk, Hellas. We're long overdue." His voice was silk.

Paper vines fluttered to the floor. Bel didn't deign to look at me. "Leave us, Mol," he said.

20

The deep freeze door curved with filigreed steel, but no handle. I knocked softly, and when nothing happened, I made a fist to knock again. I never got the chance.

The door blew outward an inch then sank back as if drawing a breath. Then it flew open with a burst of breath-stealing chill. I stepped forward and the door slammed behind me. Inside, thick blocks of ice were scattered about, coalescing into a hulking figure covered in ice crystals and chained to the wall.

Issig.

His black hair hung in a thick braid over smooth, olive-toned skin that was bare, save for a pair of uniform trousers. But his hands were pure icy white as if hewed from marble. One finger was broken off at the knuckle. His chest was anchored to the wall by a crisscross of steel chains. A shudder moved through me. Issig would never read Frigga's letters; he was nothing more than a frozen, strung-up corpse.

The ice pile lay past him.

I took a step. Chains rattled. Slowly, I turned. The dead man sloughed ice like a fisherman skimming scales off a fresh catch. A pure white stone disk hung from a metal chain around his neck. His eyes trained on me.

Not a corpse.

"Hi," I squeaked.

His hands shot out, straining toward me through his chains. I jumped back, hitting the far wall. The temperature dipped.

Scrambling, I fished the letters from my pocket. "Mail!" I shouted, and shoved the letters into his open hand. It was enough to distract him. Wincing at the bitter air, I ducked around and placed three ice cubes in my pocket.

His white disk rattled and a gust of cold came *from* him. The disk must be an artéfact. I felt a new chill that had nothing to do with the temperature. This suminaire was kept prisoner to make ice for guests.

Purple ink shone from the stack in his hands. I checked my pocket. I'd pulled out an old itinerary with Frigga's letters on accident. He ran a thumb over the inked destinations, as if he could hear the woman's voice. The paper grew brittle.

"What is this?" he said, his words a cold croak.

"Letters from Frigga."

He shook his head. "I don't know a Frigga."

Frigga clearly *knew* Issig and yet he didn't remember her. He was a suminaire. He should have his memories from inside the hotel. All suminaires did. Alastair didn't dare take them—

Because of a suminaire whose mind Alastair had erased so many times, his magic became volatile. Lethal.

Bel had told me that when that suminaire's mind had finally

snapped, an endless stream of his magic had poured through his artéfact and lashed out at everyone around him, worse than if he'd never been given an artéfact in the first place. Those who weren't suminaires had died instantly.

Bel must have meant Issig. This man was the reason Alastair stopped amending suminaire contracts. The reason Yrsa turned eyes to porcelain.

Issig thrashed and huffed. With his exhale, the stack of letters crumbled to dust. Then he looked at me, like he knew what he was, what he was capable of.

"Leave," he said, his eyes going blank again as he strained against his chains.

I had to get out.

Issig's fingertips grazed my sleeve as I scraped past him. I shoved through the door. When it slammed shut, a guttural scream ripped from inside the freezer. The door blew outward a foot then sucked back in, leaving a dusting of ice across the floor.

My frozen sleeve crumbled.

"Don't touch it." Chef appeared. With a swipe of kitchen shears, the fabric fell to the floor in a wisp of smoke. "Last time he blew up, no one could go inside for a month." She wrung her apron and shivered; the entire kitchen was freezing. "The leopards. Their meat was in there!"

"I'm sorry."

"Sorry? The maître will have my head if anything happens to Issig."

"Why does he keep him locked away?"

"He's a suminaire who can't turn off his magic." She tapped her head. "His mind is gone. That steel is the only thing that keeps us safe, and now you've gone and pissed him off."

But his mind wasn't gone. For a moment, I saw it. Now, however, was not the time to argue. The cubes were melting.

Chef caught my arm. "I don't care what Béatrice says—you're trouble, and I won't have trouble here. When we close up at midnight, I'm speaking with the maître."

"You can't," I breathed.

Chef's face contorted in rage. "Get out of my kitchen."

✳

The lobby was dark. Bel would move the hotel soon. I'd find him later, beg him to help keep me hidden, anything but have my contract amended again. If Alastair's ink worked this time, I'd lose everything.

All these thoughts fled at the sight of Frigga tucked beside the aviary. Nothing mattered until I knew if Zosa was still inside.

She held out a hand. "The ice?"

I placed the only cube that hadn't melted on her palm. Her lips parted. "What did Issig say?"

No one had warned her. "He said very little . . . but he was moved."

She swiped her eyes and pulled out a tiny key. "My end of the bargain." Her knuckles knocked on the thick aviary glass. "Made from layers of Preetian dragonfly wings. Pretty to look at, but tough as nails and nearly soundproof."

I looked around. "Where's the door?"

"Hidden in plain sight. The maître penned the enchantment for the aviary keys himself." The key touched down. Glass rippled. Out of nothing, a door appeared with a rusted copper nameplate that read *La Volière des Délices*. The Aviary of Delights.

Frigga took my hand. "Follow me."

Inside, paper leaves brushed against my cheeks. I was grateful when Frigga's fingers found mine, leading me through the press of trees to a fountain surrounded by statues. Near me, a marble man hoisted a tiny hourglass above his head. Frigga grazed a finger along it. "A suminaire."

The hourglass must be his artéfact. "All the statues are of suminaires?"

"I believe so."

A slight woman carved from green marble stood holding a round artéfact that I thought was a flattened face, until I realized the face was a reflection of the statue's own face. A mirror.

"I've seen the maître with an artéfact similar to this. A hand mirror," I said. "Do you know anything about it?"

Frigga pursed her lips.

"You've seen it?" I pressed.

"No . . . I mean, yes, I've seen it, but I haven't asked about what it does. Hellas doesn't like me to pry."

Does Hellas control everything you eat, too? I nearly asked, until a bird squawked.

"Where are the birds?" All I saw were a handful of real trees hidden among Hellas's paper creations.

"This way."

As we walked, Frigga prattled on about the chanteuses. I learned she ferried the birds between the aviary and the salon for performances nearly every day. Des Rêves performed her act so often, she forced Frigga to live in that second-floor room, because the stairwell next to the A *Verdant Enchantment Suite* emptied near the salon. Frigga didn't mind it because the older guest room made a perfect sanctuary for her birds.

"If your chanteuse is inside, she'll be through here," Frigga said, and led me through a hedge with leaves like fingers. We popped out in an open space crammed with wooden perches. High above the foliage, I could make out the birds visible from the lobby. Underneath, hidden behind a tangle of white vines, slept hundreds upon hundreds more.

I looked from bird to bird. Most of them were leached of pigment. They still had their markings, but the color was gone, leaving them gray and dull.

"What's wrong with them?" I whispered.

"They just arrive like that."

There were a few colorful birds, but no molten gold.

Nearby, a dull bird yawned, cracking one sleepy eye. Its other eye glinted in the moonlight a slightly different color.

It was glass.

21

I scanned across the birds. "How many are suminaires?"

"Not Des Rêves's chanteuses, but all the rest," Frigga said mournfully.

"That black bird from the library?"

Tears flooded Frigga's eyes. She nodded. "I think he knew what he was doing, that he'd rather disappear forever than be caged up."

He.

The library bird was a man who was willing to die rather than remain trapped.

I stared openmouthed, appalled. An anger built inside of me that threatened to consume me from within. But I didn't cry out or tear up. I felt too numb to do either.

These *people*. There were so many of them. Hundreds of men and women, and probably children. All cut off from the world and caged behind glass.

Suminaires lived long lives. These poor people had probably been trapped here for decades, or more. My god. If they all signed staff contracts, no one outside the hotel would remember them. They would be missing, just like Béatrice from that painting, just like me and Zosa from Bézier's mind.

The sight was too shocking for words, but the rational part of me also didn't understand the logic of it. Alastair hoarded artéfacts. If these suminaires' magic could be used safely, Alastair didn't need to trap them all. And nothing explained why their feathers looked as dull as they did.

Something Maman had spoken of from time to time popped into my mind. A century ago, the Verdanniere crown commissioned experiments to better understand suminaire magic and prevent it from killing people. But they were promptly abandoned when most parties involved perished. Maman always referred to it as *la semaine sombre*, the dark week. It marred Verdanne's *illustrious* nasty history.

Alastair could be doing something similar with these suminaires. Experimenting with magic. Bile rose in my throat at the thought, and I had to brace myself against a paper tree.

Then there was Issig chained inside the deep freeze. If his magic was so deadly, I didn't see why he hadn't been turned into a bird, when all of these others had. Maybe his condition excluded him from whatever Alastair was doing here, or maybe the truth was more horrible than I could imagine. Knowing Alastair, it was probably the latter.

I scanned each bird. *Where are you?*

A branch snapped. A pair of guests had wandered in alongside a leopard straining on its silk leash. Birds cawed.

I turned to Frigga. "Didn't you lock the door?"

"Lock it? I'm never here longer than a handful of minutes. No one ever tries to come in."

I rubbed my temple. I believed her, but I doubted there were often leopards with noses made to sniff out prey.

"We have to go. I'm not supposed to be in here now." Frigga tugged my sleeve, but I batted her off.

"Give me another minute."

Frantically, I searched, but there were too many birds to pick out one. If Zosa had flown out the window like the black bird, I didn't know what I would do.

I was about to turn around when a golden bird shot toward me, landing in my outstretched hands. A sob of relief wracked my chest until she started pecking at my nose.

"Zosa, stop it."

I tried to hold her back, but she wouldn't listen. Her little beak tugged at my hair. I was confused and so dizzy with happiness, I nearly toppled over. With one high-pitched keen too big for her tiny body, Zosa flew off.

I turned to face Alastair.

Behind him, Yrsa led the guests with the leopard away.

Alastair wrapped his fingers around Frigga's wrist. "You'll come with me." His face was pinched.

"It's not Frigga's fault," Hellas shouted. A moment later, he stumbled out from the bushes. "That girl must have done it," he snarled at me, then turned his attention to Frigga. There was fear in his eyes for his sister—a fear I hadn't seen from him before.

This was it—what Bel had hinted at in his room; Frigga was Hellas's *reason* for being hesitant to upset Alastair. Hellas did Alastair and Yrsa's bidding in order to keep his sister safe. Bel probably didn't understand his devotion, but I did. I understood exactly how Hellas felt.

"I'll deal with the kitchen maid later," Alastair said.

"But maître—"

"Guests got inside the aviary. Was it your sister's key or not that allowed them entrance?"

"*Please,*" Hellas begged.

"You know the rules," Alastair said. "She'll have to be punished."

I pictured Frigga's nest of hair spilling over the side of Yrsa's table, just like Red's. That swirl of not-milk. Minutes ago, Chef had sworn to report me to Alastair. I was already in trouble. I should say something—

But if anything happened to me, no one would look out for Zosa. Then Frigga started to cry, and I couldn't just stand there and do nothing.

"I did it," I said. "I took Frigga's key and came in here. She was only trying to get it back."

"Is it true?" Alastair asked Frigga.

Frigga looked at me. *Say yes,* I willed. When she nodded, Hellas let out a sharp exhale.

"Very well." Alastair gripped my shoulder. "This way."

It was eleven thirty when we reached the lobby. A stack of silver luggage stretched to the ceiling acting as a shelf for champagne. Guests took glasses and gathered to watch the hotel move. Bel leaned against a wall. He pushed away when he saw me and froze at the sight of Alastair.

Alastair didn't notice Bel. He led me to a door on the first floor and whispered a command. The door opened to a plain guest suite with no title. "After you."

I took one step inside and the door slammed at my back, locking me in the room alone. Seams filled in until the door became a solid wall. Trapped. My legs gave out and I sagged to the floor.

I didn't know what would happen, didn't know if Bel would help me now, or if he even could. My head throbbed and I wanted out of this room. Agitated, I clawed at the peeling wallpaper. At least Zosa was alive, and Frigga would keep both her eyes.

Far sooner than I expected, before I could gouge much more of the wall, the room door appeared, then opened. At the sight of Bel, relief hit me so sharp and sudden, it took my breath away. I leaped up and wrapped my arms tight around him. When he stiffened, I pulled away.

His face—a face I'd come to know as well as my own—held nothing but indifference. He looked at me like I was a stranger. It gutted me.

I didn't know why he was acting like this, but it couldn't be good. I crossed my arms, suddenly freezing.

"Well?" I asked.

"You're being sent back to Durc."

"With Zosa?"

"No."

"Then I'm not going."

"You have no choice. Your contract has been voided. The moment you walk through the lacquered door, you'll step back into that alley, same as a guest upon checkout." Then, so softly I barely heard him, he added, "You won't be demoted again, at least."

"Demote me. Tell Yrsa to take my eye. Tell Alastair to keep me."

"I won't."

Won't, not *can't.* Tears blurred my vision. "Why won't you fight for me?"

He brought a hand up and wiped my eyes then rested his palm against my cheek. I leaned into his touch, needing it in this moment like I needed air. "I'm sorry," he said.

I didn't understand it. "Why bother helping me in the first place?"

Something swept across Bel's features then disappeared in a blink. "I was curious how his ink worked and now I'm not. If Alastair discovers you had your memories this whole time, he'll find some other way to punish you. You can't stay."

Like hell.

I jerked his collar down and fished out the hotel key. "You're the Magnifique. He needs you to move the hotel. Make a deal with him."

His throat bobbed. "I already have."

I dropped my hand. I shook my head in disbelief. "*You're* sending me back? Without my sister?"

"I'm saving you."

I couldn't begin to imagine how Bel arranged that. He must have promised Alastair something obscene.

He fished in his pocket then pressed cold coins in my palm. Silver dublonnes. "For passage to your village," he said. "Congratulations. Alastair voided your contract. You get to go home."

I flinched at the word, and my heart plummeted. I'd spent years trying to get home, but I knew without a doubt that Aligney would never be home without Zosa.

"Don't you get it? Home doesn't mean anything to me without the people I love." When he was silent, my fingers curled into fists.

Deep down, I knew Bel probably had a good reason for all of this, but the idea that he would rid himself of me so easily made my lungs squeeze. My teeth clenched, and I wanted him to *feel* what this was doing to me, to know how much it hurt.

I lifted my chin, bitter anger coursing through me. "You're not just sending me back. You're pushing me away like you do to everyone inside this place. Was I always just some worker for you to use then toss aside?" My pathetic lips began to wobble. "God, I don't want to cry in front of you."

"Jani—"

"When I first came here, I thought you didn't care about anyone. But after all these weeks, things between us feel different. And now . . . now you're throwing me out like I'm nothing to you."

A muscle ticked in his jaw.

He reached out. Rough fingers smoothed over my neck.

"What are—" My words cut off with a gasp. He dipped his thumb under the neckline of my dress to tangle with Maman's necklace. His other hand stretched toward me, fingertips grazing my waist, and his eyes darkened. Slowly, languorously, his gaze slid down my face, coming to a stop on my mouth.

I held my breath until Bel shook his head and stepped back.

"You're not nothing to me," he said, almost to himself. "That's precisely the problem."

✳

A short while later, Yrsa arrived with the twins. I pulled away when she snatched my arm. "Struggle all you want. The more you do, the greater chance the maître will let me cut out one of your fine eyes before you're sent on your way." When I blanched, she smiled and tugged me along, the twins at my back.

Still before midnight, the lobby had filled with guests waiting for the hotel to move. Béatrice stood in the corner dabbing her cheeks with a hanky, whereas Bel leaned against a back wall and pretended not to see me.

The suminaire with her feather blew pink smoke over a row of guests, their ornate gowns rippling through a sunset of hues. Alastair stood with them. He caught my eyes then looked away, as if I were nothing but dirt under his shoe.

I didn't care.

I would do whatever he asked to stay on. I'd stir soup and scrub toilets until my palms bled. I could race over, beg him. I spun away from Yrsa.

"Wrong way." Her hand jerked my frock. My heel connected with a tree root and I pitched forward. My knees hit the ground, followed by my jaw, and I spat blood from a split lip onto the roots. Fitting I would leave this place under an orange tree, same as I came. Good thing I didn't manage to break one.

My eyes widened. Bel's flippant words about Alastair and the oranges raced through my mind. *If he knew you broke one, he'd never let you leave.*

When I broke an orange, he'd hid it from Yrsa, taken the blame. I didn't know if breaking another orange would buy me an audience with Alastair, but if I could touch one, knock it from the branch, it might at least buy me time.

One last tree at the door.

I reached for it, but Sazerat took my shoulders and shoved me. I brought my fist up and watched in shock as it vanished at the line of the doorframe. No, not vanished: a cold, wet breeze skated across my knuckles from somewhere on the other side.

I strained against him, boot heels slipping against slick marble. I kicked out and caught a branch of oranges with my heel. A few broke off, but I couldn't hear if they smashed because the woman's obnoxiously effervescent voice said, *"Farewell, traveler!"*

My eyes squeezed shut.

I smelled it first. Gone was the desert jasmine, replaced with a familiar tang of salt brine. I lost track of where I was in that in-between space. I *felt* Sazerat's hands on my shoulders and *tasted* Durc on my tongue. Bile inched up my throat.

"There's a girl!" someone shouted in Verdanniere. A southern accent. A fisherman's accent.

Oh god.

Strong fingers grabbed my sides, pulling me back. My eyes shot open to the slam of a lacquered door in my face. I bit back a sob and looked up. At Alastair. He panted like he'd just sprinted the length of the lobby.

The oranges from the branch I had kicked were smashed across the floor. Bel stood behind the tree, eyes locked on me, horrified.

A satisfied smile curved across Alastair's lips. "The girl stays."

22

Yrsa turned around, seeing the mess of oranges for the first time. "Maître, I didn't realize—"

"You didn't." Alastair silenced her with a single look. "Get behind the bar," he ordered. "*Now*." She nodded and motioned for the twins to follow. But Alastair put a hand on Sazerat's shoulder. "Report to my office in an hour," he said to the twin.

"Why?" asked Sido.

Slowly, Alastair turned to Sido, the vein in his forehead visible.

The twin shrank back.

"The girl knocked off an orange and your brother nearly threw her out. I almost lost her because of him. He'll have to be punished."

Sazerat was a suminaire with one eye removed. He'd already gotten his first warning. Surely Alastair wouldn't kill him over me.

"Now out of my sight. Both of you." Alastair waved his hand. Stunned, Sido took his brother and trailed after Yrsa.

A circle of staff appeared with brooms and dustpans. They ushered upset guests to their rooms and cleaned up the broken oranges. The lobby marble swallowed any pieces they missed.

I didn't move. My legs felt rooted in place while Alastair's pale eyes studied me.

"Miraculous that a kitchen maid can cause so much trouble in the span of a single day," Alastair said. "Did you know?"

"I suspected."

I whirled around at Bel's voice. Just like inside the guest suite, I couldn't read his face, but something in his eyes appeared hollower than they once had, like a bit of himself had shattered along with the oranges.

"You suspected, yet you bargained with me to send her back?" Alastair twirled an orange shard between his fingers. "The marvelous orange trees are unique to the hotel. Long ago, before the hotel existed like it does now, a suminaire created them by enchanting normal orange trees."

Before the hotel existed. I thought of the society handbook from the map room. The suminaire he spoke of could have been a member.

Alastair's mouth flattened. "I tried cutting the trees down once. But they simply spring back up, straight from the marble floor." He turned to me. "The fruit rarely releases, and only for a suminaire."

I blinked at the word. No way.

It simply wasn't possible. I'd never once felt magic flaring up. Never had any power leak out of myself, injuring those around me, like suminaire children did. Before the hotel, I'd never felt that beguiling hum of magic at all. Yet the maître thought I was a suminaire. *Bel* thought it.

The idea was ridiculous. Silly, even. I shook my head. "Impossible," I said. "The oranges are clearly misinformed."

I waited for Bel to agree with me, to laugh and make a joke at my expense. But he remained silent, avoiding my eyes.

Slowly, realization began to dawn on me. Bel wouldn't act like this . . . unless it was *true*.

I was a suminaire.

For the briefest moment, I felt like something shifted inside me and locked into place, changing me irrevocably. I looked around me, as if with new eyes. The sinister darkness of the lobby seemed to expand, calling out to me, to my magic.

My magic.

I'd seen many miraculous things inside, from that first soirée to the escape games, to the raining umbrellas and magic halls. If I were a suminaire, it meant I had the same potential building inside of me for years.

I glanced down at the tops of my hands, studied my small knuckles, the hangnail on my index finger, callused skin curving over bones and sinew. These hands looked ordinary. They were the hands of a tannery worker in Durc, a kitchen maid, a sister, a daughter from Aligney. But if Alastair were right, then these hands were also capable of wielding magic—terrible, beautiful magic— and I'd had no idea.

But Bel did.

Shock gave way to anger, rushing forth, filling up every empty space inside of me until I could barely breathe. I faced him. He straightened, his jaw set and his eyes narrowed in that calculated look I knew so well.

He knew! This whole time he knew what I was, and yet he kept it from me. He lied to me, even. I thought he was a confidant, a friend. My lips trembled. He *was* a friend. Probably my best friend here, and now—

Now the betrayal felt like a punch to my gut. I wanted to scream, to question him endlessly, but my throat tightened to a painful knot.

I stalked toward him and grabbed his collar. He jerked me off and held me at an arm's length away, his features carefully blank.

"*You knew*," I hissed through clenched teeth. Wretched tears gathered in my eyes. "Why did you keep it from me?"

"You need to calm down. Now." He gestured over my shoulder. Alastair walked over.

The sight of him turned my anger to ice, and I began to shake.

Alastair's smile was sharp-toothed. He slipped the orange shard into his pocket and placed his hand at the crook of my elbow, like I was his prize.

"This way," he said. "It's nearly midnight and the Magnifique has a job to do."

Alastair brought me to his office. I wanted to bolt from the room. It took every bit of will to remain standing, to confront what I was, what I'd always been.

I rubbed my hands together and ran my thumb over the veins on the inside of my wrist. I'd heard stories of how colorless and terrible magic was. I pictured it thrashing in my blood now, like a pitch-black snake hissing to get out, and I didn't know how to feel.

"Over here," Alastair said. He walked to his curio cabinet and took three artéfacts off a top shelf, placing them one after another on his desk.

When I stood unsure and unmoving, he snatched my hand and dragged me forward, forcing my fingertips against each one: a hazel branch divining rod, a small stone pendulum, and a bronze compass with a jade needle.

The magic from the compass tickled, cool and sharp, while both the pendulum and divining rod's magic hummed against my skin, warming it.

Alastair's mouth turned down. He dragged my fingers over the three artéfacts again and again. When nothing more seemed to happen, his nostrils flared. He threw my hand away with such force, my knuckles smacked the wall.

Wary, I took a step back. Despite the shock numbing my emotions, I couldn't tamp down my curiosity. "W—what are they?"

"Not for you, it would seem. I haven't found a suminaire who can get a good feel for any of these." He flicked the compass's jade needle. "Yrsa tries to use the compass. But she can't make it work properly. The result is unpredictable at best."

I'd seen the compass before. Yrsa held it up to me during the interview in Durc. Its needle had spun and spun. That must be what he meant by unpredictable. Maybe it was supposed to point to potential candidates, people with talent like Zosa.

Alastair returned the three artéfacts to the curio next to where that tarnished hand mirror sat propped against the corner. He didn't touch the mirror. Instead, he took out all the other artéfacts, one after another, until his desk was littered with them. Then he turned his attention to me, and a chill crept down my back.

"When each new suminaire takes a job, they choose one artéfact they'll use during their time here. A suminaire can either touch an artéfact and get a feel for it, or they can't. Other artéfacts might tug on your magic, begging you to use them, but you'll connect with one better than any others. Summoning magic through that artéfact will become second nature."

His words sounded rehearsed, like he'd given this speech a thousand times before.

He motioned to the table of artéfacts. "There's an old theory that a suminaire's ability to get a feel for certain artéfacts is determined by how much power they have, along with their soul's desire."

"Soul's desire?" The same words were written inside the cover of that society handbook. I'd nearly forgotten about those words.

Alastair nodded. "The desire could be hidden so deep, you may not realize it. But it's there, nonetheless."

I scanned the table. "What if I can't get a feel for any?"

"The more power you have, the more artéfacts you'll be able to use to some degree, but all suminaires can get a feel for one or two," he said with a smile that didn't look the least bit genuine. "Unfortunately, many here aren't useful in running the hotel."

Goose bumps rose on my arms. "What happens if I can only use one of the weaker ones? Would you turn me into a bird?" I said before I could stop myself.

"We all must do our part to keep magic safe." He parroted the same line I'd heard the last time I was here. "Enough talk. Let's see what it is you desire."

He took my hand. I winced as he forced my fingers apart. Very slowly, he ran them over the menagerie of oddities: a raven's beak, a pentacle, a carved amethyst hand, a single butterfly wing in a stoppered bottle, a lapis spike, a tiny golden porcupine, a curl of brass leaves, an engraved bone, an ivory spider, a garnet the size of my palm, an ebony coin, then vials of various things: buttons, metals, and tinctures.

Each artéfact's magic felt unique. Some magic I could barely make out, while some seemed to char my flesh. Hot, then cool, then velvet soft. The magic I felt from a small stone tangled in my fingers, earthy and ancient, and made my saliva taste like mushrooms. Pins and needles raced under my skin. A few artéfacts rattled as my hand swept over them, but Alastair didn't let me lift a single one.

"Interesting," he said when my fingers touched a topaz box studded with tiny silver teardrops, like the box itself was crying. When he released me, I didn't move my hand. I didn't *want* to.

I felt a pull like a string of spider silk had woven through my blood and tied around my heart, tethering it to whatever was in that box. The box trembled, and might have opened on its own for all I knew, because I blinked and the lid was flipped. Inside sat a circular metal gadget. It looked like another compass.

Tarnished bronze encircled a deep disk, rimmed with the zodiac, that was set with flat plates decorated with moons and constellations.

"The cosmolabe," Alastair said, pleased. "It foretold crops, taxes, the rising and falling of tides." He pointed out two protruding circles. "Altitude and azimuth. They represent the celestial sphere. This little device allowed explorers to read the skies and discover lands. A map of the stars in your palm. Some still use them, but they're considered antiquated."

"A cosmolabe." The word felt new to me. The little device was so intricately wrought, it could be mistaken for jewelry. It looked familiar. I'd seen it before, but I couldn't place where. *Le monde entier* was engraved in tiny letters across the top, the same words etched into the hotel's lacquered door. The whole world.

I ran a thumb over its delicate mechanics and it shivered against my skin. It felt like a wish and a curse, and my fingers itched to do something. But I didn't know what, or if I even wanted it.

It was still difficult to believe that after all this time, I had real magic inside me, dangerous magic that could crack spines and burst hearts.

Alastair wetted his lips. The gesture made me recoil. "Had I suspected you were a Fabricant, I would have brought you here ages ago."

A Fabricant.

He walked to his desk. Behind it, a large map I failed to notice the last time covered the entire wall. It was peppered with hundreds of misshapen swaths of land. I'd never seen such a detailed map. It had to be of the whole world. The entire surface was scribbled with purple ink. Notes. A few places were circled and many were crossed out.

I searched for Verdanne, desperate to see the dot of Aligney, to know it was still out there. But I couldn't find it. I didn't know where in the world I was, or where I'd be tomorrow. It probably didn't matter. Going home now seemed impossible.

Tears tumbled down my cheeks, but I didn't bother wiping them away.

Alastair lifted the wolf-capped inkwell from his breast pocket. He opened a desk drawer and pulled out a blank contract. I scanned the page. A staff contract this time.

"There are a number of enchantments in place that will cause unpleasant repercussions should you fail to sign a new contract soon. Considering I voided your previous one minutes before you broke the oranges, I'll have to insist," he said. "I know it's difficult, Jani. But it's for the best."

I straightened at my real name. But of course Alastair wouldn't call me Mol anymore; a voided contract meant my memories from before would have returned, and he knew it.

My old contract was an amended guest contract, but the one before me was the same contract Bel had signed, Zosa, the rest of the staff. I doubted I'd be spared again.

The reality of the situation struck me. I'd never faced death, but this had to feel close. It was as if I stood before a guillotine that would slice me away from the person I was before the hotel.

I pictured a lesser version of myself standing beside me with a face as dull as the birds' feathers in the aviary. No stubbornness in the set of her mouth. No glitter to her gaze. She looked soulless, a phantom of a girl with dark hair and dead eyes. My muscles tensed.

I couldn't stand to picture her. I certainly didn't want to become her.

But Zosa is here. You'll still remember your sister, I reminded myself. That thought was the only thing that kept me together as Alastair twisted the wolf's head and popped it off.

A sweet scent wafted out that curdled my insides. He snatched my hand and stabbed a pen nib into my thumb.

I sucked in a breath from the pain.

It didn't stop him from squeezing my blood into the inkwell. He then dipped the pen and folded my fingers around it. "Go on. It's late and I haven't got all night." When I still didn't make a move, he leaned forward. "I can always call Yrsa."

Alastair gave me no choice.

An image of Margot in her café rushed to my mind. I tried to imagine what it might be like if I'd remained in Durc, like she'd remained in Champilliers for so many years. Waking up every morning with whole pieces of myself missing. Gone forever. I braced myself, preparing for a breath-stealing emptiness that I imagined would chew me up from the inside out.

My eyes burned and the thick line next to that vile little X turned blurry. I squeezed the pen and signed.

As the nib left the page, I churned through memories from Aligney. Maman's voice. Her hands pushing back my hair, nails jabbing my spine when I slouched. Zosa's hoard of candies spilling on the floor. Scrambling to pick them up before Maman scolded her. Running my fingers through the lime-green feather grass that clumped along the village walls.

Then later. Snapping winds. A rocking ferry beneath my feet. The vieux quais sprawling out before me, and believing anything was possible in Durc.

A moment passed.

The memories nearly slapped me in the face, and the breath whooshed from my lungs.

I still remembered Durc, the smell of the port, the tannery, and Bézier's. Aligney, and my mother. Nothing was missing.

I felt an untimely laugh bubble up, so I bit down on the inside of my cheek. Alastair couldn't suspect anything.

He lifted the freshly signed contract, opened his infinite ledger, and pushed the creamy sheet inside. Then he removed his jacket and dipped into a closet behind his desk, leaving me alone.

The ledger sat before me.

A buzzing started in my ears. My contract was in there. The others'. Zosa's.

My fingers stretched toward the ledger.

A door clicked. I plunged my hands in my lap the same moment Alastair popped out from the closet. He strode across the room and lifted the ledger.

If I knew where the contracts were kept, I could come back for them. *Put the ledger away*, I willed, but he didn't. He opened it. The pages flipped and flipped. After more than a minute of flipping, he stopped on a page close to the front. Holding the book wide, he pulled out a single sheet of parchment and handed it to me. It wasn't a contract.

Société des Suminaires was printed across the top of ancient letterhead. I scanned the page. A catalogue of artéfacts ran down the side. Next to a description of each artéfact's appearance was an explanation of how the artéfact worked, along with its location.

A list of artéfacts.

A century-old list, if it had belonged to the society. This must be the list of artéfacts Bel had spoken about. The original ink was black, but a number of locations were crossed off with crisp purple, replaced with "H. M." The hotel.

"What's the list for?"

Alastair gestured to the top shelf in his curio where the compass, divining rod, and pendulum sat by themselves. "Those three artéfacts are catalogued to point in the direction of magic. The compass is said to lead you across a city and straight to an artéfact or anyone with magic in minutes."

That was why Yrsa used the compass during the interviews. She was looking for suminaires. But it must not work for her. It didn't point to anything when she held it toward me.

"Powerful suminaires have tried to use each of those three artéfacts to no avail," Alastair went on.

"But can't you use them?" I asked. He was the most powerful suminaire here.

"Just because you're powerful doesn't mean you can use every artéfact. I can use more than most, but for some reason, I could never get a feel for those three. Nor the cosmolabe." He seemed bothered by that. "But there's one artéfact that interests me above all others."

He pointed to a line item halfway down the catalogue page. A golden signet ring.

There was no location listed. The ring's ability was only described with four small, faded words: *Bestows and erases magic.*

Alastair tapped the entry. "That signet ring is lost somewhere in the world and I need to find it. Even though you can't use one of my artéfacts that could lead me directly to it, the cosmolabe could prove useful in the search."

His pale eyes looked me over and I had an urge to run from the room.

This was why he'd sprinted the length of the lobby. Now I'd be forced to help because I was a suminaire—his suminaire to be used in whatever way he wished, his tool.

The thought made me ill, but what worried me more were those four little words: *Bestows and erases magic.*

I doubted Alastair wanted to erase any of his magic. It seemed more likely that he wanted to bestow himself with more. But he already had more magic than any other suminaire in world. "Why do you need the ring?"

"For a good cause," he said smoothly. I didn't believe him for a second. "The amount of magic in a suminaire's blood determines how well they heal and how long they live. Powerful suminaires rarely succumb to mortal wounds or age." I thought of Bel's knife wound. Even though it took hours to heal, along with the paste to seal it, he didn't die on the street. "If that signet ring bestows magic, it could also gift the benefits of magic."

"You think the ring could heal?"

"More than just heal. I think it could save people, gift years to someone's life. We could help everyone," he said.

There was no possible way he cared enough about anyone to want to help them.

Then a realization struck that nearly knocked me over: I never got sick. This whole time, I thought luck was playing tricks on me, but it was the magic in my blood that kept me well. And would continue to keep me well, possibly for many years longer than a normal life span. If that ring did as that catalogue entry said, Zosa could have magic, too. She could live a long life at my side.

But even if Alastair managed to extend someone's life, they would still be magical, still dangerous. There were only a finite number of artéfacts left in the world. If they were all used up, I could only imagine what would happen.

No, Alastair didn't want to start creating suminaires from scratch. It would go against everything he preached about keeping magic safe. There had to be another reason he wanted the ring.

Bel's theories came to mind. Greed could be driving Alastair. He just admitted he couldn't use the three magic-finding artéfacts, but it was obvious he wanted to. If he had the ring, he could gift magic to himself. Powerful suminaires could get a feel for more artéfacts. With an endless stream of magic, Alastair had the potential to use any artéfact he wanted, do whatever he wanted. The thought turned my stomach.

His office door opened and Des Rêves poked her wigged head inside. "Are you almost finished with her?" she asked. Alastair walked over and whispered in her ear. She nodded then hurried away.

"Time to go," he said, and stepped to his desk. He opened the third drawer down on the right and placed the infinite ledger inside. Then he shut the drawer and touched his finger to it, murmuring a command. A lock clicked shut. The ledger was locked away with magic.

I committed the drawer to memory.

Alastair pushed the wolf-capped inkwell down his pocket and held out an arm. "Follow me, Jani Lafayette. You'll begin the search for the ring tonight."

23

Alastair led me deep into the first floor through a hall filled with a thousand paper globes, lit like lanterns, that stretched to infinity, then through a series of smaller rooms, each with its own history.

Gesturing to a settee, he spoke of the famed poet, Antoine-Martin, who would lounge there for hours surrounded by his entourage while he penned odes to everything from pastries to bespectacled women. He told me about the marmalade heiress, Colette La Rive, who once entered a soirée with lit candlewicks sparking across her shoulders for effect, only to leave early when her earlobes caught fire. He spoke of dignitaries, musicians, and queens who had graced these halls. Then he spoke of more dignitaries, musicians, and queens who would soon kiss his feet for a chance to experience magic. Not once did he mention his staff.

Alastair went silent as he took me through a hall where three liveried men sat hunched over desks like tannery workers.

One tossed a set of carved sticks, watching as they fell into a complex configuration. Another sat motionless over a scarab-shaped bowl filled with water. The third grazed bandaged fingers over a table of sharp metal chips etched with letters. They looked up as we passed by and I noticed they each had one eye slightly lighter than the other, no doubt glass.

I tried to see what the three suminaires were doing, but Alastair gripped my arm and jerked me along.

We climbed a circular set of stairs and arrived inside the small map room from a doorway opposite the main door, a doorway that wasn't there the last time I was in this room.

"How do you do it?" I asked, mystified.

"How do you think?" He patted the pocket that held the inkwell. "All the enchantments inside are written down in ink. Most are enacted with a command. As long as I'm holding the inkwell and say the correct words, I can enact whatever enchantment I wish."

He muttered a command and waved a hand. The doorway disappeared, melting into the wallpaper. But the wall didn't stop moving. It pushed back. The floor creaked. A tiny bed and tinier dressing table billowed up from nothing, turning the small map room into a modest suite.

He spoke another command and the cold hearth burst into colorless flames, lighting up the painting of the woman above it. The woman's eyes welled with tears. One dripped down the wall, sizzling when it hit the flames.

I realized where I'd seen the cosmolabe before; the woman in the painting wore it around her neck. "Who is she?"

"A suminaire who was able to use many powerful artéfacts," he said, his voice clipped.

She was someone important, that much was certain.

In that ripped page in the society's handbook, she had clutched the wolf-capped inkwell. Alastair had just admitted this woman could use other powerful artéfacts. She clearly used the inkwell and probably knew what magic went into voiding contracts.

"Where is she now?" I asked as innocently as possible.

"She died," Alastair said, his voice sharp. Well, that discussion wasn't going anywhere.

He opened the giant atlas. "Before she died, however, she used your artéfact to draw each of these maps. We haven't been able to add any since she passed away." He looked from my face to the cosmolabe. "Until now."

He wanted me to draw a map? "But I've never drawn in my life."

Alastair's eyes flicked to the painting. More tears tumbled down the woman's face. "She hadn't either, but with the cosmolabe, she could scribble maps to anything, so long as she had something to reference. She could pinpoint the geographical origin of an object that we already had, or track down the exact location of an object itself. She drew me a map to the jade-needled compass using nothing but a crude sketch in an ancient journal. I do hope you'll figure it out as quickly as she did."

"Are you threatening me?"

He didn't answer. He placed the page of catalogued artéfacts on the table and tapped the entry for the signet ring. Then I understood exactly what the cosmolabe did, how I would be *useful*.

"I won't help you," I said.

He ignored me. "There's a market at tonight's destination. It's

open late." He dumped a stack of silver disks on the table. They were curiously blank. "These coins should work for supplies. Purchase coal, ink, parchment, or vellum. Whatever you wish. I'm granting you the ability to come and go as you please, should you need more. Of course you'll have an escort waiting in the hall at all times."

Right. "A guard, you mean?"

"Semantics," he said, and smiled.

He didn't care about the black bird who flew out before midnight, or Sazerat, or Bel, or anyone else inside. Now he expected me to be his pawn.

I refused to help him have more power. In one swoop, I picked up the catalogue page and stalked toward the fire with the intent to burn it.

Alastair snatched my wrist and pried the page from my hand. "I wouldn't have done that if I were you."

He muttered another command. A bell appeared in the wall beside the door, like the service bells in some of the fancier guest suites. He snapped his fingers and it chimed.

"What's happening?"

He didn't answer me. A few seconds later, the doorknob jiggled. "Jani? Jani, are you in there?"

My heart nearly sailed from my chest.

Zosa.

"I'm here!" I ran over and pulled on the doorknob while she beat her fists on the other side. The door wouldn't budge. "Open it," I begged.

I managed to get the knob to turn. A click. The door opened half an inch. Enough for her slim fingers to push through the opening and nothing more. They scrabbled along the seam. No feathers or wings; they were real and human, and they reached for me. I touched them—I touched her. *Felt* her. For the first time in weeks.

Alastair brushed me aside.

"Let her in," I choked.

He didn't. With one swift movement, he pulled Zosa's fingers through to above the knuckle. The seam of the door grew *teeth*.

No!

It slammed shut in a sickening bite, leaving behind a smudge of red and four slim fingers in Alastair's palm.

I dropped to my knees, shaking.

When the door did open, Des Rêves stood there, a cage in her hand. Inside, a small golden bird began to keen; one wing slumped. Blood leaked from a row of missing feathers near the edge. Zosa's dark eyes watched me as tears slid down my cheeks.

Alastair held up my sister's severed fingers. Des Rêves made a face but bundled them in a silk handkerchief. "Give one to Yrsa," he said, wiping off the blood.

I looked up in disbelief. "I thought Yrsa only took eyes."

"Fingers don't work as quickly as eyes, but they do the job." When he flicked out his pointer finger with the same action as Bel's switchblade, a new wave of horror crashed through me. "I take it Bel never told you?"

People might believe Alastair to be the greatest suminaire in all the world, but he was nothing but a monster.

He pointed to the cosmolabe. "A midnight has passed. You have three more to draw me a map to that ring, so I suggest you head out now and purchase supplies. Fail to draw my map and it won't be you I punish." He took the atlas and walked away after Des Rêves, leaving me with nothing but the page from his ledger, the entry for that horrible ring.

When the door shut, I slid down the length of it. I wept until my eyes were bloodshot and swollen, until the tears ran dry and my mind was clear enough to think.

My knees threatened to give out, but I forced myself to stand. I faced the portrait. The woman stared back at me, teary eyes similar to my own.

"Did he threaten you, too?" I asked, half expecting her to flash her teeth and laugh. I probably looked as pathetic as I felt.

If I found Alastair's ring, he would have more power. He said he wanted to use it for good, but after everything I'd seen, there was no chance of that happening.

I squeezed my eyes shut and pictured that infinite ledger tucked away in the third desk drawer on the right. If I could get to it and void our contracts, this would all be over. We could walk out the door and never look back.

But even though I knew where the contracts were kept, getting there still seemed impossible. And once I was there, I didn't know how to void Alastair's ink. Bel had said it wasn't as simple as rending the contracts in two, that it required powerful magic that I clearly didn't have.

"How do I get out of this god-awful mess?" I asked the painting. "How do we escape?"

The catalogue page sat crumpled on the table. That description of the ring: *Bestows and erases magic.*

Erases magic.

The words raced across my mind. There was no way to know the specifics of what that meant. The ring might only remove magic from a suminaire, but there could be more to it. If the ring erased magic, it might erase the magic binding our contracts. If that were the case, I didn't need to know how Alastair voided them. I could use the ring instead.

I turned that thought over until the room clock chimed.

My eyes stung so badly it was hard to keep them open. But I had only three days left, and I didn't know the first thing about us-ing magic or how to work the cosmolabe. Whatever might happen after this moment, I couldn't give up until I drew a map to that ring.

I checked the wardrobe. No cloak to cover my blood-flecked frock. Only a single dress. I dragged a nail down the bodice and shivered. Black as midnight, a hundred little moons purled across its waist in silvery thread. The material was exquisite, fitting for a suminaire of the same ilk as Bel.

You're not nothing to me, he had said. This whole time he knew what I was, and yet he'd kept it from me. He betrayed me and tried to send me home, away from everyone I cared about. But I had magic thrumming through my veins. Surely I could have done something, helped him find a way out of this mess, but he clearly didn't trust me enough to tell me the truth.

A mixture of hurt and anger struck me so forcibly, I bit down hard on the inside of my cheek to keep from kicking over furniture.

I needed my wits now more than ever. Failing, unfortunately, was not an option.

Quickly, I changed and shoved the cosmolabe and the silver disks in my dress pocket.

"I'm going out for supplies," I muttered to the liveried worker stationed outside my door. His eyes were bloodshot and barely open, but he followed at my heel.

Silver disks jangled as we raced across the hotel. At the front, the doorman opened the black-lacquered door.

"Welcome to Ahnka, the heart of Preet," he said between yawns. "We suggest a scarf for the wind."

24

Ahnka was a small city high in the mountains east of Verdanne. The elevation and thin air made my ears pop and the world tilt the moment I stepped across the threshold.

Here, the hotel's façade swooped with a sharply angled roof that blended in perfectly with the carved stone buildings on either side. They all hugged a cliff, tethered to the vertical rock face with copper cables that were green with verdigris. Around me, a network of carved footpaths were lit by bronze lanterns.

Hot wind slammed up the dusty gorge. I licked my dry lips and tasted the salt from my tears. If I thought of Zosa, the tears would undoubtedly come again, so I took a long breath and concentrated on the heat, on the silver in my pocket, on the task at hand.

A switchback of narrow steps led to a series of connected buildings perched precariously along a cliff edge. Thankfully they weren't dark. Oil lamps bobbed from nearly every tall window. Shapes danced behind gilded shutters. String music drifted down from above, along with other strange sounds—including one very long, distinctive moan—that meant I could wager a guess as to what was up there.

Preetian Wish Markets were infamous, even in Verdanne, for selling everything from edible gold and scrimshawed whale teeth to kisses that could cure any illness depending where on the body the kiss was administered.

Enter with a wish in mind, leave with it granted, Maman had told us when we were little, even though the wishes were bedtime tales and certainly not real magic. We were old enough to know real magic only came from suminaires. But it didn't stop Zosa or me from counting the paper stars we'd stuck across our ceiling and dreaming up silly wish after silly wish.

The liveried worker, my unlucky guard, scratched his head. "We're going up there?"

"Wasn't in your job description?"

I felt somewhat guilty for forcing a worker who didn't know any better to follow me. Then I thought of Zosa's severed fingers on Des Rêves's square of silk and the guilt evaporated. I started up. The worker groaned, but followed at my heel.

At the entrance, a woman greeted us. Her golden-beige skin was delicately freckled and her russet hair hung in braids against a tunic made from an iridescent fabric that I wished Béatrice could see; it would make her green with envy. But unlike the head of housekeeping, each of this woman's fingers were tipped in blades like miniature scythes; apparently one did not steal from a Pre-etian Wish Market.

"Welcome," she said in accented Verdanniere, then frowned. "Are you well, mademoiselle?"

"No. Not well at all. Oh—" I clutched my ankles, gasping for breath from the climb. When I was sure I wouldn't vomit, I stood up, still a bit wobbly, and glanced downhill. The worker—my lovely guard—hovered near a bush, heaving his guts up.

I motioned to the worker. "Sensitive stomach."

"Unsurprising," said the woman. "Men tend to be the sensitive ones."

"Hard to argue with that."

I picked at the silver thread on my skirt and waited. I thought the worker was finished, but he made a strangled noise and retched again. He would be a while. I didn't exactly have a while.

I tried to push past the woman, but she put her hand up and cocked her head. "Tell me what you wish for," she said. "Savory food? A lover's kiss? Or something more spectacular?"

When I groaned and tried to step around her a second time, she flashed her blades. She wouldn't let me in without voicing a wish.

A few things came to mind, namely Zosa, but I quickly dismissed them because this was ridiculous; wishes were nothing but folklore and it was late. "Charcoal and parchment," I said.

That seemed to appease her. Her smile grew and she let me through.

Inside, I slipped through a maze of long hall after long hall filled with wafting incense and dark wood. Merchants sold their wares by candlelight. Patrons in jewel-crusted garb sat at velvet-lined tables playing a Preetian card game that looked similar to Verdanniere poker. Except the suits were composed of celestial markings—stars and comets instead of clubs and spades—and each player ended their turn by tapping their thumb against their bottom lip.

A musician drifted past blowing through a bronze instrument that looked like a flute, while a handsome dancer in elaborate silks clinked brass cymbals between his thumbs and pinkies. Nearby, a woman traced the silhouette of another woman who stood patiently behind a backlit scrim holding a candle to her masked nose.

Artisans were everywhere, woven through shops that sold whatever your heart could wish up. I spotted a gentleman pressing kisses to the tip of an older woman's ear while she handed him a fat coin.

Soon, I found a stall selling drawing supplies. I picked out a thick stack of parchment, along with a box of charcoal sticks wrapped in gold foil. Reaching into my pocket, I pulled out two of the silver disks and nearly dropped them. They were no longer flat disks but ornately carved coins stamped with an owl wearing a crown on one side and a man's profile on the other.

A merchant took the coins and bundled everything in twine. With my purchases tucked under my arm, I turned to leave but stopped in my tracks.

Bel sat at a crowded card table. He held a fan of cards, along with a glass decanter of whatever green liquor they served here.

A young woman with beautiful amber skin sauntered up to his table and ran a fingernail suggestively around his collar. I think I made an angry noise because Bel's eyes flicked up and met mine for a brief moment—long enough to know he saw me—before looking away. He took a sip of his drink and put down a card, not bothering to look at me again. In fact, he avoided looking at the entire side of the hall where I stood.

That anger I'd felt in the lobby after the oranges fell came flooding back. My jaw clenched. I strode toward his table. Everyone watched me like they were about to witness a carriage ram headfirst into a rock wall. Every person but one. Bel looked down and flipped a second card onto dark wood.

How dare you, I wanted to scream, to somehow make him pay.

Instead, I swiped his glass and threw its contents at his face. I heard him curse and his chair scrape back as I stormed away. Ten steps were all I got before he grabbed my arm and whirled me around to face him. He stumbled then righted himself.

My nose wrinkled at the sharp scent of liquor. "You're drunk."

"Perhaps."

I shoved him back. "When did you know I was a suminaire?" At the word, a pair of men looked over.

He leaned close to my ear. He didn't touch me, but my heartbeat picked up nonetheless, and I hated that he had that effect on me. "I suspected what you were in Durc. I don't exactly get the opportunity to give a contract to a suminaire every day. Why did you think I let you come in the first place?"

"You're unbelievable."

"Did you honestly think I was some selfless fool? I've been searching for ways to reverse Alastair's ink for years. Then you came along." His eyes ran down the length of me and I shivered. "I thought if I could keep you a secret, you could somehow help me understand how the ink worked."

I nodded, dumbstruck by his omission.

Every conversation we had, everything he'd shown me, told me,

every time he sought me out or gave away any information—it all raced through my mind. His mouth against my ear at the moon window, the guest rooms and halls, and in the map room when I'd trusted him enough to tell him my secrets—secrets I didn't even tell my own sister. Then in the blue city, he'd listened to my memories with such aching wonder. I'd thought Bel was forthcoming because I'd meant something to him. And I had.

I was a suminaire, after all. His *experiment*.

The thought was sickening.

"So you knew I was a suminaire in Durc. How did you figure it out?"

He sighed. "Jani—"

"Answer my question." My voice sizzled with rage.

"Not in the middle of the market," he said, and led me farther away from the table where he'd been playing cards, into an alcove, where nobody was close enough to overhear our whispered conversation. "I suspected what you were in that boardinghouse kitchen, the moment you sensed my key. Only suminaires can feel magic."

"*Only* suminaires?"

He rolled his eyes. "Then there was this."

My breath halted when Bel lifted my chin up and slid his thumb down the neck of my dress, catching on Maman's necklace, just like he had done in that doorless room. But this time, he fished it out, his eyes fixed on mine.

"An artéfact," he whispered quietly.

"*What?*"

"The magic coming from it is very subtle. But in Durc, when I touched it on accident, I recognized what it was. Any other sumi-naire wouldn't have noticed it, but I'm in the business of finding artéfacts. In the span of one minute, I suspected what you were and understood why your magic hadn't been discovered. But I didn't know for certain until the orange broke."

I remembered that moment perfectly. Bel's vague answers. Now this.

I skimmed my hand over the necklace and jerked. Something faint tingled my fingertips. Had I not just touched all those artéfacts in Alastair's office, I wouldn't recognize it now: a little vibration of magic, so subtle that I'd never noticed it before.

I could still picture my reflection in Maman's vanity mirror the moment she'd pushed my hair to one side and clasped it around my neck all those years ago. The necklace had felt warm against my skin. Special, for some reason. A *gift for my firstborn*, Maman had called it.

That night, I couldn't stop touching it. Zosa pouted about it, of course, so Maman let her wear one of her rings as a consolation. I couldn't carry a tune to save my life, but that day, I'd felt like the special one.

I *was* special, I realized, and Maman had known.

My lips trembled. Sometimes I would catch her watching me, twisting her hands in her lap, those fine creases of worry deepening around her brown eyes. Sometimes she would stay up with me long after Zosa fell asleep, feverishly telling me stories about suminaires and how she thought magic was dangerous but it could also be a gift. A gift! My throat thickened. A *true gift tends to make itself known*,

Maman had said. And she'd said it to *me*, not Zosa. I always thought she'd meant my sister's voice, but the true gift was my magic.

That whole time Maman had been teaching me about myself.

But she never warned me or told me the truth, not even on her deathbed. The ache of it made Bel's betrayal feel shallow in comparison. What I wouldn't give to have an hour with her now, to ask her about my history, but she was gone.

"How long have you worn the necklace?" Bel asked softly.

"My mother—she clasped it around my neck when I was little. She told me to never take it off." No *matter what anyone tells you, ma petite pêche,* she had said. *Even if a sweet boy whispers promises in your ear, or a man offers you a stack of dublonnes, or your fingers itch to take it off, I want you to keep it on that pretty neck of yours. It's an heirloom, after all.* "She made me promise under penalty of death." His eyebrows shot up. "Maman had a flair for the dramatic."

"Well, there was probably suminaire blood in your lineage. Your mother could have suspected what you were. Perhaps you never got sick, or you healed from something quicker than a normal child."

My lips parted.

"What is it?" Bel asked.

"When I was seven, I fell out of a tree and thought I broke my arm. I *heard* it snap. The pain was so intense, I passed out. Our village doctor took a look the next day. There was no break, just a little bruising. Maman was quiet throughout the examination. Later that night, she locked herself in her room." I remembered pressing my ear to the door, listening as she wept, and wondering why.

"She must have discovered what you were."

"But my mother wasn't a suminaire. She used to joke about it."

"Sometimes magic skips generations, even siblings. It's probably the reason she didn't keep the necklace for herself and instead gave it to her daughter, whom she obviously loved."

My fingers trembled as I ran them along the hard gold. I couldn't believe it. For years I'd walked around with a godforsaken artéfact around my neck. "What if whatever it does could have hurt someone?"

"I don't believe it can."

I glared at him. "You mean you know what the necklace does?"

"Not exactly. When I touch it, I can't get a feel for it. But I think whatever it does has to do with magic."

"You must be drunk. It's an artéfact. Of course it has to do with magic."

He sighed. "That's not what I meant. I think the necklace is somehow keeping other artéfacts from having an effect on you."

"What?"

"Think about it. There has to be a reason why you've been immune to Alastair's ink, and the only good one I can think of is sitting on your neck." He leaned forward. "I asked Yrsa about the interviews. She said that bronze compass didn't work on anyone in Durc. She can't get it to lead her to suminaires, but it still reacts when she's in a room with one. It *points* to them."

It didn't point to me. When Alastair explained how the compass worked, I'd assumed Yrsa couldn't use it properly. Not this.

"You can still use magic," Bel went on, "still feel it and see it when it's used on things surrounding you inside the hotel, but it seems

257

your body and mind are immune to magic's direct effects, probably even untraceable by my atlas."

"So my mother's necklace has been protecting me this whole time?"

"I think the necklace played the biggest role in keeping you safe, yes, but there are other ways you probably used your magic that helped you go undiscovered."

I remembered our conversation in the map room all those weeks ago. "You mentioned basic magic once, that suminaires can use it if they don't have an artéfact."

He nodded. "Some call it première magie."

First magic.

"How does it work?"

"Most of what I know has been pieced together through second-hand accounts. But I do know it just *works* without you having to summon it, like healing. There are stories of suminaires with no artéfact walking down a street in broad daylight without anyone realizing they were ever there, and suminaires finding themselves lucky in life when a normal person struggles to get by. Première magie is said to be responsible for it all. There are even stories of suminaires who kept themselves hidden and their magic controlled without artéfacts by putting themselves in dangerous situations that forced première magie to take effect," he said. "Along with healing, protection and good luck are the two other things it's said to offer."

"Good luck," I repeated.

I'd seen girls get kicked out of Bézier's for preposterous things like scattering crumbs after a meal or forgetting to lock the front door, but Bézier never bothered us. I always thought it was because she had a soft spot for my sister. *My little good luck charm*, I sometimes called Zosa.

She was the extraordinary one. The voice who could fill a flour jar with coins in minutes. The sprite who could come away unscathed after wandering by herself outside the village walls, while I worried myself sick.

But in all those instances, I was always beside her, behind her, holding her hand, searching for her, fretting about her. I was *with* her.

Then, once we were inside the hotel, there were so many times where I was able to sneak around and not get caught, like during that first soirée.

I'd thought Zosa was my good luck charm, but if Bel's theory were correct, it was the other way around, and première magie had been protecting us for years. It meant I was the lucky one all along.

"If you knew what I was since that day in Durc, why didn't you tell me?"

"Right after you'd arrived, I didn't think there was a point in telling you the truth about your magic—I thought it would be safer for you. Jani, the things I've seen . . ." The muscles around his mouth ticked. "Trust me when I say I didn't enjoy keeping that secret from you. But . . . I kept it because I'd convinced myself that if I told you what you were, you would have somehow used it to get to your sister, and everything I'd gone through to hide you would have been for nothing. Then I got to know you." His attention shifted to my face, and I felt his gaze under my skin.

"And?"

He looked down at his hands. "God, I wanted to tell you—so many times you have no idea."

"Yet you continued to keep the truth of my magic from me." My jaw clenched. "Who I *am* from me."

"I did," he said simply. "As you can probably tell, I'm not close with many people inside. The last person I spent much time with was Hellas. But we've both changed so much because of Alastair. And after everything I said to him, how it ended, it's unlikely for things between us to ever be the same." Bel's mouth tightened. "It's been so long since I've been remotely close with anyone that I'd forgotten what it was like to look forward to just . . . talking with someone."

My mouth parted, but I didn't know what to say.

"I continued to keep the truth from you because I came to realize that you were becoming important to me." His eyes flicked to mine and there was something in them that made my breath catch. He looked away. "And if I told you what you were, you would have hated me for not telling you sooner. I think a very selfish part of me didn't want to risk losing what we had."

A deep groove knotted the space between Bel's eyebrows, and my anger shifted into something that felt like an ache. I didn't know what to feel, but I certainly wasn't ready to forgive him.

"I should have told you everything the moment you came inside," he said.

"I'll say."

"Because of your magic, you became a risk to yourself without you knowing it. A self-centered experiment on my part."

"That you tried to send home."

Bel flinched.

Good. At least he felt some remorse. Even though he did it to keep me safe, it still stung. "I hope whatever you offered up to throw me out was *extremely* valuable."

Bel grunted and shifted his weight, bringing his face closer to mine. The subtle waft of brass polish along with the salt of his sweat tangled in my nostrils. If I leaned an inch or two forward, our lips might brush.

At the thought, I reeled, furious at myself for thinking it. This was pointless.

"I have to get back." I attempted to turn away, but Bel's fingers smoothed around my arm. I tensed at his touch, but he didn't let go. He forced me to face him.

"Listen. I didn't want Alastair to discover what you were and turn you into his puppet like he does to everyone else. And now he has."

"It doesn't matter. I'm still with Zosa."

"You're trapped like the rest of us. You'll never go home."

"She *is* my home."

As the words rushed forth, I was taken aback by the resoluteness in my own voice . . . and the glaring truth of it. I also knew I couldn't stand to be here another moment, this near to him. Whatever fragile thing might have been between us felt broken. He was a senseless distraction and I was losing precious time.

I tried to push past him, but his hand dropped from my arm to rest on the crook of my waist. When I gasped, he backed away, like I was a lit brazier. He muttered something incoherent, until he caught sight of my bundle.

"What's that?" He tugged at it. The parchment poked out and his eyes grew wild. "Which artéfact did you choose?"

I fished the cosmolabe from my pocket and Bel swore.

"You know how it works?" I asked.

"For the most part. Alastair locked me in a room once. He made me hold that thing for hours. I was able to see hints of places skittering on the edges of my mind, but nothing substantial enough to draw a map with. I couldn't get a good enough feel for it." His eyes narrowed. "What has he asked you to draw a map to?"

"The signet ring," I admitted. No point in keeping it a secret. I relayed the catalogue page with the ring's entry. "The description says the ring can bestow and erase magic."

Bel muttered a string of curses that would make an old man blush.

"He says he wants to use the ring for good," I went on. "He thinks if it can bestow magic, it can also gift the long lives of suminaires to normal people."

"And you believed him?"

"Do you think I'm a complete fool? Of course not. I don't think he has any intention of giving away magic. But Bel, he threatened Zosa if I don't draw a map to it." I stared at my palm, picturing Zosa's severed fingers. I blinked and blinked, but the bloody image wouldn't leave me, like it was somehow seared on the underside of my eyelids. Then I pictured that catalogue page, the ring's entry. "I've been thinking . . ."

Bel eyed me, skeptical. "I'm not going to like this, am I?"

I cut him a dirty look. "For god's sake, please just hear me out. The ring is also described to *erase* magic. If I drew a map to it tonight, what's to stop you from hunting it down without Alastair ever knowing? What if we could use it to erase the magic in our contracts?"

He looked up at the ceiling, exasperated. "There's no way to know if that would work. Most artéfacts are more nuanced. I doubt the ring is as simple as it sounds." Bel's expression darkened. "Did Alastair take you through that hall by his office?"

He'd taken me down a hall where three suminaires sat hunched over artéfacts. I assumed that was what Bel meant. I nodded.

"One uses a scrying bowl to see people across the world, another has a set of sticks that sometimes determines where we take the hotel, the third has metal letters that can answer certain questions. Nothing as direct as an artéfact that points to magic, but their artéfacts are all enough to keep them cooped up day and night. They're all searching for that ring. It could be dangerous," he said seriously. "Unless we uncover the real reason why Alastair wants it so badly, I don't think you should draw a map to it."

He didn't get it. Except . . . "Why would it matter to you? You spend your days hunting down Alastair's artéfacts."

"I'm not foolish. I never bring an artéfact back if I get a feel for it and suspect it might hurt someone."

"What about the ones you can't get a feel for? Do you bring those back?"

"You don't understand. I have to."

"I understand perfectly. You help him because you have no choice. Now I have no choice. If you won't help me track down the ring, will you at least tell me how to use the cosmolabe?" When he didn't answer, I pushed my face dangerously close to his. "Tell me how to use it," I demanded.

"I can't."

"Liar."

"You chose the cosmolabe from Alastair's collection. Using it should come as easily as breathing. You figure it out. I need another drink." He walked back to his game.

"Men can be salty when they don't get exactly what they wish for." I jumped. The market guard stood three feet from me, leaning against a stone pillar. "Do you want me to kill him for you?" She smiled, coy, then clicked her little scythes.

I shrugged. "Go right ahead."

25

My escort was still queasy from the climb. He groaned and slumped against the hallway wall, while I ran into the map room and slammed the door. Flinging parchment on the table, I ripped open the charcoal with my teeth.

Maybe I didn't need Bel to find the ring for me. If I drew a map to it and somehow convinced him to take us there, I could search for the ring myself before Alastair could get his hands on it.

Holding the cosmolabe in one palm, I ran my fingers over the catalogue of artéfacts. I traced my pointer finger along the entry for the signet ring. Nothing happened. I glanced at the painting of the woman. "This might go quicker if you told me how to use this thing."

I concentrated. The magic from the cosmolabe tickled up my wrist. I closed my eyes to see if a map would come to me, but nothing did. After each try, the magic hummed higher up my arm. Yet no map.

The society handbook was still jammed in a corner of the dusty shelf. I snatched it up and flipped through every section mentioning artéfacts, but there was nothing that told me how I might use one. Frustrated, I hurled the book across the room.

When Zosa was little, Maman would give her lessons in the most basic songs, moving up in difficulty until my sister could sing alongside her in different keys. The catalogue entry for the ring was only a small scribble. It might be too difficult for a beginner. I could try starting with something simpler.

Scanning the shelf again, I snatched a tiny vial of pink sand and poured some onto my palm. I lifted the cosmolabe. This time, when the magic drifted up my arm, I *felt* something.

Sunshine heated my tongue and a soft tickle of surf skittered up my legs. It was like the umbrellas from my first day here but different. More, somehow. I was in the room, but my mind was in Elsewhere. I poured the sand back and the feel of it was still there, in my nostrils, between my toes.

Next to the sand was an old piece of bark. At my touch, my senses filled with a winter night. Closing my eyes, I could picture a village blanketed by thick snow. Pale, hollow-cheeked children slurped watery broth. My stomach growled from hunger and I couldn't tell if it was my own hunger or conjured from the bark.

I lifted dusty object after dusty object. Places blurred together in a grotesque symphony of smells, textures, and tastes. My tongue felt thick and my stomach roiled. I raced to the toilet and vomited, then collapsed on the tile floor, a sweating mess.

It was late. My eyes were lead weights and my body threatened to ball up and sleep right there, but I refused to let it. When I could stand, I rinsed my mouth and hobbled back to the table. I pinched

more pink sand between my fingers then let that hand rest against the cosmolabe. With my other hand, I lifted a piece of charcoal to the paper. I shut my eyes. This time, when a place formed against the insides of my eyelids, I drew a map.

※

Over the next two days, I tried to picture a map to the ring. But no matter how many times I ran my finger over the ring's catalogue entry, nothing happened. So I drew other maps.

Some came easy and others only came after many minutes squeezing an object to my chest, mashing it to my throat, or pressing it tight against my jaw; the closer I got, the simpler it was. The maps took every ounce of my mind to get right. Better that way. I was too busy perfecting the rivers, the streets, the sweeping curves of land to think of much else.

I barely slept. Meals were delivered by kitchen maids I didn't recognize. I only picked at the food; I didn't wish to waste precious time rinsing charcoal from my fingers to properly feed myself. I didn't bother my rotating guard of workers, and thankfully, as long as I remained inside the room, they didn't bother me.

Alastair visited the morning of the second day, a slick smile back on his face. He was pleased I had drawn so many maps, then irritated to discover not one led to the ring. He stacked the pages neatly and took them as he left.

The next morning, I bolted awake. I must have fallen asleep hunched over charcoal and paper. My neck creaked and my eyes burned. I half expected the catalogue page to be a dream cooked up by my unconscious. But the crumpled paper lay before me, those four words still tormenting me. *Bestows and erases magic.*

Someone knocked at the door.

"Go away," I snarled. One midnight was all I had. No time for distractions. No time to even breathe.

Whoever it was didn't hear me because the door opened and a delivery cart pushed by a fair-skinned kitchen maid I didn't recognize rattled into the room.

"Where would you like your meal?"

I flung my hand toward a small table by the window.

Trays clanked. I pinched the bridge of my nose and silently cursed myself for not locking the door.

"Pretty village out there," the maid said. I watched her peek out the window. "I heard some cooks going on about the destination. Suppose to be a quaint little spot in the south of Verdanne."

"What?" I shot up and ran to the window. An old stone wall unfurled before me. Beyond it, rolling farmland stretched into the distance.

It was hard to tell exactly where we were from this view, but I had to know. I shoved my hair back and threw on my boots.

Five minutes.

I would give myself five minutes to clear my head, to be outside, then I'd come back and draw that damned map.

I rushed out of the room and halted when my guard pushed away from the wall. Sido. All by himself. He stood hunched and pale, his bald head listing to the side Sazerat would normally occupy.

"Where's your brother?"

His eye squeezed shut. He turned his back to me.

Then I remembered. Alastair had said he would punish Sazerat for nearly throwing me out. He was either a bird with dull feathers trapped inside the aviary, or somewhere much worse. I pictured a porcelain eye cracking and winced.

Alastair insisted demotions were to keep people in line, but it was obvious Sazerat didn't realize what I was before the oranges fell. Once he did, I was dragged back inside.

Alastair didn't punish Sazerat because he failed to follow rules. He did it because he was incensed, and vengeful, because he wanted that ring.

The dread that had been building over the past few days rose inside of me. I inhaled a lungful of air and forced it down, where I hoped it would remain for the next few minutes. Steeling myself, I made my way out of the hotel and into a summer day in southern Verdanne.

26

The hotel had landed between two moss-covered abandoned buildings on the outskirts of a village. My nerves sang. Stepping nimbly, I walked down the forest path leading to the stone wall. The whole time, Sido trailed a ways behind me, refusing to make eye contact.

The air was thick like it usually felt in the minutes before the summer showers I'd find myself caught in as a child. Squinting, I glanced up at the sky. Clouds had gathered. A raindrop splashed on my nose, but I refused to let it stop me.

Soon, my hair was dripping. My boot heels squished through damp soil and patches of flowers brushed my ankles. I bent and fingered a petal the exact shade of Alastair's ink. A blood poppy.

My heart clenched; we were truly in Aligney.

I never thought I would see this place again or walk this path. I turned toward the village wall. It was just as I remembered it: a monolith of craggy stone pocked with handholds that begged to be climbed. As a child, I was drawn to it. There were so many times I'd press my fingers into that stone and skin my palms as I hauled myself up, until I reached the top, until I could see over..

Drops of rain hit my cheeks as my mind skimmed across memory after memory of this place. I squeezed my eyes shut and thought of the rainy nights when I was younger, how Zosa would wiggle under my quilt, squishing between Maman and me, making sure to bury her freezing feet in the crooks of my knees. *Stop your squirming*, Maman would scold, then clear her throat and begin a tale.

In our little minds, she painted our ancient village in blood-soaked mystery, filling the surrounding farmland with marauders, bone maidens, jade-eyed beasts, and fairy queens I couldn't wait to meet.

Those stories clung to me. They sparked my desire for more. With those tales in my heart, I would sit atop that stone wall and pretend I could see across the whole world.

My legs quivered as I walked around a patch of mud and into a clearing, half expecting the ground to open up, for a voice to shout, *Behold! This is it! Where you belong! Forever!* But the only sound was the patter of rain. I'd thought if I could get us here, we'd be safe and everything would right itself. Yet here I was, far worse off than I'd ever been in Durc.

I wrapped my arms around my chest as tears rolled down my cheeks. All I felt was a deep ache for the past, how things used to be, and never would be again. I pictured a younger version of myself now, skipping alongside the stone wall and dragging her sister behind her.

God, I missed Zosa so much.

I'd never asked her if she wanted to return here. If I was honest with myself, I was too afraid to ask. She never spoke of this place like I had. I should have listened to her more, I supposed. But I was too stubborn to pay attention to what she had wanted, and now it was too late.

I lifted a leaf stuck to my boot then plunged my fingers into the ground. I squeezed the wet leaves and expected to feel Aligney in my heart, like I'd felt the objects I turned to maps. Except this place felt no different than Skaadi or Preet.

But it *should* feel different. This was my home—the only home I knew.

For the past few weeks, all I'd wanted was to crawl inside the memories of this village and live in them. But now they almost felt like someone else's life—someone I barely recognized anymore. A girl who would have been knocked down and left breathless by everything I'd gone through over the last four years.

And yet, I was still standing, still *me*. If I was honest with myself, I was probably more me than ever before.

Lifting my chin, I turned toward the dripping trees, the craggy walls circling around me. I'd convinced myself that this was where I belonged because I'd wanted so badly to belong *somewhere*, to feel safe again. But standing here, I realized that this place wouldn't make me happy.

This village felt like nothing more than a too-tight shoe cutting at a heel. A little girl's pink ruffled dress ripping at the seams.

I inhaled deeply. I knew beyond a shadow of a doubt that I wanted more than this. More than the space between these trees.

More than the distance from the north stone wall to the south.

I *needed* more.

On instinct, my fingers dug in my pocket. I sighed with relief when the cool metal of the cosmolabe pressed against my skin, the promise of it.

If a suminaire chose their artéfact based on their soul's desire, then my soul craved something other than remaining in one place for the rest of my life. Travel, perhaps. Or adventure. But those things seemed impossible now.

More tears sprang up, blurring my vision. I dragged my wet sleeve across my eyes. What I wanted didn't matter when everyone was trapped and there was nothing I could do to help.

No, *that's not true*, I reminded myself fiercely. The third desk drawer on the right was still waiting. Everything that gave Alastair power over us was in that ledger, but I needed the ring first.

A gust of wind snapped me from my thoughts. My sleeves were soaked through and my skirt was quickly on its way. Sido stood huddled in the distance under a tree. I should do the same until the storm passed.

I picked up my wet hem and ran to an archway in the village wall the width of a large doorway. It used to be an entrance, but now it was gated and grown over with weeds. Ducking underneath, I wrung out the hem of my skirt. A branch cracked behind me. I wasn't alone.

Cautiously, I turned.

Bel leaned against the opposite side not four feet away. His hair was soaked and poking in all directions.

I was still so angry with him, but I had an urge to smooth his hair down, wipe the water from his brow.

His eyes landed on me, then flicked away. "The storm should let up soon."

"Let's hope."

I pressed my back against the cold stone wall—the farthest from Bel I could stand and still remain dry—and rubbed my hands together to keep warm. Bel must have been feeling similarly because he didn't meet my eyes again, and I certainly didn't meet his. After a minute, I started to shiver. I hugged my arms across my front, but my sleeves were as wet as the rest of me.

Bel took off his uniform jacket and held it out. "I don't have a dry dress this time, but this should help until the rain lets up."

"I'll be fine," I said through chattering teeth.

"Don't be stubborn," he cut in sternly. He pulled the jacket around my shoulders.

The wool was still warm from his body heat. I tugged the collar up around my dripping ears. Even though it felt wonderful, I still made a point to scowl.

The corner of his mouth curved up. "I missed your scowls."

I relaxed my mouth and turned away from him to stare at the rain.

"I was an ass at the Wish Market," he said after a little while.

"Well, then that's one thing we agree on."

"I'm sorry."

"Sorry?" I balked. "Save your lackluster apology. It's the last thing I need right now."

My body stiffened when Bel took one of my hands in his own. He wouldn't let me pull away. "You're still freezing," he said.

"I'll survive."

"I would hope, considering you're a suminaire."

I straightened at the word, almost in disbelief.

"You'll never get used to it," he said, as if he could read my mind.

I wanted to ask him what it was like, but I lost my train of thought when he turned my hand over and gently smoothed away drips of water from my palm before kneading it with his thumbs.

My fingers smarted from drawing maps and his hands were warm. The heat of his skin felt divine.

"Better?" he asked.

I muttered something incoherent, and a smile flickered on his lips. He dropped my hand and lifted the other, continuing his ministrations. For once, I didn't mind the silence between us. It was still tense, of course, but less so than the silence awaiting me in the map room.

"How is your drawing coming along?" he asked.

"Not good. I still can't draw a map to the ring."

"Interesting," he said, and I could have sworn there was relief in his voice.

"If I can draw a map to it, won't you at least come with me to find it? We can figure out what it does before we bring it back."

Bel dropped my hand. "If Alastair suspected anything, he would punish us more."

"We'll be careful."

He shifted his attention to my face. A raindrop dripped from the

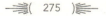

tip of my nose onto my mouth. Bel brought a finger up and wiped it away. His thumb lingered against my bottom lip, and my breath caught.

"Please," I murmured.

I inhaled sharply when his hand ran down my jaw. The hard edge of his switchblade hilt pressed into the skin below my ear. His eyes looked almost pained, but there was a flicker of something else there that I felt in my belly.

Thunder cracked.

Bel jolted. He pushed away, and I felt his absence like a sudden sting. "I'm sorry, Jani, but I won't help you find that ring."

I blinked back tears. "For a while there you had me fooled. I thought you were my friend." *And when you look at me like you are now, I know you're much more than a friend,* I wanted to add, but I was too afraid.

Bel dug a piece of wet moss from the stone wall and rubbed it between his fingers. "You know, today we were supposed to be in a forest north of here. Alastair was in a mood this morning so I promised I'd find him an artéfact to make up for changing the itinerary."

"*You* brought me to Aligney?"

"A lackluster apology," he said, repeating my own words. "I had hoped . . ." His eyes searched mine for a moment, then dropped to the ground. He shook his head. "Forget it."

I stood openmouthed as the man who had a witty remark for everything kicked up a clod of soil and stalked into the rain without another word.

Back in the room, I forced all the tangling thoughts of Bel from my mind and returned to drawing. I touched the entry for the signet ring. Still nothing. I hurled the catalogue page on the ground and paced, coming to a stop at the painting.

"Tell me where the ring is." When the woman refused to say a thing, my palm hit the wall. The painting jumped in its frame. "Tell me your secrets!" I screamed. "Tell me!"

More tears welled and dripped down the canvas. One caught on her lashes.

"I'm sorry," I muttered. I brought a finger up to brush it away and inhaled.

It will come to you like breathing, Bel had said. One breath was all it took. One intake of salt air. Had I not lived in the muck and stink of Durc for years, I never would have discerned that single breath from the air around me.

I took the painting off the wall. The frame made a heavy thump when it landed on the table. Lifting the cosmolabe, I took a few deeper breaths. With each one, my senses came alive with tastes and scents that could never occupy this small room. This woman was supposed to be dead, but I tasted her perfume along with wrought iron and brine. I closed my eyes and pictured a shop with a purple scalloped awning. When I opened my eyes, flowers bloomed in heaps around the woman's face. Silky black petals gathered along the wooden frame, raining in a waterfall to the floor. I ran a finger over the woman's mouth and a voice spoke clearly in my mind.

"Leave me be, Fabricant!"

Charcoal flew from my fingers. I backed away from the painting, eyes wide. It was the woman's voice—the same effervescent voice from the itineraries—and she was furious.

When I touched her mouth again, the same words echoed. It wasn't the ring, but it was something.

I lifted the charcoal and concentrated. Sure enough, I could picture a map—a map to this woman, the former Fabricant.

A new sheath of parchment crackled as I began to sketch. My senses ignited and my mind painted avenues and buildings faster than my fingers could draw them. When I was finished, my chest swelled at what lay on the page, what it meant.

It took too long to scrub the coal from my fingers and my face, but I made sure to get every last smudge. I pinned up my hair. Then I folded the map in two and shoved it deep in my pocket where it would remain until I found Bel.

27

Outside the room, Sido was gone. A new liveried guard stood against the wall.

"Got something for me?" he asked, a greedy look on his face.

I gave him a feline grin and fanned myself with a folded map I'd quickly scribbled from touching the rug. "I drew the maître's map."

He itched his pink, hairy ear. "That's the thing he's looking for?"

"It is. Oh, Alastair will be so pleased." I folded the map in two, then slowly trailed my fingers down the parchment. "He promised me a reward when I brought it to him." I moved to step around the guard, but he stopped me and peeled the map away.

"Give it back," I demanded.

He didn't. The guard stuffed it in his pocket. "You stay in your room. I'll deliver it myself."

"You can't," I said. "It's mine."

"It's not yours. It's the maître's. Don't worry, I'll tell you what he says." He then took off down the hall. I waited until he was out of sight before running in the opposite direction.

I tried Bel's room first, pounding a fist on his door. But the only thing that seemed to hear me were the candles. Lilac flames stretched toward where I stood, nipping at my shoulders.

"Stop it now!" I roared. Every last one of them fizzled back, shrinking from me as I raced for the lift.

Downstairs, a lobby soirée had commenced and the theme was an autumn forest, probably the same forest Bel was supposed to take us to instead of Aligney. The smell of various spices filled the air. Great gilded beasts decorated the room: wood stags, deer, and a huge bronzed bear with rubies for eyes.

Each animal was stuck through with golden arrows that held foraged fruit. Macarons dripped down like ornaments, pressed with spun sugar leaves. Everywhere, leaves were falling from high above, like snow from the heavens, turning to wisps of colored smoke as they landed across the noses of giddy guests.

The color scheme shifted between ochers and burnt oranges; fitting that Madame des Rêves would show up in a brocade gown, her enormous wig-of-the-hour shining the palest hue of plum. Her curls bounced as she spat orders at a row of waitstaff, fingering the silver talon at her bosom.

I jumped back when more performers twirled by, clothed in fabrics embroidered with vestiges of fall: berries, pinecones, and coppery cornucopias.

Bel should be inside by now. Standing on my tiptoes, I looked around, but couldn't spot him anywhere.

"There you are." I flinched when Alastair came up beside me. He pressed a cool flute of champagne between my fingers. In his other hand he held the scribbled map I'd just given away. "Your guard delivered this." He held up the map. "Where does it lead?" he asked.

It led to a small outpost somewhere in the south of Preet, the origin of the map room's rug, but it was impossible to tell from my hasty scribbles.

"Where do you think it leads?" I said, coy, and brought the champagne to my mouth.

Alastair grabbed my free hand and squeezed until a bone popped. "Where does it lead?" he repeated through his teeth.

"To the ring." My voice came out strangled.

His nostrils flared. "If we uncover the ring tomorrow, you can have your sister's finger." He tossed away my arm. "I'll even fashion the porcelain into a pretty necklace."

I dug my hands in my skirts and cursed when the map in my pocket rustled. The music was loud, but I heard it.

"Excuse me. I'm not feeling well," I said, and turned to walk away, but Alastair caught my elbow.

"I'll bring you to your room, Fabricant." He pushed an arm around my waist, brushing my side an inch above the map. My breath froze.

"Maître." A short suminaire ran over, flapping her pink hands. "A guest is looking for you."

"Tell them to wait."

"It's the emissary from the Lenore Islands. A Lord Allenbee. Yes!" The suminaire shook her head. "Or was it Bartonbee? No, Allenbee. Most certainly Allenbee . . . Esquire, I believe. He brought along the most wondrous little pickle sandwiches. We should give them to Chef, she—"

"Enough." Alastair made an exasperated noise in his throat. He released me and said, "I'll find you later."

After he was gone, I gripped the top of a tufted chair, willing my heart to calm.

"He's very handsome, isn't he?" a guest in a tightly corseted dress said to her friend while fanning herself with an oversize sequined leaf. I assumed she was speaking about Alastair, but I turned in the direction both women were looking and spotted Bel.

His shirt was unbuttoned to past his collarbone. Wet from the rain, it clung to his lean torso while his trousers were stuck with brambles and muddy leaves up to his thighs. He looked like he'd been traipsing through the rain all day.

"Find your artéfact?" I asked, catching up to him.

"Of course." He held up something gold. It flashed as he slid it into his pocket. "Don't you have a map to draw?"

"We have to talk."

He eyed my champagne warily. "Will you toss that at my face if I refuse?"

"Without a doubt."

I looked around but didn't see the maître or any other suminaires nearby so I took Bel's elbow and led him to the back of a mirrored partition. My chest tightened when he made sure to stand a distance away. I wanted to step closer, but decided against it; things were already too complicated.

"I drew a map," I said.

All amusement drained from his face. "And?"

I tugged the map from my pocket. The charcoal was smudged, but the river Noir coiled like a snake through a city fettered by canals.

"This map doesn't lead to the ring. It leads to Champilliers." I brushed my fingers over a spot in the center and felt it—a bright signature of magic. Bel did the same, his eyes widening. "I drew it from the painting above the hearth in the map room. I believe this spot of magic is that woman, the former Fabricant." I pushed the map back into my pocket. "When I touched her face in the painting, she spoke to me in the same voice from the itineraries."

"Paintings don't just speak."

I threw up my hands. "Oh, really? Look around you. We're surrounded by magic. Things speak! That woman is in Champilliers."

"Alastair himself told me the old Fabricant was dead."

"What if she isn't? There has to be a good reason why you're forbidden to take us there. I think she's alive and she knows things. I can't sense the ring, I don't know where it is, but I touched that woman's face and drew this map. You said yourself that sometimes the magical signatures are suminaires. I'm positive it's her. Bel, she's our answer."

"I don't see how."

I groaned. "In that society handbook, she's holding Alastair's inkwell. It was her artéfact at one point. She was also the Fabricant; she could know where the ring is hidden, and tell us if it could work to nullify the contracts."

"It would be suicide," he said. "Regardless, you'd have to get to the contracts first and you don't even know where they're kept."

"I do." I pictured that third desk drawer, the infinite ledger. The ring might even remove whatever enchantment Alastair used to lock the drawer. It could solve everything. When I began pulling out the map a second time, Bel pushed my hand away.

"No."

"Why not?"

He shook his head and stormed away.

I raced around a group of guests and grabbed his forearm. "You took me to Aligney. Why won't you take me here? Alastair threatened Zosa. This is my last option." My words were breathless. "Help me."

"I can't," he said. At my furious expression, Bel added, "Look. If I move us there, Alastair will take away everything he's given me."

"*Given* you?"

"He doesn't just threaten to punish me if I don't do my job. He also rewards me."

"For bringing back artéfacts?" Bel nodded. I couldn't believe it. "So whatever he rewards you with is more important than all of us? More important than my sister?"

"That's not what I meant." He picked mud from his sleeve. "I should get upstairs before I'm seen like this."

"What did you mean?"

With one swift movement, he ripped the map from my pocket and stuffed it down his own. "I'm getting rid of this thing."

I stood there like a fool watching guests jump out of his way as he bowled through them toward the caged lift.

I shot after him, but he was already on the platform. King Zelig had nearly closed the cage when I skidded to a halt. I wrenched it open. Bel tried to push me away, but I ducked under his arm and forced myself in.

"Floor?" Zelig asked.

Bel glared at me.

"Six," I replied.

"I'm ripping it up."

"I'll draw another."

"Then I'll destroy that one, too. I'm not taking you to Champilliers."

"Why? We have nothing. What are you so afraid to lose?" When he remained quiet, I slammed a palm on the cage. King Zelig backed away. "I thought you were different, but Yrsa was right. You only care about yourself."

Bel's eyes squeezed shut through an entire floor. He seemed to come to some decision because his shoulders relaxed. He exhaled and said, "Alastair rewards me with memories."

My breath froze. The distant sounds of music, laughter, the clinking champagne glasses—nothing registered as I tried to make sense of his words.

Bel idly plucked a falling leaf from outside the cage. It wisped away to pink smoke in his fingers. "With each artéfact I find, Alastair gifts me one memory. The smell of a flower, the curl of someone's hair." I flinched when he lifted one of my curls. "The memories are the reason I can't stay away from the moon window. They've made me different from the other staff."

"How?"

"Every memory I'm gifted brings me one step closer to remembering where I'm from . . . Who I am."

"But you're Bel."

"Right. Named after my title as the *esteemed* bellhop, my first position before Alastair discovered my affinity for the key."

"A bellhop?"

"Many here are missing names. I wasn't the first to lose mine, nor will I be the last." He drew in a lengthy inhale. "I had friends I trusted with my life, friends I loved, but one by one they were demoted, or they disappeared, or I drove them away myself, like in Hellas's case. Then there were those whose hearts were hardened by the maître and they no longer spoke to me because of the position I held."

"I didn't realize—"

"How would you? The memories Alastair has given back to me . . . There's nothing I'll do to risk him taking them away," he said with conviction.

Then I understood. Bel was the Magnifique; he wasn't replaceable like the other suminaires. Alastair needed another way to manipulate him, and he found it by giving Bel a taste of what he wanted more than anything, by dangling Bel's memories like goddamned carrots.

My eyes filled with tears. "Bel—"

"I'm sorry you didn't learn sooner that caring about anyone here only causes pain."

I straightened.

His words struck me with such force that they left me reeling. This was what he thought. Why he kept to himself. It was probably why he couldn't understand Hellas's devotion to his sister long ago. And why he tried to have me sent home without Zosa.

Then there were so many times I caught him looking at me then tearing his eyes away. So many instances where he shifted conversations away from anything deeper than lighthearted banter. All because he'd been hurt and was afraid of being hurt again.

The cage had opened on six. I only noticed when Bel stormed off.

"Wait!"

More leaves drifted from the ceilings, splashing the carpet with pools of colored smoke. They tickled my ankles as I raced to keep up. When Bel reached his room, I rushed around and flung myself against his door.

"You're wrong," I blurted. "In Alastair's office, I learned a suminaire's artéfact is determined by their soul's desire. Bel, I've seen your atlases. I remember the expression on your face when you moved the hotel that first night. And this—" I ran a nail along the chain that held his key. "The first time you saw le monde entier scratched into the front door's black lacquer, it called out to you like it did to me, didn't it?"

"Jani—" he started to protest.

"At first, I thought you were so arrogant, so awful," I said, cutting him off. "But you're good. You're only afraid of getting too close to people because you think it'll distract you from your goal of getting home. But if we void the contracts, you can have everything you want. Please, Bel, take me to Champilliers."

"I don't want everything," he said, resolute, then pushed his door open, brushing past me.

But before he could get far, I took hold of his hand. "Your memories can't be the only thing you want. There has to be something else."

Just like in that doorless room, his eyes settled on my lips. "I think you should leave," he said, his voice a little rough.

There was anger there, to be sure, but alongside it was something that flared inside me.

Reaching up, I touched his cheek, and his eyes squeezed shut. He looked so resigned. He'd been trapped here for years. *Decades.* He must have denied himself what he wanted countless times.

But so had I.

A surge of something bubbled up—the need to prove to him how much he could have, *deserved* to have.

"You should leave," he repeated.

"You're probably right," I said, and pressed my lips to his.

A noise caught in Bel's throat, a little gasp of surprise that soon melted into something else that made my toes curl.

I broke away to gaze up at him, amazed. "I was right. You do want this."

"Would you just shut up?" he said, breathless.

"I had thought—" I started, until his mouth found mine again. His tongue parted my lips, and all words—all *reason*—floated out of reach. Without thinking, my fingers skimmed across his back, nails dragging along his ribs.

"Careful," he whispered.

So I did it again.

He growled my name, and hooked his thumbs under me. Lifting me. Pressing me flush against a wall. No, not a wall. A book fell to the ground with an angry thump. I tore my mouth from his and glanced down. Verdanniere stood out in crisp black ink, but it might as well have been a different language entirely because I couldn't make sense of it. I was too distracted by Bel's hand as it slid under my skirt to smooth around my thigh, and his lips as they pressed kisses to the neckline of my dress, my collarbone. And stopped.

My back arched when he brushed a hand across my throat where Maman's necklace had popped out from my dress collar. He buried his face in my neck and exhaled. Slowly, I slid down the bookcase, while his fingers grazed up my sides, causing my stomach to do that silly thing stomachs do.

I gasped when he fixed the sleeve of my dress. His eyes roamed over my face. Then lower. "It's late. If I don't go downstairs now, I'll never make it," he said seriously.

Warmth spread throughout every inch of me, and my tongue—my tongue tangled in my teeth, refusing to work. I nodded and he left to go change. Then I stood there, clumsy, my thoughts muddled and molten, attempting to make sense of everything, then only one thing: Bel was moving the hotel soon.

The map.

I ran over and ripped it from the pocket of the pants he'd tossed in the hall. When he returned, I pushed it into his hands and curled his fingers over, holding his palms tight to the paper, like I'd seen

him do to the pages of the atlas. His lashes fluttered closed. I felt it, too: that tug of wrought iron and kiss of cool canals.

"Take us there."

He shoved the map away, like it was a burning flame and not a simple scrap of paper.

"I can't," he said.

"Bel—"

He stopped my lips with his thumb, and then trailed it along the ridge of my jawline. "You know I love our arguments dearly, but I don't have time to argue on this. Hide the map. Wait for me until I'm back. This shouldn't take more than a few minutes." He touched the key at his neck. "We'll figure it out later. I promise."

He wasn't taking us.

After he was gone, I threw the map across the room then paced the floor for many minutes. He didn't return. I tried sitting for a little while, but I was too antsy.

There was no clock in Bel's room, and it had been very close to midnight when I came up here. He should be back by now. Unable to stay put, I rushed out of the room and down the hall.

A hand grabbed my shoulder, jerking me around.

"Found her," Sido called out.

He wrenched my arms behind my back, his stinking breath on my face. I thrashed, clawing at him, but it didn't do a thing. "Let me go," I said, but he ignored me.

Alastair walked over with Yrsa.

"What's going on?" I asked. "Where's Bel?"

He didn't answer me. He drew a finger around my right eye and nodded at the alchemist. "Take her downstairs."

My heart thumped. "What? Why?"

"With pleasure." Yrsa grabbed me by my elbow. Sido did the same on the other arm, pulling me. They shoved me into the lift.

"You can't do this!" I shouted.

Alastair ignored me. He walked to the moon window. For a moment he stood there, staring out. Then he let out a frustrated cry and smashed his fist against the thick glass.

28

The image of Alastair stayed with me as they brought me to that terrible room behind the bar. Sido held me while Yrsa lifted her teacup with the reverence a mother might bestow a newborn babe. She then placed it on the long table—that same table Red had lain sprawled across. Bile rose in my throat. Next to the table, a single oil lamp burned beside a macabre display of curiosities I hadn't noticed the first time.

Bottles, tinctures, canisters, and glass jars filled with tiny bones dotted the shelves. Then other things: blades and feathers, vials of human hair. Teeth. A small bird skull sat on a book slick with drippings of candle wax. A glowing mercury glass vial labeled *maiden's tears* sat next to other jars labeled with various emotions like *sorrow* and *regret*. Down at the end sat a huge shelf filled with eyes.

My knees buckled. Half the shelf was stuffed with glass eyes in various colors and sizes. The other half was filled with porcelain versions, unglazed white orbs that looked out at nothing. Each one unique. Each one a person. A finishing hammer coated with porcelain dust sat next to an eye cracked in two, no doubt belonging to a corpse.

Hellas came through the door the same moment Yrsa unrolled her surgeon's kit.

"How is it out there?" she asked him.

"Messy," Hellas replied.

I wanted to know what he meant.

Yrsa nodded. "Sido, stand at the door by the bar. Make sure no one wanders back here."

I stumbled when he let me go. At the sound of Sido leaving, something rustled in the corner: a tiny golden bird in a cage.

"What's she doing here?"

Yrsa lifted a piece of porcelain, a slim finger more delicate than my own. "One outburst and I'll snap this. You can see what happens for yourself." She glanced at my sister. "Alastair said a doorway bit off her fingers. Such a shame I wasn't the one to cut them off." Her mouth slanted up.

Rage flooded every inch of me. Yrsa pulled a spool of black thread from a lower shelf and rested it beside a pair of blood-flecked pliers, a spoon, a knife, and a candle. She waved a hand over her teacup and the not-milk swirled. One creamy tendril touched her finger. She flicked it down.

Zosa shrieked, flapping at the cage bars.

My nails dug crescents into my palms. "You might think you're helping the maître's cause, but you're nothing more than a curse on this world."

My words seemed to put Yrsa in a better mood. She hummed

while she lit the blue-flamed candle. Slowly, she lifted the knife and held it over the flame, twisting it until the metal glowed red at the edges.

"Up you go. On the table." She waved the thin knife at me. "Hurry now."

The table swirled with a mess of wax drippings and dried blood. My legs shook so badly they threatened to give out. I couldn't crawl up there if I wanted to.

"So that's how it's going to be." Yrsa shrugged. "No matter. Hellas, be a dear and give me a hand."

If I had much in my stomach it would be on the floor. Before Hellas could take a step toward me, the door swung inward. Madame des Rêves stood there, plum wig and all, Sido at her side.

Yrsa turned toward Des Rêves. "What now?"

"Alastair needs you upstairs. There's a situation."

"Well? Spit it out."

"A crowd is gathering outside the door. Guests are streaming out. The crown already sent an envoy to meet with us."

"What's happening?" I asked.

Des Rêves's eyes snapped to me. "Haven't heard? We're in Champilliers."

My breath left me in one sharp exhale.

Bel.

Fresh tears welled up. I touched my lips and they were still swollen. Bel would lose everything Alastair had given him for this. All those little memories. Bel risked them all to bring me here. My chest swelled. This was for all of us.

I had to find the woman in the painting.

"Stay with the girl. I'll be back as soon as I can," Yrsa barked at Hellas, then practically flew from the room along with Des Rêves and Sido.

Hellas shuffled his cards, creating an unmovable barrier.

I wished I could summon some trick to convince him to leave as easily as he plucked cards from his deck.

When he didn't meet my eyes, I studied his face. It might have been wishful thinking, but he almost looked conflicted. Chances were good he still didn't care for me, but I hoped he didn't hate me. When Alastair threatened Frigga, it was obvious Hellas didn't have the power to spare her. I witnessed his fear. It wasn't too dissimilar from mine. I knew from experience the lengths people were willing to go to protect those they loved.

In the aviary, when Hellas had thought Frigga was in trouble, I'd seen fear in his eyes. Hellas wasn't standing here because he enjoyed working for Alastair.

He had to see the similarities between our circumstances, how we were both bound by our siblings. And if that were the case, he probably wanted many of the same things I did.

"There's a reason Bel brought us here," I said, nerves swimming inside me. I half expected Hellas leave and lock me in the room, but the Botaniste did nothing but listen. "I—I think there's a woman in this city who knows something that could help us."

"Help with what?"

I didn't mention the ring. Instead, I said, "She might know some-thing about the contracts. A way to void them. You could free

yourself along with your sister. But you have to let me out first."
When he raised a silver brow, I added, "Please."

My hands were ice-cold. I rubbed them up my arms to fill the
silence, to do something other than stand motionless. I didn't know
what else to say. I supposed I could beg. I wasn't above it.

"What would you do if it were reversed?" I said. "If Frigga was a
bird and you had the chance to save her, wouldn't you take it?"

Please let me out, I willed with everything inside me. *We're not so
different.*

He remained silent for a few more beats then held the door wide.
For me.

"What you did for Frigga in the aviary . . . She told me you lied for
her when you didn't have to. If you hadn't . . ." He sighed through his
nose. "Consider my debt paid."

He would help me.

Noises drifted down the hall, but I didn't move.

"What are you waiting for?" Hellas asked.

Carefully, I took Zosa's porcelain finger and tucked it down my
skirt pocket so it nestled beside the cosmolabe. I stepped to her
cage.

Hellas grunted in disbelief. "Surely Bel wouldn't associate himself
with a fool."

"I'm not leaving her."

"You won't make it ten blocks carrying that thing, and you'll both
have to return before the next midnight regardless."

I ignored him and bent to lift the cage.

Hellas grumbled. He took a card and positioned it at the tip of his fingers. I expected him to flick it at my throat. Instead, he stepped over and placed it atop the metal bars. Paper leaves unspooled, cloaking the entire thing in white. "At least now you might make it past the lobby before you're caught."

I straightened, amazed Hellas bothered to lift a finger. Sweeping a white leaf aside, I stroked Zosa's neck. "You have to be quiet," I whispered, hoping she would understand. She was just a bird, but she settled down, tucking her head under her wing.

Hellas motioned for me to follow. "If you don't come with me now, you won't get another chance."

I clutched the leaf-draped bars. "I'm ready."

"Good. As soon as the maître realizes you're missing, he'll send someone to look for you. Whatever you decide, I'd suggest walking as far as you can to the edge of the city and remaining there until you know what's next. Luckily it's an hour after midnight. Congratulations. You get a whole twenty-three hours before we move again."

I started down the hall, pausing long enough to check the door to Alastair's office, but it was locked, of course. I hugged Zosa tight to my chest until another thought struck.

"What is it?" Hellas asked.

"How am I supposed to walk through the front door with a cage?"

"Leave that to me. Stay in the shadows and wait for my trick. Then exit as swiftly as you can."

"What trick?"

He fanned his cards, a wicked glint in his eyes. "If you're as clever as I think you are, you'll figure it out."

Chaos gripped the lobby. It was well into the night yet revelers were out whispering about the city beyond the door. The replicated view showcased a brocade of gas lamps giving way to a night sky bursting with pink-tinged stars. Bet it looked even lovelier from the moon window.

At the thought, I searched the floor, frantic, but I couldn't see Bel anywhere. *He'll be all right*, I told myself. Because if he wasn't—

I didn't want to think. I didn't want to think about what that would mean. My only solace was the fact that we were in Champilliers, and he made it happen.

Alastair stood in one corner, gesturing wildly to a group of doormen.

Hellas took the stage usually reserved for Bel. He wasn't wearing his coat, but no one cared because the Botaniste was here to put on a show.

His silver hair spun around as he flicked out six red cards in a giant semicircle surrounding the stage. Guests gathered, but not too close.

Alastair straightened at the sight of Hellas. A steely expression came over his face and his sharp eyes scanned the room. Before he could see me, I ducked behind an orange tree.

Whatever Alastair thought didn't matter because as soon as Hellas raised his hands in the air, the entire lobby pushed in around him, crowding Alastair against the far wall until I lost sight of him.

I had to leave now.

Once Hellas's cards were in place, everyone stopped talking. The lobby was so quiet, you could pick out individual breaths. Hellas dared a glance at the shadow where I stood and raised a hand to his brow, in salute or signal, I didn't know. Then he cracked a knuckle, opened his mouth, and roared.

Two hundred guests looked to the ground in unison. *Certainly a diversion*, I thought. I could barely look away as the cards grew roots. Snaking down, they parted the marble like seedlings in wet spring soil. After the roots took hold, pale plants shot up, growing into huge paper stalks the height of the ceiling itself, tangling with the chandeliers, and turning the entire lobby into a garden of vibrant red hearts.

The crowd erupted in applause.

Only then did I grip Zosa's cage and slip out, right through the front door.

29

"Welcome to Elsewhere," I whispered to Zosa. She peeked at me through the crumpled leaves that fell away as we walked.

In Durc after midnight, the city would fill with the bawdy songs of drunken sailors. It was the same here. Everywhere, people shouted Verdanniere nursery rhymes and littered the canals with sloppy laughter.

Terrified to remain still, I made my way through the city, stopping only to catch my breath. Hours passed as I tried to picture the map—that signature of magic in the center. But without the actual paper, I couldn't tell north from south, or where I might be.

I didn't know how Bel did it. The only clear image in my mind was the purple scalloped awning, but the dark night made it impossible to see much color.

My fingers soon grew blisters from the heavy cage, and the city changed around me. Pristine marble structures gave way to ramshackle buildings with crumbling eaves. I stopped to ask directions at a blue-shuttered inn. A peeling sign lacking any hint of inlaid pearl read HOTEL DU SOLEIL.

The door groaned as I opened it. It was nearly dawn. An old woman lifted her drool-covered cheek from the front desk and squinted at the burgeoning sunlight leaking through the window.

I described the purple scalloped awning. "Is there a place where suminaires might frequent? A shop?"

Her watery eyes brightened. "There's Cheat's Alley at the end of Rue d'Arles. Careful, though, the old alley is chock-full of frauds, but there's some fluff shops dealing magic at the south end." She hissed the word *magic* like someone would say *demon* or *devil*, and it bothered me in a way it never had before. "Shops should open up soon. You could try it. Might have seen a purple awning there. Might have been pink."

Outside, the avenues teemed with people swarming in the direction of the hotel. Perspiration beaded my neck while the cage's handle sliced into my palm. But the pain focused my mind. It kept me awake and carried my feet faster. When I thought I couldn't go any farther, I turned a corner and found it.

Rue d'Arles, otherwise known as Cheat's Alley, was a cobbled passage only three blocks from the famed Noir, but it felt like a world away. Women hunched against storefronts hawking false magic. They wore makeup like masks to detract from their weeping sores and jutting ribs.

"Read your palm for a pewter, child." One crone waggled her painted eyebrows at my pockets. I tried not to cringe at her rotted gums.

"Want more kisses, love? I have just the charm to help."

"Your fortune looks filled with scandal! Hear it for a copper."

"Bottle a bit of your shadow to drink. Cures any illness!"

"Read your cards! The answers to your troubles are in your cards!"

Doubtful, I thought, especially since the cards looked to be nothing more than a tattered deck of playing cards that would make Hellas's lip curl in disgust.

A cart stocked with glowing vials and tinctures that looked straight from the bar of Salon d'Amusements took up the end of the alley. I lifted a flask topped with dripping red wax and marked with a human heart. The word *Amour* was stamped in peeling silver foil.

A young woman peered up from her stool. Freckles dotted her pale cheeks. She tapped some glowing powder from an envelope into a glass jar between her knees. The liquid turned bright orange, identical to a concoction Yrsa once mixed.

"What potion are you searching for today, madame?"

"Nothing," I said warily, and hurried past.

A small canal cut the street off at the end of the alley. I reached it and halted. A purple scalloped awning stretched before me, identical to the one I saw when I touched the painting.

Wiping a thick coating of dust from the window, I peered inside. A long counter ran across the back wall, obscured by shelves filled with mystical ephemera: vials, feathers, bowls, fossils, and iridescent crystals. Rusted hinges screeched as I pushed through the door.

Inside, stale air clung to my tongue. A display filled with dusty wooden toys leaned against a wall. SOUVENIRS MAGIQUES read a bronze sign. Curious, I lifted a few: a spyglass, a tiny hammer, a cigarette holder, a round disk carved with the zodiac.

I fished in my pocket and pulled out the cosmolabe. Carefully, I held it up to the disk. Identical, other than one was an artéfact, the other shoddy wood.

These crude toys were wooden versions of artéfacts I'd seen in the hotel. The woman from the painting had to be here somewhere, and she must still have her memories, otherwise she wouldn't know to make these.

In the back, a register sat on a marble counter. Near it, a newspaper was flipped open to the jobs section, where an advertisement stood out in vibrant purple amid a sea of black and white.

A cup of tea rested near the paper, steam curling out. Still hot. My pulse hammered in my ears. "Anyone here?"

Iron creaked. I glanced up. A woman tugged on a pair of elbow-length silk opera gloves—a bit fancy for the establishment—as she descended a wrought-iron spiral staircase in the corner. It

was her—the woman from the painting. She hadn't aged a day.

"I'm closing up early," she said as she grabbed two ratty hatboxes and threw them both on the counter. They flopped open in unison. Empty. "Can I help you?"

"I think I'm looking for you. You're the woman from the painting in the map room."

Her bright eyes studied me with new interest. Then she noticed the cosmolabe in my palm. "A Fabricant. I take it you drew a map from the painting?"

I nodded.

"I'm impressed. People tend to change with time. There's a level of skill required to draw maps to them, yet here you are. You're powerful." She walked behind the counter and scrutinized my face. "But I am curious about one thing. How are both your eyes still in their sockets?"

I pictured the not-milk and shuddered. "I've only been a Fabricant for a few days."

Zosa squawked. The woman glanced down at my sister and smiled. It was tinged with melancholy. In the painting, she didn't smile, but I'd seen that smile before.

"Who are you?"

"My name's Céleste." Her smile grew. "You're a curious thing. I sell just the charm for that. Let me find it."

She riffled through junk against the back wall.

"Ah, here we are."

She placed a wooden toy in my palm, similar to the souvenirs on display. It was rough-hewn, ugly, and in the shape of a signet ring, the letter S carved crudely on the face. A twinkle lit her eyes.

"You know about the ring?"

"Of course. Once, I would have done anything for my brother, including finding that ring, but not anymore."

"Your brother?"

She smiled again and I couldn't avoid seeing the resemblance. They had the same forehead, the same curve to their chins.

Alastair's sister.

If she were his sister, she had to know more about the ring, if it would help.

Céleste began tossing knickknacks into the empty hatboxes two at a time, packing up.

"Are you heading to the hotel?" I asked.

"Is Yrsa still there?"

I gave her a terse nod.

"The witch vowed to burn this shop down with me inside if the hotel ever came back. No, I'm not going to the hotel, and I'm not sticking around to find out if Yrsa will make good on her promise."

Out the windows, the streets were busier than they were earlier. It wouldn't take long for Yrsa to walk here, or Sido. I could hear Bel's voice in my ear. *Don't be a fool*, he would tell me. *Get out now while you still can.* But if anyone could give me answers, Alastair's sister could.

"Can you spare a few minutes?"

"Heavens, no." She darted around me to pluck a book off a dusty shelf. "There's no time. I'm leaving and you should, too."

From her words in the painting, I didn't expect her to open her arms and tell me everything. So on the walk here I thought through how I might convince her to help. I considered an outright lie, but I couldn't come up with anything better than the truth. When she reached for a hatbox, I shut it, forcing her to look at me. She made a grab for the handle, but I pushed the hatbox out of reach.

"Everyone might believe your brother keeps magic safe inside his hotel. But he also keeps his staff imprisoned with their contracts," I said, and Céleste cringed.

"I'm sorry, truly, but I can't help—"

"He threatened my sister's *life* if I fail to draw a map to that ring," I said, cutting her off. "He took . . ." My throat thickened. "He took four of her fingers and he gave one to Yrsa, who turned it to porcelain." I touched the finger in my pocket to remind myself it was still there. Céleste gripped the counter with her gloved hands, clearly bothered. Good. "No one can stop him. I don't know you. I don't have any reason to trust you, but believe me when I say you're my last hope. If the signet ring removes magic, I want to use it to nullify our contracts. Which means I have to find it first. Will you help me?"

Céleste's eyes darted to the door. "Anyone follow you?"

My muscles twitched with nerves. "Not that I saw. Does this mean you'll help?"

"It's not a simple request. I could tell you what I know, but that would take hours, and I'm heading out soon."

Her suitcase was still half empty. "Then tell me as much as you can while you pack." She opened her mouth to protest, and I knocked a fist against the counter. "Clearly you left everyone behind. If you know anything about the ring, you have to tell me."

Her face pinched. "Fine. I'll give you as much information as I can, but then you have to leave." Overwhelmed with relief, I opened my mouth to thank her, but she held up a hand. "Tell me what you know about the hotel. And hurry."

I went over the contracts, the infinite ledger. Then I told her about finding the book in the map room, that the hotel once housed a society for suminaires.

She nodded. "The building was only a hotel on the outside when I first arrived."

"The outside?"

"Yes. I found it by accident. It was a sweltering day in Champil-liers. I was walking home with Alastair and he was thirsty. That building looked like any other hotel, so we wandered inside to a small empty lobby, hoping for something to drink. On the front desk sat a sign that said the hotel was full. I stood there, drumming my fingers, waiting for someone to show up, but no one did. Not until I reached down to press a bell and it levitated to meet my finger. That wasn't the last of the magic we saw that day, not by a long shot."

"I believe it," I said, remembering the moment I'd arrived with Zosa. How the feeling of being inside thrummed through my blood like a drug. "But surely patrons wandered in just like you had. What if they'd discovered the place housed suminaires?"

"They didn't. The façade of a hotel afforded the perfect disguise.

They were easily able to turn people away. A hotel only has so many rooms, you understand."

"They told people the hotel was full."

"Yes. But not for us. When we stepped inside, I was still young. I didn't know I was a suminaire. If I'd been born into a family with a long history of suminaires, perhaps I would have been given an artéfact or schooled in the other ways to use my magic before it hurt others."

"Première magie?"

She nodded. "But I didn't know anything about using magic. The society saved my life, as they did for many children. It was spoken of among families with suminaire blood in their lineage. Parents knew that if their child exhibited certain traits, they could send them there to live a long life without the threat of being discovered. I was very fortunate to find it on my own."

"So you just moved in?"

"Of course. The only other option was going into hiding and trying to contain my magic by myself—something I certainly wasn't prepared for. The society was the best choice for me at the time. Inside, I was given my artéfact along with a job. I drew maps for them." Céleste fixed her attention on my cosmolabe.

On instinct, I shoved the metal disk down my pocket.

"If you created maps, what did your brother do?" *And please hurry*, I almost added.

"What did he not do? My brother is brilliant. The head of the society took a liking to him. He gave Alastair the job clerking along with cataloguing artéfacts. But not initially." She frowned. "It's my fault he's there, you know. I begged for him to stay on because I couldn't bear the thought of leaving him behind."

"Surely they would have seen your brother's potential and brought him on."

"They didn't bring him on, or even want him at first." She leaned forward, suddenly fearful, as if Alastair himself could hear her every word. "You see, only suminaires were allowed past that little lobby, and although he's done an admirable job convincing the world otherwise, my brother doesn't have a single drop of magic in his entire body."

30

The wooden ring tumbled from my fingers onto the marble. Alastair had no magic. "But he's the greatest suminaire in all the world."

"He's the greatest liar in all the world. Hard to believe, I know."

But I'd seen him move walls. I'd watched as he crafted flowers from air. He erased minds like plucking overripe peaches. "Your brother has magic." He had to.

"I assure you that's not the case," Céleste said solemnly. "Our parents were dead. I couldn't leave him in Champilliers by himself, so I talked the society heads into letting him come on with me." She lifted her teacup, staring at the steaming water like it held futures. "Once inside, Alastair saw suminaires old enough to be his grandfather appear no older than me. And everything was magical. Even the oranges were enchanted."

The marvelous orange trees. "Your brother said he'd tried to cut the trees down once."

"He hated them," she said. "The oranges are quite unique. Did you know their juice *tastes* like a special food you've eaten? For me, the juice always tasted like the fraisier cake from my tenth birthday. When I sipped it, everything I remembered sensing at that birthday party would come alive around me. I could even smell the smoke from freshly blown-out birthday candles."

A marvelous orange must have been the main ingredient in the juice Yrsa had given me on my first afternoon at the hotel—where she hid the drop of Truth.

"Only suminaires can pick the oranges, you know. After we'd first arrived, Alastair had hated how the trees reminded him of what he wasn't. In fact, at the mention of anything to do with magic, he would shut down. I couldn't bear to see him like that, so I began keeping things from him."

I knew exactly how Céleste felt. Often, I regretted not telling Zosa how sorry I was for bringing her to Durc. Now there were too many things I wanted to tell her and I couldn't.

Céleste tossed a couple more things in her hatboxes. One of them was nearly full and I still needed answers. "So Alastair was lonely."

"Not exactly," she said. "He had a friend, Nicole, a suminaire with barely any hint of power." She snarled the woman's name. "Nicole's artéfact was a copper spoon that could heat water one cup at a time and nothing more."

Céleste lifted the wooden signet ring. She slipped it on and off her gloved finger then held it up. Carved wood caught the light.

"One day, Alastair came across the entry for the signet ring in the society's catalogue. He brought it straight to me. He'd convinced himself that if the ring could bestow magic, it could also bestow the benefits of magic. He could be powerful *and* live forever—

everything he wanted. He begged me to draw a map to it."

That was it. That was why he wanted the ring.

He wanted to cheat death by becoming a suminaire.

"Then did you find the ring?" I asked.

"At first, I couldn't get a feel for the ring's catalogue entry. There wasn't enough to work with. But that didn't stop Alastair's obsession. The ring gave him ideas, and he soon found another artéfact in the society's vault. A mirror." Her expression darkened.

"A tarnished hand mirror?"

"You've seen it?"

"A few times. I've even seen Madame des Rêves fan herself with it."

Céleste made a face at the mention of Des Rêves. "She worked as a chamber maid for the society when Alastair and I first got there, you know. Gave herself that ridiculous title and made everyone address her as Madame. I never discovered Nicole's real last name."

I couldn't believe it. "Des Rêves was the suminaire who be-friended Alastair? With the copper spoon?"

Céleste nodded. "Her power was weak. It was the only artéfact she could get a feel for."

"But if Des Rêves could only heat liquid, how does she use the talon to turn people to birds?"

"The same way my brother pretends to be a suminaire. The mirror."

"I don't understand."

Céleste continued to grab things from shelves and toss them into her hatboxes, telling me the history of the mirror as she packed. I soon learned that after they'd been at the society for a few years,

Alastair found an account of the tarnished hand mirror in an old journal. Apparently a Verdanniere ship captain created wind from a different artéfact to sail her ship. When her magic waned halfway across a still ocean, she used the hand mirror to get a boost from a crew member who wasn't powerful enough to use the wind-creating artéfact himself. The hand mirror transfers magic from a suminaire to another person temporarily.

"Alastair was beginning to look older than the suminaires. He thought the hand mirror might work the same way he assumed the signet ring would. He brought it to me and I naively tried it on him. Instantly, he felt more youthful and he discovered he could use some of the weaker artéfacts. But the amount of magic I'd transferred to him was so small, he only noticed the effects for a few days. The transferred magic doesn't last. It wears off."

"Did you try it again?"

"Never," she said. Her eyes caught mine. Slowly, she pinched the fingertip of one opera glove and peeled it away.

At the sight of her hand, I jumped back, stumbling into Zosa's cage. My sister made an angry chirp, but I didn't look down. I couldn't tear my eyes from Céleste's palm—what was left of it.

"Using the hand mirror isn't like using magic yourself. The magic you transfer to someone else doesn't replenish. This is what giving away that miniscule bit of magic did to me."

A hole went clean through the center of her palm, the size of a dublonne, surrounded by graying flesh.

I yelped when she snatched my hand. My thumb slid into the grotesque hole. Faint wisps of smoke curled off the edges, as if she were turning incorporeal before my eyes. She let me go and replaced the satin glove.

I gripped the counter and relished in its solid feel, my solid skin.

Céleste's face tightened. "Alastair promised me he would return the hand mirror and never use it again, but he lied. Then he told *her* about it."

"Des Rêves?"

"Nicole is vicious, and my brother was a fool."

"He still is."

"Figured as much. Shortly after I'd tried the mirror on him, Nicole convinced her roommate to use it on herself, gifting both Nicole and Alastair with a rush of magic. The act, however, left a gaping hole in the poor roommate's arm, leaching her of color."

A chill slid over me. All those suminaires in the aviary, the dull feathers. The pieces were clicking together.

"Alastair later told me the roommate looked gray around the edges, her lips and eyelids the color of dust, like a corpse. She begged for Nicole to reverse it. She even tried to fight back with her artéfact, but because of that hand mirror, her magic was gone. Permanently transferred. Nicole didn't want the girl to escape, to tell anyone what happened, so with her stolen magic, Nicole used the poor girl's artéfact against her."

"What was the roommate's artéfact?" I asked, even though I could wager a guess.

"A silver talon." Céleste shook her head. "I didn't know what had happened at the time. No one did. The head of the society conducted a search. They found the roommate's suitcase missing, along with some of her clothes. Everyone assumed she'd taken off. Later, I learned Nicole had locked her in the aviary while my brother staged her things to look like she'd left. Had I known . . ."

Céleste's lips quivered. I couldn't begin to understand the guilt she felt. This whole time Alastair and Des Rêves were stealing magic from suminaires then getting rid of the evidence right under guests' noses.

Under my nose.

I knew how desperate Alastair must feel. I felt that desperation daily. I was forged in it. But he had taken it further than I ever dreamed.

"I've been inside the aviary," I said. "I've seen all the birds leached of color. All that magic—"

"Stolen. By my brother. By Nicole. Both of them needed an endless supply of it to continue the lies they'd built—for my brother to remain youthful and powerful, and for Nicole to continue to use the silver talon. Luckily for them, it was easy to hide holes with feathers."

"But there are so many birds."

"How many are there now?"

I felt nauseous thinking of the hundreds I had seen. Céleste must have read the answer in my eyes because she said, "Never mind. I don't want to know."

"So he stole from every suminaire he could get his hands on?"

"Not everyone. If you were a suminaire who connected with an artéfact useful in running the hotel or finding the ring, Alastair didn't turn you into a bird. But those suminaires were few and far between. Most suminaires he found were turned. It worked in his favor. He liked to keep a queue of still-magical suminaires in the aviary because as birds, they couldn't access their magic. It remained dormant, safe, ready for when my brother and Des Rêves needed to steal more for themselves."

She was right. I'd seen a handful of birds inside with bright feathers. They must still have their magic. But not for long.

I'd thought suminaires were rarer now than the days when the hotel began. There hadn't been one discovered in Durc in decades. It must have been because they were all trapped inside that aviary, their magic stolen. "What will happen when your brother runs out of suminaires to steal from?"

She held up the wooden signet ring.

Of course. If he could bestow himself with magic, he wouldn't need to steal it.

"My brother and I were born well over a century ago. If he stopped stealing magic, I imagine he would age and die almost instantly."

I blinked, remembering that day in the magic hall. "Once, the skin on his hand looked rippled. And I've seen him with a limp from time to time."

She nodded. "You probably caught him right before he had to steal more magic."

The cruelty of it all took my breath away. "I can't believe he can do such terrible things and still look himself in the mirror every morning."

She grunted. "Oh, he has no problem with that. He told me once that magic did more good keeping him alive than it did inside the suminaires he stole it from. He'd convinced himself the result-ing holes in their arms were nothing compared to his own life. He also promised to reverse everything he'd done, gift back the stolen magic, once he found the signet ring."

"That ring is his answer to everything."

She gave me a weak nod. "I should have noticed what my brother was doing with Nicole, but I was too busy drawing maps to pay at-tention to him." Céleste put her head in her gloved hands, blonde hair spilling over the counter.

"It's not your fault," I said as calmly as I could. When I touched her arm, she pulled it away and shot up.

"It is. He's my *little* brother."

The look on her face made my stomach clench. She blamed herself like I did every day for not keeping Zosa in Aligney. "You only did what you thought was best."

Tears spilled down Céleste's cheeks. She wiped them away then went back to the hatboxes, talking as she packed. She told me Alastair could use some artéfacts with the stolen magic, but he couldn't get a feel for as many as Céleste.

"But the inkwell was enough," she said. "Its written enchant-ments can be spectacular and addictive. Later, Alastair told me he tried penning a couple enchantments himself at first, but with each one, he felt older, which caused him to steal more magic. An endless cycle. After Nicole's roommate disappeared, four other suminaires *mysteriously* left, followed by the old head of the society. Apparently when the old man questioned Nicole, my brother used the hand mirror on him."

So that was how the society dismantled. Except everyone had to have known that Alastair had no magic. "So your brother took over the society and people blindly followed him without suspecting anything?" I didn't believe it.

"Not by himself."

"He took over with Des Rêves?"

"No," she said, a sour note in her voice. "Alastair and I took over the society together."

"*You?*"

"I thought he looked more youthful than he had, but I didn't realize what that meant. I never suspected what he was doing." She began pacing. "After the leadership vanished, the other suminaires grew edgy. I was the most powerful suminaire left. They chose me to lead. Me! The responsibility terrified me. So when Alastair came to me with a plan to run everything as a team, how could I refuse? How could I do anything but what he asked of me?"

I could picture it. The society heads out of the way. Endless supplies of suminaires. "But didn't you realize right away what was happening?" She could have stopped him.

"No," she said with a twinge of bitterness. "I was too busy. Alastair took over administrative duties and catalogued all the artéfacts, while I performed any task that required magic, like dealing contracts to new suminaires."

I froze. "You mean the society used contracts before the hotel?"

"It was how everything was kept a secret." Céleste ran a finger over the advertisement's purple ink. "When a suminaire misbehaved, their artéfact was taken away, their contract voided so when they stepped out of the society's building, they'd forget everything they'd experienced inside. They'd forget the society completely."

"That's nearly identical wording to the guest contracts."

"My brother is clever," she said. "He expanded on the society's contracts when he came up with those guest contracts. Then he drafted the staff contracts to be nearly the opposite, removing the outside world from the minds of the staff as soon as they came inside. But that wasn't until he decided to start the hotel."

"So the hotel was his idea?"

"Eventually. Finding the ring was his obsession. When we first took over the society, he used its resources to search. But it wasn't enough. He needed more resources, the ability to visit places where it would be impossible to hide. He thought if he could make the building public knowledge, a dazzling spectacle to draw in crowds, he could bring in money to pay his way into countries that wanted nothing to do with magic. The hotel was the perfect solution for everything he desired. Without realizing it, I helped him turn the building into what it is today. Have you seen the infinite ledger?"

I nodded slowly.

"I penned most of the enchantments inside."

"What?"

"Enacting the inkwell's enchantments uses less magic than

penning them. Penning them requires a lot of magic, magic my brother couldn't spare. So he told me it was my *duty* to help him make the hotel as spectacular as possible. I thought his ideas for enchantments were clever. Necessary. I was blinded."

"But the hotel is filled with enchantments. There has to be thousands. You mean to tell me you penned them all?"

She shrugged as if it were nothing. "There were some left over from the society days, but it wasn't enough. I'd sit hunched over that ledger for hours until my fingers would cramp up. But I transcribed his ideas, one after another. I penned enchantments allowing Alastair to shift walls and lock doors with a simple spoken word. I designed more magical guest rooms than you can imagine. I even added my voice to things, all with the ink." Céleste took a sip of tea with trembling fingers and cleared her throat. "*Greetings, traveler!*" she chirped. "Still got it."

She did.

"I heard you when I first arrived. Your voice still greets the guests."

She laughed to herself. "I didn't realize there would be guests when I first created that greeting. It took me until Alastair opened the hotel to figure out everything I'd enchanted was for that purpose."

"He never told you?" She was his sister.

"I found out before he got the chance. At first, I was thrilled. I knew Alastair wanted to find the ring, but I also believed him when he said he wanted to bring magic safely to the world." She ran a hand over the newspaper on the counter. "When the hotel first grew, I helped him recruit new staff by penning an enchantment that would appear as an advertisement the moment Alastair decided on our next destination."

She'd created everything, including the advertisement that started this whole mess.

A slight frown tugged down her lips. "A couple years in, I discovered the truth about the birds. I was furious, but I had no power. Once the hotel was up and running, Alastair didn't need me. Nicole and Yrsa were both powerful in their own way and supported him completely. Everyone who was left were forced to sign new contracts, erasing all knowledge of Société des Suminaires—"

She stopped speaking when the front door opened.

"Hello?" she called out.

A father and his little daughter wandered in.

"Afraid we're closing early with the hotel in town," Céleste said. "Come back tomorrow." The father muttered something, but took the girl and left.

She locked the door.

Such a paltry little lock. If Sido arrived, that bolt wouldn't make a difference. Neither would the door. Zosa shuffled in her cage as another crowd of people rushed by carrying suitcases, headed in the direction of the hotel.

"Alastair will probably hand out invitations soon," I said.

Céleste harrumphed. "If the contest is the same as it was when I was there, it's all a charade."

"It's not real?"

"Not a bit. Right before I left, Alastair confessed to me that Yrsa walked through the crowd with an old compass—a finding artéfact. It's supposed to point directly to suminaires."

"I've seen it," I said, remembering the magic vibrating off of it. "Alastair said Yrsa can't use it properly."

"She never could, so my brother gave away invitations to anyone it pointed to. He said he didn't want to risk accidentally leaving a single suminaire behind."

I reeled at her words. "Those are the people who win invitations."

"If my brother is still conducting everything the same way, then yes."

"But I've never seen anyone turned away after they've won. Surely they aren't all suminaires."

She shrugged. "I imagine the winners who aren't suminaires become guests, and if they can't afford a room, they're probably offered a job. Because unless things have changed, Alastair would never give out a stay for free. When I was there, he needed every last cent to fund his search for the ring and run the hotel."

That chest shaped from pink urd . . . "I watched him buy his way into Skaadi."

"That doesn't surprise me," Céleste said as she latched one of her hatboxes.

It all made perfect sense. Alastair needed the huge crowds. More fanfare gave him a greater chance at nabbing unsuspecting suminaires, along with making everyone excited about magic so the hotel could travel to more places.

This was why all those people in the blue city clamored for

invitations, even though many of them had no hope of paying for their stay. Why all the folk in the vieux quais rushed to that alley, wide-eyed. It was why Alastair never turned away a single winner. He needed everyone to *believe* they had a chance at seeing the world.

The hotel, the contest, the spectacle—none of it had anything to do with keeping magic safe. Everything Alastair did was to trap suminaires and fuel his search for the ring.

To stop his own imminent death.

I thought of his fist smashing against the moon window. His gut-wrenching cry. He was as desperate as me.

That day in Durc, everyone from miles around poured into the old alley. This whole time I thought it was good of the hotel to be inclusive, to conduct the contest and dole out hope to those starved for it.

My god. The winners from Durc, their tears of joy running down their cheeks. That mother with her little daughter. They could easily be rotting away in the aviary as we spoke.

"What happened after you found out what he was doing with the hotel?" I asked.

"I didn't know what to do. I stayed on for a couple of months until I couldn't take it any longer. I found the hand mirror and threatened to smash it. Nicole caught me. She brought me to Yrsa." Céleste tilted her face into a shaft of sunlight. Sure enough, one of her eyes lit up a shade brighter than the other.

"Glass."

She nodded. "Nicole wanted to kill me. She might have if Alastair

had kept me caged as a bird. So instead, he tore up my contract and banished me to this city before Nicole could make me sign a new one. Then he gave me this." She lifted a tiny spoon from the saucer beside her teacup. It was copper.

"Des Rêves's artéfact."

"The woman couldn't stand to see it anymore. And because it was the most innocuous artéfact in Alastair's collection, he let me leave with it. Aside from première magie, I've had to drink a great deal of tea to keep my magic at bay." She dipped the copper spoon in her cup and swirled it. A tendril of steam snaked out. "Alastair threatened that if I tried to go back, to interfere, tell anyone . . ."

"So he's been searching for that ring for a century?"

"As far as I know," she said.

Suminaires were more scarce than they were a hundred years ago. If Alastair used up all the magic in the world, we'd be trapped forever. No more magic to turn feathers to flesh, to retrieve missing memories. Zosa would be a bird forever. Alastair would take us all down with him.

I refused to let it happen.

"Please. How do I find the ring?" It was the only question that mattered and time was running out.

Céleste looked me dead in the eyes. "It doesn't exist."

31

Céleste walked to the back and pulled out a little book bound in green cloth. Gold foil stamped on the top read *The Touchard Brothers' Book of Verdanniere Fables*.

I recognized it instantly. Maman had kept a newer printing of it in our bookcase. Zosa and I would pull it out from time to time, but my sister was too squeamish to read most of the bloody stories.

Céleste opened it to a tale called *The Fortunate Ring*.

I knew that story. It told of a woodcutter who was tasked by an enchantress to traverse the woods he knew so well in search of a ring that gifted great power. If he couldn't find the ring before the first snowfall, the enchantress threatened to eat his firstborn. Eventually, the woodcutter found the ring. But he didn't immediately hand it over. Instead, he cleverly thought to place it on the enchantress's finger upside down. Instead of gifting her more power, the ring took all her power away and made her instantly mortal.

A woodcut illustration was printed beside the story. It depicted a woman's hand wearing a signet ring.

"I'd searched for that ring for years before I came across this book hidden in a dark corner of the library." Céleste flipped to the last page of the story. It was covered in tiny writing. "These scribbles are theories about how the fortunate ring might be an artéfact. I thought the handwriting look familiar, and it was. These notes were written by the same person who penned the ring's entry in the catalogue page."

"The ring is a fable?"

"Nothing but a fairy tale. Some of the old heads of the society believed that tales from cultures around the world held hidden truths about artéfacts. Some of the stories might have led to real artéfacts once or twice, but I'm fairly certain this one doesn't. My brother didn't believe me when I told him. At that point he'd been stealing magic for so long that he refused to accept there was nothing that could help him." There was a sadness in her voice.

That sadness struck me too, along with a deep sense of loss. It felt like a door had slammed shut before I could step through it.

I escaped Yrsa's table, the hotel. I came all this way to find something that never existed. The ring was merely a trinket in a children's story, and it broke my heart. I couldn't save my sister or use the ring to nullify our contracts.

The contracts.

If there wasn't a ring to stop Alastair's ink, perhaps there was another way.

I sharpened my attention at Céleste. "I know Alastair uses powerful magic to void the contracts. But you said you used the inkwell to dole out contracts to the society members before the hotel existed. Is there a simpler way to void them?"

There had to be something this woman knew that could help us. I couldn't have come all this way for nothing.

"I'm afraid not," Céleste said. "My brother can only command the ink while his fingers are wrapped around the inkwell. He summons his stolen magic through it to enact any enchantment, including voiding the contracts."

"What if I could steal the inkwell?" I asked, grasping for anything that might help.

She gave me a skeptical look. "Even if you somehow managed to get your hands on it, I doubt you'd be able to use it. It takes a powerful suminaire to get it to work, along with hours of practice."

My chest felt hollow. The ring was a fairy tale and I couldn't void the contracts myself. There was nothing I could do.

Céleste seemed to be thinking the same thing because she said, "I'm sorry."

"So that's it? I'm supposed to give up?"

Her miserable look was all the answer I needed.

Céleste shuffled around, preparing to leave. A voice in the back of my mind told me to go, too, but my legs felt leaden. I bent down to Zosa and stuck my fingers through her bars, stroking her feathers.

"Now listen carefully," Céleste called out. She latched her second hatbox and hoisted both off the counter. "Don't tell my brother I said anything. You might be a suminaire, but if Alastair suspects I gave away his secret, he'll do something drastic to you like he did to Issig."

"Issig?" My eyes snapped up. "What did he do?"

"Issig hated what Alastair was doing and didn't fear him like the other workers. He challenged Alastair. Even though his contract was amended over and over, his memories taken away each time, Issig kept searching for the truth. Eventually he found a way inside the aviary. When he begged me for answers, I told him a few things I wasn't supposed to."

"About the contracts?"

She nodded. "Issig is powerful. I thought he might be able to stand up to my brother. And he did, foolishly. He went straight to Alastair and tried to pry the ledger from his fingers." She grimaced. "The twins ripped his artéfact away and held him while my brother erased his mind until it snapped, then locked him behind the steel doors of the deep freeze where his magic couldn't hurt others."

"But if birds can't access their magic, why didn't he lock Issig in the aviary? It would have been the easier choice."

"It would have, but I think, deep down, Alastair likes keeping him in that freezer. With his mind gone, Issig didn't bother anyone or try anything. Besides, no one can use Issig's artéfact but him, and guests need their *precious* ice," she said bitterly. "If you try anything with those contracts, you'll be locked away—" Her words cut off.

"What is it?"

One of her hatboxes crashed to the ground, followed by the other. She turned to me. "Get down."

With a blast of shattering glass, the front door was kicked to the ground.

"Where are you, Céleste?" Yrsa drawled.

Dropping to a crouch, I peeked around the bookshelf. Yrsa stood inside the door, Sido behind her. I had to go. Zosa's cage rested against the back counter. A shaft of light pooled behind it.

Another door.

Yrsa stepped closer to the counter. "There you are. Lovely to see you, too, my dear, dear Céleste. Say. Has a girl come by asking questions?" Yrsa smiled when she noticed Zosa's cage. "Where is she?"

"I haven't seen a girl," Céleste said.

I scooted backward on my knees.

Yrsa pulled something from her pocket, a porcelain eye yellowed with age. "Alastair entrusted this to me." She twisted the porcelain piece. "If I discover you're lying, I'll drop it."

Céleste lurched forward. "Give it back."

"Where's the girl, Céleste?"

That was all it took. Céleste looked right at me. "I'm so sorry," she said.

I shuffled back until a hand clamped down on my hair, wrenching my head to the side. Sido.

"Hold her," Yrsa ordered.

The alchemist held the porcelain eye in her palm, just out of Céleste's reach. Céleste tried to grab it. Her gloved fingers came close to snatching it. Yrsa tilted her palm. The eye fell to the floor with a *crack*. "Oh, how terribly clumsy of me."

Céleste groaned. Her head dropped to the counter.

"We're adding Champilliers back to our rotation. There are too many alchemical dealers here to waste this city on your brother's pointless sense of obligation," Yrsa said as her boot heel rolled against the porcelain remains.

Crack. Crack. Crack.

Céleste jerked with each crack. Yrsa lifted her heel and stomped. With a swift snap, the rest of the eye shattered. Céleste collapsed against the counter. I couldn't see her face, only her gloved hand. A trail of blood rolled down it, dripping onto the marble floor. Sido released me to check her pulse.

Everything inside me roared. I had to go.

"What are you doing? She's dead, you fool. Get the little brat," Yrsa ordered.

I scrambled to Zosa's cage and heaved it up. The metal handle tore into broken skin. Blood trickled between my fingers as I squeezed it tightly and lunged out the back door, racing down crumbling stairs.

"Sorry," I said to Zosa when the cage tipped sideways. I winced when my sister's tiny feet scrambled and her body slammed against the bars. Her beak tapped down on my thumb. "Not now." I shifted the cage so it wasn't crooked.

She cooed. Too loud.

Yrsa shouted something to Sido. My heart raced. Hugging the cage, I dipped into Cheat's Alley.

"You might as well give up."

I turned. Yrsa stood twenty paces away. She tapped her right eye. "Only need to catch you once." Sido came up behind her.

I stumbled backward until my elbows knocked glass. The alchemist's cart. My fingers wrapped around a bottle.

Yrsa flung an arm across Sido's chest, stopping him.

I glanced down. The bottle was filled with a swirling silver mist I recognized instantly. A skeletal hand reached out, its bony claws clicking the inside of the glass, same as in the salon.

Bottled nightmare.

"Put it down," the alchemist who ran the cart said in a harsh whisper. "That stuff is undiluted. If it gets out it'll give you terrible visions."

"Don't be reckless," Yrsa shouted.

I started slowly lowering the bottle. But when Sido lurched forward, reckless was all I had left.

"Hold your breath," I said to the alchemist.

She looked on in horror as I slammed the bottle against the ground. It burst on impact and shot up in a brilliant silver plume, like a drop of ink in water, and spreading just as fast. I barely had time to cover my nose and mouth. I didn't think to shut my eyes. I only blinked when the oily silver cloud misted my face and seeped into the back of my throat. The world turned velvet black. Screams erupted and Cheat's Alley became a nightmarish scene straight from that terrible bottle.

My right hand held Zosa's cage, while my other hand felt around the alchemist's cart. I gagged. The thick mist coating my eyes made my skin crawl, but what I saw was worse.

It's not real. It's the nightmare twisting my senses, I told myself. *Just walk.*

I smelled rotting flesh as I passed things that no longer resembled women. I cried out when a massive black worm wriggled against the alley wall. A forked tongue flicked out. It lapped my neck, wet and rough. Below it, a stone statue turned to me and blinked. It lifted its clawed hand and plunged it down its own throat. A woman's scream filled the air.

In the center of the alley, a tall thing stalked forward, blood dripping from an empty eye socket, one single eye remained. The right side of its body looked as if a piece of it had been ripped away.

Sido.

He thrashed his head from side to side, backing away from the other nightmarish creatures dotting the alley. I knew Sido was still a man, and it was just the nightmare playing tricks on my eyes, but I still gagged.

"Jani!" Yrsa's voice boomed. A figure stepped forward. It looked like Yrsa but not. She was now taller than everything, looming over us.

Run, I thought. Except I stood frozen in place, watching the thing that was Yrsa. She leaned against the alley wall, wiping at her eyes.

There was nothing where her eyes should be. The holes oozed white liquid, as if she were weeping tears of the not-milk.

She walked toward me as if she could still see. Her mouth opened. Each of her teeth came to razor-sharp points.

"You can't leave us, you realize," Yrsa said. Her tongue snapped out like the lash of a scorpion's tail. Then she pulled a piece of porcelain from her own pocket, rolling it in her hand. A threat. When she held it up, everything inside me stilled.

"Who does it belong to?"

"You already know the answer to that."

A strangled noise came from my throat. I wanted to swipe the porcelain piece from her fingers, but Sido had already come up behind her. I couldn't risk it. I had to go.

"The maître wants you inside by two or he'll snap this in half himself. Now that you've seen firsthand what my teacup can do, I suspect I'll see you shortly," she said, waggling the piece of porcelain. It wasn't an eye—it was a finger, but not Zosa's petite one.

This porcelain finger belonged to a man.

32

I stumbled down more cobbled streets, through a city full of beasts, trying to stop crying.

Not real, not real, I chanted to myself, picking my way to the banks of the Noir. At the iron rail, I finally stopped running. Zosa squawked when I dropped her cage and vomited.

Even with the nightmare, Zosa still appeared the same. She pecked at my hand, quivering. "I'm so sorry," I said. I tried rubbing her feathers, but she bristled at the touch, her eyes squeezing shut. "We'll fix it all, I promise."

As soon as the words came out, I bit down on the inside of my cheek. The promise was another lie to protect her, like most of the lies I'd told her over the years.

"Actually, I don't know what to do. I'm scared to death and tired. I'm so tired I could keel over." Zosa's head peeked out from her feathers. I wiped silver from my face and blinked. "And I feel like I just let fifty snails scuttle snot across my eyeballs."

She nudged the bars.

"Don't look at me like that." Even as a bird, her dark eyes

studied me. "I can't believe I'm talking to a bird."

She squawked as if she could understand me.

"All right, all right. A very clever, very spirited young lady trapped in bird-form."

With one hand on her cage, one hand on the rail, I kept moving. After a few minutes, I found some stairs leading to the riverbank. I rested the cage on the ground so I could splash handfuls of water on my face.

"The time! What's the time?" I shouted at a row of men with fishing rods. They all took a step back except one old man. "Not yet eleven," he said with a toothless grin.

Three hours.

My hair hung in wet clumps around my shoulders. I combed through it and shoved it into a tight bun. I needed to think.

"What do I do?" I asked Zosa. I couldn't storm into the hotel; I'd be recognized in an instant. I needed a disguise, along with help.

I thought of Bel and my chest ached. I wanted help so badly. Then I remembered where we were, what it meant.

The fishermen jumped back when I walked toward them, attempting to smooth out my dripping dress. "I'm in dire need of a large, colorful wig. Can someone kindly point me in the direction of Atelier Merveille?"

✳

On the outside, Atelier Merveille was an elegant mix of frescoed stone and gold leaf. Stepping inside, however, felt like diving into a fancy, frosted cake. Gilded stairs gave way to taffeta-paneled walls dripping in a palette of sugared colors: mint, lavender, and cream. Dolled-up clerks gaped as I waltzed past, their shellacked cherry smiles dimming at the sight of my damp hair, the birdcage. Luckily no one stopped me.

I didn't find Béatrice in the shoes, or with the powders and striped tins of crème de rose. I didn't find her among the scarves, or exotic feathered hats, or near the swan tower of pearlescent macarons inside Salon de Patisserie. I found her in the dressing rooms, of course, seated amid a lavish heap of fabric. A towering pale purple wig sat beside her, bedecked with steel butterflies.

When she saw me, she jumped up. Her eyes grew at the splotches of silver on my neck. My face crumpled, overwhelmed with relief.

"Oh, I cannot wait to hear this." She swished her wrist and her gears clattered. "Don't make me force it out of you. Because I will."

A clerk in a ruffled apron arrived with a tray of iced buns. Béatrice waved the clerk away then ushered me to sit. Instead, I paced as I told her the truth about my contract and how it never worked on me, then I went over every detail since I kicked the oranges. Aside from a couple of gasps and a bit of clucking, Béatrice listened, until I came to the part about choosing the cosmolabe.

She scoffed. "My soul's desire is not fixing toilets."

Over the past few days, I'd thought through everyone's artéfact. What Alastair said made sense. "What if it's not about toilets? You genuinely care about the people who work for you. I think your desire to always keep us together, to fix any of us who feel broken, manifests in your gears."

Her mouth opened then shut, speechless for once. So I continued on with the rest of it until the moment I decided to find Béatrice here. I didn't tell her about Margot. Bel had said he'd already tried and it made no difference. Still, I was curious. "What is it about this place that made you want to come here?"

With the flick of her finger, the steel butterflies soared from the pale purple wig up to the ceiling then descended in a column of steel, stacking neatly on her palm. Then a single screw untwisted itself from the top butterfly. Béatrice rolled it between her fingers. "I made all the butterflies myself, you know, adding a screw to each one. For a long time, I wanted to perform at the soirées and use them as a prop."

"Perform?"

She shrugged. "Foolish as it was, I used to talk about it. I put together an act similar to the Illusioniste's." Her voice grew bitter. "Some saw it and called me *Mechanique* in mocking whispers."

Yrsa called her that from time to time in the kitchens. And to her face.

Béatrice threaded her fingers through the dress fabrics. She tossed a gauzy piece in the air and watched it flutter down. "I wanted a dress to practice in, so I went to speak with a member of L'Entourage de Beauté. It was the first time I'd set foot in Salon de Beauté." The edges of her mouth turned down. "And it did something to me."

"What?"

"Nothing tangible, but I felt something strange—an emptiness at the sight of it. Here." She tapped the center of her chest, at her heart. "I thought if I could visit the real Atelier Merveille, that emptiness might go away."

"Has it?"

"No. To be honest, it feels worse right now than it ever has."

Her words caused an ache in my throat. I wanted to say something to help her, but I knew there was nothing I could say that would change anything.

"Why am I even here?" Béatrice wiped her nose on a length of satin, then waved her hands. "Enough of this emotional nonsense. Tell me the rest."

So I did. Her hands balled into fists when I ended on Bel's finger. "I'm going to destroy the contracts," I said.

"You just told me only Alastair can void them."

"I'm not going to merely void them. I'm going to obliterate them."

"I see," she said, skeptical. "And how exactly will you manage that?"

Céleste didn't have the answers I wanted, but she'd given me an idea. During the walk here, a tenuous plan formed.

Quickly, I relayed how it would all play out. Béatrice shook her head. "Too dangerous."

"That's the problem," I said solemnly. "Even if we managed it, guests and staff could die, not to mention one of us. I couldn't risk it with a hotel full of people." I sank to the floor, wishing the thick carpet held all the world's answers. "I was hoping you might know what to do."

"Me?" Béatrice leaned back against the heaping pile of dresses.

Fabric billowed out around her like puffs of candy-coated clouds. "You know, I always thought you'd make an excellent suminaire," she said, sending her butterflies to the ceiling. "The stoic one who would dazzle crowds with her pigheadedness."

"Are you listening? Alastair is going to kill Bel in less than three hours if I don't turn myself in."

I realized that after everything, this would be as far as I'd go. I thought of Bel's face buried in my neck, his hands racing over my skin.

Then other images came to mind: Bel on the floor, dripping blood like Céleste, Zosa on that waxy table. My palms covered my eyes and there, right inside the famed dressing rooms of Atelier Merveille, I nearly fell apart. Until I heard Zosa flapping her wings at a whirring of gears.

I glared at Béatrice. "What are you doing?"

A steel cloud whizzed to the cage and opened the door. Zosa flew out, landing in front of me, hopping back and forth on spindly legs.

Béatrice reached over and attempted to ruffle Zosa's feathers, but my sister pecked at her hand. "You're not a very nice birdy, are you?"

No, my sister wasn't nice when she was peeved. From the sharp curve of her beak, I imagined she could be much worse as a bird.

"Come here." I tapped my shoulder. Zosa flew up and landed right at the spot I touched, nuzzling my ear.

"She listens to you," Béatrice said.

She was right. I'd noticed a handful of strange little moments over the past day. I was no Frigga, but I felt like my sister was still there beneath the feathers and she could somehow understand me. "I think she still knows me, too. Lot of good it does me now."

I ran a finger against Zosa's neck and she cooed. For the first time in ages, I wished I could ask for her advice. My sister was clever; she'd come up with something good.

"I should have listened to you more often," I said.

Zosa puffed out her chest and fanned her tail feathers like a pint-size peacock.

"Do you understand me?"

She hopped up and down and fluttered her wings.

A clerk came in, a mannequin head in both hands, each topped with an enormous pastel wig twice as large as the purple one on the floor, just like Des Rêves's. At the sight, my sister took off, pecking at the poor clerk's face. Wigs fell to the carpet as the woman ran off shrieking. Zosa perched atop a garish powder blue wig and did something that made Béatrice's jaw drop.

"Did you see what your little bird just did?" She pointed to a sludge of white dripping down the side of the blue wig. "I'll have to pay for it now."

I would have laughed had an idea not shot across my mind. That night in Salon d'Amusements the guests ran screaming, scared away by the library bird. There were hundreds more birds inside the aviary. I might be able to get all the guests out. Frigga had deftly commanded the birds in her room, and she had an aviary key. I would need her help. Along with Zosa's.

Béatrice tugged a length of ivory silk from under my heel. "You're standing on a dress."

I barely heard her, because a plan took root in my mind—a long shot at best, but it was there. "I figured it out."

As the words tumbled from my mouth, Béatrice grew quiet. After I was finished, her eyes moved down the length of me. She wrinkled her nose. "You expect to waltz into the hotel looking like that?"

Not exactly. Someone would spot me from across the lobby. I needed a disguise.

With every shred of dignity I could muster, I swallowed twice and said, "How quickly can you give me a makeover?"

33

The sun was high as I stood outside the hotel by myself, feeling rather exposed.

Béatrice had stuffed me into a vibrant ruby number with a tightly corseted waist and extravagant bustle. It spilled behind me in a tiered waterfall of crimson chiffon. I begged for her to choose a paler color. Something demure. Not so ostentatious. She didn't listen, just tutted and slapped my hand away and told me this was the color of the season. If I were to be believed as a lady from Champilliers invited to stay at Hotel Magnifique, I would need to dress the part.

A white wig powdered with gold dust cascaded down my neck and back, tickling my ears. My fingers itched to reach up and tug the thing off, to loosen the corset and scrape the layers of powder and rouge from my face. I felt like a trussed swine walking to its own spit.

At the top of the steps, a doorman pulled open the black-lacquered door and studied me.

"Oh, I can't believe I'm here!" I squealed, and waved the purchase receipt from Atelier Merveille, then fanned myself with it furiously so the doorman couldn't tell it wasn't an invitation. If he suspected a signed staff contract had allowed me entrance, everything would be over.

It seemed to work because he tipped his hat and said, "Welcome to Elsewhere."

A porter appeared. "Bags, mademoiselle?"

"My valet will deliver them to the door shortly," I said in Verdan-niere, trying to mask my southern accent.

My stomach lurched. Alastair greeted a guest across the lobby. On the outside, he looked youthful, happy even. No sign of rippled skin or bruising on his fist from punching the moon window. That meant the aviary had probably acquired another dull bird.

Alastair's eyes caught mine for a second before darting away. He didn't seem to recognize me. In fact, none of the staff paid me any attention. I slipped to the back of the lobby, dipping into an alcove behind the grand stairs. A pewter clock ticked next to my ear. One o'clock.

I glanced down at an extremely low settee. I didn't know how one went about sitting in a corset and bustle. I bent down then immediately hopped up at the sharp stab of boning between my ribs. A group of maids walked by, watching me flail.

If I survive today, I'll burn this dress, I thought. No, that wasn't right. If I survived today, I would gladly wear this dress again. I would gladly wear a thousand dresses just like it, or three-foot wigs, or stuck-on moles. So long as they were my choice.

"There you are. Oh, I thought something had happened." Béatrice rushed over and straightened the ruffles on my skirts as if she were a member of Entourage de Beauté. She gave my fingers a tug. "Keep smiling, chérie, and follow me."

We moved to a narrow hall where a laundry cart sat against a wall. Béatrice stopped me before we reached it. "I have to warn you the plans have been altered."

"What do you mean *altered*?" I looked around for a nest of hair. "Where's Frigga?"

"In her room. Do you think I'd let my sister partake in your ridiculous plan?" Hellas's silver locks were pulled into a bun, sharpening the angles of his deep golden face.

I shuffled backward, my whole body tensing at the sight of him.

"He was there before I had a chance to speak with Frigga," Béatrice explained. "He's not going to stop us."

That was a small measure of relief at least. But Hellas would never let us inside the aviary. We needed Frigga's help with the birds. I couldn't send Zosa in alone.

"We can't do this without—" My mouth stopped moving at the sound of clattering metal. A key ring dangled from Hellas's fingers.

"I'm taking my sister's place."

I couldn't believe it. After everything, he would help me again.

"I'm sorry, Jani. He overheard Frigga and me speaking then he simply took her keys and followed me."

The Botaniste met my eyes. There was something there that wasn't before—a little glint that wasn't cruel or hate-filled. But this was Hellas. "You helped me escape. You said your debt was paid. Why are you helping us now?"

He gave me a bored shrug. "I'm sick of the guests trampling my cards."

Clearly a lie. There had to be more to it. But I didn't push.

Hellas wasn't Frigga. He didn't have command over the birds, but he had an aviary key. And the minutes were ticking away.

A pair of dark eyes peeked out from under the sheet laid over the laundry cart. Zosa was tucked beside a maid's frock. I could still picture the shape of her real face. I remembered her as clear as day— always too small—but as a bird, she looked more helpless than I'd ever seen her. *But she's not*, I kept reminding myself. I would lose her if I didn't trust that she could help us now.

Part of me felt the urge to tuck her under my chin until it was all over. Instead, I bent so my nose was level with her head. As simply as I could, I whispered what I needed her to do. When I finished, she nudged my nose with the tip of her beak.

"Do you really understand me?" I asked, hoping she might answer.

She nudged me again. My clammy hands stuck to her feathers as I ruffled her neck. I winced when I brushed the scar tissue and mangled bone at the tip of one wing. She had proven she could fly, but it was still difficult to trust she could do the rest.

"Enough of this." Béatrice pulled the maid's frock from beside Zosa and shoved me inside a small storage closet. "Hurry and put it on. And don't you dare wrinkle that red dress. I plan to ask Thalia to change it to a color that will suit me better. For the price I paid, I'm going to wear it day and night when this is all over."

I grinned. "So your suminaire's name is Thalia?"

She rolled her eyes and shut the door.

After I was changed, I wiped the gold dust from my neck. Then I took off the wig. With nothing to hold it back, my dark curls spilled down my shoulders.

"What did you do with the dress?" Béatrice asked when I stepped out.

"I folded it neatly and stuffed it in a mop bucket. You can get it later."

"I don't know why I'm agreeing to this."

"You're agreeing because we have a chance."

One corner of her mouth lifted. That tiny gesture tugged at my heart. The hopeful feeling lasted until she held up the last piece of my outfit: an ivory satin eye patch we'd quickly commissioned at Atelier Merveille. I bent as she tied it over one of my eyes.

"Are you ready?" I asked.

"Not at all," she said with a half-hearted smile. She then shoved her tin of gears down my pocket. "That's half of them. Lose a single gear and I'll send Chef to braid your hair."

I threw my arms around her in a tight hug.

"Remember to wait ten minutes then meet me in the back of the kitchens," she said.

I nodded, and she kissed my cheek and left.

Only Hellas left.

My palms were slick as I approached him. "Why are you helping me again? And don't tell me it's because you're sick of your cards getting trampled."

"You were right," he said.

"Excuse me?"

"I tried to tell myself we were safe from Alastair because Frigga and I were useful. But the truth is, I hate him. I hate how he collects suminaires. He promises me he'll turn them all back one day. He uses it as an excuse, and now . . . now I can barely stand myself." His fingers curled into fists. "But I continued hiding those birds for him so Frigga and I wouldn't be next. For too long I've kept my head down and gone along with it because a part of me grew used to living with the fear, and I didn't think I could do anything to change it." He fixed his attention on me. "Then I realized a kitchen maid was braver than me, and frankly, it pissed me off."

My mouth hung open while he took Zosa's cart and wheeled it in the direction of the aviary.

After he was out of sight, I steadied myself against the wall as Alastair's face swam in my mind, his ink running across my flesh, pouring up my nostrils, choking me, until all I knew was purple and then nothing.

Taking a deep breath, I forced away the image. There wasn't time for fear. A steely determination rooted inside me. If I wanted to see my sister again, I had to move.

34

The kitchens were too busy for anyone to notice a maid wandering through. I adjusted my eye patch as I came around the corner by the deep freeze and halted at the sight of Béatrice standing beside Madame des Rêves.

She must be performing tonight, because she wore a foot-tall chartreuse wig embellished with gemstones. Her pale dress dripped over her like a glass of poured champagne.

"Béatrice told me you were recently demoted," Des Rêves said when she saw me. A smile slipped up her lips at the sight of my eye patch.

"I was," I said, and inched away from her. I still wore Maman's necklace, which meant the silver talon probably wouldn't do anything, but her long nails would, along with her commanding voice if she suspected anything was amiss.

Béatrice turned to me and cleared her throat. "I already explained to Madame that Alastair promised dignitaries from Verdanne a tour of the kitchens, and how he'd requested that you both bring Issig to his office as soon as possible." She gestured to the floor where the cage I had used to carry Zosa across Champilliers sat empty.

"I still don't understand why he didn't tell me himself," Des Rêves said.

Béatrice shrugged. "He seemed hurried. He said something about guests demanding to know why we were in Champilliers."

"Then where's Frigga? She always helps with these things."

"She was busy."

Des Rêves huffed. "Then let's get this over with. I have a show in less than an hour."

I lifted the cage and held it out for Des Rêves to take.

"I'm not touching that thing," she said. "Carrying cages is Frigga's job. Now hurry up and open the door."

She wanted me to go inside the deep freeze with her.

"I'll go," Béatrice offered, and tried to take the cage.

That wouldn't work. I needed her in the aviary. "It's all right," I said. "I can handle this."

"Then . . . I guess I'll find you later." She gave me a stern look and walked off.

Des Rêves cleared her throat. "Are we going to do this or stand around like mindless maids?" She stepped to the deep freeze door. "Where's the handle?"

"There isn't one." I rapped the steel twice.

Just like before, the door blew open with a blast of cold. We stepped forward and the door slammed, shutting us inside.

The scene hadn't changed. Issig sat chained to the wall, body still as stone.

"So he's dead." Madame des Rêves stepped toward him.

"Don't," I said when she lifted a hand to one of his broken white fingers. Ice began to chip off, but Des Rêves didn't notice. She touched her silver talon, except she didn't lift it to his flesh. Instead, she walked around him. My teeth chattered when the temperature dipped. I pointed at the talon. I needed her to turn him into a bird. "Do it already."

She didn't. Instead, she played with the artéfact, turning it in her fingers.

"It took me a little while. Béatrice is a very clever little liar."

A terrible feeling shot through me. "What do you mean?"

She glanced at my eye patch. "When Yrsa removes an eye, it's painful. Even though suminaires heal quickly, they're still laid up for more than an hour. But Béatrice wouldn't know. She's been able to avoid the whole ordeal. At least, she had, up until Alastair hears about this." She lunged forward, ripping the eye patch off me. "Just what I thought."

The sweat clinging to my neck turned icy. I took a step back. "You forget. Alastair is still waiting for us." My voice shook.

"Pishposh. Even if you weren't lying about your eye, I know he would never let anyone take Issig out of here. I just went along with it because I wanted to see Issig for myself. Alastair forbids it, you know. He lets Yrsa come in here, but he doesn't quite trust me around him." She walked in an arc around the frozen suminaire. "He was as powerful as Bel once, perhaps more. A living freezer. So much wasted magic."

"You tricked me."

I realized my mistake when she reached into the neck of her dress and pulled out the hand mirror. From this distance, the tarnished metal gleamed with an oily shine. A low, dangerous humming vibrated from it.

I backed against the wall. Other artéfacts didn't work on me, but the mirror *pulled* magic from a suminaire. It seemed different somehow. Powerful. A ringing sounded in my ears and I couldn't look away. "What are you doing with that thing?"

"I'm taking your magic for myself," she said simply. "Then I'll use a smidgeon to turn you, my sweet, into a pretty little bird." She tapped her lip with a sharp nail. "I might take Issig's magic as well. Alastair won't be pleased, but I'll have you to blame for everything."

I tried to push my way out of the freezer but the door wouldn't budge. She took a step toward me. "I know about your copper spoon," I said.

That stopped her in her tracks. "Oh?"

"Céleste told me."

"And how is Céleste?"

I swallowed hard. "Dead. Yrsa cracked her eye."

"That's for the best."

"For the best?" I tried to control my reaction, but the woman had taken advantage of her stolen power in the worst ways, and I hated her for it. "Why are you so cruel?"

She laughed. "I'm not cruel. I'm *spectacular*."

My spine drew straight at the word.

"That's it," I said, thinking through everything Céleste had told me. "When you first came to the society, you could only use the

copper spoon. No one paid attention to you, did they?"

She flinched, and I knew I'd struck a nerve.

"You would have been surrounded by some of the most awe-inspiring suminaires there ever were."

"I was weak then," she said. "But not for long."

Bel's words came to me: *You're stronger than I thought.*

He was right; I was strong. My strength was the kind of power that Des Rêves lacked, a power that had nothing to do with magic.

"Everything terrible you do is to hold on to the magic you've stolen, to make yourself *feel* spectacular. But underneath it all, you're a horrible, weak person. Probably weaker now than when you used that copper spoon."

Her face mottled. "Why would you ever think something like that? I'm not weak. I'm—"

As she spoke, Issig placed his hands around Madame des Rêves's neck.

She spluttered and reached up, trying her best to remove Issig's hands from her flesh by digging her nails into his skin. It didn't work. Her fingers turned a grayish blue then began to shatter, along with her lips, the tip of her nose. The air smelled sour. Des Rêves's mouth opened wide in an attempt at a scream, but only a cloud of ice dust puffed out. I choked, my hands going to my own throat while the veins in her neck bulged. Splintering.

Issig wasn't a corpse, but Madame des Rêves was. Frozen through, her face cracked in two when she hit the floor. That terrible mirror shattered along with the rest of her. I dared a quick glance down at

Des Rêves's corpse, the pieces of her scattered about like a smashed dinner plate.

I braced myself against the wall, trying not to lose the contents of my stomach, but the cold crept through my clothes, under my skin, and I began to shake. My gorge rose and I had to look away before I gagged.

This woman had probably been alive for a hundred years or more, all because of the travesties she'd committed. Now she was gone, and I'd had a hand in it. I felt light-headed. My legs began quaking from shock. They threatened to give out, but there was nowhere to sit, no time to waste.

I had to do something, but I didn't know what. Des Rêves was a crucial part of the plan. Forcing her to turn Issig into a bird small enough to fit in the cage was the next step. Having her turn him back once I brought him to Alastair's office had been the other. Turning my sister back. The rest of the birds—

As much as I'd hated Des Rêves, I needed her. Everything hinged on her ability to use the talon.

Béatrice would be with Hellas now, doing their part, and expecting me to do mine. If I couldn't manage it, I doubted I'd see anyone again, or walk out of this place alive. I shook my head as my plans unraveled around me.

Issig looked from Des Rêves's cracked corpse to me. The room grew colder as he strained against his chains.

Think, I told myself. There had to be something else for me to try. I forced myself to look down at the corpse a second time. The silver

talon lay on the floor two feet from Des Rêves's cracked cheek.

I swayed on my feet at a sudden swell of nausea. Breathing through my nose, I slid one leg out, my foot maneuvering around the pieces of Des Rêves. Slowly, I caught the talon's chain with my toe and dragged it toward me. I snatched it and squeezed.

"Work, damn it," I ground out. Then I felt something. Nothing like when I'd coaxed the purple awning from the painting of Céleste, but it was there. I let the magic drift up my wrist. Holding my breath, I touched the edge of the talon to the tip of one of Issig's straining fingers.

A look of surprise came over his face. He folded into his clothes, shrinking. A second later, a small arctic tern stood still amid a pile of chains that no longer kept him prisoner.

I couldn't believe it. It worked.

But there was no time to stand around pleased with myself. I shoved the talon in my pocket. Now, to get him out. Carefully, I lifted Issig and shut him inside the cage. When I carried him into the kitchen, an eerie silence greeted me.

The kitchen was empty.

I skirted around a shelf stacked with oysters abandoned in bowls of water. Tiny dishes of black caviar were smashed across the tile, muddled with cracked ivory wafers and bent silver spoons. Not a single worker in sight, until I walked through the kitchen doors to a lobby plunged into chaos.

"They did it," I whispered to myself, then jumped back when three parakeets flew toward me. A stream of steel insects followed the birds, slicing the air like knives, then disappearing behind the aviary glass where more birds were shooting out in a steady stream, raging upward.

Hellas had opened the aviary.

A flock cornered a group of women, pecking at their earrings. At least twelve white peacocks surrounded another bemused guest who could barely hold them off with a charmeuse pouf. Birds were everywhere, dipping between doormen, pecking at brass buttons, and they were followed by a whirring mass of butterflies, all crafted from steel and a single gear.

I stared in awe at the suites along the second-floor balcony. As soon as each door opened, birds tore into the room. Disoriented guests ran out, panting, lifting their skirts, pulling on their shirts. One man even took off nude, desperately trying to don a frock coat while the filigreed buttons flapped along with his other naked bits.

Then I spotted Zosa, luminous as a sharpened gemstone. She favored one wing, but it didn't slow her. Her bright gold body darted across the center of the lobby, squawking at a group of dull wrens, kingfishers, and cardinals. The birds *listened.* Zosa led them—commanded them like soldiers in her steadfast army—soaring across hallways and dipping into suite after suite.

Shrieks and screams filled the air, but the loveliest sight of all was the black-lacquered door held open by the steady stream of exiting guests.

Time for me to go.

I raced through countless hallways and ballrooms lining the lobby level. Candles burned purple flames and the carpet was dusted with feathers. My hands ached from carrying the cage, but a slow fire burned inside me, kindled by Bel, by my friends, my sister. It shone brighter than any candle flame, leaving no room for fear, only a simmering hatred stoked with every step.

I skidded to a halt in a familiar hallway and jiggled the knob on Alastair's office door. Locked. Fishing in my pocket, I pulled out Béatrice's gears.

Earlier, she'd dismantled two dressing room doors, locks and all. Then she instructed me as I took her gears and dismantled the other four doors. I didn't have the same feel for the gears as she did, so they weren't as speedy for me as they were for her, but the office doorknob was soon on the floor.

Once inside, I raced around the desk and stopped. My throat closed up. The third drawer down hung open. Empty. The infinite ledger wasn't here.

35

The other five desk drawers also proved fruitless. So did the shelves, the curio, and the small armoire in the back with handles made of bronzed claws that clasped my fingers when I flung the doors open to more nothing. Alastair must have taken the ledger.

I dropped the cage at my feet. Issig cawed.

"Sorry," I said. It was difficult to imagine such a small bird had all that power. Worthless power now.

I thought it would be enough. I'd watched Issig turn an itinerary written in Alastair's purple ink to icy dust. I thought if I could bring him here, change Issig into a man next to the drawer, he could destroy everything.

But it didn't matter. Nothing mattered until I found the ledger. *If* I found the ledger.

Before I could consider what to do next, a little golden bird flew in and perched on the edge of a chair. My eyes welled at the sight of her. I felt her porcelain finger in my pocket, silently cursing myself for not burying it deep in the ground in Champilliers where no one could ever break it.

I touched Zosa's feathers, desperately wanting to see her face. I gripped the talon and reached for her, but she hopped away.

"Let me change you back," I pleaded.

She pecked at my hand, knocking the talon to the ground.

"Stop it," I cried out when her beak drew blood. When I lifted the talon a second time, she did it again. "Don't you want me to change you?"

She took hold of a lock of my hair and jerked my head sideways toward the door.

"That hurts." I leaped up, but she was already shooting down the hall. When I didn't follow straightaway, she flew back and tugged my sleeve.

"All right, all right."

Lifting Issig's cage, I hurried after Zosa. My head pounded. But soon the tight corridor gave way to a world of white paper. We'd come out inside the aviary.

The place was a disaster. Birds still flapped inside. Plants were down, crumpled and trodden. There were great cracks in the aviary glass high above like someone had tried to smash it with furniture. A large chunk had fallen away. Another could fall at any moment.

Frigga cowered near the wall shooing birds out the door with a paper frond. We both froze at a cracking noise.

I looked up. More cracks snaked downward. Glass groaned and popped, and sounds poured in from the lobby: guests screaming, chirping, workers shouting. Shattering.

The dragonfly glass was coming down.

"Get back!" I lifted Issig's cage and ran with it to the center of the aviary. Frigga followed. We huddled together the same moment a large piece of glass fell, crunching against a paper tree near where we'd just stood.

"Is it really Issig?" Frigga stared at the cage, tears sliding down her face.

"It is. We have to get him out." I looked around. "Where's Hellas?"

She pointed to the lobby. "The maître was out there with Yrsa. Hellas . . . He went to speak with him."

"What happened?"

More tears tumbled down her cheeks.

"*Tell* me."

"He never came back."

"Do they know you're here?"

She shook her head. "Hellas didn't even know I was here until he walked in. But I couldn't just leave the birds."

Zosa swooped down and landed on my shoulder. When Frigga reached for her, my sister hopped toward my ear.

"That bird knows you," Frigga said.

I ruffled Zosa's golden feathers. "She does."

I didn't know what to do. If we stayed in the aviary and the glass came down, we'd die, but if we went out in the lobby, we'd wish we had. If Alastair were out there, he'd probably seize Issig as soon as he saw us. If I could get to the ledger before Alastair took Issig away, before he came near me with his inkwell, we could all have our lives back.

But I didn't know how. The how seemed impossible.

Keep your sister safe, I could hear Maman say. Then I heard other voices—everyone's voices—shouting and scolding and begging me to help.

Zosa regarded me solemnly. "What would you have me do?" I looked around, my eyes snagging on something. "What's that?" I pointed.

Frigga turned and took in the shelf heaped with junk. "Aviary supplies."

Beside it was the metal laundry cart Béatrice had stocked.

"I think I know how to get Issig out, but I need both of you to do as I say," I said to Zosa and Frigga, then I took off toward the wall of supplies, my sister flying close behind.

✳

My hands shook as I walked beside Frigga while she pushed the laundry cart into the ravaged lobby. Suitcases were flung about, clothes spilled, chairs broken. A few guests still rushed out the door, while a small group huddled under the remains of the red piano. Near them, weightless feathers from inside a room pillow curled up an entire wall, while flecks of blood spotted the white marble.

Sido's hand clamped down on my shoulder. "Been looking for you. We know you turned Issig into a bird. Now where is he?"

Someone must have found what was left of Des Rêves and put it together.

I nudged my chin at the cage on top of the cart. Luckily, Frigga had known where canvas was kept. We'd wrapped a length around the bars, hiding the bird inside.

Sido rattled it with his free hand. "Doesn't weigh much."

"What do you expect? It's a bird. Now where's the maître?"

"Everyone's inside waiting for you to show up." He motioned to the salon. My stomach did a little flip at *everyone*. "You'll stay here," he said to Frigga.

Her hands tightened on the cart handle. She met my eyes and a look passed between us. Sido grunted and shoved me forward.

Salon d'Amusements was in worse shambles than the lobby. Chairs were broken. Tables upended. Tea sandwiches and smashed porcelain littered the floor. Violet flames reflected off crystals in the chandeliers, flinging purple light everywhere.

Sido carried the cage toward the center of the salon, pulling me along.

As we moved, I kept my eyes peeled for the infinite ledger. Across the sea of upturned tables, three suminaires sat around a booth.

Both Béatrice and Hellas remained deadly calm. They were gagged, hands bound. Yrsa sat opposite them, her surgeon's kit opened next to her teacup, Bel's porcelain finger resting beside it. The alchemist touched the porcelain with a pinkie. It rolled to the table's edge. I held my breath when she caught it in her palm then glanced behind me with a smirk.

I whirled.

Bel sat on a barstool. He caught my eyes and blinked.

All the warmth left me.

His mannerisms were still there: how he cocked his head, the way his lips pursed, even that damned piece of hair that fell across his brow. Except his face appeared as blank as a shop mannequin. He was still him but not. Missing. Alastair risked doing that to him because he'd helped me.

I glared at Yrsa. "Give me his finger."

"Don't think so." She placed the porcelain next to that terrible little cup.

"There you are!" Alastair shouted and the chandeliers shuddered. He stepped out from the door that led behind the stage, a row of suminaires trailing at his heel. Every single one clutched artéfacts, their eyes trained on me.

I searched Alastair's hands. He held the inkwell in his fist, the infinite ledger tucked beneath his arm.

"Take Issig to the deep freeze," Alastair ordered Sido. "Chain the cage up." Sido nodded and took a few steps before Alastair stopped him. "Wait." In a sudden movement, Alastair ripped the canvas from the cage.

The cage wasn't Issig's, but an old, rusted one with a missing door I'd found on the supply shelf. It now contained a bird the color of molten gold.

"Where's Issig?" When I didn't answer, Alastair kicked a table. "He belongs to *me*."

"You're wrong. He's not yours." I turned to Bel, to the booth where Béatrice and Hellas sat. Alastair might be the one controlling the contracts, but I had people who loved me, people who I trusted to help.

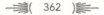

I whistled.

Earlier, I'd given instructions for this moment. Zosa flew out of the cage, flapping her wings at Alastair. His hands darted up to cover his face and he dropped the cage and the ledger. I took a step in his direction.

"Grab the girls!" Alastair shouted to the suminaires. At once, they started toward us.

I turned. Frigga was already rolling the laundry cart into the salon. In one swoop, she ripped the canvas sheeting off the top and touched her manacle to the cart's handle. Using her magic, she'd manipulated metal and fashioned the entire bottom of the cart into a cage. Twenty-two dull birds—all the birds left inside the aviary—flew straight for the row of suminaires, for Sido, while Zosa darted around Alastair, pecking at his ears.

I was almost to the ledger. I pushed chairs out of the way. But before I could grab it, someone got there first.

"Bring it to me," Alastair ordered.

Bel blinked and turned the ledger over in his hand. His dark eyes fixed on me, like he could somehow see past the haze of enchanted ink.

"The ledger. Now!" Alastair roared.

"Bel," I begged. "Please. Give it to me."

Bel's eyebrows drew together, but he didn't step toward me. My eyes burned when he handed the ledger to Alastair.

He didn't give me the ledger.

"Jani, hurry!" Frigga shouted.

I didn't know what to do, but somehow I had enough left in me

363

to race to the cart, numb. I felt numb. I blinked back useless tears. Without the ledger, Issig didn't matter. Frigga pulled his cage up. My head shook. "I—I didn't get the ledger."

"What do you mean?" Her face fell. "But your sister—"

"She knocked it away, but Bel grabbed it before I could get there. He gave it back to Alastair."

Frigga looked behind me and swore.

I turned. Alastair stalked toward us. Without hesitation, I gripped the silver talon and held it over Issig. "Stay back."

He stopped.

My eyes snapped to the ledger under his arm. Zosa flew over and landed on my shoulder. I squeezed the talon. I could still change Issig. He remembered who he was for a brief moment in the deep freeze. It might be enough.

"Don't," Alastair said, desperate, his eyes flicking to Zosa. "Your sister isn't a suminaire. If you change Issig, his cold will kill her."

He was right. Issig might have tried to steal the ledger once, but with his mind gone, he was deadly. All because of a contract.

His contract.

My free hand flew to Maman's necklace. If the necklace worked for Issig like it did for me, if it negated his contract and gave him back his mind, he could destroy the ledger himself without hurting anyone. Fumbling, I managed to unclasp it. I squeezed it. *What do I do?* There was no guarantee it would work. If it didn't, if Issig hurt Zosa—

"Don't be a fool. Give me the talon and I'll let you leave tonight.

You'll be safe, and you never have to see me again. Don't you want that?"

I did. Once. Now, his offer didn't make me feel anything. Everyone I cared about was in this room, and I needed to make a decision.

I looked at Zosa. Her dark eyes hung on mine. "What should we do?" I asked. It was her life too, after all. Tears broke over my lashes when she flew up and pecked at the talon, nudging it down, toward Issig.

Her choice.

Rarely had I listened to her. But I would now.

"Don't!" Alastair bellowed.

Cold hissed against my palms the moment the talon touched the arctic tern's head. The tern rippled. Growing. Brittle steel flung everywhere and the cage snapped away when Issig changed from bird to man.

Careful not to touch Issig's flesh, I clasped Maman's necklace around his neck. *Work, damn it,* I willed. Nothing seemed to happen to Issig. In fact, something felt wrong.

My scalp cooled as the sensation of a thick blanket of fog came over me. I blinked. The fog wasn't around me. It was inside my head, and it wouldn't clear.

I started to shiver. The room was freezing. Suminaires were backing away. Bel did the same, moving along the bar, while Yrsa scrambled up the stage with her teacup. The salon floor groaned from the cold. Zosa's tiny claws clung to the shoulder of my dress.

"You need to get back," a deep voice said.

I turned and stumbled. Issig watched me. He touched the pair of necklaces he wore. One was a white disk, the other a thin chain of ruddy gold.

That gold necklace. I'd worn it before I'd given it to him. It was an artéfact. But when I tried to remember who gave it to me, it felt like my mind was pushing against a solid wall.

"I said get back," Issig growled. The other necklace—the white disk at his neck, his artéfact—rattled. "Get to the stage now. Otherwise you'll be hurt."

Zosa shivered against my shoulder.

"Change him back!" Alastair shouted at me.

At the sound of Alastair's voice, rage flooded Issig's features. He rushed forward and ripped the ledger from Alastair's hand, just as I imagined he tried to do the day his mind had snapped. But this time, he had his artéfact.

The ledger's cover grew brittle from the cold and began to crumble away. Alastair tried to swipe it.

"Not this time," Issig said. In one swift movement, he smacked Alastair's hand and knocked the wolf-capped inkwell to the floor. It shattered on impact. Alastair cried out when the marble swallowed the broken well—wolf's head and all—as if it were nothing more than a smashed champagne flute.

The temperature dropped. I clambered over chairs toward the stage as the salon turned into a tundra. Wood splintered. My own breath grew painful in my lungs, but I kept moving, climbing.

Glass cracked across the front of Salon d'Amusements. The ground buckled as the air was replaced with a chill that froze the marrow of my bones.

I tucked Zosa under the crook of my neck, against my chest, as time itself seemed to slow. My eyes locked on Bel's from opposite sides of the room the same moment Issig opened the ledger wide. He plunged his hand inside and called up an explosion of cold right through the center of the salon.

36

I was standing, then I wasn't. I was on the stage, wedged between a frozen piece of wood and the back wall, too numb from cold to think. The only warmth I felt came from my sister, and my fingers that refused to let her go.

Bones creaked. My joints felt old, scraped and raw from a hundred summers at a tannery. I hissed as bits of ice and glass debris fell from my arms, my hair, my nose.

Zosa shivered against me. At the feel of her, I checked my pocket. My fingers grazed the rough edges of porcelain.

Zosa's finger had snapped in two.

No. I started to shake. *Look. She's alive, she's alive!* I told myself. But how? I turned and recoiled.

Yrsa had saved us in the end. Her body lay crushed under a large, splintered piece of wood that must have shot out in the blast. A ceiling beam. It ended mere inches from my neck. Next to her motionless hand rested the shattered remains of the teacup atop a frozen puddle of not-milk.

Whatever enchantment was done to Zosa's porcelain finger must have broken when the teacup smashed. I couldn't think of any other explanation.

I sat up and winced when my kitchen frock snapped like a crust of ice from the floor. Taking a painful breath, I looked around.

Salon d'Amusements lay in ruins.

The center of the room, where Issig had stood, fared the worst. Behind it, the great marble bar appeared whole, except that every glass vial had burst from the cold, contents shooting into the air and freezing solid in an instant. The thing looked like the sculptural aftermath of a great frozen fountain. It was strangely beautiful. From where I sat, I could make out a vein of silver nightmare shooting up from the colored ice.

Snow fell everywhere, drifting down from the ceiling, clumping on the floor. The glass wall dividing the salon from the lobby now hung in gnarled pieces, blasted apart. Great billows of white blew through the gaping hole, over the ravaged mess of lacquered wood tables, mangled and blanketed with snow.

I scooped a clump next to my feet and pressed it against the heat of my chest. The ice melted away, leaving behind a glob of soggy paper. My breath hitched when I caught a few pieces flecked with purple.

The paper snow blew everywhere, coating the air. The endless catalogues of artéfacts, enchantments, contracts—everything penned with purple ink inside that ledger—had been destroyed.

I touched my head, remembering that blanket of fog over my mind a mere minute ago. It was gone, my mind clear. With a shudder, I remembered how easily my mind had clouded over the moment I put the necklace around Issig's neck.

Through the ringing in my ears, I could hear shouts. My name.

Béatrice stood amid shattered bits of crystal. Her gag had fallen away. She was covered, head to toe, in clumps of paper snow as she picked her way through the broken debris. When she got to me, she stopped, staring—at my face, my hands, the trembling bird at my neck—in disbelief. Blood dripped from a gash at her brow, but otherwise she seemed unharmed. Thank god she wasn't close to Issig when he summoned the blast. I threw an arm around her. Tears flowed then froze in an instant down our cheeks.

"I remember now." A sob shook her chest. "My sister—"

"Is alive."

"What?"

"She lives in the blue city north of the continent, the one we stopped at. Bel introduced me to her."

Béatrice appeared to be at a loss for words. I wanted to ask her more about Margot, but now was not the time.

"Here," I said. The tin of gears hummed when I fished them from my pocket and placed them in her cold, open palm.

Zosa cooed.

"I should go check on the others," Béatrice said, wiping her face. "Give you two time." She turned away, shouting more names, using her gears to clear rubble.

After she left, I pulled a finger down Zosa's neck. She trembled, but when she pecked at me, I knew she was unscathed. Her tiny eyes widened when the talon touched down on the edge of her wing.

In an instant, Zosa unfurled into a person. It was so sudden, I had no time to set her down. Before I could think, I lay sprawled on the floor, Zosa seated on my chest, legs akimbo, sopping golden feathers from her dress tickling my nose. I sat up and grabbed her shoulders for the first time in weeks. She threw her arms around me and squeezed me so tight, a muscle popped.

"Too tight," I said, and she laughed until I reached down and took her hands, felt her missing fingers, felt *her*. "Can I see?" I asked, but her head shook. She dragged her hand from mine and hid it in her damp skirt. I thought about snatching it back, inspecting it, but decided against it. She'd show me when she wanted to, and in her own time.

After a moment, she looked down, suddenly shy. Besides the day she lost her fingers, it had been weeks since we'd truly spoken.

"You helped with all this, you know," I said. "It wouldn't have happened without you."

"So I'm useful?" Her mouth quirked.

I wiped a tear. "And pushy."

She pinched my nose and I began to weep, and she was laughing. Then we were both soggy and damp, dripping with tears and giddy, digging up handfuls of melting paper snow. After a few minutes, Zosa grew quiet, picking paper from under a nail.

I took her undamaged hand, the only one she'd let me see. It was freezing. "I'm sorry that I didn't keep you close in the beginning." More tears tumbled down my cheeks. "I'm sorry about everything that happened here."

"It's not your fault," she said. "At least I got to sing."

"I saw you. You were spectacular."

"I was?" I nodded, and pink bloomed across her cheeks. "I re-member some bits, but a lot of it is hazy. How long was I a bird?"

I swallowed down a lump. "A while."

"What happened to you?"

That would take hours to answer and her teeth were beginning to chatter. I helped her up. She wanted to search for her friends—the two other chanteuses that performed alongside her who were still birds somewhere—so I promised to meet Zosa later when we were both snug in front of a fire and tell her everything. I needed to find someone first.

Slowly, I picked my way over to the wreck of the bar. Under-neath, Bel lay unmoving.

The knees of my kitchen frock crunched against broken glass when I knelt and brushed a layer of paper snow from his cheek. His eyes were shut, his switchblade opened. Ice crusted his lashes, the corners of his mouth. My heart felt heavy in my chest.

Gently, I reached down and touched the bow of his lip. His lashes fluttered. He squinted and blinked away bits of frost. I hung motion-less over him, not daring to move or breathe.

Do you remember me?

He winced and reached for a lock of my hair that hung in a tangle next to his cheek, marveling at it. His mouth curved in a half smile. "I've never seen you with your hair down," he said, his throat rough. "It's . . . nice."

My face crumpled, and his smile fell away. Before I could choke out a sob, he sat up and gathered me into his lap. His fingers threaded through my hair as he looked me over.

I trembled when his hand smoothed down my back, then over my arms, my torso, and my neck, as if checking for cracks. "Hold still."

"I'm all right, you fool," I said, my voice thick.

Gently, he wiped tears from my cheeks. "I thought I'd never get to argue with you again."

"You missed your chance at a boring life."

He laughed. Then his warm arms wrapped so tightly around me, I could feel his heart thump against my own, like he was afraid I might vanish into air. We sat like that, tangled up together under the bar, until we were shivering from paper snow.

"My sister is herself," I said, burrowing into his warmth. "And Béatrice is unharmed."

He glanced to where the alchemist's broken body lay crumpled. "Yrsa?"

"Dead. Her teacup shattered. And I haven't seen Sido."

He nodded and pushed a clump of sodden hair away from my neck. A tremor moved through me as he stroked the skin below my ear. "Alastair?"

Alastair had been standing beside Issig. I didn't see him run, but I was trying to get away myself. "I don't know," I said.

"Then we should look."

Wincing, Bel rose and pulled me up alongside him. Together, we picked our way out of the salon and into the wrecked lobby.

Glass had scattered everywhere. Chairs were cracked. A cluster of guests still huddled together underneath the ravaged top of the bright red piano. Paper snow covered every surface. But unlike the pillow feathers, the snow fell *down*. It dusted the chandeliers and arched alcoves. It clumped on waxy branches of marvelous orange trees. It snuffed out all the colored flames.

"It's gone," Bel said with wonder, eyes fixed to the spot where the great glass aviary once stood. Above us, birds flitted through the gusts of snow.

A cluster of staff stood in the center of the lobby. Issig stood with them, draped from head to toe in canvas from the aviary supplies. He whispered to Frigga. She smiled and touched his collarbone where my mother's necklace still hung. Issig took Frigga's hand, twining their fingers together. I looked away when he pressed a kiss to her knuckles.

"Incredible," Bel said. "Someone finally freed Issig."

"Must have been a foolish soup girl," I said.

Bel's brows shot up.

A moment later, someone cried out, joyful, and Issig wrapped his arms around a man in a cook's uniform, like they were old friends. The contracts were destroyed. All the workers had their memories back.

Soon everyone clustered around a crumpled body on the floor.

Alastair.

His eyes were closed, his pale eyelids so blue-tinged they appeared translucent. A bit of blood leaked from the corner of his mouth and dribbled down his cheek.

Hellas toed his arm. "Is he dead?"

Bel checked his pulse. "His heart's beating. He might have

tried to run, but the blast must have knocked him out."

I looked from worker to worker, people who Alastair imprisoned. Hurt. I half expected someone to dash Alastair's head against the marble and end it. But no one moved. None of us wanted any more torture or pain today. Besides, without the hand mirror, Alastair didn't have any time left once his stolen magic wore off.

"I have an idea," Issig said. He stepped over Alastair's prone form and hoisted him up by the shoulders. "I know of a room that's no longer in use, where we can lock him up for a bit until we decide what to do." A small smile slipped over the suminaire's chiseled features. "Hellas, be a doll and take his feet. We'll move him to the deep freeze."

✳

Over the next few hours we rounded up birds. A large flock had holed up near the moon window. Even more flew out from various hiding places around the hotel. Hundreds squawked. I stood beside Bel and touched wing after wing with the silver talon.

Two dozen or so came out whole. The rest appeared just as Céleste had described, their appearances leached of color, their limbs spotted with holes.

Most holes were covered by clothing. A few were not. One scrawny child, no older than ten, fingered a hole in her pale arm the width of her wrist. And a brown-skinned man walked around with a misshapen hole in his calf.

That must have been where the hand mirror touched down. It was sickening to know that Des Rêves and Alastair did this for years. I remembered the feel of Céleste's hand, that wisp of tendon, and felt ill.

At least no one seemed to be in pain. Instead, all the trapped suminaires unfurled from birds into people too bewildered to do a thing but step out of the way.

The hotel was mostly empty of guests, but soon the freed suminaires took their places. Some were still dressed as performers in evening wear. Others were decked out in glittering frock coats, silken capes, and corseted gowns from another time. Some even wore stiff kitchen uniforms splotched with soup stains. But most were clothed in the garb they had arrived in.

I touched a bright emerald bird—one of the suminaires who still had magic—and it unfurled into an old woman with deep olive skin. She wore a cook's uniform from a different era. Bel stared at her, awestruck. She flung her arms around his shoulders. "We can all find our homes now," she said.

His home.

My chest tightened at what that meant.

After the cook left us to find more friends, Bel was curiously quiet. He seemed reluctant to leave my side, but a long line of birds were still waiting their turn. I swallowed down a knot in my throat. "You probably have more people to find. I can take care of the rest without you."

"Are you sure?" Slowly, he trailed the pad of his thumb up the side of my neck. I closed my eyes and let myself relax into the touch, just for a moment. I didn't want him to leave me here yet.

But soon he'll leave for good, for his home, I reminded myself. I forced my fingers to brush his hand away. "We'll talk later."

He hesitated for a moment, then he gave me a tight nod that twisted my stomach. "Later, then."

After Bel left, I changed the last of the workers. Zosa found me when I was finished. I took her hand and led her up the grand staircase. Together, we searched for a place to dry off, to rest, to figure out what came next.

Save for the mangled door, the *Ode to a Fabled Forest Suite* was immaculate. Two dressing robes hung in the wardrobe, each monogrammed with the letters "H. M." in shimmering purple thread. Zosa peeled off her dress. She donned the robe and climbed under the thick bedsheets, pulling them up to her chin.

I lifted a pot of tea to pour a cup, but no steam came out. I dipped a finger in the water. Lukewarm. The enchantment that had heated the teapot was written in the ledger. All the enchantments were. All the magic that had made this place so wondrous was gone.

I sank down beside Zosa, relieved to feel her body beside me. "What do you remember?"

I expected her to smile, carefree, like that day in Durc when the hotel came to town. But the corners of her lips turned down and she refused to meet my eyes.

"I don't want to talk about it now," she said through a yawn, fiddling with a silk tassel on her pillowcase. She still hid her other hand from me, but I could see it dancing beneath the sheets. "Do you think that doorman could make me something like his wooden finger?"

She didn't know about Bel's switchblade. I pictured Zosa with fours knives for fingers and tried my best not to let the idea of it show on my face.

I kissed her damp hair. "I'm sure he could figure something out."

We remained in the *Ode to a Fabled Forest Suite* for a handful of days. Zosa didn't want to leave and I refused to leave her. Béatrice stopped in often, bringing us food along with information about everything that was happening in the hotel. She shared stories of people who had found each other after decades, and even people who had never met befriending each other. After a little coaxing, she even told me the story of how she wound up here.

Years ago, her father had tried to marry both Margot and Béatrice off separately to the same wealthy neighbor. But since Margot wasn't interested in marrying and Béatrice wasn't interested in men, they ran away to Champilliers and took jobs at Atelier Merveille. Margot played piano around town at night, while Béatrice worked on an act hoping to join her sister onstage. The hotel appeared during a holiday they both took up the coast. That was the last time she remembered seeing her sister. She was angry, of course, but beneath it, there was hope baked into all her future plans—a hope I hadn't heard from her before. She wanted to visit Margot as soon as possible.

In fact, I'd learned that many of the trapped suminaires wanted to look for family members who might still be alive.

Béatrice also told me that she spoke at length to Issig about the explosion in the salon. Apparently his memories had rushed back the second I'd put the necklace on him. I could kiss that necklace. I didn't want to think about what would have happened if it hadn't worked.

Issig made sure it was returned to me the day after the explosion. I doubted it would ever again be as useful as it had been over the past few weeks, but that didn't stop me from promptly clasping it back around my neck.

Truthfully, I liked the weight of it against my skin, how the subtle vibration of magic soothed me. I also appreciated how it served as a reminder of how lucky I'd been. Sometimes I found myself touching the necklace and replaying different outcomes in my mind, and thinking about what was lost.

Despite our best efforts, there were casualties that day. Others had died in the explosion besides Yrsa, but no one I knew well.

The twins were gone. Frigga spotted Sido running out the front door right after the blast, and no one knew what happened to Sazerat.

Bel came into our suite from time to time, but Zosa was always with me, so we never said more than a few stilted words. I didn't want to know when he would leave for his home, and clearly he wasn't ready to tell me.

After a week had passed, I convinced Zosa to wear something other than a dressing gown. She hid her damaged hand in strips of bedsheets as I took her into Champilliers.

We dipped inside patisseries, and perfumeries, then Atelier Merveille, where we sat amid piles of lace and ruffles, promptly leaving when a clerk brought in a selection of enormous multicolored wigs.

Afterward, I showed her the hotel I knew. I led her through the back of the kitchens. I wove her down the maze of service halls. Then I introduced her to King Zelig, who insisted on continuing to operate the lift, even though it clanked and stuttered louder than before.

Later, when Zosa was nestled in bed, she turned to me. "Is it really over?"

"For now," I said, trying to convince myself of the same thing.

I reached up and ran a finger along a molten gold feather tucked behind my ear. I'd found it after the blast and couldn't seem to part with it. Whatever came next, Zosa and I would face it together.

✳

The following day, I found myself in the kitchens dressed in a soup-stained frock that had only appeared in the wardrobe of the *Ode to a Fabled Forest Suite* because Béatrice had put it there. I stood over a boiling copper pot helping Chef, whose real name was Gerde.

When my frock was thoroughly stuck to my back, I took off my apron and pulled down my hair. Then I crept up the many flights of stairs to the sixth-floor landing where Béatrice told me he might be.

Bel stood by himself at the moon window.

I wiped slick palms down my skirts and walked up beside him. For a few minutes, neither of us spoke. When I couldn't stand it any longer, I cleared my throat. "I heard Hellas found a large safe in Alastair's suite stuffed with Skaadan urd."

Bel nodded. "It's a fortune."

Béatrice had told me as much. She said a group of workers wanted to purchase building supplies, hire help, and repair the damage to the building. But money couldn't repair everything.

"How are the suminaires doing?" I asked.

"As well as can be expected. We handed out artéfacts to those who still had magic."

I had thought of that. Besides spending time with Zosa, thinking was all I'd done over the past few days. But mostly, I thought of the future, and what it might look like. "Do you think there are enough suminaires with magic left to perform tricks that could make this place . . . interesting again?"

He gave me a wry look. "What's going on inside that thick skull of yours?"

"Do you?" I pressed.

He rubbed the space between his brows, considering. "Nothing like Alastair's ink. But you wouldn't believe all the astonishing things some of the artéfacts can do." He took one of my hands and ran his thumb along my wrist. I tried not to tremble and failed miserably. "Why do you ask?"

"Béatrice told me that many—" I took a breath. "Many suminaires have been trapped for so long, they're not sure they have a home to go back to. Some didn't even know they were magical before being plucked from the crowd, and many who still have magic want to learn about it." I looked down at his hand twining mine. "Those without magic . . . Some of them are okay with it, but the majority of them are angry. They want whatever was done to them to be reversed."

"They told Béatrice that?"

"I'm sure it was the only way to get her to stop fretting over them," I said, picturing the worried look on Béatrice's face when she explained everything. "And I plan to do something about it. That's why I'm here."

His brow arched, but I didn't let it bother me. I'd be surprised if he wasn't a little bit skeptical.

"I want to keep this place up and running like it was. The signet ring might be only a fairy tale right now, but Céleste said herself that there was truth behind stories, and someone in the Société des Suminaires believed in the ring enough to add it to the catalogue of *known* artéfacts."

He dropped my hand. "You want to search for that godforsaken ring?" His voice was flat.

"Not just the ring. Even if it doesn't exist, the world is vast and unimaginable. Who's to say there isn't something else out there—another artéfact that might help? Those suminaires have been trapped behind glass for years. I think they're at least owed a chance to search for something." Bel opened his mouth, but I held up my hand. "Don't look at me like that. People died here because of what Alastair did. As long as we're repairing the hotel, we should at least try to do something." *And I want you to stay by my side and help*, I desperately wanted to add, but I couldn't get the words past my tongue.

His switchblade tapped his lip. "But I had thought you wanted to take Zosa to Aligney."

I managed a laugh for the first time that day.

"Don't laugh at me," he said.

I snorted. "I did want to take Zosa to Aligney, more than anything, but it's not where we belong. Right now, this place is my home as much as Aligney or Durc ever was. All the people I care about are here. This place . . . I want to make it a home for anyone who wishes to stay."

Bel didn't answer. Instead, he lowered his gaze to the pair of artéfacts around my neck. The weighty cosmolabe now hung from Maman's chain.

After too long a silence, Bel lifted his hand. "Can I?"

I nodded and flinched when his warm fingers grazed my skin to inspect the cosmolabe's elaborate mechanics. I didn't brush him off or push him away, even though I could barely breathe.

"I suspect you could get a feel for my key. You could try to use it if you wanted. You might like it." He looked at me from the corner of his eye. "And if we're going to search for an artéfact to help all those suminaires, it might be nice to not have to work every single midnight for the foreseeable future."

He would stay.

"But you wanted to leave so badly. Your family—"

A painful expression crossed his face.

"My mother came from a family with suminaire blood in her lineage, but she never told my father. She didn't have an artéfact, but she knew enough about première magie to keep my magic from hurting others. It probably would have been fine, but she decided to tell my father what I was when I was still so young—long before my magic ever had a chance to show itself—and my father grew afraid of me. He told me . . ." He swallowed. "He told me that he wished I was never born. My mother had heard about Alastair, that he took on suminaires and helped them. So when the hotel came to town . . ." His words trailed off. A haunted look came over his features.

"I'm so sorry."

He reached up and tucked a strand of hair behind my ear. "It was long ago. I doubt any of my family is left, and even if they are, I'm not sure I would want to see them." I gasped when his fingers grazed the inside of my elbow. "I want to stay on. To help."

"As the maître?"

His mouth slanted up. "You don't strike me as someone who would ever take orders from me, and I doubt I'd be able to work under you."

"Probably true. I imagine if I ever gave you an order I'd likely end up with a knife in my rib."

"Naturally." I yelped when his switchblade hilt tapped my waist.

Neither of us could oversee the other. If anything, we were equals. He seemed to be thinking the same thing because he said, "I want to work with you." His fingers threaded mine. "Alongside you." He pulled me close—so close I could feel each brass button of his uniform press against my chest. The beat of his heart was fast, just like my own. "You could even be the maître if you want the title.

After what you did for everyone, people are expecting you to take it." He leaned down, his mouth brushing against my ear. "Just don't let it go to your head."

Bel froze at the sound of the lift's cage opening. But whoever it was didn't stay long. They took a quick look out the moon window, not wishing to disturb the couple beneath it.

After they left, I grazed a finger along the ornate carvings of his switchblade hilt. I wanted to ask so many questions, and there would be time for those later, but there was one particular answer I couldn't wait for. "What's your name?"

"Bel," he said without pause.

"Don't you dare tell me you can't remember."

"I do. It's tied to a place that's no longer my home. Maybe I wanted to know it a little too desperately, once. I thought it was who I was, but it's just a name. Bel has been my name for most of my life. It's who I am now." His thumb stroked along my bottom lip. "I like when you say it."

I arched a brow. "I thought you like it better when I keep my mouth shut?"

"Only when I'm kissing you," he said. "If I have my way, you'll remain silent for the foreseeable future."

I buried my face against his neck and smiled.

"Where did you go?"

"Hiding. Go away."

"Silly girl." He dragged me up and wrapped his arms tighter around me.

I shivered against him. "Don't you want to at least visit your home?"

"Perhaps one day. For now, I guess I'll have to settle for this place. Do you want to visit your home?"

The question lingered. I gazed out at Champilliers and thought of my last home, the sun on Durc's port and the stink of fish in the air. "Maybe for a day."

EPILOGUE

A tasseled curtain was pulled across Salon d'Amusements with a sign that read CLOSED INDEFINITELY.

No one minded. The guests were too eager to be here, to see the magic of the legendary hotel and visit the places it would take them.

Around the lobby, the guests mingled. Some wore glittering gowns, some wore their frilliest homespun dresses. A handful even had dye on the ends of their fingertips, slinging foul words that would never be heard inside the fancy shops along boulevard Marigny. One thing was common among them all: they each had an equal chance at an invitation and were chosen fairly, paying whatever price made sense for their situation, even if it was nothing more than a single coin.

Everywhere eyes glinted as guests waited, with bated breath, to experience magic firsthand. Because tonight was the lobby soirée, when the greatest suminaire in all the world—the Magnifique— would take the stage.

A guest in the front clutched a program to her breast and pointed to a slight girl with light skin and gleaming blonde curls. She wore the most elaborate dress of all, a diaphanous confection of silver and cinched ribbons, probably purchased from some fancy atelier in Champilliers.

Breaths caught. People blinked, not because they couldn't remember, but because they never wished to forget the sight of the slight girl's lace-gloved hands tossing hundreds of steel insects into the air. Beside her, an old woman who looked so similar to the girl that she could only be her grandmother began playing a bright red piano.

Metal wings flapped, swarming the lobby, landing on furniture, on shoulders, on noses. They fluttered in glinting clouds around huge paper trees sprouting up from playing cards across the floor. They flitted among the chandeliers. Then, when the girl raised a gloved hand, a column of roaring silver split the air and fell like sand to her open palm.

The applause kept coming, signaling to everyone who wasn't in the lobby that now was the time.

In a steady stream, more guests spilled out. They came from the endless library. They wandered from the curious paper garden in the center of the lobby, not confined behind any speck of glass, but open to everyone. Guests descended the caged lift. They slinked with their silk-leashed leopards down the grand stairs from the balconies, and also from the galleries, dabbing at the tears on their cheeks from the magic of it all.

"Is that man the maître d'hôtel?" One older woman gestured to a darkened corner, clutching a pair of lorgnettes that did nothing but magnify. "Heard the old one disappeared somewhere."

"I believe the new maître is a woman," her companion pointed out, but he looked over anyway, at the peculiar man who leaned against a wall.

The man stood there, not turned to the stage but facing the audience, watching the soirée play out. He tapped his chin with an odd finger that, from where the couple stood, appeared to be nothing more than a carved and polished piece of wood.

Above the guests, birds flitted freely through the chandeliers, but no one dared look up. All eyes were trained on the black-lacquered door.

"Shouldn't there be a stage?" a young girl remarked as the maître d'hôtel dipped out from the audience. *She's just a slip of a thing*, the young girl thought. *She's not much different than me.*

But she most certainly was different.

She wore a simple blue dress the shade of a storming sea and a small bronze trinket on a gold chain around her neck. Her dark hair bounced as she walked, spilling down her back in a tumble of waves, catching the light off flickering oil lamps being lowered on cranks and pulleys around the door. She was exquisite in her simplicity, a stark beacon in a sea of colorful guests. In fact, the only frivolous thing on her was a single feather the exact color of molten gold tucked behind her ear.

The woman who held her lorgnettes leaned over to her companion. "Where's the Magnifique? It's minutes to midnight."

Her companion didn't answer because the peculiar man from the corner now stood before the maître. He brushed her neck to push a curl out of the way, but his thumb rested against her pulse a beat longer than was proper, before whispering something in her ear that caused her cheeks to flush.

"What do you suppose he's saying?" the woman asked.

"Shush," her companion said, although he was wondering the same thing.

A row of tittering women in front swooned when the man leaned in and kissed the maître, soft and slow, his fingers replacing the feather in her hair before handing her the key from around his neck.

The woman tutted to her companion. "A little indecent, don't you think?"

"Shush," he said. "It's nearly midnight."

ACKNOWLEDGMENTS

This book has been on a journey almost as magnificent as the hotel within its pages. When I first sat down to draft it, I didn't realize how many wonderful people I'd meet along the road to publication. You have all convinced me that magic does, in fact, exist.

To the genius editorial duo of Casey McIntyre and Gretchen Durning—I'm still pinching myself that I have not one but two amazing editors on my team. You immediately put me at ease, and your edit ideas helped create some of my favorite moments in the story. I'm incredibly grateful to have you both by my side.

To my agent dream team, Hillary Jacobson and Alexandra Machinist— thank you both for embracing this extravagant world and pushing me to shape it into something greater than I ever thought possible. Your brilliance is only equaled by your kindness. I'm constantly amazed and so appreciative of everything you do, and I can't imagine better agents to have in my corner. Thank you to everyone else at ICM who has touched this book, especially Lindsey Sanderson, and my film agent, Josie Freedman. Thank you to my foreign agents at Curtis Brown UK, Roxane Edouard, Savanna Wicks, and Liz Dennis.

Thank you to Kristie Radwilowicz, Theresa Evangelista, and Jim Tierney for a cover that made me gasp and sit down the first time I saw it. Thanks to Tony Sahara for the stunning interior. To the rest of the Penguin Young Readers team, Jayne Ziemba, Amy White, Marinda Valenti, Sola Akinlana, Alison Dotson, Nicole Wayland, Olivia Russo, Felicia Frazer, Deb Polansky, Shanta Newlin, Emily Romero, Alex Garber, Felicity Vallence, Shannon Spann, Jen Klonsky, Jocelyn Schmidt, and Jen Loja—thank you for making this outlandish dream of mine a reality.

I cannot wait to see the fantastic places *Hotel Magnifique* will go.

A thousand thank-yous to Joan He and Mara Rutherford for picking this book to mentor. Those few months during Pitch Wars still stand as a favorite moment of this journey. Endless gratitude to Brenda Drake, Heather Cashman, and everyone involved in Pitch Wars 2017, especially my fellow mentees. The rumors are true; the community is everything. I wouldn't be the writer I am today without that experience.

Thank you to those who have shaped my writing in profound ways. To Elizabeth Runnoe, you're the best CP and friend a girl could ask for. To Allison Brink, therapist extraordinaire and all-around incredible human, you've been a continual bright spot. To Janelle Erickson and Angie Beckey for reading early drafts and still being my friends. To April Smasal for the fangirling and the flowers. To Tim Blevins, the first person I pitched this idea to on that fateful day in January all those years ago; your reaction lit the fire. To Sovanneary Sweere, one of my oldest and dearest friends, for the lake walks and listening. To my sweet cousin Jessica, and the rest of the ladybugs, for your endless enthusiasm.

Thank you to all my friends and work friends for your support during the creation of this book, especially Emily Lane, Denise Lorenz, Adam Ridgeway, Anna Mercier, Jenny Pinion, Renee Kallio, Lindsey Wright, Joanne Torres, Amanda Clark, Alea Toussaint, and Tom Sebanc.

Before writing books, I worked as an art director alongside some of the most talented writers I've ever known. My deepest gratitude to each of you for teaching me what words can do.

Thank you to my No Excuses critique group, especially Eliza Langhans, Brook Kuhn, Lyla Lawless, Jeff Wooten, Brighton Kamen, Ryan Van Loan, Erin Fitzgerald, and Margie Fuston for being a sounding board of positivity during our monthly video chats. Extra thanks to Emily Thiede for the eleventh-hour read that changed this book, and to Melody Steiner for your fierce enthusiasm. To everyone in my Loft critique group, Paul Bachleitner, John Sheahan, Erin Gallas, Jennifer Granneman, and Mohammad Seifi—thank you for all your excitement and feedback.

A huge thank-you to everyone at The Loft Literary Center in Minneapolis. The evening classes allowed this working mom a sacred space to dream. This book was born at the Loft. And in many ways, so was my writing.

At the heart of this book is a sister story, and I wouldn't have been able to write it like I did without having a sister of my own. To the amazing Caren, thank you for all your encouragement. You are magical. I love you so much. To my mother, Carolyn, and her husband, Arnie, thank you for being a backbone during this lengthy process. Mom, I now give you permission to go forth and tell all your friends on Facebook about my book. To Pat, Jerry, Christine, and the whole Milwaukee squad, thank you for cheering me on. Love you all.

To my husband, Eric, this book would not exist without you. You didn't have to sacrifice weekends to watch babies while I shut myself in a room to write, and yet you did. Thank you for making this work that is important to me also important to you. This journey would be awfully lonely without you by my side. I love you. This book was always for you.

To my little boys, Rogue and West, sorry for all the on-deadline mac 'n' cheese. I love you both! Keep on reading weird stories and dreaming.

Finally, to my dad, Svika, who left this world when I was barely a young adult myself—there isn't a day that passes that I don't miss you. I wish you were still here to see all the astonishing things I've done. Especially this thing.